"Take it from a real-life Pirate Hunter—reading one of Mack's books is just like being there."

—"PO," U.S. Navy boarding team support, USS *McFaul* (DDG 74)

"While assigned to CTF 151, fighting real Somali Pirates in the Gulf of Aden, there has been no more welcome diversion than reading Mack Maloney's tales of Team Whiskey. He makes every effort to blend action, excitement, and reality into one of the most prevalent and enduring maritime issues of our time."

—Special Agent Chris "Shakespeare" Ahr, Naval Criminal Investigative Service, senior law enforcement adviser, USS *Mason* (DDG 87)

"Mack Maloney clearly did his homework when it came to this book. As a Naval VBSS member and trainer, I know this great read will get the attention of anyone interested in fighting modern-day piracy."

—Intelligence Specialist Third Class "Junior" Lawson, USN

"An awesome book! A thrilling take on this modern-day scourge of the high seas. Those of us fighting piracy out here every day love it!" —"LURCH," VBSS team member, USS *Mason* (DDG 87)

"*The Pirate Hunters* is nonstop action. Whiskey does what I wish America could do. A take-no-prisoner, don't-mess-with-us attitude to the world." —"DEXTER," VBSS team member, USS *Mason* (DDG 87)

Operation
Sea Ghost

Mack Maloney

A TOM DOHERTY ASSOCIATES BOOK
New York

OPERATION SEA GHOST

Copyright © 2012 by Mack Maloney

All rights reserved.

Edited by James Frenkel

A Forge Book
Published by Tom Doherty Associates, LLC
175 Fifth Avenue
New York, NY 10010

www.tor-forge.com

Forge® is a registered trademark of Tom Doherty Associates, LLC.

ISBN 978-0-7653-6523-1

First Edition: February 2012

Printed in the United States of America

0 9 8 7 6 5 4 3 2 1

For SEAL Team 6

Thanks to NCIS Special Agent Chris Ahr and
the real pirate hunters of Combined Task
Force 151, USS *Mason*, DDG–87,
and to Al Picardal and everyone at CENSECFOR,
LS Pearl Harbor, Hawaii.

Operation
Sea Ghost

1

Airfield 414
Udorn, Thailand
March 1968

THE C-130 CARGO plane took off in a violent rainstorm.

It was 2350 hours, almost midnight, and the monsoon that had battered Southeast Asia all day was still intense. The wind was fierce and lightning flashed everywhere. The thunder was like artillery booming in the distance. This was dangerous flying weather, but the C-130's mission was a top priority. It was going to fly no matter what.

The aircraft rose from its secret base on the eastern edge of Thailand and turned north, over Laos, heading toward Vietnam. The four-man crew was wearing standard U.S. Air Force flight suits, each with his name tag attached—DAVIS, LEE, RUBY and JOHNSON—but the crew members were not military personnel. They were civilian employees of the CIA.

Five containers were stacked in the plane's cargo bay. Four were made of plain thin plywood barely held together by tiny screws. At six feet long and about two feet wide, they looked like bargain-basement coffins.

The fifth container was an SMT. About the size of a footlocker and officially known as a "Sensitive Materials Transport," these containers were used by the CIA to move highly classified material around the war zone. Built of the same nearly indestructible material as an airplane's "black box," SMTs had small, sealed-environment enclosures to preserve their contents over long periods of time, be they documents, important items taken from the enemy or even secret experimental weapons.

Several SMTs had been captured by communist troops during the recent Tet Offensive, causing the loss of valuable war intelligence. Since then, SMT containers were supposed to be accompanied by at least two armed guards at all times. But this one was traveling alone.

There was no paperwork attached to any of this cargo; no manifest or ID tags were in evidence. The only writing was on the SMT: The letter "Z" had been faintly stenciled onto it, next to an almost imperceptible keyhole.

The C-130's crew did not know what was inside any of the crates, though their collective gut told them some kind of secret weapon was probably involved. The plane's pilot was carrying sealed orders issued by their CIA station chief in Bangkok. These orders were not to be opened until the cargo plane reached a so-called control coordinate about 100 miles from the border that divided North and South Vietnam.

Only then would the crew know the details of their mission.

• • •

FIVE MINUTES AFTER takeoff, the C-130 reached its cruising altitude of 10,000 feet. It had now gotten out of the worst of the storm—though the weather was still harsh over most of Indochina.

It would take forty minutes before the plane reached the control coordinate where the crew's orders could be opened. To help pass the time, the flight engineer produced a thermos of coffee. He poured cups for the pilot and the copilot and himself. The cargomaster had his own thermos. He preferred tea.

With the crew settled in, the cargomaster pulled out a copy of *The New York Times,* dated two weeks before. He showed the others a small story, stuck deep inside the third section. Its headline read: "Nixon hints at nuke use in Vietnam."

The pilot saw the headline, nodded to the SMT in back, and joked, "Is *that* the ticking sound I hear?"

The flight engineer was quick to dismiss this notion. He'd been on the flight line when the SMT arrived and said none of the people handling it had worn radiation suits. However, he said they might have been wearing gas masks; it was hard to see in the torrential downpour. If so, perhaps the SMT contained some kind of secret poison gas.

But now the copilot disagreed. He, too, had been close by when the SMT was being loaded and he thought he saw the people handling it wearing hazardous material suits. That indicated some kind of deadly material, a powder or something, might be involved.

"But if that's the case," the pilot said, "where are *our* suits?"

• • •

THEY REACHED THE control coordinate just after 0035 hours.

The others looked on as the pilot tore open the orders envelope and removed a single sheet of paper.

He read it quickly, then whispered, "This has *got* to be a joke. . . ."

He passed the orders to the copilot, who read them aloud.

"You are to proceed one hundred miles due north of your present position. Prior to reaching that coordinate, you are to reposition the four wooden crates near the flight deck. On reaching the assigned coordinate, you will purge all but two hundred pounds of fuel from your tanks. You are to put your aircraft on automatic pilot and then the entire crew should leave the aircraft via parachute. The pilot shall be the last to leave the airplane. Prior to leaving, he is to remove the contents of the four wooden crates and then dispose of the crates. Upon reaching the ground, the entire crew will make its way to the Special Forces camp at Lo Nimh, on the Laotian border, for retrieval and return to Udorn. You will not disclose the details of this mission to anyone."

It took a moment for the words to sink in.

Then the flight engineer said, "They want us to let the plane *crash*? On purpose? That doesn't make sense."

The pilot reread the orders, then shook his head.

"This is Vietnam, boys," he said. "Nothing makes sense over here."

• • •

THE FLIGHT ENGINEER and the cargomaster went back to the cargo bay and, per their orders, dragged the four wooden crates to the front of the aircraft.

Then, five minutes before reaching their coordinate, the baffled crew climbed into their parachutes and prepared to bail out.

With one minute to go, the pilot set the plane's controls as ordered and then told the others to jump. Each man stepped out the side access hatch and disappeared into the blustery dark night. The pilot could just barely see their parachutes open.

Returning to the flight deck, the pilot unscrewed the lid of the first wooden box. He was shocked by what he found inside.

It was a dead body. Male, Caucasian, with a bloody chest wound, the corpse was wearing a flight suit exactly like his own. Most astonishing, though, the flight suit's name tag read DAVIS, his own name.

Totally confused now, the pilot rolled the crate over and let the body fall out. That's when he noticed the corpse had a chain around its neck with a small key attached. The pilot had no idea what it was for and, at the moment, didn't care. He hastily took the lids off the three other wooden crates, finding three more bodies, each wearing an ID tag bearing a name identical to one of his crew. He guessed the bodies belonged to soldiers recently killed in battle.

He emptied them onto the deck as well and then kicked the four plywood boxes out the open door. All this took him about a minute and it was very disturbing and weird.

"Why do they want someone to think we're all dead?" he thought, once the four makeshift coffins were gone. Then he looked back at the SMT, still sitting at the rear of the plane, and added: "And what the hell is inside that thing?"

He didn't have any time left to think about it. He rechecked the plane's controls, purged its fuel tanks to just 200 pounds, and then jumped.

His chute opened quickly but roughly, jerking both his shoulders up and nearly cracking his collarbone.

The C-130 continued flying north, toward North Vietnam, the bodies and the mysterious SMT still on board.

The pilot figured by that course, and at that altitude and fuel load, the intentionally doomed plane would crash about twenty miles north of the DMZ, well inside communist-controlled territory.

But just as he was preparing himself for his landing, the pilot saw a sudden flash of light rise up from the dense jungle below. It exploded under the C-130's right wing. It took the pilot a moment to realize an antiaircraft shell had hit the cargo plane.

The last time he saw the C-130, it was disappearing into a cloudbank, its right wing completely engulfed in flames.

2

Gulf of Aden
Present Day

THE SWARM OF paparazzi helicopters finally dispersed around sunset.

The armada of fast boats and Zodiacs carrying even more photographers left shortly afterward. Those villagers who'd gathered on the nearby cliffs at Ghadir also called it a day and went home. The western end of the Gulf of Aden was calm again at last.

The center of attention was a 210-foot Blenheim & Koch mega-yacht named *The Immaculate Perception*. At the request of the U.S. consulate in Aden, the giant luxury craft had skirted the Yemeni coast for about twenty miles, allowing a few people in the highly troubled, impoverished country, as well as the crush of international media, to get a fleeting glimpse of the vessel's very famous passenger, American film star Emma Simms.

Now that the show was over, the yacht's captain turned away from the barren coastline and headed toward Bab el Mandeb, the narrow strait that separated Yemen and Djibouti and served as the southern mouth of the Red Sea. Ordering the yacht's running lights turned on, he upped his speed to seventeen knots and settled in behind the steering wheel.

It was an ideal night for traveling; the early moon had set and the stars were coming out. The weather was clear with hardly any wind.

The sea was like glass.

• • •

THE PLAN FROM here was for *The Immaculate Perception* to sail up the Red Sea, through the Suez Canal, into the Mediterranean and then on to Italy where Emma Simms was to begin shooting her next movie. The film's production company was already in place in Rome, set construction was finished, her costars were rehearsed and waiting. All they needed was for Emma Simms to arrive.

However, she'd just completed a whirlwind publicity tour of Africa. In the span of forty-eight hours, she'd visited an AIDS hospital in Kenya, dedicated another in Cameroon, cut a ribbon at a girls' school in Liberia, read to blind children in Botswana and visited an orphanage in Nigeria. She'd posed for so many pictures and done so many interviews, she'd lost count.

After the colossal two-day media blitz was finished, she'd declared herself too stressed to fly directly to Italy. She'd opted instead to lease the enormous mega-yacht out of Oman and sail up to Rome instead, a trip of seven days. It would be a relaxing way to spend the week, plus she would arrive fashionably late for her first day on set, something that made her high-powered publicists very happy.

Such was life for the person *People* magazine had christened "the world's favorite movie star." Emma was gorgeous; that was beyond dispute. Just twenty-six years old, five-foot-five and nicely shaped, she was impeccably blond, redhead or brunette depending on her mood. Her image regularly graced the covers of every celebrity magazine on the planet. Her movies were hits everywhere; they'd already grossed more than a billion dollars worldwide, and that included dirt-poor places like Yemen where she was extremely popular. Her celebrity spanned religious, ethnic and cultural barriers. Though thoroughly American, she was considered a citizen of the world. Her Facebook page received a million hits a day and millions more around the globe followed her every move on Twitter. She was a certified international phenomenon.

But being Emma Simms was not easy. She spent five hours every day in the gym working with her personal trainers. Another three hours were devoted to creating new hairdos and makeup schemes with her stylist. Her life coach took up another two hours, as did her personal spiritualist and her nutritionist. Hundreds of millions of people adored her, so all the hard work must have been paying off.

Still, she could be demanding. Her morning toast had to be exactly 76 degrees Fahrenheit or she would not eat it. Bad for digestion, her nutritionist had told her. She had to have exactly five one-inch-square ice cubes in every glass of Bavarian spring water she drank, as anything less would not provide the optimal temperature for proper skin hydration. The clothes closets on the rented yacht—which she insisted undergo a $100,000 redesign overnight before she agreed to step on board—were organized in four distinct categories: day of the week, time of day, disposition of the moment and strength of aura as calculated by her ever-present shaman.

Anywhere she traveled, the hired help were told not to look at her directly—after all, that's how auras were stolen. The help also had to be white, or at least not too dark. She'd told the mega-yacht's owners that after her recent tour, she'd "had enough of Africans for a while," leaving them to scramble to find fifty-three Caucasian maids, cooks, butlers and crewmen on just a few hours' notice.

Her own lily-white entourage numbered in the dozens, and her luggage consisted of more than a hundred suitcases, many filled up with her extensive collection of sunglasses, which simply had to go with her wherever she went. And to keep herself centered at all times while on the yacht, whatever outfit she was wearing up on deck, all the pillows and cushions within her line of sight had to be of the same color or they damn well better be made up of complementary hues.

There had already been a couple of tirades about this, and heads had rolled.

• • •

EMMA SIMMS WAS intensely sure of herself. She had more balls than any of her leading men. She rarely forgot her lines. She could play happy just as well as sad, light as well as dark. And though she'd starred in a couple of romantic comedies early in her career, her bread and butter was the action-adventure film. She looked her best on screen when she appeared to be kicking someone's ass. She even hoped to do her own stunts someday, to get a deeper connection to her characters. But at the moment, her management was dead set against that idea. Stunt doubles still threw the punches, took the tumbles, crashed the cars.

Emma was just too valuable to do them herself.

• • •

THE IMMACULATE PERCEPTION sailed through the evening, gliding atop the quiet sea.

It was not entirely alone. The Omani Navy had provided an armed frigate, currently sailing a quarter mile behind, to watch over both megastar and mega-yacht during this part of the journey. A favor from her friend, the Sultan of Oman, the warship was scheduled to stay with her until an Egyptian patrol boat met the yacht off the Red Sea island of Perim around midnight. From there, the Egyptian navy would take over escort duty right up through the Suez Canal.

A small glitch arose in this plan, though. Emma was below in her luxurious cabin, staring at proofs of her new children's book, *Everyone Wants to Be Me,* when word arrived that the Egyptian boat had been slightly delayed due to some celebrity reporters demanding they come aboard and record its cruise. Her personal physician had just left, having injected her with her nightly cocktail of mood elevators and sleeping aids, and she was already feeling the effects.

The plan now was for the Egyptian vessel to rendezvous with the mega-yacht just before 1:00 A.M., a little north of Perim. This was not a problem. Though low fuel had forced the Omani frigate to turn back at 12:30 A.M., by that time, the Egyptian patrol boat was just ten miles away. Considering the two vessels were heading right for each other, *The Immaculate Perception* would be without escort for less than twenty minutes.

But that's all it took.

Because just as soon as the Omani ship disappeared over the horizon, the pirates struck.

• • •

THEY'D BEEN LURKING off Perim, hidden among the rocks near the island's treacherous south side.

Using two fast boats, each carrying six heavily armed gunmen and extra fuel tanks, they'd come up behind the yacht and, hidden by the darkness, climbed aboard unmolested. Only when two of the pirates appeared in the yacht's control room did the crew know something was amiss. The vessel's onboard security team, four bouncers from Ankara, vanished in an instant. Once the yacht's captain realized how quickly they were being overrun, he ordered his fifty-five-man crew not to resist. He also suggested Emma's entourage do the same.

It all happened very fast. Sixty seconds after climbing aboard, the dozen Somali pirates were in control of *The Immaculate Perception.*

• • •

WHEN THE FIRST pirate walked into Emma Simms's cabin, she thought he was one of her waiters, inexplicably dressed in blackface and rags.

"Why are you in that getup?" she'd asked him.

The man didn't speak English, but he didn't have to. He simply raised his AK-47, fired a burst into the ceiling. Then he yanked her to her feet and began to drag her up to the main deck.

"No!" she screamed, terrified—but it was no use. He pulled her up top where she saw the crew had been made to kneel against the railing, her own contingent right beside them. The pirates' two large speedboats were tied up alongside the yacht, which by now had stopped dead in the water.

Armed men were everywhere: up on the bridge, on the fore-deck, up on both helicopter pads and along both rails. From what Emma could see, everyone else on board had been aware of the pirate attack long before she was.

"So what the hell is this?" she suddenly bellowed to no one in particular. "These guys came looking for me *last*?"

Two pirates blindfolded Emma and her stylist and forced them into one of their speedboats. Emma complained loudly, slapping and kicking the gunmen, but to no avail. The rest of the pirates looted the yacht, robbing everyone on board and stealing Emma's extensive sunglasses collection. They disabled the yacht's engines and shot out its radio equipment, then left.

Had it been another time and place, the pirates might have stolen *The Immaculate Perception* itself.

But not tonight.

Emma had been their target all along.

3

THE TRIP TOOK two hours, a lot of it over choppy water.

Emma was only aware of sounds. The speedboat's engine, her captors laughing, waves thumping against the bow. Loudest of all was her stylist wailing. At first, the woman tried to hold on to her so tight, her fingernails dug into Emma's flesh. Finally Emma just pushed her away.

Once they'd reached their destination, the pirates drove the speedboat right up onto a beach. Still blindfolded, Emma was pulled out kicking and screaming, dragged across the hard sand and thrown in the back of a loud, rattling truck that squealed away in a cloud of exhaust. And suddenly she was alone. Her stylist was no longer with her.

The truck rumbled along for about fifteen minutes. Emma heard waves crashing along the way. She was on a coastal road somewhere; she prayed it wasn't Somalia, the most horrible place in Africa. Just the thought of that made her sick to her stomach.

Eventually the truck stopped and she was hauled out and tied to either a pole or a tree, it was hard to tell. There was a lot of noise around her now: people cursing, fighting, weapons being fired; voices yammering in some strange language, spoken a mile a minute.

Someone eventually tore off her blindfold; her eyes adjusted to the bare light. She was in a clearing surrounded by dense jungle. A campfire was burning at its center. About a dozen wooden shacks were nearby. Three smaller shacks were standing a couple hundred feet away.

There were about thirty pirates in the camp. All were heavily armed and, oddly, many were wearing her sunglasses, even though it was night. This infuriated her. She screamed at them to take them off, but the pirates ignored her. They were so arrogant and dirty; she vowed never to wear any of the sunglasses again.

The pirates had picked the perfect place to hide—even she could see this. The thick forest concealed the camp from the ground, from the sea nearby and almost entirely from the air. She could just barely make out the stars above the over-hanging jungle canopy. Their shimmering reminded her of her jewelry box back on the yacht.

The pirates began to build the campfire into a bonfire, adding wood and trash to make the flames go higher. A white female suddenly appeared among them. She was dressed in threadbare coveralls with a kerchief drawn around her nose and mouth, and a fisherman's hat pulled over her forehead. Only her eyes were visible.

The pirates were ordering her about, making her carry firewood, and kicking her when she did not move fast enough. She was obviously another captive.

When she came close, gathering more wood for the fire, Emma whispered to her: "Do you know who I am?"

The woman barely acknowledged her. "I do," was her muf-fled reply. She had a slight British accent. "Everyone does, I suppose."

"Then don't worry," Emma told her. "When people find out *I'm* missing, they'll come to rescue me. And they'll res-cue you, too."

But the woman hissed back to her: "No one comes here to rescue anyone. You better learn that right away. You leave here only when someone pays your way out. I've been here two years and I'm *still* waiting. Others haven't been so lucky. Some were shot just for taking up too much space."

But Emma began arguing with her. "These filthy mon-keys must know *who I am*," she insisted. "They *must* realize I'm more valuable to them alive than dead."

"Oh, they know *all* about you," the woman replied, pre-tending to fuss with some scraps of wood. "Too much in fact. They knew you were in the area because you made such a big deal about it. So, they were just waiting to snatch you. You mean millions to them."

"Well, you see then," Emma boasted. "If they're not going to kill me, I have no reason to be afraid, right?"

The woman just shook her head and moved on.

• • •

THE PIRATES SMOKED cigarettes, chewed qat and passed around Emma's sunglasses. They drank alcohol from old oil cans, and the more they drank, the more boisterous they became. After a while, several began fighting, cutting each other with knives. Others were so drunk they were barely able to walk.

Emma cursed at them the whole time. She demanded to be untied. She demanded water. She demanded they stop wearing her sunglasses. She called them criminals, gangstas—and worse. But the pirates continued to ignore her, preferring instead to watch their bonfire grow. Some even stuffed pieces of cloth in their ears, just so they wouldn't have to listen to her.

After an hour, another truck arrived. A tall black man in jungle camos climbed out. The other pirates flocked to him, calling him "Captain."

This man had a copy of *People* magazine and showed it around to the delight of the other pirates. Emma caught a glimpse of it: July 7, 2011. Her face was on the cover.

The captain walked over to her. He smelled awful and she told him so. He had a digital camera and began to take her picture. She tried to look away, tried to hide her face, but the man grabbed her hair and made her pose. When she spat in his face, he raised his hand to strike her, but stopped.

"You can't hurt me!" she screamed at him. "I'm worth too much!"

The man wiped the saliva from his face and glared at her, but then he turned and went back to the bonfire. Emma mocked him as he retreated. Even in this precarious situation, she felt in control, invulnerable and above it all.

Then the woman in the kerchief passed by her again, carrying more wood for the fire.

"You're only making it worse for yourself," she whispered to Emma. "If you just shut your mouth, they might get so drunk, they'll forget about you for a while."

Emma laughed. "I'm not making it that easy for them. Why should I? They're animals. And like I said, they won't dare kill me. So I have nothing to worry about."

"Oh, but you do," the woman warned her. "And instead of insulting them, you should be praying very hard. Because what they're planning for you will be *worse* than dying."

Emma laughed at her. "Nothing is worse than dying," she said.

Clearly Emma wasn't catching on, so the woman pointed to a pair of pirates sitting close to the raging fire. They were holding a steel rod over the flames. It was nearly white hot.

"They are going to use that on you," the woman told her starkly. "To *brand* you—understand? Mark you up like a blooming pig or a cow. *That* makes you *their* property. And after that happens, they'll rape you. Sodomize you. All of them, and more than once. And God be with you, because while you might survive, you will never be the same. . . ."

But Emma simply refused to believe the woman. She challenged her: "How do you know all this? Maybe you're just crazy."

" 'How do I know?' " the woman spit back at her. "Let me show you . . ."

The woman pulled down her kerchief to reveal horrific burn marks all over her face. Strange symbols and inverted numbers were permanently branded into her cheeks and forehead. Then she lifted her shirt to expose her chest, which was covered with horrendous cuts and bruises; on her stomach was what looked like a crude cesarean-section scar.

Then the woman said to Emma: "I know all this because at one time, I was just like you."

Then the woman ambled away.

• • •

FOR THE NEXT ten minutes, Emma fought very hard to keep her composure.

But the woman's words would not stop echoing in her ears and the sight of those scars was burned into her retinas. Emma's face was beautiful, and that beauty was her life. Even if she did get out of this somehow, what good would it be, if she were made ugly? If she was scarred? She began to panic. She began fighting against the ropes. Her spirit was abandoning her; her aura was draining away. Fear was taking over.

The gang's leader walked over to her again; this time his eyes were red and glassy. He motioned to the pirates closest to the fire. They retrieved the hot branding iron and brought it to him. All the pirates gathered around Emma now. Some were drunkenly poking her breasts with the tips of their assault rifles.

She screamed; she tried to kick them. But the pirates just laughed at her.

"Rich American bitch," the captain sneered in thick English. "Think you own everything? Think you own the world?"

He raised the branding iron to her face. The heat was so intense, it melted away her mascara.

"*We are* going to give you something now," he told her, his breath putrid. "Something to make sure you remember us forever."

Emma fought and screamed and kicked, but it was all to the pirates' amusement. And after a short while, she could scream no longer, fight no longer. She could do nothing more but shut her eyes tight and wait for the pain . . .

But the pain never came.

Just as the hot iron was about to sear her cheek, a mighty explosion rocked the compound from one end to the other. Emma opened her eyes to see the gang leader and the half dozen pirates closest to him had been vaporized, leaving only a bloody pink mist behind. Many more pirates lay broken and bleeding on the ground around her. Emma couldn't believe it. More than a dozen bad guys had just been killed, yet she was untouched. Just like in her movies.

An instant later, one of the wooden shacks blew up, filling the camp with smoke and flames. This explosion was so violent, it knocked the remaining pirates to the ground. Then another shack blew up. Then another, and another.

Emma's vision became partially obscured by the dust and smoke, but she could see some pirates getting to their feet and stumbling about. Others ran in panic. One man was covered in blood from his head to his feet. Another was on fire and disappeared screaming into the woods.

Yet some of the pirates had survived the mysterious blasts unscathed. They were shoving aside their horribly wounded comrades and scrambling toward the trucks, determined to flee the camp. But three of them began staggering toward Emma. And this time they weren't carrying branding irons, but long, razor-sharp knives.

In the middle of all this came an amazing sight: A helicopter appeared out of the darkness, flying below the jungle canopy. Its guns were firing. It was shooting missiles—these were causing the explosions. Streams of phosphorous bullets were flying in every direction, hitting pirates all around Emma, but leaving her untouched.

This helicopter disappeared and another larger one came into view overhead. Armed men were hanging out of its doorways, firing weapons at the pirates below.

This copter, with its engines screaming, slammed down for a sudden, violent landing. The armed men jumped out and began firing on the pirates at close range. These men were wearing huge battle helmets equipped with weird goggles and heavy blue battle suits. They looked like aliens from a bad sci-fi movie.

Some of the pirates tried to surrender, but the attackers weren't taking prisoners. Other pirates tried to fight back, but to no avail. They were firing directly at the attackers, but their bullets seemed to be bouncing off them. The attackers were staggered by the gunfire, but it was not slowing them down.

They moved through the camp like automatons, mowing down the pirates one by one.

Another explosion went off; a missile had hit the camp's ammunition shack, causing the most powerful blast of all. More streams of gunfire went by Emma; they looked like fireworks all going off at once. With each fusillade, though, the bullets seemed to get closer to her.

And then, the three pirates she'd spotted before emerged from the smoke and confusion. Wild eyed and screaming, each one was bleeding horribly from various parts of his body. But they still had their knives with them and they were still coming toward her.

These men didn't care about ransoms anymore. They were going to kill her, Emma could see it in their eyes. They were even pushing and shoving each other for the opportunity to stab her first.

But just as the first pirate raised his knife to slit her throat . . . he suddenly stopped, looked directly into her eyes, then fell away, a bullet hole in his skull.

The instant this happened, a soldier literally fell out of the sky and landed right in front of her. He put himself between Emma and the two remaining pirates and shot them both dead, just like that.

Then he cut her ropes, causing her to fall into his arms.

She looked up at him and said: "Who the hell are *you*?"

The man took off his battle helmet to reveal a handsome face marred only by a patch over his left eye.

He said, "Snake Nolan. At your service . . ."

Emma looked him up and down, especially studying his bright blue combat suit.

Then she said, "Well, 'Snake' . . . that's a *very* ugly uniform. . . ."

• • •

TEAM WHISKEY HAD little time to prepare for the rescue mission.

They'd just returned to their headquarters at the Port of

Aden after an extended gig in the Caribbean when they got the news: Somali pirates had snatched the American actress Emma Simms from her mega-yacht and would undoubtedly be holding her for a huge ransom.

Horn of Africa politics being what they were, no armed force, military or private, had ever attacked the Somali pirates in their homeland. But this was different. These particular pirates were believed part of the Shaka Clan, and the Shakas had well-known links to al Qaeda in Africa. In fact there was a good chance the Shakas had done the kidnapping on the terrorists' orders.

Having snatched the big time movie star, the gang was sitting atop a two-fold bonanza: They might get tens of millions of dollars in ransom money *and* generate an avalanche of publicity for the jihadist cause. But for that very reason—that such an incident would generate so much attention worldwide, meaning so many fingers could soon be in the pie—the situation might become drawn out forever, during which time anything could happen.

So, before the political or diplomatic wheels could even start turning, a consortium of movie studios had come up with a ten-million-dollar reward, payable to anyone who retrieved Simms unharmed.

Whiskey took the job.

• • •

THEIR OFFICIAL NAME was Ocean Security Services, Inc. They'd been in the business of fighting pirates for less than a year. Their core group was made up of Delta Force veterans—call sign Task Force Whiskey—who'd fought together throughout the 1990s and right up to the invasion of Afghanistan following 9/11. In fact, Whiskey had been pursuing Osama bin Laden himself, had him *in their gun sights* at Tora Bora when they were inexplicably ordered by the top dogs at the Defense Department to back off. Whiskey refused. It was a brave but tragic decision, because in addition to getting two of them seriously wounded, disobeying those direct orders got them bounced from the military, and their CO, Snake Nolan, jailed for several years and banned from ever stepping foot inside the U.S. again.

Fronted and financed by the marine transportation giant, Kilos Shipping, Whiskey's anti-pirate services had been a huge success, defeating brigand gangs from Indonesia, China, Africa and the Caribbean, and getting well paid for it. But when the ten-million-dollar offer came in, they just couldn't say no.

Because of the time crunch, their plan had to be simple. Find the Shakas' compound, lay down a surgical barrage of Hellfire missiles, then land a ground force and roll up the pirates before they knew what hit them.

If everything went right, they would rescue Simms and any other hostages the gang was holding, and then fly directly to the movie's star's mega-yacht, which, its engines repaired, had reversed course and was now back in the Gulf of Aden, speeding south.

And everything *did* go just about how they planned. Whiskey first found the gang's pair of speedboats pulled up on a beach near Kushu, the Shakas' home village. Then they'd used their OH-6 attack copter's night-vision capabilities to find the hideout and blow it apart as intended. Utilizing some new body armor they'd agreed to test for a private arms manufacturer, their modest ground force had killed most of the pirates and scattered those few who remained, without getting so much as a scratch. Simms was free and now it was time to get the hell out.

But then, suddenly, they had a problem.

• • •

THE TEAM'S XO, Batman Bob Graves, had piloted Whiskey's attack copter on the mission. After firing a half dozen Hellfire missiles into the heart of the pirates' compound, he'd swung around to the trio of smaller buildings located nearby. The team believed more hostages were being held here.

Batman landed the OH-6 and, after shooting the locks off

the doors of the three small buildings, indeed found more hostages. Counting Simms's stylist, there were thirteen in all.

Whiskey had guessed that, at the most, they'd find ten hostages here, Simms included. The rescue force itself was comprised of ten raiders—and that was the problem. There was only room on their two copters for twenty-two people maximum, pilots included.

But now they had twenty-three.

• • •

ONCE ALL FIRING had ceased at the compound, the team's ground force made its way over to the hostages' location. The second copter landed; it was a Bell X-1 the team had borrowed, along with its pilot, from the Kilos security force. Batman had the hostages ready and waiting to go. He started hustling them onto the Bell as quickly as possible. When the copter was at its limit, he tried to stuff the rest into the much smaller OH-6 attack copter, leaving room only for the pilot. But no matter how they worked it, they still had one person too many.

Only three people in the rescue force could fly a rotary craft: Batman, Snake Nolan and the pilot of the Bell copter. Batman huddled with Nolan and made a suggestion: "You fly the gunship. Take the queen of the universe and four other people with you. Everyone else can go on the Bell."

"You mean you're staying behind?" Nolan asked him.

Batman nodded. "It's no big deal. Just drop everyone off, get some gas and come back. I'll stay in the area and I'll have my GPS locator on full power and my sat-phone, too."

Nolan started to protest. Leaving someone behind *did* seem to be the only solution. But that didn't mean Batman had to be the one.

"Why are you assuming I shouldn't be the one to stay behind?" Nolan asked him. "Because I only have one eye?"

Batman held up his left hand. It was a metal claw prosthesis; he'd lost his real hand in the team's action against a band of Indonesian pirates. "And I shouldn't be, because I'm a one-armed paperhanger?" he replied.

The impasse lasted just a few seconds.

"You're the leader of the pack, man," Batman told him. "You need to be there to deliver that piece of ass back to her handlers, so we can collect immediately. I'll be okay; I need a nap anyway."

It was a bullshit explanation, but they had no time to waste. If anyone could survive out here without getting into trouble, it was Batman.

So Nolan tapped him twice on the shoulder and said, "It will take about an hour to get to that yacht and then an hour to get back here. Add in twenty minutes to tank up, and that means we're looking at some time just before sunup. So, go hide somewhere and we'll be back ASAP. Capeesh?"

Batman gave him a mock salute.

"Capeesh," he said.

• • •

BATMAN WATCHED THE copters go over the horizon, disappearing among the stars to the east.

He studied his GPS locator and hoped he knew how to work the thing manually. It took him a few moments to override the commands previously programmed into the device. Finally, it began to behave.

He cleared the memory and then reactivated it. He zeroed in on his own position, then hit the enter button. A faint green light began blinking on the command screen. He breathed a sigh of relief.

Next, he checked his sat-phone. The charge was at three-quarters, which was plenty for the next few hours.

Now, all he had to do was wait someplace safe.

He walked back to the burning pirate camp, knowing it was best if he stayed deep in the bush. He checked his watch and rechecked the time line. It was close to 0300 hours. If Nolan was right, it would be just before dawn when they came back to retrieve him.

Making his way around the bodies of the pirates, he could see no suitable war souvenirs worth taking from the dead.

"Mooks," Batman murmured, strolling around the smoldering camp. "Small time clip artists . . ."

He reached into his ammo pocket. Among some 50-caliber shells he found what he was looking for: a partially smoked marijuana cigarette.

He lit it off a piece of burning wood and drew in deeply.

"Breakfast of Champions," he said.

A moment later, four bullets hit him in the back. . . .

• • •

NOLAN WAS ABOUT thirty minutes into the flight when he realized he'd made a huge mistake.

True, he could fly the attack copter. He'd done it many times since the team had come together. But he was also at a disadvantage because he didn't have use of his left eye. This led to depth perception problems, especially at night, issues that were somewhat rectified by a specially built night-vision scope attached to his battle helmet and placed in front of his good eye.

But he still couldn't relax, not even for one moment. During this dark flight over water, navigating by both the stars and dead reckoning, constantly looking for the mega-yacht and listening for the radio signal it was supposed to be sending out, all while checking his dwindling fuel supply, he caught himself thinking maybe he *was* the one who should have been left behind. In this case, two eyes were definitely better than one.

His very famous passenger was not helping the situation. In fact, she was making it worse just by her presence.

Emma Simms was sitting right next to him, strapped into the copilot's seat. She hadn't stopped fidgeting since they'd taken off, which was distracting him. Even worse, like a little kid, she kept asking Nolan, over and over: "Are we there yet?"

When she wasn't bugging him on their ETA, she'd spent

the time contemplating her reflection in the copter's side window, fussing with her hair, trying to manually curl her eyelashes, pinching her cheeks for color and trimming her fingernails by biting off the tips.

She'd asked him not once, not twice, but *three* times if he knew whether any paparazzi would be waiting for her once they arrived on the yacht. He'd replied each time with a simple, "I don't know," to which she responded with a pout.

So, half the time Nolan was wishing he'd stayed instead of Batman; the other half, he was wishing *she'd* been the one they'd left behind.

By contrast, the four ex-hostages riding in the back couldn't have been more grateful. Two were Swiss nationals, one was Indian, the other Austrian. They were marine biologists snatched from their research boat by the Shaka pirates four months ago. Several times during the flight, each one had reached forward and patted Nolan on the back, thanking him for getting them released from their little hell.

Emma Simms never noticed. She was more interested in her cuticles.

• • •

NOLAN FINALLY LOCATED the mega-yacht sailing about 180 miles off the northeast tip of Somalia. The vessel had all its lights on and had been sending out radio signals to the copters for the past hour.

Both the OH-6 and the big Bell went into a loose orbit around the vessel. It had two helipads: a large one at its stern and a smaller one on its bow. Nolan let the Bell land first, using the larger stern pad. He watched as members of the yacht crew swarmed toward the Bell, helping the hostages out and guiding them below.

Nolan then set down on the bow, his fuel reserves running out just as he hit the pad. He disengaged the engine and was heartened to see other members of the yacht's crew were standing by, ready to pump his copter full of gas for the return flight to retrieve Batman.

Once his primaries were shut off, he told his passengers they could open the doors and get out. Again, each hostage in the back took the time to awkwardly hug Nolan, endlessly thanking him for their rescue.

Emma Simms did no such thing.

She simply opened the door and got out without a word.

4

Somalia

CHIEF BOL BADA had seen it all: The pirates tying up the young white woman. The beginning of her torture. The sudden attack from the sky. The slaughter of the Shakas.

Bada was the leader of the Ekita Clan, a family of two hundred who lived on a piece of land bordering what used to be the Shaka base.

The Ekita despised the Shaka, but like many Somalis of the countryside, and especially those who lived near the sea, they had few traditions of war or conflict. They were nothing like the pirates. Whenever the Shaka came to this place to do their evil deeds, the Ekita melted into the jungle and waited for them to leave. Sometimes it took a few hours, sometimes days. Sometimes, the Ekita had to stay in hiding for weeks.

This time, with the other members of his clan safely hidden away, Chief Bada had slipped down close to the Shaka base, as he'd done many times before, to keep an eye on the pirates until they left.

But this night, he'd seen something incredible.

For once, someone had actually attacked the Shakas on their home turf. The men in helicopters, falling out of the sky, dressed like monsters—they had overrun the Shaka, who could do little to stop them. The pirates shot at their attackers, but with no result because the strange warriors seemed unaffected by bullets—*that* was the amazing thing. They looked like Americans, the people from the sky. But bullets did not hurt them? Bada knew America was highly advanced. But had they reached the point where bullets did not harm their soldiers?

All this would have made a great story to tell the family around the campfire, but a new twist had been added. One of these strange warriors had fallen right into Bada's arms. His comrades had left him behind for some reason, and he'd been shot, in the back, and he'd collapsed into the same bush where Bada had been hiding.

His assailants were riding in a caravan of pickup trucks that appeared off in the distance just before this man had been shot. Someone in the caravan had fired at the lone soldier, and then all the pick-up trucks had raced toward the burning compound.

Chief Bada wanted no part of these new people. They were not Shaka pirates; they were their sponsors, the much-feared Jihad Brotherhood, Muslim fundamentalists who had taken over just about every major city in Somalia. As vicious as the Shaka could be, they were mere insects compared to what these religious fanatics could do.

Bada knew he'd have to get out of there quickly if he ever wanted to see his family again. If these people caught him, they'd cut him up alive.

But he could not leave the wounded warrior behind.

So Bada recalled one of his family's oldest chants and whispered it, over and over.

And that's how he and the wounded warrior who had fallen on him became one with the jungle.

• • •

THE CARAVAN OF pickup trucks arrived at the devastated Shaka compound just seconds after Chief Bada had finished his chant.

Three dozen in all, many of these Brotherhood gunmen weren't even African—they were Arabs from Yemen, Syria and Iraq. They were dressed better than most religious fighters in Somalia, with crisp green camo uniforms and spiffy black boots. It was important for their reputation to be recognized instantly wherever they went; this outfit filled the bill. And though it was against the will of Allah to wear jewelry around one's neck or in one's earlobes, the Brotherhood were known for wearing gaudy silver rings. Some had them on every finger—the bigger and thicker, the better.

The Brotherhood was allied with the Somali pirates for one reason only: money. They'd sent the brigands out looking not for ships to hijack, but for high-profile persons to kidnap and hold for ransom. In exchange for guns, ammunition and the blessing of the Brotherhood to ply their trade, the pirates would snatch whomever they could from yachts and other pricey vessels and hold them for as long as necessary.

It had worked out well so far. They'd kidnapped several Dutch priests, the son of an Indian industrialist and a handful of marine scientists. The Brotherhood had been counting on somewhere around two million dollars when these people were finally ransomed.

But they'd been *very* excited to learn that earlier this night the pirates had managed to kidnap a very famous American movie actress—someone who would bring in *tens* of millions in ransom. Yet on arriving at the pirates' base camp, the Muslim fighters were stunned to find the place destroyed, their allies dead—and all those valuable hostages gone. Also missing was the man they'd just shot from far away, because they thought he was a police officer or maybe even a UN peacekeeping soldier.

None of this made sense. The jihadists were here to see the movie actress in the flesh, confirm her identity, then discuss with the pirates' leader how big of a ransom they should ask for.

But instead, they'd found little more than a smoking hole in the ground, and a lot of dead pirates lying around.

The leader of the jihadist gang was baffled. Who could have done this?

He spat twice on his hand and wiped it on his brow, a jihadist custom.

"Oh Allah," he said. "Please have mercy on us."

• • •

BATMAN WAS TERRIFIED.

He was being dragged through the brush and razor-sharp vegetation was cutting him all over. It was dark and he was disorientated and weak. He'd lost his weapons; his GPS locator and sat-phone were also gone. From his shoulders to his tailbone, his back felt like someone had hit him four times with a sledgehammer.

Every part of the past twenty minutes seemed hazy. He recalled that Whiskey had squashed the pirates, that they'd freed the hostages and that he'd agreed to stay behind to make room in the helicopter. He remembered lighting up the roach . . . and then suddenly, boom! He was out like a light.

But then, someone fell on top of him and hid him or made him invisible or something. Next thing he knew he was looking at some bad actors in green camos and polished boots who were inspecting the devastated pirate camp not ten feet from where he lay. Their rings—they all wore many silver rings. *That* had stuck in Batman's mind. And that these guys didn't look like Africans at all.

Then, he was being dragged through the bush, and was too stunned and weak and sick to fight back.

He was finally hauled to a stop and only then did he realize he was not in some lion's den, but in a small village of straw huts, hidden on all sides by high foliage.

Several dozen people had gathered around him. By their clothes, or lack of them, and their painted faces, he knew they were people of the bush. Some were kids; they were poking him, touching his arms and legs, checking to see if he was real. The adults stayed back, though, studying him as if he'd just fallen from the stars.

Finally, he turned over to see that he'd been dragged here by a fierce-looking Somali man.

"You are now among the Ekita," this man boasted to him in broken English, beating his own chest with every word. "Chief Bada has brought you here and you are a very lucky man."

Somehow Batman managed to unfasten his battle armor and crawl out of it. The chief produced a broken mirror and showed him the four large bruises on his back. They were purple and hideous, but Batman knew, had it not been for the body armor, the bruises would have been bullet holes, and he would be dead.

The chief sat him up.

"You are the first magical warrior to visit Ekita in three hundred years," he told Batman gravely. "You fly. You defeat bullets. You kill the Shaka and you wear a suit of enchantment. We must know: How do you do all these things?"

Batman was just getting his senses back. He took off his gloves to reveal that his left hand was missing and that a mechanical prosthesis was in its place.

The villagers gasped. The chief was fascinated. "So you're made of metal?" he asked Batman.

Batman waved his comment away.

"Just this hand," he said. "The rest of me is bone and muscle."

The chief translated for his villagers. This animated them further.

"Then we must learn from you," the chief declared. "We must heat you and consume the result."

Two women appeared carrying a wooden cup. It contained a blood-red liquid with what looked like tiny tulip bulbs floating in it. The chief urged Batman to drink it in one gulp. It smelled awful, but thinking it was some kind of pain reliever, drink it he did. But he quickly became even woozier than before.

Then he heard the chief say: "Now for the heating, so you will be one with us."

The crowd of villagers parted to reveal a giant campfire blazing away in the middle of the village. On top of it was a huge steaming pot.

Two men picked up Batman and began carrying him toward the steaming cauldron. The villagers became very excited. But Batman was getting concerned. He could actually see vegetables floating around inside the pot.

"What are you going to do?" he asked the chief anxiously. "Put me in that?"

"Yes—we are," the chief replied. "It's part of the process. It will change you . . . and it will change us."

"But—it looks too hot for me to go into," Batman said, becoming very alarmed.

The chief put his finger in the steaming water, tasted it and laughed.

"For our purposes," he said with a grin. "It is the perfect temperature."

5

Gulf of Aden

REFUELING WHISKEY'S ATTACK copter took just fifteen minutes. This was lightning quick for the yacht crew, who were not practiced in the art of quick aircraft turnarounds.

In the time the copter was getting serviced, Nolan had a chance to down two amphetamine pills and reset his weapons. Then he took off again, got a bearing via his rudimentary navigation system, turned west and hit the throttles. The mission to retrieve Batman had begun.

Gunner and Twitch were with him. They were the other half remaining of Team Whiskey. Gunner LaPook was a giant of a man from Cajun Country in Louisiana. He was the team's door breaker; whenever Whiskey assaulted a fortified position, Gunner went in first. His weapon of choice was the Streetsweeper, essentially a machine gun that fired shotgun shells. He was a tall, beefy individual and fierce looking. All tats and muscles, he looked like a WWE wrestler.

Twitch was a Kanaka, a native Hawaiian, and he was as diminutive as Gunner was tall. His nondescript Asian features, as well as a talent for languages, were a great advantage for the team, as he was able to go undercover just about anywhere in the world and blend in. He was a little off kilter, though; "edgy" was a polite description. He'd lost his leg during Whiskey's ill-fated pursuit of bin Laden in the mountains of Afghanistan. Just as Batman wore a prosthesis on his left arm, Twitch wore one for his right leg.

Both Gunner and Twitch were still wearing their experimental body armor, as was Nolan. It had worked well in their assault against the Shaka camp; though both Gunner and Twitch had been hit by pirate bullets, deep bruises were the only result.

Indeed, the mission earlier that night had gone off extremely well. The hostages had been freed, no one on the rescue force had been seriously hurt, the equipment had made it through unscathed and the world had one less pirate gang to worry about.

But now, as they were roaring back to retrieve Batman, Nolan was not getting a signal from his colleague's GPS locator. Even worse, Batman was not answering his sat-phone, even though Gunner was punching the number repeatedly.

They knew this part of the Somali coast was infested with pirate gangs, criminal clans and al-Qaeda-linked terrorist groups. Had their wayward associate really been able to avoid all of these dangerous sorts? Had Whiskey been too caught up in their victory earlier not to think clearly about leaving Batman behind? What kind of hot water could he have gotten into?

"Or maybe it's just like he said," Twitch said dryly. "Maybe he's just taking a nap."

• • •

THE SUN WAS barely up when Nolan spotted the coastline of Somalia again.

They'd hit a fog bank about ten miles out and it stayed

thick right up to landfall. Nolan was doing his best to get them to the same spot where the rescue mission had taken place. They were hoping that Batman was still in the area and, on hearing the copter, would send up some kind of signal so they could swoop in and pick him up.

But Nolan was prepared for the worst.

"Lock and load," he told Gunner and Twitch. Twitch checked his M4 assault rifle, stringing out its extended ammo belt. Gunner did the same with his massive Streetsweeper. Nolan reached down and pushed an oversized ammo clip in his own M4. Experience told them they had to be ready for anything.

So it was with great surprise that when they broke out of the fog and zoomed in on the nearby beach, what they saw was not a murderous gang of gunmen ready to shoot them down, but a lone figure in a bright blue battle suit—doing jumping jacks.

It was such a surprising sight, Nolan yanked the copter into a sudden, violent turn. Flying parallel to the beach a moment later, he was looking down through the lingering mist at this person: blue suit, rock star hair, and prosthetic hand at the end of the left arm.

There was no doubt about it: it was Batman.

But what the hell was he doing? Nolan had known Batman for more than twenty years. He'd never seen him as much as eat an apple, never mind do calisthenics.

Nolan turned the copter again just as Batman broke from his jumping jacks and started running wind sprints up and down the beach. Again, his colleagues were shocked.

"Is this a trick?" Gunner asked. "Some way to get us to land and ambush us?"

Nolan had half expected to be picking up Batman's bullet-ridden or hacked-up body. But this?

Batman had stopped his wind sprints and was now doing a handstand—on his one good hand.

"My guess is he got hit on the head and went nuts," Twitch said as they came in for a landing.

"Whatever it is," Nolan yelled back, putting the copter down with a thump, "just grab him and let's get out of here."

But Batman had spotted them by this time and was actually hand-hopping over to the copter. Then when he was about twenty feet away, he did a tremendous backflip, soaring some fifteen feet into the air before landing squarely on his feet.

"He's fucking crazy!" Nolan yelled to Gunner and Twitch. *"Grab him!"* They were out of the copter in an instant, tackling Batman just as he was breaking into another round of jumping jacks. They dragged him to the aircraft and threw him inside just as Nolan engaged the controls and prepared to take off again.

Throughout it all, Batman was laughing hysterically.

"What *the fuck* is the matter with you?" Nolan yelled back at him.

But Batman never stopped laughing. "Besides feeling great you mean?" he replied. "And clean? And warm? And one with the earth, and the sky and . . ."

Nolan looked him over for a moment. He knew Batman loved smoking marijuana. But though his skin seemed slightly singed, at the moment Nolan could not see any of the telltale red-eye side effects usually associated with getting high.

His friend just looked, well . . . *different.*

"Let me fly this goddamn thing," Batman yelled up to Nolan, trying to climb over the seat as Gunner and Twitch fought to keep him in the back. "C'mon! Let me bring us back in class. . . ."

Nolan just shook his head, pulled up on the copter's collective and took off.

"Strap him down," he told Gunner and Twitch. "And sit on him if you have to. If not, he might jump out and try to fly back on his own."

6

Aboard *The Immaculate Perception*

TEAM WHISKEY RETURNED to Aden once they had retrieved Batman.

But they stayed only long enough to make sure their payment from Hollywood had arrived, to wash up and get into clean clothes. Then they flew back to *The Immaculate Perception,* which by this time was sailing off the southern tip of Yemen again, five Omani warships in tow, providing security overkill.

Whiskey returned to the mega-yacht not for another mission, but for a party. The vessel's very famous passenger was throwing herself a bash to celebrate her own rescue. The crème de la crème of the Persian Gulf's wealthiest characters were invited, along with a lot of Euro-trash, as well as a sizable contingent of A-list Hollywood types who happened to be vacationing in Israel, Greece, Italy, even as far away as the Riviera. While the oil people had their own transportation, many of the Hollywood crowd had to make the trek in leased jets and then helicopters, a particularly expensive way to travel. But this was a party no one wanted to miss.

Few of the guests even knew what the party was for; the news of Emma Simms's dramatic kidnapping and rescue was not yet public knowledge. However, a *People* magazine correspondent had also been invited to the festivities—and offered an exclusive interview. This guaranteed that Emma's harrowing adventure would dominate the news cycle around the globe within twenty-four hours. And that meant more headlines, more cover photos, and more need to have that morning toast served at precisely the right temperature.

As for her multimillion-dollar movie shoot in Rome?

That would have to wait at least another week, maybe longer.

• • •

NOLAN FLEW THE OH-6 copter out to the yacht, setting down on the rear helipad, relieved to survive another copter landing.

It was just sunset, not quite twelve hours since the end of the hostage rescue, but already the yacht was full of people ready to celebrate far into the night.

Nolan had barely shut down the copter's engines when Batman bounded out of the aircraft. The yacht's stern helipad was elevated about eight feet off the rear deck. Without prompting, Batman stepped to the edge of this pad and launched himself into another spectacular aerial backflip, spinning high in the air before landing with the precision of a trapeze artist, feet first, onto the main deck.

Those guests nearby gave him an enthusiastic round of applause and welcomed him like one of their own—a celebrity. The other Whiskey members were simply bewildered. Batman had been acting extremely strange since he'd been lifted off the Somali beach that morning. First, he hadn't shut up about his time with Chief Bol Bada and the Ekita clan. They'd heard several times about how the chief had saved him when the Jihad Brotherhood unexpectedly showed up, how the clan had nursed him through the early morning hours, how they'd bathed him, *cleansed* him, given him all kinds of potions and herbs and tulip bulbs, anointings, on and on.

In the course of this, Batman had become the exact opposite of what he used to be. His cynicism was gone. He was suddenly talkative, trusting and compassionate. The chip was off his shoulder and the bitterness about losing his hand, always bubbling below the surface, was nowhere in evidence.

Nolan wrote it off to the excitement of the rescue mission combined with an overindulgence of the killer pot Batman always seemed to have access to.

But this didn't explain the twenty-foot aerial backflips.

After his grand entrance, Batman headed straight for the middle of the party. He was absorbed into a clutch of beautiful people who were just oozing with fascination at meeting a real-life pirate hunter, especially one with a mechanical hand.

More typically, Gunner and Twitch made a beeline for the obscenely sumptuous buffet in the process of being served on the second deck. Twelve pheasants, seven cows, four geese and at least one octopus had given their lives for this spread. Mangosteen, African cucumbers and jackfruit were also in abundance, as were large bowls of Chinese black ice cream. Magnums of Krug Clos du Mesnil champagne were lined up like soldiers nearby, waiting to be popped. A vast array of scotch and other liquor was also on hand. Gunner and Twitch were among the first in line for this exquisite feed.

Nolan was just happy to feel his feet on something solid again. He was here only because the other guys wanted to come. Parties were just not his thing. He felt self-conscious about his eye patch and was no good at making chitchat. But he was here now and vowed to make the best of it.

He went down the helipad's access ladder and walked toward the second deck midships, grabbing a glass of beer along the way. The mega-yacht had looked spectacular as they were flying in; it appeared even more so now. It was lit up stern to bow with thousands of tiny white lights strung in intricate patterns all over. The bridge was bathed in red. The swimming pool was a light green. Each of the vessel's many cabins had an amber glow coming from within. A fine, rose-perfumed mist was being generated throughout the yacht's ventilation system, settling on everybody and everything. Live chamber music was playing somewhere.

The middle deck was where the action was; it was about the size of a football field and was overflowing with gorgeous women wearing incredibly sexy party wear. The female wait staff, in miniskirt tuxedos and serving drinks and miniscule bits of food, were knockouts as well. There were even 3-D holographic images being randomly projected throughout the yacht, some showing tranquil aquatic scenes, others depicting clips from famous sci-fi and horror films, still others of Emma Simms in a variety of erotic poses. The sweet scent of pot was also in the air.

Nolan had never seen anything like this. It was like stepping into a real-life movie.

The beer went right to his head and he started to get caught up in the swirl—it was hard not to. The beauty, the glamour, the smell of money mixing with the rose-scented mist and the marijuana; it was intoxicating.

Maybe I'll like this more than I thought, he mused.

But at that moment, the ship's headwaiter appeared from nowhere and growled at him in French: *"Ne restez pas là imbécile. La cuisine doit être nettoyée!"*

As in: "Don't stand there you fool. The kitchen must be cleaned!"

Nolan looked at the guy like he was insane. But then he realized his bright blue Whiskey fatigues looked exactly like the one-piece suits worn by the yacht's maintenance crew.

He was instantly pissed. He tossed his beer glass over the side, then grabbed the headwaiter by the collar. He pulled his jacket open to give the guy a peek at the massive Magnum handgun he was carrying. Then he spat back at him: *"Je suis le gars qui a sauvé votre patron - tête de merde!"*

As in: "I'm the guy who saved your boss, shithead . . ."

The waiter almost had a myocardial infarction right there on the spot. He began babbling apologies, bowing and scraping as he hastily retreated below decks. But it was too late. Nolan had received the cosmos' message loud and clear.

Hero or not, he was just another part of the hired help here. This whole scene was way out of his league.

He grabbed another designer beer, then retreated to portside amidships and slipped into the shadows.

• • •

THE ITALIAN PHOTOGRAPHER drew in a lungful of pot and nearly collapsed to the deck.

"My God," he gasped. "Where did you get such great stuff?"

Batman used his mechanical hand to retrieve the joint and pass it on to the stunning British model. Though she took only a baby toke, she, too, was instantly legless. Her icy demeanor melted away as she became a hopeless ball of laughter.

Batman caught the joint just as she was dropping it and passed it on to the Austrian movie director, who imbibed and then passed it to the two gay French musicians. The doobie made one complete lap around the circle of Batman's new best friends, being reduced to nothing by the time it reached him again. Everyone had a toke and everyone got quite high—except Batman himself. When the model asked why he wasn't partaking in his own weed, he replied with a shrug, "I just don't need it anymore."

Giggling and chattering, the group commandeered a table up on the top deck where the Italian photographer produced a large vial of cocaine. Once again, everyone in the newly formed coterie partook, but Batman. Yet he seemed the highest of them all.

Between snorts, sniffs and gales of laughter, he regaled them with details of his recent adventure with the Ekita clan. The battle. The rescue. The potions. The cleansing. The tulip bulbs. He even showed them his bare back, where the four bullets stopped by the body armor had left a quartet of huge bruises, contusions that had already vanished.

The Dutch plastic surgeon opined any Ekita potions Batman had ingested were probably coca-based, with some sort of hallucinogenic property added in. He also guessed that the hot cleansing waters he'd simmered in probably contained a significant amount of aloe, or something akin to it that had taken care of his wounds.

But Batman good-naturedly dismissed the explanation.

"I like to think it was pure magic," he told them.

• • •

BATMAN EVENTUALLY EXCUSED himself from the table and made his way to the tip of the yacht's extended bow. There was no one up here, which is just as he wanted it.

His spirits were soaring into overdrive. The night sky above seemed to be on fire, with the stars revolving and dancing and moving in elaborate patterns. The air itself smelled glorious. The water below looked like a lake of champagne.

He felt all this, truly and deeply, even though he'd not had a drop of alcohol or any drugs since coming aboard. These things really *didn't* interest him anymore. He was naturally high. Feeling like a huge weight had been lifted from him, he was seeing life as it really was for the first time. And life was wonderful.

He whispered under his breath: "Thank you, Chief . . . thank you for saving me."

That's when he sensed someone behind him, someone close enough to touch him. He turned, expecting to find the Italian or the Austrian, looking for another joint.

Instead he saw a strange glowing figure materializing before his eyes. The figure was dressed all in white, yet Batman could see right through him.

A ghost . . .

Was that possible?

The apparition looked him in the eyes—and Batman felt his knees turn to rubber.

This was no ordinary phantom.

Batman knew him well. . . .

• • •

NOLAN HAD DRAINED four beers in thirty minutes. He was still hanging back from the rest of the guests and constantly checking his watch.

The encounter with the headwaiter had burst his bubble. Now he was counting the minutes before they could get off this tub.

A woman approached him out of the dark. She was not a

model, but then again not unattractive. Maybe in her forties, blond, with a good shape and a nice tan.

California . . .

Nolan knew it the moment he spotted her.

She introduced herself, but Nolan didn't really catch her name. She was with *People* magazine.

"I was just briefed by studio publicity about this rescue mission," she said. "And someone told me you were involved?"

Nolan was nonchalant. "I was," he replied.

"Do you know that Miramax is already talking about a movie?"

"Seriously?" he asked.

"You sound shocked. . . ."

"I shouldn't be, I guess," he said. "Things move pretty quick these days."

She took out a small tape recorder. "So, how did it go?" she asked him. "During the rescue mission?"

Nolan shrugged. "We got the gig, flew in, found the bad guys' camp, blew it up, rescued the hostages and flew back."

"And how many pirates did Emma herself take out?" she asked.

Nolan laughed. But then he realized the reporter was serious.

"None that I saw," he replied. "She was tied up until the battle was over."

"Interesting," the reporter said. "Can I use that?"

Nolan shrugged again. "Sure, why not?"

Suddenly all activity on the yacht came to a stop. Everyone's attention was drawn to the center of the mid deck where a dozen people had been led up from below. None of them were wearing party gear; just the opposite, in fact, many were dressed in rags. Nolan realized who these people were: the twelve other hostages Whiskey had rescued earlier that day.

A half dozen photographers followed them up on deck, all from *People*. The hostages were made to line up in two awkward rows, the photographers turning them this way and that. Then giant flash reflectors were put in place. Strobes were tested. Light readings taken. Soon enough, they were ready to take a picture.

But someone was missing.

Emma Simms.

Thirty seconds later, she appeared across the deck, making a grand entrance as usual. But to say she looked beautiful was like saying the ocean was wet.

Radiant. Striking. Transcendent . . .

Even those words didn't come close.

She was wearing an elegant white gown, with a plunging neckline—but nothing too drastic. Her hair was flowing blond curls. Her face angelic.

But she also looked terminally bored and totally uninterested in her own party.

She was ushered to a spot in the front row of the hostages. Once she was settled, she gave her publicist a curt nod and the photographers started snapping away. A warm smile came across her features, as she looked left and right, up and down. The dozens of strobes flashing on fast advance made for an interesting special effect.

Then, just like that, it was over. The cameras stopped, the strobes died away. Emma stood up and, without a word, disappeared below, a small contingent of handlers following in her wake.

The other hostages were led over to the starboard-side gangway. A small ferry leased out of Aden was waiting below. With no ceremony, the hostages were put aboard and dismissed. The last one to go was the woman who'd been horribly scarred by the Shaka. Once loaded, the ferry pulled away and disappeared into the night.

Nolan couldn't believe it.

"That might have been the coldest thing I've ever seen," he told the reporter. "Miss Perfect was there for about two hours. Some of those people had been held prisoner for years."

"Welcome to 'Emma's World,'" the reporter said. "And we're all just visiting."

She pulled out her small tape recorder and sighed. "Time to go to work. Can't keep the Princess waiting."

With that, she, too, disappeared belowdecks.

• • •

NOLAN WENT LOOKING for the rest of Whiskey. He wanted to get off the yacht in the worst way now. But as he was climbing up to the top deck, he ran into Gunner and Twitch on their way down.

Both looked rattled.

"You gotta come with us," Gunner said. "And I mean, *right now*."

Nolan followed them to the forward top deck, probably the only spot on the mega-yacht devoid of guests. They stopped at the starboard lifeboat station and pointed beneath it.

"Take a look under there," Twitch told him.

"Is this a joke?" Nolan barked back.

"Just look," Gunner urged him.

Nolan looked under the lifeboat—and saw Batman squeezed into an incredibly small space underneath, curled up in a fetal position and shaking violently.

"What the fuck . . ." Nolan gasped.

"We can't get him to come out," Gunner said. "Something is wrong with him, big time."

Nolan reached in, grabbed his colleague by the collar and, with much effort, eventually slid him out. But Batman was still trembling mightily.

"What the *fuck* is the matter with you?" Nolan demanded to know.

"I'm not sure," Batman answered, barely able to speak. "Something very fucked up just happened. . . ."

Nolan looked into his eyes. "What did you take tonight?" he asked him. "What kind of drugs?"

"Nothing. . . ." Batman just managed to whisper. "I swear, no drugs. . . ."

"How much booze then?"

But Batman was shaking his head no.

"Not a drop," he insisted. "I've been drinking nothing but water since you guys picked me up this morning."

Nolan detected no stink of alcohol around him. Nor were his pupils dilated or his eyes overly red.

Nolan told Gunner and Twitch to stand fast, and make sure no one, especially the magazine reporter, got past them.

Then Nolan led Batman up to an isolated point of the bow, out of earshot of the others.

"OK, what the hell is going on?" he asked him.

Batman's face was ashen. His eyes were watery and sunken. Nolan asked him again: "What is it? Tell me. . . ."

Batman wiped his brow, cleared his throat, then looked Nolan straight in the eye.

"I just saw Crash," was all he said.

• • •

CRASH . . .

The name went through Nolan like a knife.

These days Team Whiskey consisted of four members. But they were once five.

Jack Stacks, aka "Crash," had been their team's sniper back when Whiskey was part of Delta Force. A surfer dude from southern California, he'd been a SEAL transfer when he first joined Delta, and eventually wound up fighting with them through the Balkans, Iraq and Afghanistan.

When the team was hung out to dry after their bin Laden debacle, Crash was the only one who stayed in the business, working as a mercenary. It was he who put the team back together; it was he who kept it going. No argument, Crash was the heart and soul of Whiskey.

He was also the first to die, drowned by a renegade SEAL team who'd hijacked a U.S. Navy nuclear sub in the Caribbean. Nolan and Twitch were the ones who'd found him, floating face down near some isolated Bahamian islands, beyond resuscitation. After recovering the hijacked sub, the first thing Whiskey did was bury Crash at a veterans cemetery in Florida, a temporary interment until relatives could claim his body. All that had happened not a month ago. The team hadn't been the same since.

"So, you've lost your mind?" Nolan finally said to Batman. "*That's* what you're telling me?"

Batman was shaking his head. "I *saw* him, Snake," he insisted. "Right up there, on the top deck, near the tip of the bow."

"You know how fucking crazy that sounds, don't you?" Nolan growled.

"Of course I do," Batman shot back, eyes welling up. "But it happened. It *just* happened. I saw him just as I'm seeing you right now. It was him."

Nolan knew what was going on. Batman had been tabbed by someone at the party—LSD being the most likely culprit. Either that, or he was suffering delayed side effects of his time with the Ekita Clan back in Somalia. Or an avalanche of PTSD symptoms had just claimed him. Whatever the case, this was not a good situation.

"We're getting out of here," Nolan told him. "We're going back to Aden right now."

But Batman shook his head. "I can't fly," he said. "I can barely walk. And you stink of booze, plus you can barely drive the copter in the daytime. Who's going to fly it now, in the dead of night?"

Nolan knew he was right. Trying to fly now, in his condition, with his limited sight and high anxiety—he might wind up killing them all.

So, if flying was not an option, then they had no other choice. They'd have to stay on the yacht and baby-sit their troubled colleague all night, making sure he didn't harm himself or cause a disruption at the party.

Nolan said as much to Batman. But his friend was barely listening. He had his head in hands and was sobbing.

"There's more," he said. "Crash told me something. Something very strange."

Batman looked up at him. "Do you want to know what he said?"

Nolan shrugged wearily. Any buzz he'd had was long gone now. "You mean, do I want to know what this figment of your imagination told you?" he asked.

Batman caught his breath and began slowly. "He said we're about to be 'blinded by the light.' And that you're going back to jail. And that we should be careful if we ever hear the word 'moonglow.' "

Nolan just shook his head.

"Dude, climb onto one of the lounges up there and get some sleep," he said pointing to the unoccupied top deck. "That's the only way you're going to come out of this."

7

Off West Sumatra

THINGS WERE NOT going well for the Indonesian pirate gang known as the Kupak Tangs.

It was a few hours before sunrise. They were sailing on a leaky coastal freighter near a treacherous part of the Indian Ocean known as the Indischer Bank. The pirates were trying to elude a sea-borne posse, while fighting to keep their one remaining engine alive and preserving what little fuel they had left.

For the Tangs to be in this predicament would have been unthinkable a year ago. Back then, they were part of Zeek Kurjan's immense pirate gang, a criminal enterprise that had just about all of western Indonesia under its thumb.

But two unlucky events had cursed the Tangs recently. First, their leader, Zeek the Pirate King himself, had been killed by the American mercenary group, Team Whiskey.

Not a month later, Zeek's godfather, and the patron saint of all Indonesian pirate bands, Shanghai mobster Sunny Hi, had been assassinated, most probably by the same people who'd iced Zeek.

With their two powerful patrons gone, small brigand bands like the Tangs had little chance of survival. They'd been pursued by the Indonesian state police, no longer being paid off by Zeek's bagmen, to the point where the gang was forced out into international waters in order to escape.

Two weeks before, the Tangs had stolen the leaky freighter from the port of Balang in the Malacca Strait. Desperate to leave Indonesia in hopes of plying their trade elsewhere, they couldn't have picked a worse ship. A relic from World War Two, its engines were shot, its seams were splitting and its electrical systems were frayed and dangerous. Worst of all, its fuel tanks were half empty when the Tangs made off with it.

They'd sailed south, toward Jakarta, but one engine died two days into their journey. Then the other started leaking oil. By the time they slipped through Bakauheni Harbor and started sailing up the west side of Sumatra, all nonessential systems aboard the vessel had been turned off, including those in the tiny galley, which made little difference because the twelve-man pirate band had almost no food aboard.

Bad weather, a dwindling water supply and fights among themselves left little doubt that, at the moment, the Tangs were probably the most unsuccessful pirate gang on the planet.

This was the situation when the leaky freighter reached the Indischer Bank. This place was known for two things: its brutally thick fog banks and for being a massive spawning ground for the Indonesian short fin eel, considered a delicacy throughout Asia. It was also situated directly over one of the deepest parts of any ocean, anywhere: the 25,000-foot Java Trench.

Desperate, the Tangs had come up with a somewhat workable plan. They wanted to enter the Indischer Bank at its foggiest, find a good-size fishing ship there, hijack it and then quickly flee the area. This way they could not only get a clean vessel to escape on, they might possibly find its cargo hold full of something they could eat.

Their porous coastal freighter had only the most rudimentary sea surface radar, something bought at a RadioShack. Still, the Tangs had it working at full power as they approached the Indischer around 0300 hours. As expected, there was an enormous fog bank this morning. Pointing the radar into the mist, they were hoping to find at least a dozen fishing boats working the misty waters.

What they found instead was a U.S. Navy warship.

• • •

IT WAS THE USS *Messia*.

Six hundred feet long, with a crew of 350, it was, at least officially, an Aegis cruiser. But it had satellite dishes and VRL transmitters poking out of many places where one might expect to find naval guns, and its bridge and superstructure were covered with antennas of all types and shapes and sizes.

The best description of the USS *Messia* was probably "armed intelligence-gathering vessel," because while the ship did carry tons of eavesdropping gear, it was also equipped with surface-to-surface missiles, antiaircraft weapons and even a naval cannon or two.

Essentially, it was a spy ship—and whenever any kind of covert operation involving the United States was happening anywhere in the waters of Asia, the *Messia* could usually be found lurking close by, taking it all in.

That's what it was doing here this night, moving very slowly on the edges of the Indischer fog bank.

• • •

IT WAS TOO late to change course by the time the Tang pirates spotted the warship.

And it was their bad luck that they were heading right for it, because they knew there was a good chance their leaky rust bucket would be recognized as a pirate vessel. But they also knew turning around would be such suspicious behavior, they might as well had just run a skull and crossbones up the main mast. They had no choice but sail right past the Navy ship and hope for the best.

They were within a thousand feet of the warship when they blew their foghorn twice. A few seconds passed, then they heard the warship blast its own mighty horn twice in return. A short radio conversation ensued, discussing the distance between their two ships. The pirates blew their foghorn again at five hundred feet away from the warship, and received two more blasts in response.

Not a minute later, the pirate vessel sailed past the Navy ship, a hundred feet off its port side. The pirates blew their foghorn again, and the warship replied in kind. Moving much faster than the almost stationary warship, the pirates disappeared back into the mist thirty seconds later unmolested.

The Tangs couldn't believe it. They'd risked certain capture and had gotten away with it.

• • •

DEEP IN THE heart of the fog bank five minutes later, the pirates came upon another ship. Its name was the *Pacific Star* and, though old and rusty, it was the answer to their prayers. It was a hybrid cargo vessel and fishing boat, 250 feet long, with a deck covered with huge eel traps. It was moving very slowly to the east and sending out an SOS, asking for help.

Why the U.S. warship had not come to its aid, the Tangs did not know. But they couldn't resist. They contacted the ailing vessel, told them they would come alongside and render any assistance they needed. The captain of the stricken ship quickly agreed.

The Tangs tied up to the ailing vessel minutes later and swarmed aboard. They were met by a crew of ten sailors, all of them Vietnamese.

The captain came forward to greet the Tang gang leader warmly. But on noticing the Tangs were armed, the captain said in broken English, "I was told real guns were not part of the plan."

The Tang leader was confused. They all were.

He told the ship captain, "We're taking over your vessel. If you don't fight back, no one will be hurt."

The Vietnamese captain stared back at him. "Are you saying that you're pirates?"

The Tang leader shrugged and replied: "Yes—we are."

But still, the Vietnamese captain was confused. He said: "But you're not Filipinos. I don't understand your role in this . . ."

Now everyone on board the ship was confused. The Tangs had no idea what the Vietnamese captain was talking about.

"We are taking your ship, we are hijacking it," the Tang leader emphasized, trying to clarify the situation.

But the Vietnamese captain just shook his head. "But this ship has already been hijacked. *By Filipinos.* We've been waiting for them—but they're late."

"'Waiting for them?'" the Tang leader asked. "Who waits for pirates to take over their ship?"

The Vietnamese captain shrugged uncomfortably. "But that's what we were told to do," he said.

"By who?"

The Vietnamese captain replied testily. "By *you*—you're CIA—aren't you?"

Now the Tang leader was totally baffled—and he was getting mad. He finally pulled the arming bar back on his AK-47. That's when the Vietnamese sailors knew something was *very* wrong here.

With little more than a nod from their captain, the entire crew suddenly jumped overboard, hurling themselves into the foggy waters below.

• • •

THINGS WERE JUST as confused on the bridge of the USS *Messia,* one mile away.

The captain and his executive officer were huddled over the spy ship's ultrasophisticated sea surface radar. While the XO was studying the images coming in from the fog bank, the captain was consulting a highly classified document marked: "Operation Sea Ghost."

"Where the hell are they?" the captain finally asked with no little agitation. "According to this, they were supposed to be at the coordinate five minutes ago. They must have blown by it."

"Expand the screen coverage again," the XO told a nearby technician.

In an instant, the screen was displaying a ten-mile-square area of the Indischer Bank. It clearly showed about a dozen small fishing vessels and a large blur in the middle.

"What's with that anomaly?" the captain asked the technician.

The tech replied, "A blur could indicate two ships so close to each other it skews the equipment."

"But isn't that where our mark is supposed to be?" the captain asked, putting his finger on the blur.

"And if it's two ships, who is the other one?" the XO added.

The tech thought a moment. "Maybe that ship that went past us a few minutes ago?" he said.

"Not unless they collided out there somewhere," the XO replied. "Other than that, what would one have to do with the other—unless they answered their distress call?"

The captain was growing agitated. "Whatever happened, our Vietnamese friends don't appear to be following the plan."

The XO could only agree. "What should we do?" he asked.

The captain studied the radar screen again, then said: "Better send in the playboys. Maybe they can straighten it out."

• • •

THE XO LEFT the bridge and quickly headed aft.

He went by a sealed-off section where accommodations for the Vietnamese crew had been laid in.

Food, clothes and money were waiting for them here. The XO took a moment to peek inside the large cabin and thought, *Like a party no one wants to come to.*

He kept moving until he reached the aft portion of the bottom deck. Two fast-boats were waiting here, along with a dozen SEALs, all dressed in battle gear and mission-ready. Also on hand were five Filipinos, mercenaries hired by the CIA for this unusual occasion.

This compartment had a recessed panel on its aft wall. This panel was open and looking out onto the foggy sea.

The SEAL team commander saw the XO coming and got his men to their feet.

"What's our status, sir?" the SEAL CO asked.

"Status is officially unclear at the moment," the XO replied.

He briefed the SEALs on the situation, how there was some confusion sorting out ships inside the fog bank.

"The captain suggests you guys deploy, get into the soup and see what's going on," the XO told them.

"How about our little friends?" the SEAL asked, nodding toward the Filipinos.

The XO just shrugged. "We might have to give them a box lunch and send them home. We'll see."

"Should we bring the UDT gear?" the SEAL CO asked.

The XO eyed the three duffel bags he knew held enough explosives to sink a good-size cargo ship.

"Maybe best you guys go in first," he told the SEAL officer. "If you need the heavy stuff, we'll get it to you."

The SEAL CO just nodded.

"OK," he said. "But just in case you lose sight of us, we'll leave a trail of breadcrumbs."

• • •

FIVE MINUTES LATER, the two SEAL fast-boats were heading into the thickest part of the fog bank.

They were equipped with a smaller version of the sea surface radar. With surprisingly little difficulty, they were soon approaching what everyone had been calling "the target." At first, it looked exactly as it had been described to them: a rusty old ship.

One of the SEALs' boats came up alongside the elderly vessel and several SEALs rappelled up to it. But as soon as they were on board they knew something was wrong.

This ship was *way* older and *way* smaller than what they were expecting. Plus, there didn't seem to be anyone on board.

They searched the bridge, the cabins and the engine rooms, but found no one. And there was certainly no large shipment of old M-16 rifles or small black box that had a big "Z" stenciled onto it.

The SEAL team leader called back to the USS *Messia* with some very disturbing news.

"I hate to be the one to tell you this, sir," he said to the *Messia*'s captain. "But this ain't the ship we want."

• • •

BACK ON THE *Messia,* the captain had retreated to his cabin, hoping to figure out what had gone wrong.

He received a subsequent report from the SEALs saying they'd picked up a bunch of Vietnamese seamen in the water, but no one was exactly sure quite yet who they were.

The ship's communications officer appeared at his door a moment later holding a dispatch he'd just written.

He passed it to the captain who read it aloud: "On this date, in the area of the Mentawai Islands, the USS *Messia* engaged a cargo vessel of Vietnamese origin which had been taken over by pirates twenty-four hours before. A brief battle using five-inch naval guns ensued. The hijacked ship was sunk during this action but its captive Vietnamese crew was rescued. All pirates either died in the exchange or are missing."

The captain gave a grim laugh.

"Let's make sure we delete *all* copies of this right now," he told the communications officer. "And that's an order. . . ."

8

Aboard *The Immaculate Perception*
Gulf of Aden

THE MORNING DAWNED hot and humid.

The sun was crimson bright, turning the Gulf of Aden blood red. There was no wind. No waves. No sound. It was an uneasy calm.

The Immaculate Perception was still off Yemen, its Omani escorts in tow, doing long meandering figure eights at barely five knots.

Nolan, Gunner and Twitch had spent the night taking shifts up on the yacht's bow, keeping Batman quiet and away from the other guests. It hadn't been that difficult. While the party had grown wilder and noisier throughout the night, it finally ended with a whimper a couple hours before sunrise. Those guests who'd lacked the stamina to make it to their cabins still littered the decks. Sleeping off their inebriation, they looked like dead soldiers in the aftermath of a battle.

The sound of a helicopter approaching stirred Nolan from a half sleep. He opened his good eye just in time to see the aircraft fly overhead. It was a UH-61 Blackhawk, painted dark silver, with no markings, but with lots of antennas sticking out of its roof, nose and tail.

Nolan groaned. Only one outfit flew helicopters like this: the CIA.

Splayed on the lounge chair next to him, Gunner was now half awake, too. He saw the copter and instantly knew its origin.

"Why are *they* out here?" he asked with a yawn.

"Taking pictures," Nolan guessed sleepily. "Looking for someone topless."

They both expected the copter to just fly on past, but it

suddenly turned sharply and came in for a landing on the yacht's stern-mounted helipad.

"They're making a house call here?" Gunner asked. "Really?"

Nolan was fully awake now. "Maybe they want to talk to the ice princess about her ordeal," he mumbled, stretching his legs. "Or get her autograph."

The copter settled down and a lone passenger climbed out. Nolan and Gunner pegged him right away: the off-the-rack clothes, the bad haircut, the cheap sunglasses, an overall disheveled look; there was no doubt about it. He was from the Agency.

"Freaking spooks," Gunner mused. "They really *do* all look alike, don't they?"

The man signaled the copter pilots to kill their engines. They heard him yell: "This might take a while . . ."

Then he approached two of the yacht's clean-up crew and had a brief conversation. At the end of it, the workers pointed not toward Emma Simms's cabin below, but up to the bow where Whiskey was stationed.

"Oh fuck," Nolan grumbled. "What do they want with us?"

Gunner woke Twitch and Batman while Nolan met the man halfway up the bow.

"You're Whiskey?" the visitor asked him.

Nolan nodded. There were no handshakes, no introductions.

"I've got to talk to you and your guys," the man said urgently. He was middle-aged, bald and paunchy. This guy was a station chief, Nolan thought. And definitely not a field officer.

"Talk? Before breakfast?" Nolan asked him.

"Yes," the man replied sternly. "As in right now."

They climbed up to the bow. The others were waiting at a table right below the bridge deck. Everyone sat down.

Nolan pulled his chair next to Batman.

"How are you doing?" he asked him in a low voice.

Batman gave him an enthusiastic thumbs-up.

"One thousand percent improvement," he whispered in reply. "Nothing beats sleeping it off."

Nolan believed him. Batman looked much better than the night before.

The CIA man got right to the point. "We've been following your activities since yesterday," he said. "The kidnapping. The Somalis. The rescue mission. We figured you'd still be out here."

"But you're a little late," Gunner told him, pretending to look at his watch. "The party ended a couple hours ago."

The agent ignored him. "I'm here because we've got a major problem in Asia and, as much as it goes against my nature to admit it, we require some expert assistance."

"Just for the record, who's 'we?'" Nolan asked him.

The agent just stared back at him. "Who do you think?" he asked.

Then the agent began a strange story. Two months before, the wreckage of a C-130 cargo plane was unearthed in a remote area of Vietnam near the Laotian border. The aircraft had been shot down in 1968, crashing into a rice paddy. Apparently the paddy had become flooded soon after, as a result of heavy monsoons, causing the wreck to sink in the mud and hiding it for more than forty years. It was discovered only when local villagers looking for metal to make cooking pots began digging in the area.

Four skeletal bodies were found in the wreckage; the villagers quickly buried them. But they also found an unusual cargo container. This container was made of highly reinforced material and was marked only with a single "Z." The villagers repeatedly tried to open it, but failed each time. Eventually they turned it over to authorities.

Old hands in the Vietnamese military recognized the container as an SMT, something the U.S. used during the Indochina War to carry anything from classified documents to secret weapons to hazardous materials. Because this one was marked with a "Z", which they interpreted as meaning "hazardous," the Vietnamese wanted nothing to do with it. Their military intelligence service asked Swiss intermediaries to contact the CIA's Bangkok station and inform them of what had been found.

News of the container's discovery rippled through the Bangkok office, where a couple of semiretired contract workers remembered what the Z-box mission was all about. In fact, the Agency had looked for the Z-box for years after the war, using satellite surveillance, infiltrating U.S.-Vietnamese body recovery teams, and even sending in undercover agents to scour the Vietnamese countryside.

Now that it had been found, the Bangkok office wanted to get it out of Vietnam and dispose of it as soon as possible. But they wanted to do it in such a way that no one in the CIA would actually come in contact with it. Their reason: The box's contents were so potentially embarrassing, no one in the know wanted to get their fingerprints on it.

So they cooked up a plan. The idea was to have the Vietnamese put the container on a ship leaving Haiphong. The ship, called the *Pacific Star,* would also have a few tons of weapons stashed aboard, captured M-16s left over from the war that the Vietnamese also wanted to get rid of. These were referred to as "the bait." After a few days at sea, and once the ship was approximately twenty miles off the west coast of Sumatra, it would be taken over by "pirates," who were actually Filipino seamen in the CIA's employ. At that point, a U.S. Navy warship would engage the vessel, battle the "pirates," rescue the crew, and then sink the ship right over the Java Trench, sending it and the Z-box to one of the deepest parts of the seven seas.

"So, what happened?" Nolan asked the briefer. "I'm guessing it's not a happy ending."

The agent shook his head no.

"Our 'pirates' never made it onto the ship," he said. "The

freaking thing was taken over by *real* pirates before our guys could get into position. So now the ship, the old M-16s and this Z-box are floating around out there somewhere, but we've got no idea where."

Nolan looked at the other Whiskey members. They were all on the verge of laughing. They'd all heard some crazy CIA stories before, but this one was crazier than usual.

The agent went on. "Now, this thing was hatched strictly by the Bangkok office. No one in the White House or the Pentagon has any idea the operation was going on. The cruiser we used is assigned to us for special ops, and ninety-nine percent of its crew didn't have a clue what was up, either. But what was supposed to be a mission to avoid embarrassment for the Agency has now become an incident that could draw *huge* negative publicity for everyone involved. Just because no one ever counted on the ship being seized by *real* pirates . . ."

Finally the team burst out laughing—they couldn't help it. Lamebrained didn't come close to describing the scheme.

But the briefer surprised them by saying: "Let me finish, because it gets worse. The people in charge were so sure this would work, they'd prepared a press release to be sent out once the 'pirate ship' was sunk.

"Now, thank God the people on the Navy ship were smart enough not to issue it—but some dumb-ass in our Bangkok field office discovered his computer might have been hacked and now this press release might be out there, somewhere, too. At any moment, the world might hear the U.S. Navy sank a pirate ship off the coast of Sumatra, rescuing its Vietnamese crew in the process. The press release even says something like the 'first full-scale U.S. Navy sea battle with pirates since the 1800s.' But when it gets out that there was no battle, no heroes, no pirate ship sunk . . . it will be very bad for all involved."

There was a long, uncomfortable silence.

"So, why are you telling us this?" Nolan finally asked him.

The agent wiped some sweat from his forehead; he seemed a little out of his element here.

"Isn't it obvious?" he replied. "You're the Pirate Hunters. We want you to hunt down these pirates and get this Z-box back, before they realize what they have."

"And what do they have exactly?" Nolan asked; it was the question on everyone's mind. "What's in the box?"

But the agent shook his head gravely. "I can't tell you," he replied. "In our own lingo, the box, and what it was doing on that plane that night, has been described to me as both 'catastrophically compromising' and 'potentially horrific and beyond any plausible deniability.' If you speak the language, you know what all that means. But *what's* inside is no concern of yours. It could be feathers and popcorn for all you care. Just get it back and we'll pay you handsomely."

"OK—then can you define 'handsomely?'" Gunner asked.

"How's a hundred million sound?" the agent replied.

The team gasped.

"A hundred million *dollars*?" Gunner whispered.

The agent nodded. "You heard right . . . that's how bad we want this thing back."

The team was stunned into silence. It was an enormous figure.

"And that's tax-free," the agent went on. "But, there are guidelines you must follow or there will be no payment."

"I knew there'd be a catch," Twitch muttered, speaking for the first time. "There's *always* a catch. . . ."

"Well, this is a big one," the agent told them. "Like I said, no one in the Pentagon or in the White House is aware this Z-box has been found—and it *must* stay that way. This means no help can be asked of *any* U.S. military units or any *other* U.S. government agency in looking for this thing. *None*. If word of this leaks out from you guys, the whole thing goes down the drain—and I don't care if your fingers are three inches away from grabbing the box. The lid on this has to be sealed tight and you should all go down fighting before anyone gets a peep out of you."

Twitch raised his hand—his way of asking if he could ask a question.

"Why doesn't the Agency just go after this thing itself? You got a worldwide network; you got spies, informants, satellites. It seems you could find it quicker than us or anyone else."

Once again, the agent was shaking his head. He seemed anxious—and disorganized.

"I know that makes the most sense," he said. "But again, this thing, the original 'Z-box mission' was so off-the-reservation, that even forty years later, the Agency can't be seen anywhere near it. We can't put our fingerprints on it, we can't have a paper trail, we can't even breathe next to it. Had we dug it up ourselves that would have been a different story. But now that it's out of our control—well, that's why we'll pony up so much money for you guys to get it back."

Another silence. Then Nolan summed it up: "So if we find the pirates, the hijacked ship, and get your box back without any outside help, you'll pay us a hundred million dollars."

The agent nodded. "And I don't want to know how you are doing it, what methods you're using, what happens to the pirates, nothing. In fact, I was never here. My name is Audette, but that's all you have to know. I'll give you two sat-phones, a number and a code word. Once you've found the box, or can confirm its whereabouts, call me and give me the code word. And that's how I'll know what's happened. Agreed?"

Nolan looked at the team. They all nodded quickly. For a hundred-million-dollar payday, they'd swim to the moon and back.

The agent smiled nervously. "I'm hoping you guys hit gold right away, so this thing will be simpler than we thought."

But no sooner were those words out of his mouth than his sat-phone started beeping. The agent did all the listening in the conversation that followed.

When he hung up, he had to wipe some newly formed perspiration from his brow.

"There's been a development," he said, slowly. "Not a pleasant one . . ."

He held up his sat-phone. "That was my contact in Bangkok. Apparently the Prince of Monaco is now involved in this thing."

The team members laughed again.

"The *Prince* of *Monaco*?" Gunner exclaimed. "How the fuck . . ."

The agent explained: "We just got word that not too long after that target ship was hijacked, a sat-phone on board made seven calls, all within five minutes. One was to a number in Germany, a place called Bad Sweeten. Ever hear of it? It's a dumpy little city, some place still stuck in the old East Germany. But it's also a hotbed for al Qaeda types, as well as people who in the past have brokered ransom deals for Somali pirates. We believe many of these brokers are ex-Stazi agents—you know, the old East German secret police?"

"That's not good . . ." Gunner said.

The agent went on. "Another call from the same cell phone went to the Prince's Palace in Monaco. Then the rest went to other phones at unknown locations within Monte Carlo."

"Monaco? Monte Carlo?" Gunner said. "What could all that possibly mean?"

The agent shook his head. "I've got no idea—but we were able to track down the phone by satellite. They found it, still turned on, left adrift on a small raft not far from where the target ship was hijacked."

Whiskey groaned as one. There was no mystery to this part of the story. It was an old spy trick. By setting the sat phone adrift, the pirates were trying to confuse anyone in pursuit. It also confirmed they were smarter than previously thought.

"This means *they* know they have something more important than a bunch of old M-16s in their possession," Nolan said. "They must have found the box and determined it has value to somebody. But how?"

The agent shook his head. "Who knows? Those Vietnamese sailors might have mentioned the Agency in the confusion. That's all it would take, maybe."

Nolan said, "Well, for whatever reason, if they're talking about it to money brokers in this Bad Sweeten place, and in Monte Carlo, then I'm guessing they're trying to sell it somehow. I'm also guessing they'll try to get rid of that ship they hijacked as quickly as possible."

At this, the team nodded as one; the agent detected something.

He studied them for a moment and then asked, "So now that you have all this information, is there any chance you guys know where these mooks might be heading?"

Nolan shrugged. "Nothing is exact in our business," he said. "Most pirates are drug addicts and drunks. Few of them have ever been educated. But—if they think someone is out there looking for them, someone with the resources of the U.S. Navy or the CIA? Yes, they'll want to dump that ship quick, quiet and permanently. And for that there's only one place they'll go."

"And where is that?" the agent wanted to know.

"Ever hear of Gottabang?" Nolan asked.

• • •

GOTTABANG WAS A place where old ships went to die.

It was a vast scrap yard located on a beach in northwest India.

The place had unusual tide changes, thirty feet from high to low, which made it an ideal place to "break" ships.

An old ship destined to be broken—that is, cut up and sold for scrap—would appear off Gottabang and ride in on the high tide at full speed, intentionally beaching itself. As soon as the tide ebbed, a small army of workers would descend on the beach and, armed with cutting torches and sledgehammers, would tear into the ship like vultures, carrying it away one piece at a time until there was nothing left.

Many of the ships that met their end like this were thirty years old or more. This meant they were full of hazardous materials such as asbestos, PCBs and highly toxic hydraulic fluids and fuel.

When a ship was gutted, a lot of these harmful contents spilled out onto the beach—and most of them stayed there, to be eventually burned, which simply spread their toxicity over an even larger area. In fact, fires big and small burned along Gottabang's beach day and night, providing a poisonous atmosphere for the 20,000 people who worked and lived there.

As a result, Gottabang looked like a doomed landscape where industrialism and pollution had run rampant. On any given day, more than 100 ships sat offshore, waiting to be called to their death.

There were a few other places in Asia where ships could be broken, larger places. But Gottabang had a special distinction: It was the least regulated of all the ship-breaking operations. If pirates or anyone else wanted to get rid of a ship with no questions asked, Gottabang was the place to go.

The procedure was simple: A typical-size 500-foot cargo transporter could produce enough scrap metal to see a million-dollar profit or more. But if a pirate band wanted to quickly lose evidence of a hijacking, they could bring a ship to Gottabang and get it broken in return for a mere fraction of that amount, if anything at all, letting the bulk of the profit go to the millionaires in Bombay who owned the ship-breaking operation.

The important thing was, if such a deal could be struck between the pirates and those owners, then the ship in question would be moved to the front of the line and would cease to exist in a matter of hours.

• • •

THE CIA AGENT listened intently. Southwest Asia was not in his purview, but he'd heard of the notorious ship-breaking operations at Chittagong in Bangladesh and Arang in southern India.

"New ones opened up in Pakistan and Turkey in just the past year," Nolan told him. "It's the same situation at all of them. A few people make a lot of money by using near-slave labor and polluting a piece of the planet."

"So much for being 'green,'" the agent said.

"Only the money is green," Twitch interjected.

Nolan went on: "The pirates realize the stolen ship has more than those weapons on board, but they'll also want to cover their tracks. The people who run Gottabang are corrupt as hell. They'll have no problem breaking the hijacked ship, no questions asked."

"Let's say your scenario is correct," the agent said. "What will they do with the Z-box?"

Nolan replied. "Before that phone call just now, I would have said that maybe they'd make like old-time pirates and bury it with those M-16s someplace. Or maybe they'd try to unload it on to the crooks at Gottabang. But now, contacting those ransom brokers and people in Monte Carlo? They've got to be trying to sell it for big bucks."

"But how can we find out for sure?" the agent asked.

"First thing is to find the pirates," Nolan replied. "And that means getting to Gottabang fast. Maybe we can beat them there. But even if we don't, we can find out if they've been sniffing around and that will at least let us zero in on their location. And that sure beats looking all over the globe for them."

The agent was growing very anxious.

"Well, all this means you guys got to get cracking," he said. "And I mean, immediately."

• • •

HE LEFT THEM with two sat-phones and a business envelope holding his secure number and the code word.

The agent then retreated to the silver helicopter, looking more disheveled than before. The copter took off and, as it gained a little height, it swung back over the mega-yacht. Flying low and slow, the team was surprised to see one of the pilots was indeed taking photos. He had a camera sticking out the cockpit window and was snapping pictures of the top deck.

Once the copter had departed, only then did the team get serious about planning their new mission. From the start, they knew it wouldn't be easy.

"It means we'll have to split up," Nolan said. "The time element demands it. Half of us will have to go to Monte Carlo, while the other half goes to Gottabang."

There was murmured agreement around the table.

"But the question is, how?" Nolan added. "Those places are about two thousand miles in opposite directions. That's way beyond the range of our copters, without a hundred refuelings, that is."

"Even on a fast ship, it would still take us days to get to Monte Carlo," Gunner said, adding, "And it isn't like you can fly commercial to Gottabang."

It seemed like a huge problem.

"So, how are we going to do it then?" Twitch asked.

At that moment they heard another voice. A female voice. It was coming from right above them, not five feet away, on the bridge deck, the highest point on the yacht.

"For God's sake, tell them they can use the seaplanes if they'll just stop yapping down there. The tone of their voices is stressing out my epidermis. . . ."

Nolan just looked at the others, stunned.

The voice unquestionably belonged to Emma Simms.

And this meant only one thing: she'd been up above them the whole time, sunbathing—and listening to everything.

"Well," Gunner said dryly. "Now we know what the spooks were taking pictures of."

• • •

A MINUTE LATER, an elderly man in a flowing white gown and a gray beard climbed down off the bridge. He looked like a character from the Old Testament. He was Emma Simms's on-call shaman. They'd seen him at the party.

He approached the team, gleaming wide smile in place.

"You know in our business we shoot people who eavesdrop on private conversations," Gunner told him.

The man smiled even wider. "And in my business, people are smart enough to keep their voices down and be discreet."

The team was mortified. Here they were laughing at the CIA for their fake-hijacking-gone-wrong fuckup, and they themselves had just committed one of the biggest rookie mistakes possible: assuming they were out of earshot of everybody.

"But let's not dwell on negatives," the shaman went on. "As it turns out, my dear friend Emma has already arranged for two seaplanes to ferry some of our guests to the mainland. Once they are free, you can have use of them for as long as needed."

He pulled a BlackBerry from his robe and showed them a photograph of the planes in question.

"Will these do?" he asked.

The team looked at the photo and was shocked again. It was an image of two P-1 Shin Meiwas. Originally built by the Japanese military for antisubmarine duty, the more commonly called Shin was one of the world's last modern amphibian aircraft. It was a large plane, 108 feet from front to back with a wingspan almost as long. Though powered only by four propellers, it could fly nearly five miles high while cruising at a respectable 230 knots. Most important, the Shin had an unrefueled range of nearly 2,500 miles.

It could hardly be called a seaplane, though. A more apt description was "flying boat."

But whatever the size, a couple Shins would certainly solve Whiskey's problem. It's just that they were coming from the most unlikely source.

And that made them highly suspicious.

"What's the catch?" Twitch asked the shaman directly.

The man smiled again. In fact, he never stopped smiling.

"My good friend Emma is merely appreciative of your assistance yesterday, that's all," he said diplomatically while retreating back toward the bridge. "Besides, 'why does *everything* have to have a catch?'"

• • •

THE PAIR OF *Shins* arrived thirty minutes later.

Between a shuttle service of private helicopters and the two flying boats, the revelers were off the yacht by midafternoon, all without so much as a good-bye wave from their very famous friend.

Whiskey spent the time planning their operation. Basically, they were facing two separate missions: an armed recon to Gottabang, and an undercover intelligence-gathering mission to Monte Carlo. So, splitting up *did* make the most sense. But who would go where?

After some discussion, it was agreed that Nolan and Gunner would make up "Alpha Squad." They would fly to Gottabang in the first Shin and hopefully find evidence that the pirates were there or had been recently.

Meanwhile, Batman and Twitch would become "Beta Squad." They would take the second Shin to Monte Carlo, the other end of this trans-world puzzle, and snoop around, trying to figure out who the pirates called in the prestigious playground of the wealthy and how they might be connected to the Z-box.

The only hiccup was the matter of Batman's mental state. Nolan was able to talk to him privately late in the morning when the others went below for coffee. While Batman had just about convinced Nolan that he was back among the living, and that whatever happened the night before was already ancient history, the one-handed copter pilot didn't squawk when Nolan suggested he honcho the more subtle, "Beta" side of the plan.

"You'll look better in Monte Carlo than I will," Nolan told him.

• • •

THE ATTACK COPTER they'd used in the hostage rescue, one of two the team owned, would not play a role in the upcoming mission. Whiskey arranged to have it ferried back to Aden by the same pilot who'd flown the Bell helicopter during the attack on the pirate base.

When the Bell arrived on the mega-yacht to drop off the ferry pilot, it was also carrying another important component of Team Whiskey: The Senegals. The five seagoing soldiers of fortune, employees of the team's parent company, Kilos Shipping, had been a vital cog in Whiskey's success. But because their names were so hard to pronounce, the team just called them the Senegals, after their country of origin. Preferring a day of rest to attending a poofy party, the five West Africans had stayed in Aden after participating in the hostage rescue, relaxing at the team's headquarters high atop the Kilos Shipping building.

But now that the team had a new mission, they were back. All five would fly out with Alpha Squad.

• • •

WHISKEY WAS READY to go by sunset.

The two Shins had come alongside *The Immaculate Perception,* one tying up in front, the other in back. Up close, they were odd-looking birds. They had outrageously angled wings, and a radar dome that stuck out from under the raised cockpit, looking like a swollen red nose. And truly, they looked more like boats with wings than airplanes that could land on water. But Shins also had an unsurpassed reputation for ruggedness. And they were a breeze to fly.

The yacht's crew helped load Whiskey's gear into the flying boats and then fueled the OH-6 and the Bell for their trip back to Aden. Through it all, the mega-yacht's very famous passenger never showed her face.

Finally, as the others climbed aboard their respective planes, Nolan and Batman had one last thing to do before they went their separate ways. Standing on the mid deck gangway, Nolan gave one of the sat-phones provided by the agent to Batman, taking the other for himself. Then he opened the business envelope the agent had given him. Inside he found two index cards. Written on one was the agent's secure phone number. Written on the other was the all-important code word they would use if and when they found the Z-box.

Nolan read it first—and suddenly froze.

Then he said the code word aloud: "Moonglow."

Batman almost fell over. Nolan immediately felt his metallic hand digging into his arm.

Moonglow . . .

The exact word Batman said he'd heard from the apparition.

"Stay cool, man," Nolan told him now, pulling Batman's metal fingers out of his skin. "It's just a coincidence. It means nothing."

But Batman wasn't so sure.

"You know what they say about coincidences," he whispered. " 'If they don't mean anything, how come they happen all the time?' "

9

Above the Indian Ocean

THE *SHIN-1* WAS a flying penthouse.

This was no surprise, considering the airplane's owner was the Sultan of Oman.

A few years earlier, unhappy that his personal 767 jetliner was restricted to landing at airports, too far from his fleet of battleship-size yachts, the Sultan approached the Japanese military, which sold him two civilian versions of the Shins, making His Highness's transition from air travel to water travel that much easier when he was in the mood. It turned out the Sultan also had many friends in Hollywood, Emma Simms being his favorite. Whenever she was in his part of the world, he gave her unlimited use of the amphibians for whatever she wanted.

Of course, the Sultan *had* to travel in style, it was in his genes. That's why the *Shin-1*'s interior contained a hot tub, a big-screen TV, a half dozen private sleeping cabins, a deluxe galley, a full-sized bar, even a small disco—all furnished with luxurious leather seats and lambs-fur couches.

Everything but the hot tub was on rollers, though, and moved easily to the front of the plane, freeing up a significant amount of space deep in the cargo hold. This is where Alpha Squad stowed its gear.

Conversely, the plane's pilots were definitely un-posh. Both were ex-members of the *Stormo Incursori,* the Italian Air Force's special operations unit. Among the crème de la crème of the world's secret operators, the SI had enjoyed a string of anti-terrorist victories around the Mediterranean over the years, few of which were ever publicized.

Nolan had no doubt the Stormos would get Alpha Squad where they had to go. The flying boat had an impressive array of navigation gear, both ground-based and GPS-slaved, plus specialty equipment such as anticollision radar and even an advanced air defense system, just in case someone wanted to take a shot at their ultra-wealthy employer.

Once at their destination, though, the Stormos' skills would have to be extra sharp. They would have to avoid any local radar networks while Alpha reconned the target area from above—and that would be the easy part.

Landing off Gottabang would be a major challenge. The waters were known to be extremely rough, a nasty side effect of the area's high tidal forces. It would be like coming down in a typhoon, even though the weather might be perfectly clear. One wrong move, one rogue wave, or the slightest loss of power at the wrong moment, and the big Shin would flip over, come apart, and everyone on board would be killed.

It would only get harder for Alpha once they'd set down and left the *Shin-1*. There was the question of breathable air at Gottabang. Anything that couldn't be salvaged from the ships on the breaking beach was burned. Asbestos, PCB pipes, a galaxy of different plastics and carbon-based coatings and wire—all of it went up in flames. But because of Gottabang's location—it was carved into the side of a mountain—the resulting smoke tended to stick around. This made the local atmosphere highly toxic even for short exposures.

For this reason, the Senegals had brought a box of small oxygen tanks and masks with them from Aden. But the tanks had an endurance of just under an hour, so whatever Alpha Squad was going to do at Gottabang, they'd have to do it in less than sixty minutes.

And there was an additional time constraint: Alpha had to complete their recon of the site while still under the cover of darkness. This was especially important because in an effort to keep its near-slave-labor force from escaping, the people who ran Gottabang employed a small army of thuggish Indian mercenaries, some of them veterans of the brutal wars in Kashmir and Sri Lanka. These people were well armed with armored cars and technicals, and possibly an armed helicopter or two. They had to be avoided at all cost.

Alpha Squad's mission required a lot of moving parts. If just one of them ran into a snag, it would mean an unsuccessful mission and good-bye to Whiskey's big payday.

It might get them all killed, too.

• • •

THEY ARRIVED OVER Gottabang just before midnight.
The *Shin-1* was flying at 20,000 feet. Once on station, the

Stormos throttled down to just 120 knots and started a long, slow circle high above the notorious ship-breaking beach.

Nolan was looking out one of the plane's many observation blisters via his specially adapted one-eye nightscope. The many fires he saw below made Gottabang look even eerier and more noxious than he'd imagined. It really *was* like looking down on another planet.

The best for all concerned would be if Nolan was able to spot the missing *Pacific Star* from this height. That way, Alpha could set down close to it, dispatch a boarding party, pop any pirates they could find and then, ideally, reclaim the Z-box, all in a matter of minutes.

But this notion was quickly dismissed when Nolan realized Gottabang's highly polluted bay was absolutely crammed with ships waiting to be broken, many more than he'd expected. There were *so* many, it wasn't possible to concentrate on just one for very long from this height, never mind trying to read the name on its hull. Making a bad situation worse, the wind was blowing the lethal smoke in swirls over both land and water, further obscuring the soon-to-be-broken fleet.

Under these conditions, and the fact that the CIA, even though they'd arranged for the *Pacific Star* to be used in the botched Z-box operation, never bothered to record its dimensions or any recognizable characteristics, trying to find it from four miles up was virtually impossible.

So Nolan and Alpha had no choice. They would have to set down and look for the missing ship up close.

• • •

NOLAN WENT FORWARD to the Shin's cockpit and briefed the Stormos.

Gottabang was some distance away from any airport or Indian military bases, so the chance of them being picked up on local radar at the moment was remote. But just to be safe, the Stormos would have to bring the Shin almost straight down to the water's surface, so as not to show up on the edge of someone's long-range radar.

With this in mind, the pilots announced that everyone on board should strap in. Then they put the *Shin-1* into a long, slow spiral dive, aiming for a point about a mile off Gottabang's north side. Nolan went back to his observation blister for a moment, his night-vision scope on full power as the big plane fell out of the sky. The closer they got to Earth, the more apparent it became that the waves off the breaking beach were indeed turbulent, again a by-product of the extra-high tides that ran the dying ships up onto the sand for their final disassembling.

Add to this an ink-black night with all the smoke obscuring an otherwise bright three-quarter moon. Nolan swallowed hard. He got nervous anytime he had to fly one of the team's copters at night. Now he was plunging almost straight down, toward a dark, unruly sea, in a multi-ton airplane, its four propeller engines absolutely screaming in protest.

He finally scrambled back to his high-quality leather seat and strapped in—but he was quickly pressed up against its back cushion, absorbing g-forces like those in a supersonic jet. Only once did he manage to look across the compartment, and that was to see distress on the faces of the Senegals.

Normally very cool customers, if *they* were concerned, then everyone should be.

It seemed to take forever, but then one of the Stormos yelled over the plane's intercom: *"Preparatevi a dire una preghiera!"*

Brace yourself and say a prayer. . . .

They hit the water a moment later.

It was like going through an airplane crash in slow motion. The giant flying boat bounced once, came down again, bounced a second time, more violently than the first, came down a second time, skidded left, skidded right, bounced again, went nose up, then came down hard for a third time.

But this time, it stayed down.

They careened along the choppy water, still banging around violently, but at least they didn't go airborne again. The engines were screeching so loud, Nolan couldn't imagine anyone within a hundred miles not hearing their arrival. But that didn't matter to him at the moment. He just wanted the big plane to come to a stop.

And it did, finally. Out of nervous habit, the first thing Nolan did, after exhaling, was check his watch.

It was exactly midnight.

"Right on schedule," he thought.

He looked around the cabin, wondering how all the luxury items had managed to survive landings like that. Everyone gave him a reassuring thumbs-up.

"Les prières ont travaillé!" one of the Senegals said. Rough translation: The prayers worked. . . .

Now, on to phase two. Alpha had given themselves five minutes to get ready for their recon. They began by aligning their GPS units. Then they would start climbing into their standard armored battle suits.

But first, Gunner went looking for the head.

That's when things started to go wrong.

• • •

GUNNER HAD MADE his way almost to the front of the huge plane, when he spotted a door with Arabic writing on it. The door was unlocked, so he went in.

But instead of finding the lavatory, he realized he was in one of the plane's private cabins.

And it was here that he found Emma Simms.

Feet propped up on a chair, iPod earbuds in place, she was calmly painting her fingernails.

She looked up at him nonchalantly, seeming neither concerned nor frightened. Even after the violent touchdown, not one hair was out of place.

Gunner couldn't believe it.

"Have we landed yet?" she asked him, taking out the earbuds.

"What *the hell* are you doing here?" he roared back at her.

She ignored his question. Instead she asked him, "Can you bring me a chilled water then?"

"What are you *doing here*?" Gunner demanded of her again.

She went back to doing her nails. "I decided I wanted to see this Banging Place you girls were going on and on about. It will be good character research. End of story. Now—five ice cubes in that water, please. . . ."

Gunner called out for Nolan: "Snake—get up here *quick*!"

The Whiskey CO arrived seconds later—but he couldn't believe what he saw either.

Even as he stood in the doorway, looking at her in her silk top and tight jeans, all baubles and bling, in full princess mode, his brain refused to process what his good eye was taking in.

"She says she wanted to see Gottabang," Gunner told him feebly.

Nolan was speechless for ten long seconds.

Then he finally growled at Gunner, "Tell them . . ."

"Tell who . . . what?" Gunner replied, confused.

"The pilots," Nolan said through clenched teeth. "Tell them to take off again and go back. . . ."

But Gunner asked: "Go back? Go back where?"

He was right. Turning around and leaving now would fuck up everything. They'd have to return to Yemen, land, refuel, take off, find her yacht somewhere in the Red Sea, land, refuel, take off, fly back to Yemen, land, refuel, take off, then fly all the way back to the west coast of India.

They'd lose at least twenty-four hours screwing around like that. And with this mission, time was of the essence.

When all this became clear, Nolan gave Gunner a look. He got the hint and left the cabin, closing the door behind him.

"Is he still getting my water?" she asked once he'd gone.

Nolan was beyond furious.

"This cannot be," he told her sternly enunciating every

syllable. "You *cannot* be here. This is a serious mission, for serious money, and . . ."

She laughed a little, interrupting him. "*That* depends on what you consider 'serious money' home-boy. I made a hundred million last year just on DVD rentals . . . and I didn't have to lift a finger."

Nolan was so livid, he had to fight for his next breath.

"*Why* are you here?" he managed to ask her. "And spare me the bullshit about seeing one of the worst places in the world."

She blew on her recently coated fingernail. "OK, how about this then: Maybe I just like helping out the common people."

"Like those hostages, you mean?" Nolan shot back at her. "For all you know, that ferry sunk on the way back to Aden."

"I'm sure we would have heard if it sank," she replied in an annoying sing-songy voice. "And for your information, I believe I gave them all airfare home, too."

"Well, considering many of them were from the Gulf area anyway, that must have set you back, what? A few hundred bucks?"

"They should be grateful they got out with their lives," she said, blowing on her nails again. "They were rotting away there until I got kidnapped. If it wasn't for me, they'd still be with those Somali monkeys."

Again Nolan had to fight to take a breath. It came slow and hard, but he used it to calm down. Then he started again. "OK, please explain to me why you're here. The real reason."

She shrugged again as she applied more polish. "Maybe that whole kidnap thing was kind of a rush. I mean, skydiving? Bungee jumping? Doing meth? Same old stuff gets old pretty quick. And I get bored easily, so I got to keep feeding the monster."

"So you're an adrenaline junkie? Is that it?"

"Is that so hard to believe?" she replied. "Swimming with

the sharks. Running at Pamplona. Getting kidnapped. Getting rescued. Real stuff gets the heart pumping—and it's good for the street cred. Plus, it looks great on Twitter."

She blew on her fingernails again. "Hey, what do you think is in that Z-box thing?" she asked him out of the blue. "I'll bet it's porno of Kennedy or someone."

Nolan still couldn't believe this was happening. "Do you have any idea how dangerous this is going to be?" he asked her sharply.

"They're just pirates," she replied. "I read a pirate movie script once. They're not so scary."

"These pirates have guns," he corrected her. "Just like the last ones you saw. And they're desperate people. If you really thought deeply about this . . ."

She cut him off. "No one in my business ever 'thinks deeply' about anything," she said. "You should remember that. My world is all surface and bullshit. I do what I want to do—and that's the way I like it."

"But you have to realize what we do *is* real," he shot back. "You saw it for yourself in that pirate camp. Bullets fly. Explosions go off. Things go zipping through the air and when they hit you they can kill or maim you for life."

He pointed to his eye patch. "How do you think I got this?"

She looked him up and down for a few moments.

Then she said: "I'm guessing in your business you have to make a lot of deals? Come to terms with unsavory people?"

"What's your point?"

"OK then," she said, dropping the whole wealthy Valley Girl affectation. "You asked what the catch was? Well, here it is. I may be queen of the ball now, but I have three coke-sniffing whores nipping at my heels back in LA. One of them went to Afghanistan last month and was lucky enough to be there when they bombed her air base. Another one just bought her sixth AIDS baby. The third got grazed by a bullet in a shoot-out at a hip-hop club last week. And *then,* some asshole told *People* magazine that I was the little damsel in distress while those Somali apes had me tied up, after I wanted to tell them I fought back.

"There's a script making the rounds about a female CIA agent from the future who kicks ass. I want that script, but I also want a lot of money to do it. Which means I'll do anything to make those two things happen, and going on a real CIA mission will ace it for me.

"Now, you got to use my yacht. And now you're using my seaplanes. You're getting to use *my people,* and anything else that goes along with my name. So in return for all that, I get to go with you to this Banging Beach place. And you're going to take pictures of me there, helping you out on this mission thing, whatever you're doing. And if you say no, then *I'll* tell *my* pilots to turn around—in both planes. Or did you forget they serve at my pleasure, not yours."

Nolan was frozen to the spot, stunned by her arrogance.

"You realize that this isn't a movie, don't you?" he said. "This is real life. Can you understand that?"

She looked up at him and smiled. "Listen, my very dopey one-eyed friend. When you're in my business, *everything* is a movie . . ."

She painted one more fingernail, then said: "So . . . is that guy coming back with my water or not?"

Nolan just shook his head.

"What a bitch . . ." he said.

• • •

NOLAN RETREATED TO the rear of the plane and explained the situation to Gunner and the Senegals. They already knew Emma Simms had stowed aboard. But now she was demanding to go with them to Gottabang and wouldn't take no for an answer.

The Africans were more astonished that she'd somehow made it through the harrowing descent and landing without making a peep.

"*Elle est probablement tres médicamenteux,*" one of them said. "She is probably heavily medicated. . . ."

"I'll have what she's taking then," Gunner commented.

They agreed they had to think of a way to dissuade her from coming with them. The mission was going to be dangerous enough as it was. Having her along could turn it into a disaster.

But it was a short discussion. In all their years of special ops work, they'd never faced a situation like this. She held all the cards. It *was* her airplane, her pilots.

So, they were stuck with her.

She finally emerged from the cabin, designer jeans, silk blouse and thousand-dollar sneakers—everything she'd been wearing before, including her bling. She was also carrying a digital camera.

Nolan, Gunner and the Senegals were putting on their battle-wear when she appeared. Big helmets, flak jackets, elbow and knee pads, combat boots, ammo belt, trouble light and weapons.

She didn't say a word to them. She just looked at Nolan, expecting him to wait on her. He threw a rucksack in front of her. Inside was an extra battle suit.

"Hurry up," Nolan told her. "We're on a timetable."

She took one look at the bulky combat gear and said: "I'm not wearing this stuff."

"You are untrained, unarmed and unwelcome," Nolan shot back at her. "There's no way you're going out there with us unless you're protected to the max. End of discussion."

She stalked off—not back to her cabin, but up to the flight deck. A heated conversation ensued, half English, half Italian, between her and the Stormos. Nolan guessed she believed the pilots were her only allies and needed their support. But the Stormos told her quite clearly only one of two things could happen: either she wore the armored suit to Gottabang or she stayed on board with them. If she refused either, they would simply turn around, take off and fly away on their own call as commanders of the airplane. Then no one would go.

She was wearing the mother of all pouts when she emerged from the flight deck. Nolan's spirits lifted a little. Maybe an assault on her fashion sense was all they needed.

He was praying that she'd lock herself back inside her cabin—and allow them to proceed unencumbered. But no such luck. She stomped her way back up to the team and reluctantly started putting on the battle suit.

Nolan and Gunner groaned in unison. Even the Senegals were shaking their heads.

Nolan rubbed his tired eye. "What the hell have we gotten into?" he thought aloud.

It took a few extra minutes for her to get dressed. Of course, nothing fit to her liking. Everything was just too big for her, too tight, too heavy.

Even after she was in the battle suit, she couldn't stop complaining.

"I can't go anywhere in this thing," she said, her voice muffled by the helmet's mouth plate. "It's like a suit of armor."

"No kidding," Nolan replied, angrily fastening it a few places in the back that she couldn't reach.

When she was done, Gunner and the Senegals looked her up and down—then put their hands to their mouths to stop from laughing. They couldn't help it. All encompassing helmet, thick black visor, oxygen mask. Full torso body armor with shoulder pads, elbow pads and highly armored gloves. Kevlar bottoms with padding on the knees and ankles. Thick armored "ski boots."

She looked like a kid wearing a *RoboCop* costume.

"I will confiscate any camera that takes a picture of me besides mine!" she bellowed from behind the mask.

"Don't worry about it," Nolan said, pushing her to the rear of the plane. "No one here cares that much about you."

• • •

TIED DOWN AT the back of the cargo bay was Alpha Squad's next mode of transport: the RIB.

Standing for Rigid-hull Inflatable Boat, it was a combination rubber raft and speedboat designed by the British Special Air Service, the famous SAS. Jet-black and almost impossible to see at night, Whiskey had been lugging one around since they'd gone into the pirate-busting business. Now they would get to use it.

Upon inflating the RIB, they would slip out of the back of the flying boat's large rear hatch and dip into Gottabang Bay. Then, after one last check of their equipment, the search for the *Pacific Star* would begin in earnest.

The Stormos kept the *Shin-1*'s big engines turning, just in case a quick getaway was needed. But the RIB inflated with no problems, and its powerful near-silent engine came to life right away. The squad and Emma Simms climbed in, and finally, they were off.

Gunner piloted the boat. Nolan and the five Senegals sat around the edges with Emma Simms smack in the middle. Body armor or not, the arrangement guaranteed that if the RIB was fired on, someone else would catch the bullet before her.

They were soon moving in and out of the traffic jam of ships clogging Gottabang Bay. They had to act like detectives now, looking for one vessel among many. Though some of the ships had had their names scraped from their hulls, the remaining silhouettes were fairly easy to read via the team's night-vision scopes. Many of the ships also appeared devoid of crew. Very few had any lights burning—and all of them looked like they were barely able to stay afloat.

Nolan was trying to look in every direction at once, but there was a lot to take in. The only clue they had besides the missing ship's name, which the pirates might have changed anyway, was that the *Pacific Star* was a combination cargo ship and fishing boat. But in this floating graveyard, where virtually every ship looked the same, that wasn't much to go on.

The RIB was highly maneuverable and Gunner knew how to put it through its paces. Through all the swishing and shushing, though, Nolan could hear Emma Simms loudly complaining under her helmet that she was going to fall out, that they were going to capsize, or they were going to hit something and she would sink to the bottom, so heavy was her armored body suit. But everyone in the squad just ignored her.

The waterborne search took almost thirty minutes, weaving around the ghostly fleet of ships, checking their hull conditions and trying to decipher their scraped-off names. In the end it all proved fruitless. None of the vessels was named *Pacific Star*, and none of them fit the barebones description the CIA had given them.

This meant on to Plan B. Alpha Squad would have to go ashore and look for evidence of the phantom ship there.

• • •

THEY APPROACHED THE beach slowly, not wanting to kick up any kind of visible wake.

Though it was the dead of night, a lot of noise was coming from the shore: The idling engines of heavy cutting machines, soon to be made ready for their morning work. Static and foreign voices blasting from radios up in the workers' shantytowns. The continuous baying of an unseen foghorn. There was so much smoke coming from the beach fires, it had settled on the shoreline like a toxic blanket. Nolan ordered everyone to connect their oxygen masks. Where they were going next, the air was not breathable.

Prior to leaving the *Shin*, Nolan told one of the Senegals that if Alpha had to go to the beach, he should pretend to stay behind to watch the RIB—and that he would try to make Emma Simms stay behind with him. But as soon as they made it to shore, she was the first to jump from the boat, ruining the plan. She had her camera out and was demanding someone take pictures of her. When no one would, she stormed off, marching up the beach alone, in full view of anyone who might be looking in their direction.

Nolan ran after her, practically tackling her and pulling her back into the shadows. "This place is lousy with people who won't mind shooting any of us—and not with a camera," he told her sternly. "Why can't you just stay with the goddamn boat?"

She waved him off. "Because I got this goddamn suit on," she snapped back at him. "Nothing's going to happen to me."

He kept hold of her arm, though. "If you move more than two feet away from me," he told her, "I'll shoot you myself."

Hiding the RIB in some shore vegetation, by this time the rest of the squad had caught up to them. Nolan told them to check their weapons and their breathing masks. Then they began their search of the grimy beach.

They made their way slowly at first, moving carefully among the heaps of cut steel and burning trash. The beach reminded Nolan of a battlefield that war had passed by. The carcasses of dozens of ships lay tossed about as if discarded by some giant hand. Some were in pieces; others had yet to be broken. There seemed to be no rhyme or reason to it. There were also hundreds of tools scattered about—sledgehammers, huge hacksaws, acetylene torches. Apparently once quitting time arrived, all of Gottabang's 20,000 workers just dropped whatever they were using at the moment and walked away.

All this clutter, plus the smoke and the night, made moving around the beach slow and difficult. Nolan soon realized they had to split up. Two Senegals would search the water's edge along the southern part of the beach. Two more would take the northern end. Gunner and the fifth Senegal would take the midsection. Being stuck with Emma Simms, Nolan would search the area closest to where the RIB was hidden.

He was hoping this would be the safest part of the mile-long beach to check. Because it was far from the cutting yards and the workers' shantytowns, it seemed the place where they were least likely to run into Gottabang's security thugs.

Once the squad dispersed, Nolan and Emma Simms set out, staying close to one another but not talking, which was fine with him. They passed dozens of pools of discarded fuel, oil and bloody-red lubricants. The beach was so polluted, the sand was luminescent green in some parts, so soaked through it was with toxic chemicals. Sky-high piles of insulation and mountains of ship's wall paneling soon surrounded them. Random jagged pieces of metal, lit by countless fires, big and small, were everywhere.

They reached an area jam-packed with giant pieces of broken ships. Bows, sterns, midsections. Some were cut neatly in sections, others were torn and jagged as if they'd been blown apart. It was like walking through a city where the streets contained block upon block of nightmarish buildings. These pieces towered over their heads, blotting out the night sky as effectively as the ever-present cloud of toxic smoke.

They moved along like this for nearly a half hour, Nolan checking for a ship name on every stern they came to. Every few minutes he would feel his sat-phone click twice, the signal from the other search teams checking in. But nothing beyond those two clicks meant they had no good news.

One part of Nolan was actually hoping they *wouldn't* find the remains of the ship on the beach. It was pretzel logic, but if the ship was not here, then that meant it was still out there, somewhere. If it *had* been broken already, then the contents and the pirates would be scattered by now.

Besides, if they didn't find evidence of the missing vessel here, they could leave quickly, dump Emma Simms, and resume the search somewhere else.

• • •

NOLAN WAS CERTAIN the recon mission was a bust when he returned to the water's edge and saw the other search parties all heading in his direction.

Each group reported the same thing: not even the barest clue of the *Pacific Star* had been found.

So much for Plan B.

Now they had to return to the RIB and get out of there. But when Nolan turned around to tell this to Emma Simms, she was nowhere to be seen.

"Where the fuck did she go?" he bellowed through his oxygen mask.

They fanned out immediately and began looking for her.

All kinds of thoughts were going through Nolan's mind now, not the least of which was that she could still get them all killed. But then after running about 100 feet back into the canyon of broken ships, he suddenly found her.

She was standing at the back of a severed stern they'd missed somehow, looking at the name painted below the intact railing.

She saw him coming and simply pointed up.

Nolan adjusted his nightscope and read the name.

Pacific Star . . .

She handed him her camera.

"Make sure you get my good side," she said.

10

SHADEY HADARI WAS Gottabang's Master Cutter.

He'd been employed at the breaking yard since it opened nearly twenty years before. This was substantial longevity as the Gottabang operation averaged one death, and usually a dozen mangling injuries, per day. Due to its outrageously hazardous working conditions, people looked up to Hadari as a sort of holy man, simply because he'd lasted so long at the most dangerous job in the world.

All these years of work had taken a toll on him, though. He was missing his left arm up to the elbow. He had just two fingers and a thumb on his right hand. His right foot was devoid of toes; his left ear was gone, as was all his hair, including his eyebrows and eyelashes. He had exactly two teeth left in his mouth.

He needed the help of a cane to walk and an ancient hearing aid to carry on a conversation. Though he was just thirty-eight years old, he looked twice that age at least.

He resided in a shack that was close to the beach and set away from the shantytowns where the rest of the cutting crews lived. Though built like the others, of wood and leftover ship paneling, the shack's location was considered a perk, the only reward for Hadari's long service to the multimillionaires who owned the ship-breaking operation. Its location was ideal only because most of the toxic smoke that rose from the beach did not usually blow in his direction.

Still, Hadari rarely slept, so numerous were his ailments. That's why he was wide awake when Benja, his second cousin's half-nephew, came to his shack in the dead of night asking if they could talk.

Benja was just twenty years old, but he, too, was covered with scars and bubbled skin, the result of coming in contact with so many harmful chemicals. He'd worked at Gottabang just six years, but in the day-to-day operations, he was considered a senior man as well.

Hadari motioned him inside, indicating he should close the rickety door behind him so no rats would get in.

"Visitors are here to talk to you," Benja told Hadari. "They are looking for a missing ship."

Hadari did not understand. Visitors? No one ever visited Gottabang.

"I found them, or I should say they found me, down at the water's edge," Benja went on nervously. "They want to know about a certain ship that came here to be chopped. I told them you were the wisest man on the beach. That if anyone knew, you would."

But Hadari still didn't understand. He'd been hit on the head by various objects so many times over the years, some things just didn't register. He was still stumped by Benja's news that visitors had come to the beach.

"I don't want to talk to anyone," he finally replied, his voice raspy and barely above a whisper. "If they are looking for a ship, let them float around in the bay, searching for its name. If it's not here, let them walk among the junk piles on shore and see if they recognize what's left of it."

Benja fidgeted a bit. "They have done that, uncle, with only partial results. They are pressed for time and they feel they shouldn't really be here in the first place."

"And if they are outsiders, then they are right," Hadari shot back at him. "So why did you bring them to me?"

Benja replied by taking something out of his shirt pocket. It was a hundred-dollar bill, the equivalent of a year's pay for him.

"Because they gave me this," he said. "And they said they'd give you even more, if you would talk to them."

Hadari's eyes went wide at the sight of the bill.

"Well, then bring them in, you fool!" he roared. "Why do you delay?"

Alpha Squad squeezed itself into the tiny shack a moment later.

Hadari's expression said it all. This was not what he'd been expecting. He'd assumed the "visitors" were just some steamer bums looking for their lost wreck—rich steamer bums, but bums nevertheless. These people were soldiers, dressed in battle armor and carrying enormous weapons.

"My God, are you Americans?" Hadari asked them.

"We're working for Americans," Nolan corrected him.

"Not those cursed environmentalists, I hope?" Hadari said.

Nolan emphatically shook his head no. "Not a chance."

"Is that a woman with you?" Hadari asked, looking at the heavily armored Emma Simms.

"She's just along for the ride," Nolan said, hastily pushing her to the rear of the group. He couldn't imagine what would happen if word got out that the world's most famous actress was here, in the worst place on earth.

Hadari looked her up and down again, but bought the explanation.

"You people lost a ship?" he asked them in creaky English.

"We are looking for one, yes," Nolan replied. "We know it's already been broken."

"Then you really haven't lost it," Hadari said with a tooth-less smile.

"What we need is information on it," Nolan said. "We think pirates were involved in bringing it here. Can you help us?"

Hadari hesitated. Talking to the Americans alone could get him severely punished, if not killed, by Gottabang's bru-tal overseers. Adding the topic of pirates would only seal a painful death.

But Nolan had assumed as much, so he pulled out a wad of cash—his best weapon of all—and peeled off a hundred-dollar bill.

He stuffed it in Hadari's ragged shirt pocket.

"This is for your trouble," Nolan told him. "For start-ers . . ."

Hadari considered the money for a moment and then yelled to his half-nephew. "Get outside and keep a watch out. If you see any guards coming, you must tell us before you run away like a little child. Do you understand?"

Benja understood. He disappeared out the front door and took up station just outside the little shack.

"Now, we can talk," Hadari said. "There *was* a ship that came in here late yesterday. And yes, it had a crew of pirates—they called themselves the Tangs. The whole thing was very hush-hush, though. Their ship went to the head of the line of those waiting to come up to the beach.

"Our men tore it down in just a matter of hours. The big boss put every available person on it. It ceased looking any-thing like itself within the first hour."

"What about the cargo it was carrying?" he asked Hadari.

Hadari nodded slowly. "It is so unusual that a ship arrives

here still bearing cargo. When one does, it's a bit of news. And yes, this ship was full of guns and something else."

Nolan got excited. "What was the 'something else?'"

But Hadari just shook his head. "Something strange, very unusual. But at least to me, something unknown. Before the ship was cracked, the pirates made arrangements to transfer their guns and this unusual thing to another ship. Something along the lines of a seagoing tug, I believe. Pirates favor such boats, especially if they are on the run, because they tend to blend in."

Hadari lit a cigarette. "What is it that you're really looking for then? The guns or the unusual thing?"

Nolan took off his helmet and rubbed his tired eye.

"The 'unusual thing,'" he replied wearily.

Hadari used his cane to tap him twice on the shoulder. It was almost a fatherly gesture even though they were close to the same age.

"You are looking in the wrong place," Hadari said. "Whatever the 'unusual thing' is, it's gone from here by now."

Nolan peeled off two more hundreds. He passed them to Hadari, whose eyes welled up at the sight of the money.

"Thank you, sir," Nolan told him.

"Good luck in your quest," Hadari started to say . . . but he was interrupted by Benja bursting through the door,

"The security guards are coming!" he said breathlessly.

"How many?" Hadari asked anxiously.

"At least twenty," Benja replied. "They have their machine guns and machetes. They might be heading for the Black Hole."

Then as predicted, Benja ran away.

"Go . . ." Hadari told Nolan and company urgently. "Out the back door and through the worker's settlements. Make your way back to the beach from there. But don't stop for anything—no matter what you see!"

• • •

SUDDENLY, THEY WERE running.

Gunner was up front. Then came Emma Simms, the Senegals still in a protective formation around her. Nolan was bringing up the rear.

In their previous line of work as special operators for Delta Force, Nolan and Gunner had stolen into many unfriendly places, gathered intelligence and then gotten out, sometimes clean and smooth, sometimes with an army of bad guys on their heels. They excelled in both means of escape, but never with an uninvited guest along.

As soon as they went out the back of Hadari's shack, they tumbled down a hill and found themselves on the edge of a massive slum. This was the Gottabang workers' shantytown. It was a horrible sight, thousands of decrepit hovels stretching for as far as Nolan's eye could see. Most were made of tin sheeting and cardboard, or leftover materials from the broken ships. They were crowded together in conditions that seemed impossible to support even the lowest of animal life, never mind humans. Yet, here they were.

The stink was unbelievable, even through the breathing masks. There was no sanitation here, no running water, certainly no electricity. Trash and excrement were everywhere. Even worse, the smoke from the toxic fires burning on the beach nearby hung over the slum like a cloud that refused to blow away. Animals—small dogs, cats, rats, chickens, snakes and some unidentifiable—scattered or slithered away as Alpha ran past.

Then there were the people. Nolan saw them only as eyes, staring out of the shadows, watery, frozen, *unaffected* as Alpha went splashing on by. With weapons pointing in all directions, night-vision goggles, heavy body armor and oversized Fritz helmets giving them an otherworldly appearance, Nolan would have thought, in the heat of the moment, these people would have shown some emotion: fright, wonder, amusement.

Something . . .

But they all looked dead inside.

Nolan could hear Emma Simms's muffled voice screaming out complaints throughout this dash. They were moving too fast. The body armor was hurting her knees. The smell was making her sick. She was going to catch some disease because the people here were *looking* at her.

Truth was, had she not been with them, Alpha would have been able to move a lot quicker.

Finally Nolan shouted an order and the Senegals on either side of her, reached under her arms and began half carrying her, half dragging her.

This did not stop her from complaining, though. She began yapping faster and more virulently than before.

They were totally unfamiliar with the lay of the land; all Nolan knew was they were heading north, which was the general direction of where the Shin was waiting. He'd looked behind every few seconds to see if anyone was chasing them, but saw no one.

It took Alpha five minutes of flat-out running but Nolan finally spotted the other edge of the slum terminating at the base of a sandy hill. Beyond, he could see the water and the waiting Shin.

If they could just make it over that hill . . .

• • •

GUNNER WAS THE first to reach the top of the rise.

Even with all the confusion going on around them, Nolan clearly heard his colleague cry out. Not in pain, but in surprise.

The Senegals went over next, two carrying Emma Simms between them. They, too, cried out and came to a halt. Seconds later, Nolan scrambled up the crest—and he stopped cold as well, finally seeing what had frozen the others in their tracks.

It was another slum, much smaller, and separated from the one they'd just run through. Here, the shacks were clustered in a rough circle with a sewage ditch splitting it down the middle. But the shacks themselves looked more like cages. Most were fashioned out of cargo crates only two or three feet high.

It was obvious there was no running water here either, no electricity, no sanitation facilities. And, if anything, the stink was even more overwhelming, the conditions more putrid. It made the shantytown Alpha had just passed through look luxurious by comparison.

The Black Hole . . .

That's what Hadari's nephew had called it.

At first, though, Nolan thought the place was empty, only because he couldn't believe anyone could actually live in a place like this.

But then he started seeing faces in the blackness. They looked especially eerie through his nightscope. They seemed to be floating in space at first. Initially a few pairs, then a few more. Then a dozen, then several dozen.

Gunner was the first to take out his flashlight and shine it into the center of the camp. What they saw was revolting.

There were about a hundred people here, staring out from the crates.

Auschwitz . . .

That was the first word that came to Nolan's mind. These weren't humans looking back at him as much as they were collections of bones wrapped in loose skin. They were emaciated beyond belief. Sunken eyes, sunken stomachs. Loose teeth. Many had lost their hair.

More grisly, though, many also bore the marks of being beaten—with fists or sticks, and maybe even slashed with machetes. Their wounds were infected and some still running with blood. It was also apparent that just about all these people were women and girls, with only a handful of males mixed in.

That's when another word came to Nolan: *Untouchables*. Those people at the bottom of India's caste system, people traditionally forced into the lowest kind of labor and rigidly demonized on the subcontinent.

Just what they were doing here at Gottabang also became apparent. There was a mountain of twisted pipes at one end of the Black Hole, barrels of sickly yellow powder at the other. All of the pipes had been taken from the broken ships, all of them were coated with the yellow insulation material. These people scraped the insulation from the pipes and then separated the two.

The problem was that many of the ships broken here were so old, their insulation materials almost always contained asbestos or some other equally hazardous substance.

So these people weren't just hungry and mistreated by having the worst jobs at Gottabang, they were ghastly sick as well.

"I can't take this," Gunner cried out. It was too much for all of them. "We gotta get out of here. . . ."

But at that moment Alpha heard another sound. One that was all too familiar.

Gunfire.

Suddenly tracer bullets were flying all around them, coming from all directions.

Then came the sound of explosions, and bright flashes lighting up the appallingly smoky night.

Alpha Squad hit the dirt, dragging Emma Simms down with them. Nolan looked up to see the trails of high-caliber tracer ammunition going right over his head. And with each second those streaks of light were coming closer to them. It was clear. Gottabang's notorious security forces had found them.

But everyone kept their cool—or at least the experienced members of the squad did. All her bullshit and bravado gone, Emma Simms was screaming through her battle helmet, absolutely terrified to suddenly be in the middle of yet another gunfight.

Nolan took stock of the situation. The incoming fire was unfocused and random, so he knew that whoever was shooting at them didn't have them locked in, at least not yet.

On the far side of the Black Hole was a high sand dune,

and beyond that was the sea. Even if the squad were unable to retrieve the RIB, if they reached the water, they would be able to summon the waiting *Shin* close to shore and get out that way. So, Nolan started the squad moving again.

They splashed their way through the center of the Black Hole, the sullen lifeless eyes seeming to burn right through them. Most of the gunfire was going by right over their heads, yet none of the Untouchables even flinched. To be shot, or not shot, didn't seem to make a difference to them. They were dead to it all.

Nolan tried not to look at them as he rushed by, once again bringing up the rear, but it was impossible. He'd been to a lot of bizarre places in his career—but he'd never seen anything like this.

The squad finally made it to the top of the dune, the Senegals depositing the still-screaming Emma Simms face first in the sand and holding her there.

But then came something else.

Another noise. Mechanical. Whirring, yet also like a great gust of wind.

Was that a helicopter?

Nolan had heard that the goons who guarded this awful place might have a couple civilian copters converted to gunships. But this didn't sound exactly like a helicopter. It seemed like something else.

But whatever it was, it was coming their way.

They'd just started moving to the other side of the dune when the dark object appeared above them. There was so much smoke, and so much tracer fire going over their heads, it was hard to see exactly what it was.

"Son of a bitch," Nolan whispered, trying to make it out through the smoke and gunfire. This was the last thing they needed.

Actually, the *second* last thing.

Because at that moment Emma Simms decided to freak out for real.

She managed to scramble away from the Senegals, then stand up and whip off her battle helmet. Throwing the helmet away and with her blond hair wild and flying, she began screaming at Nolan and the others, demanding they get the gunfire to stop, demanding they get her away from the awful Black Hole, demanding the people living there, just down the dune, *stop looking at her. . . .*

She was hysterical—and if Nolan had been within reach of her, he would have slapped her back to reality. But she was about twenty feet from him, fists clenched, feet stomping like a child throwing a tantrum.

She was going to get them all killed . . .

But at that moment, with the object hovering not fifty feet above them, and with the violent downwash and smoke covering them all, one of the strangest things Nolan had ever seen happened.

A shaft of blinding light exploded out of the sky. At first Nolan thought someone on the mystery craft had turned on an extremely powerful searchlight. But whatever it was, it hit Emma Simms square in the face and knocked her off her feet.

Nolan couldn't believe it. The light was *so* intense, she'd dropped like she'd been shot.

At first it seemed like the weight of the battle suit prevented Emma from getting up. But actually she lay there for a long time, the bright light burning into her eyes, she looking up at it, paralyzed.

Finally Gunner lifted his huge weapon and fired at the light. There was a loud explosion—and suddenly the light went out, and the helicopter, if that's what it was, disappeared into the smoke again.

Only then were Nolan and Gunner finally able to scramble over to Emma Simms, retrieving her discarded battle helmet along the way.

She was not moving. She was on her back—eyes wide open, but lying completely still. Neither was she breathing.

"Jessuz, we killed her . . ." Gunner cried.

He peeled off his helmet and started giving her mouth-to-mouth.

But nothing happened.

He tried again, checking for a pulse.

Still nothing.

Nolan took off his battle glove and banged her hard, once in the chest.

No response.

Gunner tried mouth-to-mouth again. *Nothing . . .*

Nolan banged her chest a second time. She did not move. For about ten seconds.

Then suddenly . . . she roared back to life.

She sat up and began shaking and gasping, like someone who'd been drowning suddenly coming up for air.

Nolan and Gunner couldn't believe it. It was like she'd come back from the dead.

They tried to lift her up, tried to put the helmet back on her, tried to drag her toward the water, but she immediately started fighting with them.

"C'mon—we have to get out of here!" Nolan screamed at her.

But five sharp fingernails were suddenly piercing their way through his thick combat suit and into his skin. She had grabbed on to him and would not let go.

He tried to shake her, tried to tear her hand away. She was looking all around her, her expression confused and horrified. It was as if she didn't know where she was, or even who she was.

Then her eyes fell on the Black Hole—and she screamed: *"We can't leave!"*

"We *have* to leave!" Nolan yelled back. "Those goons are right on our asses . . ."

"We're *not* leaving," she insisted, her voice sounding different than before. "Not without those people . . ."

Nolan just stared back at her. She looked different, too.

"What people? What are you talking about?"

"*Those* people," she said, pointing at the pitiful collection of humans huddled in the Black Hole below. "We *have to* save them. We *have to* get them out of here!"

"Save them?" Nolan yelled back, totally confused. "Why?"

"Because they're human beings . . ."

Gunner took a look into the Black Hole.

"I don't think *any of them* will be buying your latest DVD anytime soon," he yelled at her.

She took a swing at him, missing widely, but causing all three of them to tumble to the ground. It was a good thing, too, as another stream of gunfire went over their heads a moment later.

"This is not about that!" she screamed at Gunner.

"Then what the hell *is it* about?" Nolan shouted back at her.

She was trying to look in all directions at once, even though she could barely keep her head upright. She looked totally confused and totally out of it.

"I don't know!" she screamed back at them. "I just know we've got to do it!"

"But how?" Nolan shouted.

She started looking around again—it was obvious she was making it up as she went along.

Then she pointed out to the harbor. "We'll take one of those old ships," she said excitedly. "There's plenty of them out there. We'll take one—and we'll load these people on. And we'll get them away from this horrible place!"

Nolan almost couldn't speak. He started stammering. It was like she was a different person.

"But . . . but . . ."

"But what?"

"But that's just too . . . complicated," he heard himself say.

"Why?" she asked. "Why is it complicated?"

Nolan was completely flustered now. "I don't know," was all he could say. "It just is . . ."

She was furious—and crying—at the same time.

"I thought you guys were supposed to be heroes," she said angrily.

Gunner started yelling at her. "Is this the part where you tell us you hit your head and can't remember who you are?"

She swung at him again—missing again, but knocking them all off their feet a second time.

She roared back him, "For the first time ever, I *know* who I am. . . ."

They ducked another barrage of tracer fire, this one extremely close.

Nolan said to her, "Look, how about if we come back for them?"

"Come back?" she replied. "When? And with who? When will you get them a ship if not now?"

She never gave Nolan a chance to answer. She started screaming: *"Bolay! Bolay!"* to the startled people below.

Then she grabbed Nolan's M4 out of his hands and ran back down the dune and into the Black Hole, yelling at the emaciated people to follow her.

Nolan and Gunner just looked at each other, totally bewildered. The Senegals were simply stunned.

"Elle est devenue folle!" one of them yelled. She's gone crazy . . .

But Alpha Squad had no choice. They couldn't leave her here.

So they ran after her.

• • •

Gottabang Bay

THE *TAIWAN SONG* was a general-purpose cargo vessel.

Seventy years old, rusty and devoid of paint, it was 510 feet long, with a bridge at middeck and ancient loading cranes front and back. It was of utilitarian design, built decades before the first appearance of the super-sized modern ships, and ordinary in just about every way.

It had sailed around the world innumerable times, but

now its engines were shot, it was leaking in dozens of places and its electrical systems barely worked at twenty percent. Filled with asbestos-coated pipes, paneling like flash paper and even a lead-lined water tank, its Malaysian owners decided it was time to give up the ghost. They'd made a deal with the Gottabang cutting operation to have the ship broken for a payment of $150,000 cash.

There were only four crewmen remaining on board tonight. The captain had left the day before, taking a dozen hands to a new command out of Singapore. The four who remained, South Koreans all, would stay with the ship until the end, which was scheduled for shortly after sun up.

In fact, the *Taiwan Song* was first in line to be broken that day. When the call came from shore, the small crew would start the ship's balky engines and rev them up to the highest possible RPMs. Eventually steering toward the beach at absolute high tide, they would force the old ship up onto the sand as far as it could go—and that would be it. Once the vessel reached the beach, it would no longer be considered a sailing ship. At that moment, it would simply be "pre-scrap material."

Or so they thought.

The four crewmen had spent this last night up on the bridge, mixing coffee with *cheongju*, getting buzzed while staying awake. It seemed the right thing to do for this ship that would soon cease to be a ship. Most merchant sailors had gruff, hardcore exteriors, but many were sentimental about the ships they'd served on. These four had crewed the *Taiwan Song* for a long time. They were sad to see her go.

But around 0100 hours, strange things began to happen. The crewmen had just brewed another pot of coffee and were sweetening it with their potent rice wine when they heard what sounded like gunfire coming from the shore.

They retrieved their rudimentary night-vision glasses and the senior man put them on. The first thing he saw were fireworks—or what he thought were fireworks—about a quarter mile away. There were dozens of red and orange streaks crisscrossing the sky over a small hill just up from the beach. He watched these pyrotechnics for about a minute—then he saw a helicopter. Or at least he *thought* it was a helicopter. There was so much smoke and fireworks going off, he couldn't see it very clearly. Whatever it was came into view just above all the commotion, going into a lower hover. Seconds later, it illuminated a piece of ground with an extremely powerful light, something brighter than the senior crewman had ever seen coming from an aircraft.

This display lasted just a few seconds before the bright light suddenly went out. There was a chance that this aircraft was shot at, and possibly even shot down. Either way, the sailor lost sight of it a moment later.

About the same time, the fireworks doubled in intensity— but then just as quickly, they faded down to nothing and it was dark again on the other side of the hill.

The sailors knew the ship-breaking beach employed a ruthless security apparatus to keep its 20,000 laborers in line. Maybe some of these gunmen had been drinking too much and things got out of hand.

But then the senior man saw another curious sight. At least a hundred people were making their way over the hill, through the greasy saw grass and down to the beach. Women and children mostly, they were all dressed in rags and many seemed sick. Some couldn't walk and had to be helped by others.

The senior crewman's first thought was that these people were somehow responsible for all the tumult he'd just seen and were about to be executed by the Gottabang security forces. But how exactly? Were the security people going to shoot all these women and children? Or slash them to death? Or walk them into the dirty water and drown them?

None of the sailors wanted to see that.

But just as the senior man was about to turn away, another weird thing happened. Off to his left, a huge plane came into view.

It roared over their ship, its large nose pointing toward the water's surface. Just when it seemed the plane was going straight into the sea, the sailor realized it was an amphibian and it was *landing* on the water.

But why?

The hundred people were on the beach by now, and the seaplane was moving over toward them. But the senior man knew that a plane that size could hold maybe forty people tops.

The attention of the four sailors was so locked on what was happening on the beach for the next few minutes, they never noticed the two shadowy shapes sneak onto the bridge behind them.

It was the reflection in the ship's windshield that finally gave them away. The sailors turned to find two huge individuals in combat suits and giant helmets holding enormous weapons on them.

"We're really sorry, boys," one finally said in English, "but we have to borrow your ship."

11

FROM TWO MILES up, Monte Carlo looked like something from a dream.

Dozens of glittering high-rise buildings sprouting almost naturally from the side of a stately mountain; long, winding, tree-lined streets wrapped like ribbons around the city's undulating topography; a harbor full of yachts, mega-yachts and even giga-yachts, surrounded by water that shimmered like Perrier.

Batman and Twitch were up on the *Shin-2*'s flight deck, noses pressed against the cockpit glass, looking down on it all. Everything below them was clean, shiny and new. A magical place, captured permanently by a Nikon Starlight lens.

Five minutes later, they were down with a splash in Monte Carlo Bay. It was just after nine in the morning. The place was even more enchanting from eye level. The flying boat sped past the fleets of magnificent multimillion-dollar vessels; some were as big as warships and some were even bigger. A few made *The Immaculate Perception* look like a rowboat.

It was enough for Batman to forget all the weirdness from a few hours ago. He'd never been here before, but he was particularly in awe of this place. After being kicked out of Delta Force, he'd gone to work on Wall Street before getting caught up in the Wall Street meltdown and then the Madoff scandal. He'd seen wealth flaunted before; it provided a strange excitement to him. But he'd never seen anything like this.

The *Shin-2* slowed and taxied toward the inner harbor. Its arrival had not gone unnoticed. Passing two rows of fireboats, the crews sent out great plumes of water, greeting the grand seaplane. Cruise ships and nearby mega-yachts sounded their horns in welcome. Fireworks were shot off. Somewhere a band was playing.

"Is all this for us?" Twitch asked the *Shin-2*'s pilots. Unlike the people flying *Shin-1*, they were civilian pilots from the U.S.

"My guess it's more for who people *think* is aboard," the first pilot replied.

"The Ice Princess, you mean?" Batman asked him.

"More like Ice Bitch," Twitch said.

The cockpit erupted in laughter.

At that point, a formation of police helicopters went overhead trailing long red and blue streamers. More fireworks went off.

"Or, maybe this is how every flying boat is greeted here," the copilot mused. "After all, Monte Carlo is a very special place."

The *Shin-2* glided through the inner harbor. Its destination was a specially appointed dock that housed a bevy of smaller, but no less impressive amphibian aircraft.

Gazing out on all this, Batman whispered to Twitch: "This is an unlikely place for a bunch of pirates."

"There's more than one kind of pirate in the world," Twitch replied.

• • •

WHILE MONTE CARLO was famous as a place to see and be seen, Batman and Twitch were here mostly to listen.

Twitch was Whiskey's computer whiz. His laptop contained an assortment of intelligence-gathering software that he'd been carrying around since the team was reassembled. One program was a patch he'd hacked from an NSA site. It allowed him to track and isolate dozens, even hundreds, of phone conversations by intercepting key words or phrases. In this case, words such as "pirates" "Z-box" and so on would be keyed in. Once identified, the software could not only narrow down who was making the call and to whom, it could also pinpoint their location.

Beta's plan was to use this technology to set up a listening post somewhere in Monte Carlo. The pirates had made at least five phone calls to someone in the city shortly after they'd seized the *Pacific Star*. To Whiskey's thinking, they, or their confederates, would probably be making more calls to someone here, just on a different phone. Twitch's special software would allow them to identify these people and move in on them, up close and personal. And if some sort of interrogation was needed? That would not be a problem. In their Delta Force days, both Batman and Twitch had learned how to be very persuasive.

But no sooner had the *Shin-2* reached the inner harbor than Batman and Twitch realized they had a big problem on their hands.

They'd passed a sign hanging above a dock that announced the upcoming Monte Carlo Grand Prix, the famous

Formula One car race. In fact, the town was wallpapered with these signs, as the beginning of the four-day event was just forty-eight hours away. An elaborate photo shoot was taking place on the dock beneath this particular banner featuring a dozen of the powerful and sexy Formula One cars, each one draped in a couple of bikini-clad models.

As they continued into the inner harbor, the *Shin-2* passed another banner display. This one was trumpeting the first annual Trans-Atlantic Grand Prix. The banner indicated this was a competition pitting heavily modified high-speed yachts in a race from Monte Carlo to New York City. Below this banner were the two participating vessels. Both looked like overgrown speedboats on steroids.

A yacht race across an entire ocean?

"How fast can those things possibly go?" Batman asked, studying the souped-up racing yachts.

"A year ago, the fastest yacht in the world could go seventy miles an hour," one of the pilots said. "These days, they can go almost eighty miles an hour, day in and out. They are powered by gas turbines and they have plenty of fuel. They're like jet fighters, except they fly on water."

Batman tried some quick calculations. By sea, New York City was about 4,400 miles away from Monte Carlo, give or take. At eighty miles an hour, and favorable weather, a racing yacht could make it in . . .

But Twitch already had the answer for him. "About fifty-five hours," he said.

"That's the record they're going for this year," the pilot told them. "The Big Apple in a little more than two days."

Batman was amazed.

But that's when it hit him. They'd spent the entire flight here formulating their eavesdropping plan and going over a list of actions they would take if indeed they found out who the pirates were talking to. But, with not just one, but *two* Grand Prix races in town this week, he realized Monte Carlo would be absolutely mobbed and all its lodging absolutely booked.

So, where were they going to stay? And where were they going to set up this listening station?

He told this to Twitch, who was immediately on his laptop, banging the keyboard. It took less than a minute for him to confirm their worst fear: There were no rooms available within fifty miles of Monte Carlo. They'd all been sold out months ago.

And unlike *Shin-1, Shin-2* was just a taxi. The pilots were dropping off Beta Squad and then going home. Staying aboard the plane was not an option.

"Son of a bitch," Twitch said as all this was sinking in. "There really *is* no room at the inn."

* * *

BEFORE LEAVING *THE Immaculate Perception*, Batman and Twitch had borrowed civilian clothes from the crew. They might have been the best threads either had ever worn: Omani silk shirts, Versace slacks, Italian suede loafers. And these were items that belonged to the yacht's kitchen crew.

But aside from these clothes, a single debit card, Twitch's laptop, their side arms and a small backpack each, they had nothing else with them. For this last-minute mission, they were traveling very light.

The Shin finally reached the pier and a gangplank was put in place. Batman and Twitch momentarily considered just going back with the flying boat to somehow devise a Plan B. But go back where? To *The Immaculate Perception?* What would be the point of that? Besides Batman never wanted to see that particular mega-yacht again. They could return to their headquarters in Aden, but then what? There was nothing they could do there to help the situation here.

So they finally just thanked the pilots and disembarked. They watched the Shin turn around and make its way out to the harbor. Within two minutes, it was airborne again, winging its way back east, leaving them alone on the pier with no place to go.

"Do you think they have any homeless shelters here?" Twitch asked.

Batman took a look around and replied, "Maybe for people with bank accounts under a million bucks."

But at that moment, a black Mercedes SUV suddenly roared up the pier and stopped in front of them. The doors flew open and two men in trench coats jumped out. It was a balmy eighty degrees and sunny. Hardly trench coat weather.

Twitch whispered to Batman: *"Gestapo?"*

One man stayed with the vehicle. The other walked over to the Whiskey members.

"You are Major Robert Graves?" he asked Batman, noting his missing left hand. Oddly, the man's accent was mid-American.

"I used to be," Batman replied.

"And this is Mister Kapula?" he asked, turning toward Twitch.

Twitch lifted his pant leg to show he had a prosthetic leg.

"Proof enough," the stranger responded snidely.

"Who are you?" Batman asked him.

"Let's just say I'm a friend of a friend," he replied.

"But we don't have any friends here," Twitch said.

The man's facial expression did not change.

"A friend in high places, shall we say?" he replied.

Batman and Twitch looked at each other and mouthed the same thing: *Emma Simms?*

Is that who he meant?

The man indicated the SUV; its rear doors were open.

He said, "Gentlemen? If you please . . ."

• • •

SECONDS LATER, THE SUV was speeding through the streets of Monte Carlo, its driver apparently auditioning for a spot in the upcoming Formula One race. Batman and Twitch were in the back; the two trench coat men were up front. The

Whiskey members were pressed against the seats, the g-forces keeping them glued there.

"Reminds me of a ride I took in Shanghai recently," Twitch said under his breath.

Though they were going by in a blur, the streets of Monte Carlo looked surreal nevertheless. Preparations for the big road race were going on everywhere. Signs, banners, flags, advertisements, race cars, support vehicles and hundreds of media-types were all over the place. So too were flocks of the Beautiful People. Every woman they could see flashing by looked like a model. And every man looked like a billionaire.

But many of these people were walking around wearing earmuffs, even though the weather was warm and the sky was cloudless. Why? Because it was so noisy in the city, people needed ear protection.

Very strange . . .

Five minutes into the journey, Batman became convinced they were actually being brought to a police station for questioning; the guys up front just seemed like cops.

But questioning for what?

Were the Monte Carlo authorities on to them? Did they know who they were, or why they were here? Would they even care?

Batman's visions of being hit with rubber hoses faded, though, when they passed first one, then two police stations without even a pretense of slowing down. The SUV continued driving very fast through the narrow streets, passing the all-encompassing preparations for the big road race.

Throughout it all, the men in the front seat said nothing.

• • •

THEY FINALLY CAME within sight of the Prince's Palace. Sitting up on a hill, looking out on it all, this was the seat of the 700-year-old Grimaldi royal family, the nominal rulers of Monaco and, by extension, the principality Monte Carlo itself.

The palace was well named. It was huge, ornate, and lit up even though it was the daytime. It was a typical-looking Old World European castle with some modern additions.

Who the hell do the pirates know in there? Batman wondered.

The SUV sped right past, though, and another magnificent building soon came into view. This place made the Prince's Palace look like a simple apartment building.

The first indication Batman and Twitch had that this place was like nowhere else, was when they roared past the front entrance and saw a line of Rolls Royces waiting outside. They were taxis. Their drivers were wearing tuxedoes. It was the Grand Maison Casino.

The place was well named, if an architectural contradiction: very modern in materials—gold-lined revolving doors, gold-tinted windows and subtly hidden solar panels—but very much classic in design, with great columns, balconies, turrets and towers. A huge fountain shooting multicolored streams of water high into the air was the centerpiece of its ornate entrance. Many smaller fountains dotted the surrounding gardens. It was as if the building and its grounds had been built in the eighteenth century and whisked into the present day, where everything underwent a modern makeover.

Once past the main entryway, the SUV stopped at a smaller, private entrance in the rear of the fantastic building. This was obviously their destination, though Batman and Twitch had no idea what they were doing here. A tuxedo-suited doorman opened the SUV's rear door, and at his urging Batman and Twitch got out. The SUV immediately took off.

They were met by a gorgeous young Asian woman in a business suit. An earphone was partially hidden by her hair. She smiled warmly and indicated they should follow her. She guided them through this side door and to a hallway on the edge of the casino's grand lobby. They could see the lobby walls were adorned by precious art. The ceiling was an enormous fresco. There were marble columns and floors that looked like glass. Everyone seemed to be gliding rather than walking.

It looked more like a cathedral than a casino.

"This place makes the Sistine Chapel look like a dump," Twitch observed.

Separating them from this lobby, though, was a hallway still under construction. Scaffolding and lots of brushes and cans indicated a painting job was underway. Their guide led them to an elevator close to the entrance. On its door was a sign written in French: PRIVÉ—EN COURS DE RÉPARATION

Private—under repair.

The woman indicated they should ignore the sign. "Keeps the tourists away," she explained. She, too, had an American accent.

She gave them a four-number pass code that opened the elevator door. Climbing in, they rode the elevator up a handful of floors. It opened directly into a huge, lavishly appointed penthouse. Again, it was like walking back into the past— medieval artwork, oriental rugs, even some stained glass windows—but with a couple big-screen TVs, a Bose music system and other modern conveniences mixed in.

In one corner was a table with enough food for a small army. In another corner was a well-stocked bar. A gigantic picture window right in front of them looked out onto the casino's grand concourse, which boasted yet another giant fountain and pond, plus an Olympic-sized swimming pool.

And sitting out on the balcony, sunning themselves, was a quartet of bikini-clad young women drinking champagne and eating grapes. They smiled and waved at Batman and Twitch when they walked in.

Batman turned to the stunning Asian woman.

"What is all this?" he asked her.

She smiled. "It's your living quarters, of course. You needed a place to stay—correct?"

"Yes, we did," Batman replied.

She opened her arms wide to indicate the huge penthouse.

"Well then, here you are," she said. "Room for twenty—plenty of room for two."

She indicated the women on the balcony. "Those are your tour guides," she went on. "They'll show you around, and explain where things are. Now, we have lunch at the Queens Kitchen at 1:00 PM, dinner at the Château Freeye at seven and then a night of wagering begins at nine. We'll get you some clothes by that time."

She took out a silver box and opened it. Inside were two credit cards made of platinum.

"These are your most favored player cards," she said, handing one to each. "Anything you want, just show these to the manager and it will be taken care of."

Then she took two keys from her breast pocket: one silver, one gold. "You'll also need some transport, I assume?" she asked. "Do you prefer a Lamborghini or a Maserati?"

Batman and Twitch just stared back at her, dumbfounded.

She laughed a little and handed the gold key to them. "Take it from me," she said. "The Maserati is a lot more fun."

With that, she began a graceful exit by stepping back into the elevator—but Twitch stopped her.

"Who's paying for all this?" he asked her.

She just smiled again. "Your friend, of course," she said, putting her finger to her lips, hinting she could say no more.

Batman and Twitch just looked at each other again.

Emma Simms?

Who else could it be?

The woman resumed her retreat onto the elevator, smiled again and was gone, just like that.

When they were alone again, all Batman could say was: "What the hell just happened here?"

12

Indian Ocean

"ANY IDEA WHAT'S going on here, Snake?"

Nolan nervously checked his ammo clip and then looked out on the hot and hazy sea.

"I wish I did," he replied, "but I don't have a clue."

He and Gunner were sitting atop the bridge of the *Taiwan Song*. They were both armed, sweaty and anxious. Gunner had binoculars and was scanning the sea in all directions. Nolan was doing the same with his specially adapted one-eye night-vision telescope, set for daylight.

Down on the bow, two of the Senegals had set up gun slots for their M4 assault rifles. Two more Senegals were covering the stern. The fifth Senegal was on the bridge with the freighter's crew helping them steer the purloined bucket of bolts. The weather was brutally hot.

It was now late morning. They were sailing about thirty miles off the coast of India, barely making five knots. This part of the Indian Ocean was regarded by mariners as particularly treacherous waters. The area had a propensity for freak storms, waterspouts, whirlpools and tsunami-sized rogue waves. Even worse, it was a haven for pirates. Lots of them. Next to the Gulf of Aden and certain places in the Java Sea, this area had the highest concentration of pirates of anywhere in the world.

This was not a very good place to be at the moment and Nolan knew it. Twenty-four hours ago he'd been a guest on one of the most luxurious vessels on the planet, dealing only with snobs and ghosts. Now he was here, in this devil's lake, on a ship that was moving so sluggishly, the slowest fish in the sea could pass it with ease.

And for what? That was the biggest mystery.

Nolan looked out on the vast expanse of water again and thought: *How the hell did we get here?*

• • •

ESCAPING FROM GOTTABANG had been the easy part.

Once they'd stolen aboard the *Taiwan Song* using a rowboat found on the dirty beach, Nolan and Gunner had no problem getting the drunken Korean crew to do what they wanted. And what they wanted at that moment was to make Emma Simms happy and load the poor souls from the Black Hole onto the soon-to-be-broken ship.

The squad had been able to get the Untouchables onto the beach in the first place only because the Senegals had realigned themselves atop the sand dune and brought massive firepower down on the Gottabang security troops who'd been firing at them from the edge of the workers' shantytown.

But once on the beach, it was soon clear that there was no way to get the escapees onto the *Taiwan Song,* anchored 500 feet offshore. The ship didn't have any lifeboats remaining on board, and the team's RIB had been left way down near the breaking beach and thus was irretrievable.

Just about the time Nolan and Gunner were realizing all this, the ship's radio crackled to life. It was the Gottabang beachmaster, confirming the *Taiwan Song* would be the first ship broken that day and that the crew should start making preparations for it now. He ended by saying he'd be calling back in twenty minutes with further instructions on how the crew should run the old ship up onto the beach.

Of course, this was crazy. There had just been a gun battle less than a mile from the breaking operation. Tracer fire was still streaking through the sky occasionally, a few small explosions still going off. Was the beachmaster simply unaware of what was happening?

At the time, Alpha Squad didn't want to find out. They told the ship's senior crewman to reply that he was awaiting the beachmaster's further instructions. Then Nolan came up with the only way possible to get the Untouchables aboard the creaky *Taiwan Song* quickly.

The *Shin-1* had landed about halfway between the ship and the beach, thinking they would be retrieving the squad. Nolan radioed the *Stormos* with his change in plans. Moving in the fading darkness and using the pervasive smoke as cover, the pilots maneuvered their airplane right up to the beach and took on all of the Untouchables, as well as Emma and the smartly retreating Senegals. Though too overloaded to fly, the plane was still able to taxi its human cargo over to the stern of the *Taiwan Song*, where Nolan and Gunner were stationed with an access ladder. They hastily pulled everyone onto the ship.

Just as the last Untouchable was brought aboard, the ship's radio came to life again. It was the beachmaster, with his further orders. The sun was just coming up, and even though there were some small fires still burning from the gunfight, it was apparently business as usual with the breaking operation.

The beachmaster's instructions were direct. The crew was told to raise anchor, start its engine and—oddly—head out to sea. But that was only to build up speed. Once the ship was three miles off the beach, they would then turn around and head for the shore at full throttle, building the momentum needed to properly run the 30,000-ton ship aground. After hearing the instructions, Nolan told the ship's crew to follow the beachmaster's orders.

All this time Nolan had been watching the breaking beach come alive with workers, arriving for another day of hellish labor. Though it seemed one hand didn't know what the other was doing, he was half expecting some kind of armed boat to come out and challenge them at any moment. Or maybe the security troops would begin shelling them from the north beach. The emptied-out *Shin-1* had taken off and was circling high overhead by this time, giving Alpha some eyes in the sky. But no one really knew what the flying boat could do if any unfriendlies did appear.

But . . . nothing happened. There *was* no opposition. No gunboats. No counterattack from shore. The only explanation was that the people who ran Gottabang simply believed the wretched souls taken from the Black Hole just weren't worth fighting over.

With the Senegals looking over their shoulders, the ship's crew got the *Taiwan Song* moving. Zigzagging through the heavily polluted harbor, it finally made it to the less congested bay beyond.

But when the ship reached the three-mile limit, and the point where they were supposed to turn around, Nolan ordered the crew to just keep on going.

The beachmaster went ballistic. Screaming in a variety of languages, he repeatedly ordered the ship to turn around and come into the beach as instructed. But the *Taiwan Song* just kept on going.

After a few minutes, the angry calls from shore suddenly stopped. The radio went silent for a minute and then they heard the beachmaster's voice again, sending out instructions to the next ship in line to get ready to beach itself.

They never heard from Gottabang again.

• • •

FROM THERE, THE immediate plan was to get as far away from the ship-breaking beach as possible.

But it wasn't just the power plant on the *Taiwan Song* that proved difficult. It was also the steering; it was like something found on an amusement ride. The Senegals were expert seamen, but they discovered the ship's controls were so out of whack, it took all their strength just to move the wheel even a quarter way. Eventually, though, they got it heading southwest.

In the meantime, Gunner had walked through the ship, taking stock of their situation. He'd returned with nothing but gloomy things to report.

One of the ship's engines was not working at all; in fact, its bearings had already been removed. The second engine was working, but only at half speed. They were diesel-powered, but the ship's fuel tanks were less than one-quarter full. The electrical systems on board were down to running at ten percent; everything on the ship was dim. The bilge pumps weren't working at all. They had very little drinkable water, and practically no food. Finally, there was so much seawater in the bottom hold, the ship was sailing at a ten-degree list.

Gunner's conclusion: there was a good reason the *Taiwan Song* was about to be broken.

It was falling apart.

• • •

THE *SHIN-1* STAYED with them for the first hour. Circling overhead, the pilots used their radio to call the bridge and report to Nolan what they could see from 5,000 feet up.

But soon enough, the flying boat had reached its bingo point. It had to leave and fly the 1,000 miles back to Oman before it ran out of gas.

As the whole affair had been woefully unplanned, all Nolan could do was ask the Stormos to refuel and come back and meet them near the Lakshadweep Islands. This isolated chain was about 200 miles off the southwest coast of India and roughly 150 miles south of the ship's position at the time. It was just about the only landmass other than India itself for thousands of square miles.

Though they knew nothing about the place, at the time it seemed to be their only chance at safe haven.

• • •

ALL THIS HAD happened about thirty minutes ago.

Nolan and Gunner had taken up their stations atop the bridge soon after the *Shin* departed and had been looking out for trouble ever since.

They'd done a lot of talking in that time, but Gunner finally asked Nolan the question that was on everyone's mind:

"What do you think happened to her back there, Snake?" he said. "She's not the same person."

It was just about the only topic they hadn't discussed since leaving Gottabang. Emma Simms's sudden transformation from Bitch Princess into . . . well, into what?

"I got no idea," Nolan said. "I know I've never seen anything like it—that's for sure."

"Concussions can do weird things," Gunner offered. "Or drug withdrawals. Meth, coke, do weird things when you don't feed the need. Or maybe the Shakas gave her a Mickey like the Ekitas gave Batman? The change was just as radical. Even more so."

Nolan just shook his head. They had ninety-nine Untouchables on board. Confused and frightened, they'd been led down to the ship's mess. All of them were either sick or malnourished, and none of them spoke a word of English. Even worse, when they were first brought aboard, they were convinced they were going to be thrown overboard once the ship reached deep water. Apparently this had happened to others like them who'd lived and worked at Gottabang.

The Senegals took a long time using pantomime trying to explain to the unfortunates that they weren't being transported to their deaths, but rather they were being liberated. Still the Untouchables were terrified. It was only when Emma rose to talk to them that they calmed down and came alive.

Nolan and the others wouldn't have believed it if they hadn't seen it, but Emma had thrown herself body and soul into helping the sickly ninety-nine. She'd helped get them settled in the mess. She'd scoured the ship for sleeping mats, blankets or anything that would make them more comfortable. She'd taken Alpha squad's MREs, as in "Meals Ready to Eat," divided their contents and distributed the meager result to the starving people. She gave away her own ration of precious water, so there would be just a little more for them.

It was baffling and it was weird. The actress had done a 180-degree turnabout from her former self and they really didn't know why.

"Was it a 'Road to Damascus' moment?" Nolan wondered. "Or . . ."

"Or . . . what?"

"Or maybe people like her *can* change . . ." Nolan said.

Gunner just laughed.

"I'm just afraid if she whacks her head again, she'll turn back," he said. "Then what will we do?"

• • •

THEY SAILED ON for another hour.

The heat became even more vile. The sea was almost too calm.

They could see nothing on the horizon in any direction. The radio had fallen silent; the only noise was the constant chugging of the ship's single balky engine.

Suddenly Gunner elbowed Nolan. He nodded toward the railing on their port side.

Nolan saw that Emma had come up on deck, taking a break from the overcrowded mess hall below.

"Maybe this is your chance to get the 411," Gunner said.

Nolan had to agree.

"If I'm not back in ten minutes send a search party," he told Gunner.

Then he climbed down to the deck.

She was sitting against the bulkhead, her head on her knees. Her clothes were dirty and damp. Her hair was a mess. She was either asleep or quietly crying.

He approached her slowly. This would be the first time they'd spoken since the bizarre incident back in the Black Hole.

Suddenly he was at a loss for what to say to her. Sitting there, crouched almost into a ball, she looked like a different person.

"I think we should check you for a concussion," he finally said.

She looked up, surprised to see him. Her makeup was smeared, and yes, she'd been crying.

"Why?" she asked him simply.

"Sometimes concussions can change a person's behavior," he said, "And the condition could get worse."

But as he was saying this, he knew he was making a big mistake.

She thought a long time, then put her head back down on her knees. "If that's the case, I don't want to know."

He almost sat down next to her, but fought the temptation.

Instead, he told her their current position, speed and direction, and said that at their present course they would be near the Lakshadweep Islands sometime the next day.

Then as diplomatically as possible, he asked, "Unless there's somewhere else you'd like us to go?"

She didn't reply for a long time. And now he saw she was crying again. Finally, she wiped her eyes and looked back at him.

"I have plenty of rich friends around here," she said with a sniffle. "And they owe me plenty of favors. If I could just get in touch with them, we'll be OK. They'll help us out."

Nolan knew the ship's radio was in bad shape. It was old, and like the rest of the ship, was about to be canned. Plus, the electrical power was at such a low point on the ship, the radio was barely emitting static anymore.

The only other communications device Alpha had was the sat-phone the CIA agent gave them.

The agent had warned them strenuously not to use the phones unless they'd found the Z-box or found out what happened to it. But their mission of locating the mysterious box seemed like a dream at the moment.

Nolan decided this was an emergency and, basically, screw the CIA.

He pulled out the sat-phone and handed it to her.

"Do you know their telephone numbers?" he asked.

She wiped her eyes again, a bit surprised, and then took it from him.

"I can call anyone in the world?" she asked with another sniff.

He nodded. "That's the theory."

She thought a moment, then tried a number—but nothing happened.

She tried again. Still nothing.

She looked up at him helplessly.

"Try another number," he suggested.

She started dialing again.

But again, to no result.

"I'm not even getting a dial tone," she said finally.

Nolan took the phone back and removed the rear panel. He was instantly pissed. The battery was corroded beyond belief.

He looked the phone over and saw it had been made in China.

"Freaking spooks," he said under his breath. "How to wave the flag . . ."

He yelled up to Gunner. He was soon on the deck with them and Nolan showed him the phone. It was so frustratingly stupid Gunner couldn't help but laugh.

"This Z-box could have fallen out of the sky and hit us on the head," he roared. "And there wouldn't have been any way for us to tell them. If that ain't typical."

Nolan threw the phone into the ocean. "This cheap crap has totally screwed us, though," he said soberly.

Gunner got serious again, too. "Now what are we going to do?" he asked.

Before Nolan could answer, one of the Senegals came running down the deck. He interrupted the conversation by saying in French, "You must come to the stern, right now."

Nolan and Gunner hurried to the back of the ship, Emma trailing behind. The other Senegals were already there. They directed Nolan's attention to the northeast horizon.

"*Brigands—beaucoup d'entre eux,*" one said.

Translation: *Pirates—lots of them.*

Nolan saw a dozen motorboats heading in their direction. Each boat was brightly colored; each had a flag billowing from its back. Nolan knew who these people were right away: the *Bombay-Katum-Velay* pirate gang. Better known as the

Bom-Kats, they took their name from a small chain of islands located about twenty miles off Bombay.

Recruiting small-time criminals from India's ports, the Bom-Kats had an almost unlimited supply of manpower to draw from. They preyed mostly on coastal freighters along the west Indian coastline and luxury vessels sailing between India and the Maldives Islands. Just like pirates of old, the Bom-Kats usually killed the crew of any ship they attacked and rarely showed mercy to any passengers. Of all the Indian pirate gangs in the area, they were the most ruthless.

"Maybe this is why no one chased us out of Gottabang," Gunner said, looking at the pirate fleet through his binoculars. "Those cutters might have tipped off these guys to get their ship back."

"Either that or they're just bored," Nolan said.

To her credit, Emma wasn't scared. She was angry.

"What would they want with us?" she asked hoarsely. "The people on this ship are in rags."

Nolan just shrugged. "I guess they want the rags . . ."

He motioned to one of the Senegals to take Emma and the ship's crew below.

"Hide them and stay with them," Nolan said. "No matter what happens."

When they departed, he gathered the remaining Senegals and Gunner together. Each man checked his ammo supply. Nolan and the Senegals had half-full magazines in their M4s, with three magazines each in reserve. Gunner's Streetsweeper was about 80 percent full, plus he had a belt of C-80 ammunition, small incendiary shells that exploded like mini hand grenades.

It was a lot of firepower.

So, Nolan told them simply: "OK—you guys know what to do."

• • •

THE FIRST BOM-KAT boat came alongside the freighter five minutes later.

Those pirates on board it were sure the *Taiwan Song* would be easy pickings. It was moving at barely five knots, its engine was smoking and it was sailing with a noticeable list. It was obviously wounded and in trouble.

The Bom-Kats weren't expecting to find a mother lode aboard the rusty old ship. Rather, at the moment, it was the ship itself they were after. Their allies among the Gottabang security force had asked them to be on the lookout for the crippled vessel. If they found it, they could do whatever they wanted with whomever and whatever they found on board. The important thing was they'd get a payment for returning the vessel to the notorious ship-cracking beach.

It wasn't typical pirate work. But it was a payday, so why not take it?

The first pirate boat had reached the ship with no problem. They'd seen people scrambling about on deck as they drew closer, but that was routine. Whenever they seized a ship, the resulting panic and confusion always worked to the Bom-Kats' advantage.

The first boat tied up to the freighter's port-side access ladder. Here it lingered until a second boat arrived. Each boat had four pirates in it. Two more boats were waiting off the ship's starboard side, being held in reserve. The remainder of the pirate fleet stayed about a quarter mile away, simply to watch.

Once everyone was in position, two pirates from the first boat started to climb the steep access ladder. Ten feet from gaining the railing, the pirate first in line looked up to see an African man looking down at him from the railing.

The pirate thought the man was part of the crew and wanted to surrender. But an instant later, he saw the barrel of a huge weapon pointing down at him. He actually saw a bright flash from this weapon—but then he saw no more.

The pirate behind him took almost the full blast from this same shot after it had nearly decapitated the man in front of him. Both dead men fell back down the ladder, hitting the water with a sickening splash.

All this happened in a heartbeat. The pirates in the second boat immediately pulled out their AK-47s. They hadn't expected any resistance from this ship's crew. They'd been told four drunken, unarmed Koreans had stolen the ship. Besides, in situations like this, the imperiled crew usually fled to the engine room and locked themselves inside, letting the pirates do their dirty work unchallenged.

But now shots had been fired and two of their comrades had been killed. The Bom-Kats were forced to fight back.

As soon as the first two pirates had been shot down, three more gunmen, two Africans and a white man, appeared at the midship railing and fired at the second boat. This fusillade was so powerful it punched a hole in the brightly painted vessel, sinking it in an instant. Its four occupants were tossed into the sea and quickly caught up in the ship's wake, drowning them.

Two pirates were left in the first boat; they tried frantically to rev their engine and get away, but a fourth African gunman appeared on the railing directly above them. He fired straight down onto their heads, killing them and blowing the speedboat to bits.

The pirates on the third and fourth speedboats, waiting not far away from the ship, were stunned by what was happening. It wasn't supposed to be this way. They turned to escape.

That's when another figure appeared at the railing. He was a large white man holding a huge weapon. He started firing at the two speedboats, expertly spitting out small incendiary projectiles on high arc trajectories. Both boats were hit in seconds, exploding into flames.

And that was enough for the Bom-Kats.

The remainder of the fleet, watching this from a quarter mile away, turned south and quickly fled.

• • •

FIVE MINUTES AFTER the battle ended, Emma was back up at the railing. The other Senegal and the ship's crewmen were close behind.

Even though none of the pirates had made it aboard the ship, Emma was greeted by a grisly scene. The freighter was moving so slowly, and the sea was so calm, a couple of the dead pirates had been caught in the current and were ghoulishly keeping pace with the ship. Also some of the water around the vessel was faintly pink with blood.

"Was this all necessary?" she asked, looking over the side and shuddering.

"They weren't coming for milk and cookies," Gunner replied. "They just didn't expect a tub like this to be armed."

Emma was close to tears.

She grabbed Nolan by his arm. "We have to get that radio working somehow," she said. "I have to contact my friends and get us out of this."

At the same time, the ship's original crewmen were also surveying the post-battle scene, especially noting the bodies still floating around the slow-moving ship.

They were incredulous. They knew well how pirate-infested these waters were. They also knew how brutal the Bom-Kats could be. Yet the brigands had been dispatched in a matter of seconds.

The crewmen looked at Nolan, Gunner and the Senegals.

Then one asked in broken English: "Who *are* you people?"

• • •

ABOUT A MILE away, the lead boat of the Bom-Kats gang lingered behind as the rest of the fleet retired.

Aboard was Bompat Kalish, the commander of the pirate group. He was a large man with many tattoos and body piercings. At the moment, he was furious—and baffled. He'd just watched a number of his men being killed in the unsuccessful attack. Why was such an old wreck of a ship so heavily defended? According to his contacts at Gottabang, it was supposed to be barely crewed and not worth fighting for.

Kalish had been pirating for thirty years. He knew whoever killed his men were professionals, not just tramp seamen with rifles.

His conclusion: There was something different about this ship.

He held a pair of very powerful binoculars to his eyes, studying the freighter as it chugged its way southwest. He focused in on the railing near the bridge—and couldn't believe his eyes.

There was a blond woman up on the bow, talking to one of the gunmen. But this was not just any blond woman. Kalish thought he recognized her.

His binoculars had a small camera built in. He could take a photograph of anything he saw through the eyepieces. He zoomed all the way in on the blonde and then snapped a couple pictures.

Then, he showed the photos to his second-in-command.

This man couldn't believe it.

"Do you believe in God?" Kalish asked him.

"No—not until now," the man replied.

They went below to the captain's cabin. Its walls were covered with photos of a young blond girl.

Kalish held the photo in his binocular screen next to one of the wall photos.

"It is her," Kalish said. "I'm sure of it."

"I am, too," the second-in-command said. "But what would the world's most famous actress be doing on that old tub?"

Kalish shook his head and licked his lips.

"God be praised, I don't know," he said. "But this changes everything."

13

Grand Maison Casino
Monte Carlo

"ANY LUCK YET, girls?" Batman called over his shoulder.

The quartet of bikini-clad beauties was sitting at the penthouse's rococo table, huddled around Twitch's laptop. They were timidly pecking at the computer's keys and studying the screen with great uncertainty.

"Nothing," one cooed in a French accent. "No Wi-Fi anywhere . . ."

A second added: "Monsieur Bat? You need to find another way to amuse yourself. This is boring."

Batman poured himself another glass of mineral water and contemplated her comment.

"I'm not so sure about that," he said to himself.

He was sitting out on the penthouse's immense balcony; Monte Carlo, in all its opulent splendor, was spread out before him. This was the life—and he knew it. His divan was layered with thrice-spun Egyptian cotton; his robe was the finest Iranian silk. His sunglasses were Dolce & Gabbanas his cigar was a Cohiba Behike. There were a dozen bottles of expensive liquor less than an arm's length away. Courvoisier cognac; Macallan Whiskey; Romano Levi grappa. In the top drawer of the balcony's Leptis Magna marble table was a cube of Moroccan hashish. In the bottom drawer, a bag of pure cocaine. Both were courtesy of the management.

But still, Batman was not partaking; even his cigar wasn't lit. He was getting high in another way: by inhaling the sweet smell of success all around him. It was in the air. In the trees. In the glare of the sparkling buildings he saw everywhere he looked. The surroundings alone were intoxicating him. And whether this had to do with Chief Bada's bubble bath, or something else entirely, Batman was definitely jonesing on them.

The view from the balcony was spectacular. It overlooked both the casino's giant pool and its rear concourse, where everything was either gold, green, white or aqua blue, and everybody was one of the Beautiful People. Beyond the casino's grounds was Albert Boulevard, the *l'avenue principale* of the upcoming Monaco Grand Prix. Batman could clearly see both the race's starting point and its finish line from here. Farther out, beyond the wavy tree-lined streets, was the magnificent harbor, jammed with mega-yachts. Beyond that, the sparkling Mediterranean Sea.

In between getting thrown out of Delta and starting up their pirate-busting business, Batman had made a killing on Wall Street. He'd wheeled and dealed his way through hundreds of exotic financial transactions, earning his trading company tens of millions of dollars on a daily basis and growing himself a small fortune. When he was at the height of his Master of the Universe powers, he'd stayed and played in places like this. He knew the taste of the good life was hard to get rid of once it's been on your tongue.

Seeing all this glamour and wealth, and knowing it substituted for oxygen in Monte Carlo, made him realize just how much he missed those days.

And how much he wanted them back.

• • •

THE CHAMBERMAID HAD finished clearing away Batman's snack of pâté de foi gras and grilled bald eagle eggs when Twitch returned to the penthouse. He'd just received his third massage since arriving here that morning.

"When it comes to rubbing, the babes here are way better than the ones in Shanghai," he told Batman, looking refreshed—again.

He began browsing the bar's medley of champagnes.

"We got nothing better than this 1965 *Jamre de Grape* crap?" he asked.

Batman stretched out on his divan.

"Drink it through a straw," he said sleepily. "It tastes better that way."

Twitch grabbed a La Vielle Bon-Secours beer instead, and then pulled up a chair next to Batman.

"In the win-win department," he said, "we've been invited to three parties tonight."

"Who's throwing them?" Batman asked.

Twitch shrugged. "Models, modeling agencies, race car companies," he said. "What more do you have to know?"

Batman sipped his water. "Nothing, I guess."

Twitch eyed the four girls across the room. "Any luck with the Wi-Fi?"

"Not at last report," Batman replied. "But I'm hoping it gets fixed somehow, eventually. You know, with time."

"I just hope the Z-box stays in one place while we're waiting," Twitch said.

Batman pretended to yawn. "That 'Z-what?'" he replied wryly.

The main reason they were here—to establish an eavesdropping station—was on hold at the moment. Twitch's ultrasophisticated spy stuff only worked when his laptop was able to get Wi-Fi, and that hadn't happened since they'd arrived. It was somewhat curious that a place like the Grand Maison Casino didn't have Wi-Fi in every suite and apartment, in every nook and corner, but that was not the case. The chambermaid told them it was being installed as part of the ongoing renovations downstairs and could come to life anytime.

"How long have we been here?" Twitch asked Batman after a while. "It seems like a week."

Batman adjusted his sunglasses. "Seven or eight hours, I guess," he replied. "I've already lost track."

"Well, no Wi-Fi aside, don't you think it's getting a little odd?" Twitch said.

"The free booze, food, lodging, and gorgeous women, you mean?"

"Exactly," Twitch said. "Why are we getting all this royal treatment? Just because we happened to fly in on the plane that the bitchiest actress in the world uses?"

"You got a better theory?" Batman asked him.

"I guess not," Twitch replied.

"You want to ask someone for one?"

"And ruin the party? No thanks. . . ."

"Then drink up. . . ."

Twitch drained his beer and reached for another. "But how about we contact Snake and the Gun, then?" he suggested, still antsy about their situation. "See what's shaking with them?"

Batman yawned for real. "You know the rules," he said. "They'll call us if they have anything to report. And the same for us."

Batman looked over at the four bikini models again.

"Anything to report yet, ladies?' he asked.

They giggled, and one replied, "Not yet, Monsieur Battie."

Batman looked at Twitch and said, "Any more questions?"

The balcony phone rang; Batman answered it. A woman with a thick German accent who said she was calling from the front desk told him a visitor was on his way up to their suite.

"Who is it?" Batman asked her.

"The man to fix the Wi-Fi," she replied.

• • •

A MINUTE LATER, a small man in his mid-sixties stepped off the elevator.

He was dressed in a plain white shirt, slacks and loafers. His gray hair was a bit long for someone his age, but other than that, he looked like the most ordinary person in the world. He was smoking a cigarette—and he wasn't carrying a tool bag.

He nodded to the four girls, then walked out onto the balcony. He handed Batman his business card.

"With my compliments," he said. His accent was thick French.

On one side of the card was printed MAURICE PHILLIPE, INTERNET SPECIALIST, MONTE CARLO.

But on the other side was scrawled *We must talk Z-box*.

Batman nearly fell off his divan. He passed the card to Twitch, who was equally shocked.

"How do *you* know about *that*?" Batman whispered to the visitor.

The man eyed the four girls nearby and touched his ear. Batman got the message.

Batman called over to them: "Hey girls—why not go for a swim so we can take turns drying you off?"

The foursome had no qualms with that. They were soon in the elevator and gone.

Maurice then pulled up a chair and sat down.

"I'm your Agency contact," he told them point-blank, his accent suddenly turning very American. "I'm here to help you guys get this thing done."

Then he opened his arms to indicate the expansive suite.

"So? What do you think of all this?" he asked. "Pretty good for the setup, isn't it?"

"The 'setup?' " Batman asked. "What 'setup?' "

"You know, the 'setup,' " Maurice said with a smile. "To make you guys look like high rollers."

"As in gambling 'high rollers?' " Twitch asked him innocently.

Maurice smiled again, but now it was with some uncertainty.

"Well, that's what you're here for," he said. "The game. You know, the *big* game . . . the *Grand Gagnant?*"

Both Batman and Twitch shrugged.

"We got no idea what you're talking about," Batman said bluntly.

Maurice studied them for a moment. "You *are* the pirate-hunting guys, right? Ex–Delta Force and so on?"

Batman held up his prosthetic hand, while Twitch wiggled his prosthetic leg.

"That's us," Batman said.

"We're hard to miss," Twitch added.

Maurice looked puzzled. "And you weren't briefed on this? The game? The buy-in? All that?"

Batman and Twitch just shook their heads no.

Maurice crushed out his half-smoked cigarette. Suddenly he was very pissed.

"Who *the fuck* was your initial briefer?" he asked them harshly.

"Some guy named Audette," Batman replied.

"Emphasis on the 'odd,'" Twitch added.

Maurice shook his head. "Never heard of him."

"I think he's a station chief somewhere," Batman told him.

"And he didn't give you a wire transfer notice for ten million dollars?" Maurice asked.

Batman and Twitch just laughed at him.

"Ten million dollars?" Twitch said. "No freaking way."

Maurice's face turned red. "Jessuzz, *that's* the whole reason you two guys are here," he said heatedly. "It's the reason you've been set up in this place. It's the reason we're putting on this whole show. It's the reason for *everything* . . . And now some paper-pushing asshole station chief, with no fucking time in the field, has screwed it up."

Batman reached out and put his good hand on the man's shoulder, calming him down. "Look, we're quick learners," Batman told him. "Just start at the beginning. What game are you talking about?"

Maurice took a breath, composed himself, then inched his chair closer to them.

"OK," he said. "There's going to be a game played here, in Monte Carlo, on the night before the big race starts. It's called the Grand Gagnant, which, loosely translated, means: the big winner. It's a very secret, very exclusive card game that's being held at a very secret, very exclusive location some-where in town. It happens here every year when all the zil-lionaires show up, they play it at exactly midnight, meaning about thirty-six hours from now. What makes it not your typi-cal card game is that instead of money, priceless items make up the pot. Stolen artwork. Stolen jewelry. Moon rocks. Entire companies. Things like that. It's just one hand, just one prize. The big winner takes all."

He lit another cigarette and then continued.

"We have solid information the prize this year is going to be the Z-box. That's why we set you up in this place. You're Americans, you got distance from the Agency and you can keep your mouths shut. You were supposed to infiltrate the game, pretending to be hedge fund billionaires or some-thing, and you were going to make it look like you wanted to win this thing. But to do so, you gotta look good to everyone whose anyone in town this week. You gotta look like you have money to burn."

He held out his arms again. "That's why we arranged for this place."

"So this gagnant game is what all the calls between the pirates and those Monte Carlo phone numbers were about?" Batman asked him.

Maurice nodded. "Yes—the pirates, who we believe were part of a gang called the Tangs, and those characters from Bad Sweeten in Germany, *and* the people who run the game. They're the ones who were doing all the flapping. That's how we found out about all this."

"But how does it work?" Batman wanted to know. "You say the Z-box will be the game's big prize, but the pirates have the Z-box. Why would they make it available for this gagnant? What's their motivation?"

Maurice smiled darkly. "Well, at this point, the Tangs are either all dead or they've been paid off—most likely the for-mer. But whichever it is, it was done courtesy of those ex-Stazi middlemen from Bad Sweeten. *They* now have control of the box. They contacted the people here who run the gagnant, knowing in past years people have won giga-yachts, or Gulf-streams. Oil wells. Oil tankers. Entire oil fields."

But Batman still didn't understand.

"OK, but if the ex-Stazi guys have the box," he said, "how do *they* make money on this game?"

"From the buy-in," Maurice explained. "That's why I asked you about the entry fee. To play in the gagnant, each partici-pant has to put up ten million in cash, and then a surety for another forty million. Fifty million dollars each—that's the buy-in. By providing the Z-box as the grand prize, the Stazi guys will split all that entry money with the people running the game. This year they're expecting at least ten people to be buying in ahead of time. And if someone shows up with the full fifty million at the time and place of the game, well, they're not going to turn them away. So, do the math. They'll be splitting at least a *half billion dollar* payday, maybe more."

Batman let out a long low whistle. "Fifty million each, on one hand of cards?" he said. "Some serious bread."

"And therein lies the problem," Maurice went on. "Because the consensus is this Z-box thing is some kind of terror weapon and now, only someone who's *filthy* rich can win it—or some-one who's in league with someone who's filthy rich. And let's just say there are a lot of not-so-friendly types who live in the Middle East who are filthy rich. And if the person who eventu-ally wins it is without scruples or has ties to terrorism, then we're sure they'll use the box against the U.S."

He took another serious drag of his cigarette.

"Now, there is another scenario," he continued. "If some-one filthy rich who might *not* be linked to terrorists but is still without scruples wins the box, then they can always ransom it back to the United States. But they could also just sell it to the highest bidder—and make a nice profit that way. And believe me, though everyone in this game will be super wealthy, none of them will be upstanding citizens, I guaran-tee you that."

"The filthy rich get filthy richer," Twitch said.

"Precisely," Maurice agreed. "So, you see, if there were going to be any heroes in all this, it was supposed to be you guys. You were to get in the game, or at least pretend to, because we're pretty sure once the ten million dollar entry fee is paid, you get the location of the gagnant. And once we had that info, we were going to move in, raid the place, bust some heads and either retrieve the Z-box, or at least find out where the hell it is. Then you guys would've gotten paid for your troubles, the USA would have stayed safe and we would have all gone home fat and happy."

He crushed out his cigarette and checked his watch.

"There's a deadline for sending in the entry fee," he said. "And it's less than a half hour away. But if that asshole didn't give you the wire transfer notice that means time will run out, we won't know where this game is being played, and the whole thing is fucked."

Batman sipped his water. "As far as we could tell, this guy was just getting word of the Monte Carlo connection while he was briefing us," he said. "That's why this is all very new to us."

"Let me tell you something," Maurice replied irately. "I'm used to that kind of bullshit inside the Agency with these station chiefs. Something gets fucked up, you have someone call you, 'Oh—really—I'm just hearing about this now.' In the Agency, it's not only what you know, but when you can deny you knew it. In this case, I guarantee something got fucked up along the way."

"But, what's the problem?" Twitch asked. "Just get us another ten million and we'll go ahead with the charade."

Maurice was shaking his head.

"But don't you see?" he said, lighting yet another cigarette. "We *can't* get you another ten million. We were lucky to scrape together the ten million that asshole was supposed to give you, and that was by pure stealing from other departments. No one at Langley or at the Pentagon or in the White House even knows this goddamn thing is happening—and believe me, the way things are now in Washington, if we filched *another* ten million from somewhere, inside two minutes, a hundred people would know and they'd start asking questions about where it went."

"So, do you think Audette stole it?" Batman asked him. "Had it wired into his own account or something?"

Maurice just shrugged. "I have no idea," he admitted. "But nothing would surprise me at this point. I mean, this thing has been screwed from the start. That much I *do* know. The whole thing with staging a fake battle with the pirates? Sinking a ship over the Java Trench? I mean, they don't even do stuff like that in James Bond movies. It's crazy."

Batman opened another bottle of mineral water.

"But what if we had bought a seat at the game," he asked Maurice. "And you couldn't sniff this thing out before the game started? What would have happened then?"

Maurice shrugged again. "Then we would have found you both tuxedoes, you would have showed up for the game, infiltrated the location, then identified and pursued whoever won the box."

Batman thought a moment. "And what would have happened if we'd made it into the game and actually *won* the damn thing?"

Maurice laughed.

"Well, that would have been heaven," he said. "Neater and sweeter. You would have gotten your fee, we would have gotten the box and western civilization as we know it would have been saved. The money would have flowed then, my friends—and whatever the Agency said they were going to pay you, you would get. But it's back to the drawing board now."

Maurice looked genuinely disheartened. He eyed the bar. "Do you mind?" he asked.

"Help yourself," Batman told him.

Maurice poured out two fingers of Macallan and downed it.

"And you don't know what it is?" Batman asked him earnestly. "The box, I mean?"

Maurice slowly shook his head no. "My pay level doesn't go that high. Just some kind of scary weapon someone dreamed up long ago that might still be functional. That's all I know and frankly, that's all I *want* to know. Anything beyond that is just too disturbing to think about."

Batman thought deeply about all this. The sun was reflecting off one of the shiny buildings nearby, warming his face in a very pleasant fashion. Words started coming to him, phrases from the past: One for ten split; Low risk assessment; Cash-rich environment; Government-backed funds upon transaction completion; No tax exposure.

Suddenly he said: "OK—let's do it."

Maurice was confused. "Do what?"

"Do the buy-in," Batman said. "We got money in the bank. We'll pay the entrance fee and we'll pretend to get into the game."

The little man didn't believe him. "You're kidding, right?"

Batman shook his head. "If you know so much about us," he began, "then you must know that we just made ten million for saving America's sweetheart—and that was just one of a few very lucrative jobs we've had lately. You must also know that before I got into busting pirates I was busting nuts on Wall Street. If someone came to me and said I could put up ten million to make a hundred—*and* get my initial investment back—all of it tax-free? I'd do it in a heartbeat. In fact, I used to do it all the time, sometimes overnight. In the business it's similar to a Shearson Short-Stake Derivative. And they work all the time. So, let's do it. Let's save the country and make some money. Unless it's too late to pay the fee?"

Maurice was suddenly excited again. He checked his watch. "We have about ten minutes. If you can access your account online, we can do it all right here. I have the secret gagnant Web site address; it's just a matter of transferring the funds."

Batman turned to Twitch. "Do you have any problem with this?"

Twitch shrugged. "Hey, we have a pile of money in Aden

and it's as much yours as it is mine. Plus the other guys might appreciate you saving their big payday for them."

"My partner has spoken," Batman told Maurice.

The little man pulled out a BlackBerry Torch.

But then Twitch groaned.

"Wait a minute," he said. "We can't do it here."

"Why not?" Maurice wanted to know.

Twitch spread his hands to indicate the suite. "Because there's no Wi-Fi here," he said. "We've been trying to get it ever since we arrived."

Maurice smiled; he looked very relieved.

"Not a problem," he said. "Watch this."

He snapped his fingers twice above the BlackBerry, then showed them the screen. A Wi-Fi icon had suddenly appeared and was pulsating with vigor.

Batman and Twitch were puzzled.

"*How* did you do that?" Twitch asked him.

Maurice just smiled again. "You guys have been out to sea too long. Wi-Fi is all around us. Just because you can't get it on a laptop doesn't mean it isn't here. You just got to know where to look."

He opened a page on the BlackBerry, then passed it to Batman. Two minutes of key punching later, ten million dollars from Whiskey's account at the Bank of Aden had been deposited in the secret account of the Grand Gagnant.

"Now what?" Twitch asked.

"Now we wait," Maurice replied. "Hopefully, we'll get the location of the game in a couple hours and then we'll start the ball rolling on this. I've got a good crew with me—seven people holed up at seven different places around the city. If everything goes right, we'll either have the Z-box or a pretty good idea of its location in less than forty-eight hours. Then you guys get your money back *and* your big payday, all without breaking a sweat."

There was a short silence. Then Batman asked, "One last question. How did you know when we were coming here, I mean enough to have all this waiting for us?"

Maurice smiled again. "The pilots—of that flying boat?" he said. "They're on our payroll. It's surprising how much you learn flying rich people around the Persian Gulf."

He snuffed out his cigarette. "Now I suggest you guys relax, take a snooze, whatever—but keep a low profile. I'll be back in a couple of hours after I put out the word on this asshole Audette and see what his sorry excuse is. In the meantime you've got to maintain this façade that you're mysterious high rollers. The people running the game have no ethics when it comes to *who* plays, just as long as they have the cash. So don't let anyone see you drinking cheap beer, OK?"

Maurice got up to go. He shook hands with both of them, thanking them profusely.

"It's funny," Batman told him. "All this time we thought we were getting this royal treatment just because we flew in on Emma Simms's airplane."

Suddenly Maurice's eyes lit up.

"So I've heard," he said. "What's she like, by the way? As advertised?"

"If you're interested in the lifestyles of rich and bitchy, sure," Twitch said.

Maurice seemed embarrassed for a moment.

Then he lowered his voice and said, "Listen, when this is all over, if you guys could arrange for me to meet Emma Simms in person, I'd consider it a *big* personal favor."

14

Indian Ocean

THE SECOND PIRATE attack on the *Taiwan Song* came as a total surprise.

The hours following the first assault had been hectic. Thinking the pirates were gone for good after being bested in their initial attempt, Nolan had washed the blood off the sides of the ship, just for Emma's sake.

Once done, he'd headed for the bridge where, by switching around some of the dying electrical circuits, the ship's crew had finally gotten the shortwave radio working well enough to produce static. When further adjustments were made to the ship's battered antenna, the radio, like a small miracle, screeched to life. After a little more fine-tuning, the ship's crew declared it able to reach stations along the west coast of India and even up into Pakistan.

Emma spent the long afternoon trying to get a message out to personal contacts she had in the area, asking them to accept the ninety-nine Untouchables as refugees, the first step in getting everyone off the leaky, dangerous ship. And she had a fairly impressive list of people to contact.

Her first choice was friends at the Pakistani headquarters of the Red Crescent, the Muslim version of the Red Cross. This considerable organization was headquartered in the city of Karachi. Two years before, in return for a sizable fee, Emma had done a series of photo shoots for them, posing with starving kids in one of Pakistan's largest refugee camps. The Crescent's donations skyrocketed, at which time, the charity's executives told her if they could ever return the favor, all she had to do was ask—and she'd believed them.

She had no idea, though, if the Crescent's headquarters' communication center had a shortwave radio, or if they did, what channel they could be contacted on. But as this headquarters was situated in Karachi, and Karachi was a port city, with Nolan's help, she contacted the city harbormaster on a channel found in the *Taiwan Song*'s radio handbook. It took forever, but finally someone was able to tell them the radio channel on which to contact the Crescent's Karachi location.

So far, so good. But after spending an hour getting someone to actually reply to her radio call, the person she spoke to—a low-level functionary—said the Pakistani Crescent was too overburdened to take on the care of ninety-nine more refugees—especially *Indian* refugees.

This was just the beginning of an exasperating six hours. After the Pakistani connection went nowhere, Emma used the same tactics to contact the Indian Red Cross's Mumbai office. The previous year she'd lent her image to an assortment of their ads, again for a large fee. It took more than two hours and many repeated hailing calls until she finally got the radio channel she needed from the Mumbai District Police. But while they were glad to talk to her, once she explained why she was calling, no one at the Indian Red Cross office wanted anything to do with the ninety-nine Untouchables, especially after they heard they'd come out of Gottabang.

She did not give up, though. She began taking a series of long-end-around routes to contact political figures she knew in both India and Pakistan, but all to no avail. Then she found a phone exchange in Gujarat that could patch her from the shortwave right into the Indian phone system. Through this, she tried contacting movie stars, pop stars, and moneymen she knew in Bollywood. But none was interested in helping her.

In sheer desperation she even tried to contact Tamil Nadu—the location of the Mother Theresa Mission. Though she got through to them, after first contacting the local police, the person she talked to just kept repeating: "We have no boats. We have no boats." Finally, they just hung up on her.

This was how she spent the long, uncomfortable sweltering day. Nolan was always close by, but Emma did all the work—and bore the burden of the maddening indifference as each contact on her list turned her down.

By the time the sun started to set, it was clear that, while Emma had managed to rescue some of the most unfortunate people on the planet, no one wanted to take them in.

Night fell. It was still many hours before the *Shin-1* would return, and they weren't sure what would happen when it arrived. Even if the flying boat could take some of the refugees, where would they bring them?

"Have you ever heard of the SS *St. Louis*?" Emma asked Nolan, once she finally twitched off the radio.

He told her the name sounded familiar.

"I read a script about it once," she went on. "This ship full of Jewish refugees somehow got out of Nazi Germany right before World War Two began. When they set sail, they were sure that some other country would take them in. But every time they reached a destination, the refugees were barred from going ashore. With each stop, it got worse—even the United States wouldn't let them in.

"Finally they had to go back to Europe. When the war started many of the passengers wound up in the concentration camps and were murdered."

She looked up at Nolan. Tears were streaking the last of her eye shadow. "I'm afraid that's what's going to happen here," she said.

Without thinking, he took her hand. It was curiously cold.

"It won't," he told her. "I promise."

She looked at him with unadorned eyes. He realized for the first time just how huge and blue they were. There was an awkward silence between them. Her eyes were locked on him. In a way it felt like he was meeting her for the first time.

That's when one of the Senegals suddenly appeared on the bridge.

He shouted: *"Brigands . . . encore!"*

Pirates . . . again.

Nolan couldn't believe it.

"Are you sure?" he asked the man. "After what we did to them this morning?"

The Senegal pointed to the rear of the ship. Nolan activated his nightscope and was disheartened to see at least a dozen lights approaching the freighter in the dark, coming from the east. They had the same markings as the ones that attacked earlier. Each one was also flying what appeared to be a colorful flag.

No doubt about it. It was the Bom-Kats, again. . . .

"What is this?" Nolan groaned. "Didn't these guys have enough?"

The Senegal said in French: *"Quelques brigands n'obtiennent jamais assez."*

Some pirates never get enough. . . .

Nolan grabbed a pressurized foghorn they'd found on the bridge and blew it three times. Gunner was belowdecks trying to get the electrical systems working better. The other four Senegals were attending to the ship's balky bilge pumps. Within seconds of hearing the horn, they were up on deck, weapons ready.

Emma looked at Nolan; her eyes were watering up again.

"You know what you have to do," he told her. He realized he was still holding her hand.

She hurried down to the mess hall; Nolan motioned for one of the Senegals to follow her, the ship's regular crew was right behind.

• • •

THE PIRATES' ATTACK was coming from the rear this time—a change in their tactics.

The Bom-Kats knew the old ship was heavily defended, yet they appeared intent on doing a second assault—a notion that baffled Nolan.

The pirates might have speculated the ship was carrying drugs or weapons, and that was the reason for all the firepower on board. But drugs and guns were readily available in this part of the world, both were cheap and plentiful. The Bom-Kats were crazy to attack the ship again, thinking that sort of treasure awaited them.

But that's exactly what they were doing.

And Alpha Squad had to get ready for them.

• • •

TEN MINUTES LATER the pirates' speedboats were just 500 feet from the stern.

Nolan had set Alpha's defensive positions the best he could.

Because Gunner was holding the most individual firepower, Nolan suggested he hide behind the aft railing support beam, a thick strut of metal which looked out over the dead astern.

Nolan put two Senegals behind the starboard lifeboat station, which was now empty but still gave them adequate cover. The two other Senegals Nolan positioned atop the aft power shack, a five-foot-high hump located right behind Gunner's location.

Once they were set, Nolan climbed up to the second work railing—a sort of crow's nest where the ship's crane could be operated. It was about twenty feet off the rear deck. From here he could see everything from midships back.

Everyone had his nightscope goggles on and working. They could clearly see the pirates creeping up on them. Everyone knew to hold fire until they could determine exactly how the Bom-Kats were going to attack.

The pirates' speedboats finally passed through the ship's weak wake. There were four of them this time. Nolan counted six men in each, three times the strength of the pirates' first attack. As before, the majority of the Bom-Kats fleet stayed off about a quarter mile away.

Alpha Squad allowed the pirates to throw hook ladders up to the aft railing. The hooks were large and three-prong; the ladders were made of reinforced clothesline. Four of the ladders quickly latched on. The pirates were ready to climb.

Nolan did one last check of the squad. Each man was ready, weapon up, just waiting for his order to fire.

The pirates began climbing; this was their most vulnerable position. Alpha Squad was well hidden in the dark, aiming right down at them. Few things in combat came this tidy, Nolan thought.

But he didn't hesitate for more than a second.

He cried out: "Now!"

The resulting explosion of gunfire was so bright, it lit up the entire back of the ship. The five M4s plus Gunner's Streetsweeper tore into the pirates, killing most of them instantly. As before, those not killed outright were thrown back into the sea, most of them horribly wounded, to be swept away by the current.

It all took just ten seconds. Two dozen pirates were dead, and none of them had come within six feet of getting aboard the *Taiwan Song*.

So, what was the point of this?

No sooner had Nolan called out ceasefire than he knew something was wrong.

Pirates weren't soldiers. They weren't in the business of doing massive armed assaults on ships. And certainly not a ship as worthless, yet heavily defended as the *Taiwan Song*.

Something wasn't right here.

He yelled for the rest of the squad to stay in position. Then he ran full tilt away from the aft section, past the cargo bay, past the bridge, up to the bow. He looked over the edge—and saw six pirates, dressed in black, climbing up a rope ladder. Each one was armed with an M-16. Each was also carrying a camera and a strap around his neck. Weird . . .

It was clear the attack on the aft section had been a diversion. *This* was the main raiding party.

Nolan opened up on them. Two of the pirates didn't even see him standing above them. He killed them immediately then shot two more as they became entangled in the rope ladder. The fifth and sixth men fell into the water. He shot them as well—two short barrages each—finishing them off.

But with the last squeeze of his trigger, Nolan heard a disturbing click!

Damn . . .

He was out of ammo.

15

Monte Carlo

THE FOUR BIKINI models had been a fixture in the Grand Maison penthouse since Beta Squad's arrival.

They'd tried valiantly to get Twitch's laptop connected online via Wi-Fi. They'd kept the penthouse's bar well-stocked. They'd made the luxurious surroundings that much more luxurious just by lounging around and looking gorgeous. They'd also used a lot of towels.

But now, almost two hours had passed since Maurice's visit and yet the girls never returned from their swim.

But that was OK with Batman and Twitch. Maurice's last instruction to them was to sit tight, stay low, and await further information on the time and place of the grand gagnant.

And that's what they were doing, without the girls distracting them.

• • •

THEY WERE OUT on the balcony again when they heard the penthouse elevator coming up.

Batman was waiting when the door swished open and a thirtyish somewhat world-weary man stepped out. He was dressed informally for Monte Carlo—jeans and a t-shirt—but because he looked like someone who made a living working with his hands, Batman's first thought was that he might be the real technician, really here to fix the Wi-Fi.

Then the guy said: "Maurice sent me. I have some information for you."

Batman and Twitch led the visitor out to the balcony and had him sit down. Batman poured him a Portuguese Sagres beer.

"So, what can you tell us?" Batman asked him. "You have the details on the grand gagnant?

"Even better," the man replied—like Maurice, he was an

American. "I have details about the Z-box itself. What's in it, what it's all about."

"You're joking," Twitch said.

The guy shook his head no. "I've seen it myself, just recently," he said. "Maurice had me flown in just to brief you guys."

Batman and Twitch were suddenly paying rapt attention.

"Tell us everything," Batman urged him.

"I work the docks on Little Nicobar Island," the guy began. "Ever hear of it?"

Batman and Twitch nodded yes. Little Nicobar, aka "Little Nicky," was part of an archipelago off the northwest coast of Sumatra. Though physically closer to Indonesia, it was claimed as part of India. It was a weird little place, a real tropical paradise but also notorious as a smuggling center for everything from drugs and weapons to stolen luxury cars and jewels. A lot of human trafficking also took place there. Extremely high Acapulco-style cliffs made up its northern coastline and many of the natives spent their time diving off these peaks into the ocean below, near suicidal behavior for anyone less than an expert. It was said anyone who lived there was wacky because Little Nicky seemed to be hit by tsunamis, typhoons and/or major earthquakes on almost a monthly basis.

"I was in the U.S. Navy until a few years ago," the visitor went on. "We stopped at Little Nicky on a tsunami relief mission and I fell in love with the place. It's really paradise. When I mustered out, I went back to visit and decided to stay.

"But as you must know, there's also a lot of illegal activity happening there. Drugs, stolen merchandise, forced prostitution—weapons. Lots of weapons. The Indian police do very little because the place is so far away from the mainland.

"I was there about a year when the Agency contacted me and asked if I could keep an eye out for anything terrorist-related transiting through Little Nicky's port. They said they'd pay me a couple hundred bucks a month, so I signed on."

He took a long swig of his beer.

"Fast forward to just a few days ago. These guys come to us; they're pirates, Indonesian types, though they're sailing a Vietnamese eel boat. They had some rifles they wanted to put in storage. That sort of thing is done a lot on Little Nicky, too. My boss on the docks asked me to help unload these things. They were crates that looked pretty old; I'm not sure any rifle inside them would even work.

"Once everything was off loaded, I saw these guys had this other thing, something they were keeping with them. It looked like a little metal coffin. It had a large 'Z' carved into it and a weird locking device that looked like it needed a special key to open it.

"Three of these guys were just grunts fooling around with this box while their boss was helping store their weapons. One of them had a battery-powered screwdriver and wanted to use it to open the box. They argued for a while about whether they should try to break the lock, to see if the box would open.

"They finally decided to do it. But as soon as they did, as soon as that lid opened, this green glow came out, and seconds later these three guys standing closest to it all dropped dead."

Batman and Twitch were stunned. *"Dead?"* Twitch asked. "As in no-longer-breathing dead?"

The guy nodded emphatically. "I don't know if it was radiation, or some kind of biohazard? Or something chemical? Maybe a combination of all three," he said. "But they were DOA, just like that."

"Son of a bitch," Twitch groaned. "So, it *is* a weapon."

"How close were you to this box?" Batman asked the informant.

The guy sipped his beer. "I'm not sure," he replied. "Maybe ten feet or so."

"And the inside of this box—you said it was glowing?"

He nodded. "Like something from a horror movie."

"Pretty powerful stuff," Batman said.

The guy nodded again.

"Who finally closed the box?" Batman asked him.

"I did," he said. "Shielded my eyes. Tried not to look at it. Just kicked it closed."

Batman glanced over at Twitch. His expression told him he was beginning to smell a rat, as was Batman.

Twitch then asked: "So you got pretty close to it."

"I did . . ."

"Then how come *you* weren't killed? Or affected at all?"

The man suddenly tensed up.

"I don't know," he sputtered. "Beats me."

Batman came nose to nose with the man.

"You want to tell us why you're *really* here?" he growled at him.

The guy half smiled.

"You wouldn't believe me if I did," he replied.

Then without another word, he stood up, climbed onto the balcony's railing and to the astonishment of Batman and Twitch, did a perfect dive off the railing and into the huge pool, six stories below.

"What the fuck?" Batman yelled.

The man expertly hit the water, swam a bit under the surface and then got out of the pool at the opposite end. He took a gracious bow to the delight of those people sunning themselves poolside. Then he saluted Batman and Twitch up on the balcony and ran off.

"Fucking guy?" Twitch cried out. "He was a *disinformation* agent? A 'disinformant?' "

The wholly invented word, created right then and there, just tumbled out of Twitch's mouth. But it applied.

Batman repeated the word. "A disinformant . . . trying to punk us."

"But why us?" Twitch asked, scratching his head. "We're bit players in this. Unless one of Maurice's guys just went nuts or something. . . ."

Batman thought a moment, then said: "Let's find out. . . ."

"Find out how?" Twitch asked him. "I'm not jumping off here."

Batman retrieved his Glock 9 from his travel bag, and said, "Maybe it won't be so hard to find the only soaking wet guy running around Monte Carlo."

• • •

THEY WENT DOWN the elevator, Twitch also grabbing his handgun as they were leaving.

They arrived in the hallway just off the casino's main lobby. As before, the lobby was mobbed with guests and dignitaries in town for the Grand Prix.

The repair sign was still on the elevator's door and the hallway leading to the lobby was even further blocked off by yellow tape and scaffolds and what now appeared to be equipment belonging to plasterers. All this conveniently separated Batman and Twitch from the rest of the casino.

They went out the side door and ran around to the main entrance. The area in front of the casino was just as busy, just as hectic, as the inside. Many Rolls taxis were coming and going. Some were carrying celebrities traveling with large entourages and dozens of pieces of luggage; others were full of models and model wannabes. But everyone they saw was well dressed—and absolutely dry.

They made their way through the crowd, finally locating the attendant in charge of retrieving guests' cars. They tried to explain that a car had been reserved for them, a Maserati. But the man did not speak English.

They used sign language to urge him to call over a nearby coworker. This man understood some English. Batman showed him the gold key. The man then asked them in a thick accent: "Which color Maserati would you prefer?"

"Any color is good," Batman told him hurriedly.

"Convertible or hardtop?" the coworker asked. "It's a bit hot today, but it might rain, so . . ."

But Batman cut him off by growling: "Whatever—just get us a car!"

Chastened, the man ran off, returning a minute later with a solid gold Maserati GranTurismo Stradale hardtop. It looked like a car from twenty years in the future.

But then . . . another problem.

Batman started to climb into the driver's seat, but stopped. He could fly a helicopter with one hand—but how was he going to drive this ultraexpensive car? He had to shift with his right hand, meaning he'd have to steer with his mechanical hook? It wasn't going to work.

Yet the thought of Twitch driving the $250,000 beauty was downright scary. It was just not in his skill set.

But they had no other choice.

"I guess I go shotgun," Batman said. He'd been high as a kite—still intoxicated on life itself—until the guy went off the balcony. Now his buzz was long gone.

Twitch happily switched places and jumped behind the wheel. He took off with a screech, startling everyone huddled around the casino's main entrance. Some even hit the ground.

No surprise, Twitch was a maniac behind the wheel. Batman was soon holding on for his life as they rocketed through the narrow, winding streets of Monte Carlo. The noise, the faces, everything started going by in a blur.

"How *the fuck* do people *race* on these streets?" Batman cried out.

"You should try it in Shanghai," Twitch yelled back, laughing crazily.

Batman finally got his shit together and began navigating. He got Twitch going around the immense block that housed the Grand Maison Casino. The disinformant had disappeared to the rear of the casino's concourse, heading west. So, they had to go west too.

This necessitated a right onto Avenue des Beaux-Arts and then a very sharp left onto Avenue Albert I. They made both turns and stayed in one piece—and then, almost immediately, Batman spotted their quarry.

He was walking on Avenue Albert I, hurrying away from the casino grounds, trying to look inconspicuous, though he was still dripping wet.

"There's the asshole—right there!" Batman yelled, pointing.

But Twitch was driving so fast down Avenue Albert I, that by the time he heard Batman, he'd completely overshot the man.

Batman yelled for him to stop and turn around, but Twitch just wound up spinning the sports car in a triplet of screeching 360-degree turns.

Even in a place where Maseratis were common, this display attracted a lot of attention. The soaking wet man saw it all and ducked down the nearest alley.

Twitch finally got the car under control. They sped off toward JFK Drive hoping to catch the dripping man on the other side of Regent Square. By the time they made their way through the traffic, though, there was no sign of him.

They drove up and down De La Costa Boulevard and then D'Ostende Avenue, but still no luck.

Then Batman got an idea.

He told Twitch to stop. They pulled over to the side of Boulevard de Suisse and just waited.

Monte Carlo was more like a small town than a city. There just weren't many places a soaking wet man could go. So, what would happen if they stayed still, just another Maserati parked along the curb, and waited?

They sat there for two minutes, engine idling, handguns on their laps. Then, sure enough, they spotted their prey again.

He'd popped out of an alley three short blocks away and began walking west again, this time toward Avenue Saint-Laurent. Twitch jammed the Maserati in gear, hit the gas and resumed their pursuit. But after fighting traffic and blasting the horn all the way up the Escalier des Fleurs they were stopped by a line of policemen cordoning off a section of the roadway for a practice lap of Grand Prix cars.

Once more the dripping man managed to lose himself in the crowd. But Twitch was not going to let him get away so easily this time.

Steering around the policemen, he again slammed the Maserati into gear and started driving right on the famous racecourse itself. And for a third time, they actually caught up to the mystery man. Walking through a crowd of Japanese tourists, still dripping wet from his dive, he stuck out easily from everyone around him.

They had him . . .

But . . . at that moment the sky darkened. Where just minutes earlier there were no clouds, now a huge black overcast had moved over Monte Carlo. It opened up and the sunny place for shady people was suddenly treated to a massive downpour.

People scattered. Windows were slammed shut. Awnings were quickly lowered. Even the policemen ran, as if they would shrink if they got wet. The deluge was so intense it was impossible to see much of anything. Twitch had to pull the car to the curb again to wait it out.

The torrent lasted just a minute, and then the clear skies returned. But now everything had changed. Now, just about *everyone* within their view was walking around soaked to the skin.

Batman couldn't believe it. This was crazy. . . .

I knew I should have gone to Gottabang, he thought suddenly.

But then came a bit of luck. Just as they were about to give up, a taxi went by them, weaving through the post-storm traffic. As it passed by, the passenger in the back seat looked out his window and right into the Maserati.

It was their dripping man.

"Son of a bitch!" Batman cried. "There he is . . ."

The taxi immediately accelerated with a squeal and was off.

Twitch turned to Batman and asked: "What do we do?"

"Chase him!" Batman yelled.

Another deafening screech, and Twitch was again in pursuit.

The taxi was really moving. Apparently in Monte Carlo during Race Week, everyone thought they were in a Formula One car and, therefore, drove like a madman.

But Twitch was a madman all year round. He wheeled his way in and out of traffic like a pro. Riding the curb, downshifting, upshifting, double clutching, triple-clutching—he was doing it all, and with a prosthetic leg no less. It was madness—and they weren't doing the Maserati any favors either. But Batman could do nothing but hold on and hope for the best.

And somehow it worked. Because by the time the taxi reached the outskirts of Monte Carlo, the Maserati was only a few blocks behind.

But then the game changed yet again. The taxi began climbing one of the steep winding roads that led out of Monte Carlo, heading toward France.

Now the advantage was greatly in the taxi driver's favor. Not only was he driving as insanely as Twitch, his little Fiat was more than a match for the powerful sports car at taking turns, especially when traveling at more than 100 mph. They lost sight of the taxi within seconds.

Still, the chase continued. The sun was gone and suddenly it was night and Twitch had a hard time finding the Maserati's headlamps switch. Batman tried to help, but he had his seat belt pulled so tight he couldn't move but a few inches forward. These few particular moments of madness, driving on the incredibly twisting, recently wet road, with no lights, going in excess of 100 mph, with Twitch at the wheel, were simply terrifying. Batman found himself wondering if such a fancy sports car might have an ejection button he could push.

Finally, Twitch found the headlights switch, and suddenly the road was illuminated, just as they were going around a very sharp bend at warp speed.

That's when they saw the taxi again.

It went cruising by them—going in the opposite direction.

Twitch made yet another heart-stopping 180-degree maneuver, overtaking the taxi, then turning wildly a second time. There was dust, smoke and burnt-rubber fumes, but when it was over, the Maserati was blocking the road. The taxi could not get by.

Batman and Twitch jumped out of the steaming car, weapons in hand, and rushed up to the taxi. But they quickly discovered only the driver was inside. No one was in the backseat.

Twitch yanked the driver out and threw him to the pavement. Batman vigorously searched the backseat and even the trunk. But there was no sign of the passenger, other than the backseat was soaking wet.

"Where did you drop him?" Batman screamed at the driver.

The driver was frightened—and he couldn't speak English. But he knew what they wanted.

With shaking hands he pointed to the top of the mountain.

"Drop off!" the driver was telling them. "Right there . . . top of mountain."

The top of the mountain was a gradually sloping rock that ended in a conical peak jutting up into the night sky. It almost looked like a naturally formed Tower of Pisa.

"There!" the man insisted. "Crazy man, all wet, jump out."

They let the driver go, climbed back into the Maserati and resumed driving up the steep mountain.

Inside a minute, they were close enough to see the peak clearly. And climbing up the face of the weird rock formation was the dripping man.

Twitch cried, "Who *is* this guy? And what's he going to do up there? Dive off?"

Batman said, "We got him cornered. He can't come down from there without us catching him."

They jumped out of the car, weapons in hand.

"After all this," Batman growled, "I'm going to personally kick his ass—*then* ask him what the fuck this is all about. . . ."

They ran up the sloping field and were soon approaching the rock formation. They could see the dripping man's silhouette against the night sky. He seemed to be waiting for something.

Then they heard an awful roar behind them. The ground started shaking. The air around them felt like it was vibrating.

Batman and Twitch looked over their shoulders and saw an amazing sight.

A jet fighter was passing right over their heads.

It was not a typical jet fighter. It was a Harrier jump jet, one of the few airplanes that could take off and land vertically, without the need of a runway. It was also devoid of country markings or tail numbers.

Batman and Twitch watched in astonishment as the hoverjet stopped right above the rock formation and, with admirable skill, put its nose wheel on the rock itself. Its canopy slowly opened.

The dripping man clambered up the last bit of the peak and, with some impressive dexterity himself, scrambled up onto the wing and crawled into the open cockpit. The canopy was just closing as the pilot started moving away.

Then the plane quickly picked up speed and roared off into the night.

• • •

THE MASERATI'S DASH back down to Monte Carlo was even more terrifying than the trip up.

There was no conversation. Twitch was focused on getting to the bottom of the mountain as quickly as possible. Meanwhile, Batman had two enormous questions spinning around his head. Who could call in a Harrier *jump jet* to get them out of a jam like that—an unmarked Harrier no less? And why would someone with that kind of capability go to such great lengths to mislead them with such a lame sci-fi story of glowing boxes and death rays killing people?

None of it made sense.

He was sure of only one thing: Whoever the dripping man was, he knew about the Z-box and he at least knew Maurice's name.

This meant Beta Squad had to find Maurice.

The problem was, they didn't know how. They had no phone number for him, they had no idea where he was staying or even his real name.

But they knew four people who probably did.

• • •

THEY FINALLY REACHED the city and sped back to the Grand Maison.

The same car attendant took their Maserati, doing so without a word. They headed straight for the penthouse, hoping the four girls had returned. The reasoning was simple: If Maurice had arranged for the penthouse, he must have somehow arranged for the four bikini models as part of the ornamentation. They might know where to find him.

There was also a chance that Maurice himself had returned to the penthouse in the time Beta Squad was out chasing the dripping man. Perhaps they had a message from him waiting there. Either way, they were in a hurry to get back to their luxury digs.

They used the casino's side door again and headed for the elevator. But right away they noticed all of the plasterers' equipment was gone from the hallway, as was the yellow caution tape. For the first time, they had an unobstructed view of the casino's bustling main lobby.

Arriving at their private elevator, they saw the work repair sign was also gone. More surprising, before they could enter their pass code to call the elevator down, it arrived on its own. The doors opened and a couple stepped out. She was young and beautiful; he was middle-aged and wearing a cowboy hat. They brushed by Batman and Twitch as if they weren't there.

The elevator doors closed before Batman could jam his foot between them. So they punched in their pass code, hoping to retrieve it quickly. But the code didn't work. They tried a dozen times, with the same result.

Left with no other choice, up the stairs they went. Ten steep and narrow flights in all. They were seriously out of breath by the time they reached the sixth floor.

Here they found a hallway full of unmarked service doors. Because all of the penthouses on this floor had private elevators, none of the doors had numbers on them, only computer locks accessed by encrypted card keys carried by the casino's service staff. Batman and Twitch had no such key, so they spent the next twenty minutes trying to figure out which doors belonged to their suite.

After using rough triangulation, they finally estimated where the six service doors leading into their penthouse would be. They tried all six, but each one was locked.

So, they knocked on one—and were heartened to hear female voices and someone padding their way to the door.

"Ten bucks it's the blonde," Batman said.

The door opened, but it was not one of their bikini model friends on the other side. It was a chambermaid. One they'd never seen before.

They'd guessed correctly, at least—this *was* their penthouse. They were looking through one of the bedrooms and could see the familiar balcony, the empty liquor bottles and spectacular view just beyond.

But the chambermaid would not let them in.

Not without proper ID.

Batman tried to explain to her that while, yes, they had no ID, that they really *didn't need* any.

But she was adamant: No ID. No entry.

Both Batman and Twitch fingered their handguns—but hesitated.

What were they going to do? Shoot the woman?

In that moment of indecision, she ended the conversation. She slammed the heavy door in their faces and locked it from the inside.

• • •

THEY HURRIED BACK down to the lobby. The place was crowded, hectic and drunkenly festive. The line waiting at the front desk was a dozen people long, so Batman and Twitch tried to stop ordinary employees to explain their plight. But no one wanted to help them.

Finally Batman grabbed a floor manager and wouldn't let go. The man barely spoke English, but it didn't matter. He was clearly uninterested in their story. Batman was persistent though, allowing the man a glimpse of his handgun. His request was straightforward: Who'd reserved the royal penthouse and how could they get in touch with him? Finally the manager told them to wait in the lobby while he disappeared to check the occupancy records. When he returned he told them the penthouse was not listed in either of their names. Nor was it listed under anyone named "Maurice." In fact, he claimed the penthouse had been unoccupied for the past six weeks while it was undergoing renovations and would not be available for another week or so.

Batman insisted the man accompany them back upstairs, threatening to shoot him if he didn't. The manager reluctantly agreed. He overrode the elevator's pass code, and Batman and Twitch rode up filled with nervous anticipation, hoping this was all some huge mistake.

The elevator doors opened, and again, they could see it was undoubtedly their penthouse. But now, from this vantage point, looking directly into the main living area, it was clear the place had been cleaned of all evidence that they'd been there. Plus, it was full of scaffolding, paint cans and plastering materials. And there was absolutely no sign of the four bikini models.

Again, Batman began to protest, but the manager cut him off this time. The penthouse was obviously under repair. And even if it wasn't, where was their luggage? Their clothes? Their personal effects?

Batman began to sputter, but he had no good answer. The manager hit the "down" button and they were soon back in the casino lobby. The manager told them he'd been working double shifts for the past week and he'd never seen either of them until just a few minutes ago. When they tried to explain that they were always separated from the main lobby by workman's equipment, he started to walk away in a huff.

Batman caught him by the arm and said: "OK—what about these?"

He and Twitch pulled out the platinum cards the Asian woman had given them when they first arrived at the penthouse; supposedly the cards gave them carte blanche at the casino.

But the manager just looked at them and laughed. "I don't know what those things are," he said. "But I can assure you they have no currency here."

With that, he finally disentangled himself from Batman and walked away.

Two burly security men appeared a few moments later. They firmly escorted Batman and Twitch out the casino entrance and off the grounds.

Then they made it clear—in several languages—that neither should come back again.

If they did, they'd be arrested and put in jail.

• • •

BATMAN AND TWITCH couldn't believe this was happening.

They were suddenly out on the street, with barely any money, no shelter, just the clothes on their backs and their handguns. They didn't even have Twitch's laptop with all the spy gear on it.

Someone was messing with them, that much was clear. And it was imperative that they track down Maurice. However, they couldn't do so by wandering the streets. They had to find shelter first, and then figure out what was going on.

Batman did have his debit card with him, and that meant they could at least withdraw funds from the team's private bank account in Aden and proceed from there.

All they needed was an ATM.

They made their way through the crowded streets looking for the nearest money machine. It didn't take long to find a bank with an ATM out front. They began the process of withdrawing $5,000, feeling that would be enough to start with. But then came a problem . . . the debit card wouldn't work. As soon as Batman punched in his PIN, a message flashed on the ATM screen in French: CONNEXION REFU-SÉE.

Connection Refused.

Obviously the ATM was malfunctioning. They walked a few more blocks, found another and tried a second time.

But once again they wound up staring at a screen flashing: CONNECTION REFUSED. No matter what they did, no matter how many different ways they inserted the card, or how slowly or quickly they punched in the PIN, the same message kept coming back. They found and tried a third ATM, and then a fourth. But they received the same message every time.

Was something wrong with all the ATM machines in Monte Carlo? If so, it would be an apocalyptic problem. They hung around the last ATM and waited for the next person to approach it. A German couple appeared soon after and used the money machine with no trouble. Behind them, a man from a crowd of Chinese tourists withdrew money, just as easily, as did a couple of American college students after him.

But when Batman and Twitch tried again, the result was the same: the machine just would not connect.

• • •

THEY MADE THEIR way down to the harbor and found the Sun Casino, advertised as Monte Carlo's "American Casino."

The place was crowded and everyone seemed to be wearing

a cowboy hat. They went to one of the casino's cashier cages. Their plan was to use the debit card to withdraw money in the form of chips, and then cash in the chips for the real stuff.

The cashier was friendly and cute, but no matter what she did, including calling a 24-hour bank hotline, the same message kept coming back: CONNEXION REFUSÉE

This was getting serious now—and Batman and Twitch were running out of ideas. They discussed returning to the Grand Maison Casino to press the issue with management. At the very least they could make a case that they'd been robbed of their possessions. But the way things were going, they didn't want to risk being arrested.

They decided a more direct route would be to simply use a public phone to call the Kilos Building in Aden and ask for the cavalry to come to their rescue.

Batman used his last five Euros to purchase a phone card. They found a public phone inside the Sun Casino and started to place the call. But as soon as Batman began dialing the number, the phone ate the card.

They both snapped at that point. Twitch punched the phone, then pummeled it with the handset. Batman took over and did everything but rip the phone off the wall in an effort to retrieve the card. But nothing happened other than them creating a huge scene.

Security arrived to escort them out. But as this was happening, a casino customer walked up and used the same phone with no problems.

Kicked out of their second casino in just thirty minutes, Batman and Twitch knew the time had come to break the rules. Batman took out the special sat-phone the Agency contact had given them back on *The Immaculate Perception*. They were going to use it not to call the Agency, but to call Aden—and deal with any fallout later.

But though Batman repeatedly dialed the number, the call would not go through. When he finally removed the back of the sat-phone, he discovered the battery was corroded beyond all hope.

"I think I'm going crazy," he said, hurling the useless phone into the harbor. "I think I'm actually going insane."

Twitch shook his head. "Welcome to my world."

They both collapsed to the curb, feeling and looking homeless.

"I guess we're not going to any of those parties," Twitch groaned.

"Someone is *really* fucking with us," Batman said. "They get us into the city's best penthouse, then make it seem like we don't exist? They have us chase some maniac—and he gets picked up by a fucking Harrier? I swear they're fucking up the ATM machine and pay phones too."

"But why play with us?" Twitch asked. "Wouldn't it just be easier to kill us?"

Batman shook his head. There were no answers.

Only their situation was clear. They had no sat-phone. No place to stay. No money. No nothing . . .

And there was a good chance they'd been taken for ten million dollars.

16

Indian Ocean
0200 hours

THE SEA HAD become motionless.

There was no wind. Not even a breeze.

The night sky was clear; the stars above were sizzling. It was still brutally hot.

Nolan had spent the last hour on the bow of the *Taiwan Song,* at the very tip of the ship, looking out at it all, *feeling* it all.

Waiting . . .

This was the calm before the storm and he knew it. The only question was, what kind of a storm would it be?

Why did the Bom-Kats attack the second time?

That was the question that kept coming back to him. He could understand the first attack. They saw the old ship as easy pickings. But they were met with enough firepower to deter a small army. Still they came back again—and with a diversionary plan yet. And cameras.

Why?

After a lot of thought, Nolan knew there was only one explanation.

Gunner was suddenly beside him. He handed Nolan a cracked cup holding something warm and soupy.

"What's this?" Nolan asked, trying to identify the steamy brownish liquid.

"It's coffee and cheongju," Gunner told him. "This is what the ship's crew was drinking when we broke up their party. I found a little left in the pot."

Nolan sipped it—it was awful.

"Fuck me," he said with a grimace. "You sure this isn't from a bilge pump somewhere?"

"It wouldn't be this tasty if it was," Gunner said, drinking a cup of his own.

They were quiet for a few moments. Nolan felt the cheongju making its way through his system. It had a slightly numbing effect.

"They know," he told Gunner unexpectedly.

"Who knows what?" Gunner asked.

"The Bom-Kats," Nolan said. "They must know we have a very special passenger on board."

Gunner thought about it. "It *would* explain why they hit us the second time," he said. "But how did they find out?"

Nolan shrugged. "We've been lax on security," he said. "They were probably watching us through high-power binoculars, and after the first attack, she was up on deck when we should have kept her below. I'll bet they started listening to our radio traffic after that and figured it out. Why else would they come aboard with cameras if not to take a picture of her in case they couldn't kidnap her? As dopey as that sounds, I can't think of anything else that makes sense."

He wiped the sweat from his brow. "And that means they're going to hit us again," he went on. "They'll try to roll over us, then take her and God knows what. Asking for a ransom will be just a small part of it, I'm sure."

Gunner knew Nolan was right. "So what are we going to do when that happens?"

Nolan looked out at the motionless water and just shook his head. They were still chugging along, still trying to make it to the Lakshadweep Islands. But at the moment, they could have been halfway to Africa for all he knew. The ship's condition was getting worse by the minute. The electricity was failing steadily. Every pump on board had stopped. The leaks below had become endemic and the remaining engine was close to its last gasp. And they were now battling a fifteen-percent list.

"We got to fight them off again," he finally replied. "Somehow . . ."

"That won't be easy," Gunner said. "We're just about out of ammo. Not just you, all of us. It could be a big problem."

Nolan sipped his laced coffee again.

"Actually I think the biggest problem we have is below," he said.

Gunner knew what he meant. Emma Simms. "If it dawns on her that *she's* the cause of this . . ." he said.

"She'll go nuts," Nolan finished the thought for him. "Or get even nuttier."

"If that's possible," Gunner said.

Nolan drained the last of his drink.

"I'll bet in a million years she never dreamed she'd wind up here," he said. "With us, with those poor people below, with a bump on her head or a lesion on her brain or whatever the hell happened to her."

He threw his cup overboard.

"I guess being the world's most famous movie star isn't all it's cracked up to be," he said.

• • •

THEY WENT UP to the bridge where they found the five Senegals. They were just as hot and exhausted as he and Gunner.

Nolan expressed his thoughts on the Bom-Kats' actions. The Senegals could only agree.

"Le monde devient fou sur une belle femme," one said.

The world goes crazy over one beautiful woman . . .

Nolan laughed grimly. He replied: *"Toute ce qu'il faut est une . . ."*

All it takes is one . . .

They spent the next few minutes taking inventory of their ammunition supply. The results were disheartening.

They had six M4s between them, all of them adapted to be belt fed. The problem was they had more empty belts than full ones. In all they had just 223 rounds. Split six ways, that was not a lot. In any kind of major firefight, 223 rounds could be gone in a matter of seconds.

Gunner's ammo supply was especially low. He'd gone ashore at Gottabang with a full load in his Streetsweeper—but he'd expended 95 percent of his shells in the battle against the beach's security forces and while repelling the first two pirate attacks. Now he had just three shells left, all of them of the incendiary variety.

Each man also had a Beretta sidearm—but there were no extra clips for them. And there were definitely no other firearms on the ship, nor were any of the Korean crewmen armed.

At the end of it, Gunner said, "We might be kinda screwed here."

Nolan could only agree. "We've got to come up with some other kind of weapon," he said. "Something outside the box."

Gunner looked around the barren bridge. "Something like what? There's not much of anything on this tub."

Nolan asked one of the Senegals to retrieve the ship's original crew. Within a minute, the four Korean sailors were on the bridge. Though they'd stayed in the mess hall with Emma and the ninety-nine refugees during the previous two attacks, after viewing the aftermath of those battles, they were well aware what Alpha was capable of.

Yet, they were hardly soldiers, and when Nolan told them he thought the pirates were going to attack again, the Koreans became very nervous. Then Nolan asked them: Were there any other weapons aboard the ship? Anything at all?

The crew members settled down enough to think. Through hand signs and rough English they confirmed there were no guns aboard. Nothing along those lines.

But maybe . . .

The four men disappeared below deck, but within another minute, two were back. They were carrying a bucket filled with a thick red liquid.

Though it looked like blood, Nolan recognized it as hydraulic fluid.

The sailors explained that in one of their last bits of duty, on the day before the ship was due to be broken, they had drained all hydraulic pipes on board, simply to save the workers on the beach from doing the messy job. The fluid itself had been poured into empty diesel barrels; four were now located in the ship's cargo hold.

But what good would this be?

"Make hot," one of the crewmen said. "Dump on bandits. Burn skin . . ."

Nolan looked at Gunner, who just shrugged.

"Boil that stuff up and pour it on someone coming up a ladder?" he said. "Could be nasty."

The other two Koreans arrived. They were carrying a box containing an array of kitchen knives, ranging in size from a dinner knife to a butcher's cleaver to something that resembled a cutlass.

A chill went through everyone on the bridge. If a fight ever came to the point of using some of these things as weapons, then it really *would* be a battle for their lives.

Nolan started to thank the Korean sailors, but then each one took a couple long knives and put them in their belts.

Again through rough English one explained: "This is still our ship. This time, we will stand and fight with you."

• • •

NOLAN DRAGGED HIMSELF to his feet and left the bridge. There was something else he had to do. He had to talk to Emma.

He went below, hoping to find her asleep. Like the rest of them, it seemed as if she hadn't stopped moving for more than a few minutes since they'd embarked on this bizarre voyage.

He headed to the mess hall where most of the Gottabang refugees were sleeping on cots and blankets. Nolan had spent a good deal of his adult life killing people. Throughout his years in Delta Force, on both large and small ops, and then in his second career hunting down pirates, there had been only one objective: Get rid of the bad guys.

Now, he was realizing that saving lives actually took a lot more energy than taking them.

He went through the mess hall, but Emma was not there. He walked past the ship's tiny sick bay, but she was not there either. He finally went to the makeshift hospital they'd set up in the ship's galley. This was where he found her.

She was sitting in the corner with an infant in her arms, frantically applying cold water to the baby's forehead. The baby was crying, but even as Nolan approached he could tell its cries were getting faint.

Emma would not give up, though. Water to the forehead, slipping bits of food between the lips. Hugging the infant, rocking back and forth, she was trying to keep herself together and save the child at the same time.

But it was not to be.

The infant let out a weak cough, and then stopped crying for good.

Emma didn't want to accept it. She continued to hold the child close, in whispers imploring it not die. But it was too late. The spirit had passed. Nolan had seen many things in his adventuresome lifetime. But this might have been the saddest thing of all.

He waited a respectable amount of time, then took the infant from Emma's arms. He walked back to the mess hall and returned the child to its mother.

Then he went back to Emma. She was collapsed against the wall, tears rolling down her cheeks.

Nolan put his weapon aside and sat down beside her.

"I wanted them all to survive." She started sniffling. "It was so important that *none* of them die."

"*All* of those people would have died if you hadn't saved them," he told her. "You have to think of the others who are still alive. You're their guardian angel."

She looked up at him with her huge blue eyes. All her makeup was gone by now, yet Nolan realized she was even more beautiful without it.

"Do you really think that?" she asked him tearfully. "Do they really think of me as their 'guardian angel?'"

He smiled at her. It had been so long since he'd smiled for any reason, it almost hurt.

"I'm sure of it," he said.

Suddenly, she was embracing him tightly.

"I've been such a fool my whole life," she said. "And I know I can never make up for it."

He was frozen on the spot, at a loss for words.

"You're just a kid," he finally sputtered. "You've got a long way to go."

This made her laugh. And he began to hug her back.

That's when the Senegal came into the room—the same one as before. The bearer of bad news. But he didn't say anything this time.

He didn't have to.

Nolan just looked at him and asked: *"Ils sont à venir?"*

The man nodded grimly.

They were coming again. . . .

• • •

NOLAN RAN UP to the main deck, jammed on his battle helmet and pushed his night-vision telescope into place.

He looked to the east and saw lights that stretched almost horizon to horizon, all of them heading for the *Taiwan Song*.

Gunner was soon beside him.

"There's a lot more of them than the last go-around," he said to Nolan. "They must have gotten some new recruits."

Nolan nodded. "If they're here for the reason we think they are, they probably had no problem picking up new blood. There's hundreds of small pirate bands up and down this coast that would be more than willing to help them out for a fee."

Nolan zoomed in on the fleet and could see the Bom-Kats' distinctively shaped boats and billowing deck flags. There were at least three dozen speedboats heading their way, each one carrying at least a half dozen pirates.

"How much time do you think we have before they get in range?" he asked Gunner.

"They're moving pretty quick," Gunner replied, adjusting his own night-vision goggles. "I'll say five minutes. Maybe less."

Nolan had to think fast, not easy to do with no food or sleep in almost three days. He let out a high whistle; this brought the Senegals up deck with him. The ship's Korean crewmen were close behind.

The sheer size of the approaching flotilla left no doubt this would be an all-out assault. So, Nolan had to come up with a defensive plan, making sure it was workable but also as simple as possible.

It took a couple minutes, but finally each man knew what he had to do. The situation was *so* desperate, though, they could not afford to send one of the Senegals back down to protect the people in the mess hall. Everyone who could shoot a weapon or wield a knife would be needed up top.

Gunner divided up the ammunition. Each Senegal got forty rounds for his M4. Nolan was left with twenty-three. They all had huge Beretta handguns as well, with eight-round clips. Basically their last ditch weapon, they would have to make every bullet count with these, too.

Each Senegal then took a carving knife from the box of cutlery the ship's crew had uncovered. Using wads of duct tape, they attached the knives to their M4s like bayonets. Then Nolan assigned them positions around the ship: one Senegal at the bow, two at the stern, one amidships starboard and one amidships port. He and Gunner would fill the gaps at the railings on either side of the bridge.

Nolan checked the approaching fleet again and then took one of the steak knives himself.

He was sure of only one thing at that moment: Two hundred and twenty-three bullets would not be enough to win this battle.

• • •

NOLAN HURRIED BACK down to the galley.

Emma knew what was happening, just by the look on his face. He got her back to the mess hall and told her to put all the refugees in one corner, turn out the lights and not move until someone came for her.

"These people are depending on you," he said. "Stay with them, keep them safe."

He started to go, but she grabbed his hand, stopping him. In the dim light of the passageway just outside the mess hall door, she looked up at him, but didn't say a word.

If this had been a movie, they would have kissed here. But it didn't happen. Nolan simply brushed her cheek, catching a tear just as it was rolling off.

Then he told her again: "Don't move until one of us comes for you."

He gently nudged her into the mess hall and closed the

flimsy panel door. He waited until he heard her lock it from the inside. Then he looked down at the threshold and saw the light go out.

He took the added measure of killing all the lights in the passageways around the mess hall, hoping to discourage any pirates who might actually get aboard the ship, the ultimate nightmare scenario.

Then he ran back up on deck.

• • •

HE FOUND GUNNER at his position, port side next to the bridge. He was checking over his Streetsweeper. Again, the bad news was he had just three explosive projectiles left.

"More than anyone, you've got to be smart in how you use those," Nolan reminded him.

They looked out on the water. The Bom-Kats were only about a mile away and closing fast.

"Roger that," Gunner agreed grimly.

The four Korean sailors reappeared on deck. They had something rarely seen on a ship: a wheelbarrow. Two of them, in fact.

They explained that while getting the *Taiwan Song* ready to be broken, they'd used wheelbarrows to dump debris ripped from the walls over the side.

Now the wheelbarrows could be used for another purpose. The sailors had carried the four barrels of hydraulic fluid up to the deck. They'd also put a fifth empty barrel right behind the bridge, along with some mop buckets. They indicated they were ready to do their part.

Nolan took assorted trash from the bridge and threw it into the empty barrel. Then he told the crewmen: "OK, let's light a fire in here. . . ."

But the four sailors hesitated. Intentionally lighting a fire aboard a ship was not only dangerous, it was considered the height of bad luck.

"It's OK then," Nolan reassured them. "I'll do it."

Once the fire started, the sailors put a brace across the barrel from which a pail full of hydraulic fluid could be hung and heated up. The wheelbarrows were placed nearby, ready to transport the hot liquid once it was bubbling.

Inside a minute, the crewmen had one bucket of the fluid already starting to percolate.

"Hot quick," one sailor said, pointing to the boiling liquid.

"But once we start, you must keep it coming," Nolan urged them.

The four men understood right away.

"Count on us," one said firmly. "We stand with you."

• • •

THE PIRATE FLEET began to split up about a quarter mile off the *Taiwan Song*'s stern.

Nolan had climbed halfway up the ship's forward mast by this time. With his night-vision telescope turned up to full power, he counted thirty-eight speedboats in the pirate fleet, along with three larger vessels. These were *dhonis*, traditional Indian fishing boats. They looked like diminutive Viking ships, about twenty-five feet long, with a large engine and stack at the rear, a small-enclosed bridge at the front and a sail in the middle. Like everything Bom-Kat, they were intricately constructed and had many flags adorning their masts and aft sections.

The divided fleet began moving up on either side of the old freighter, just out of the M4's range. With this maneuver, the pirates' strategy was confirmed. This was going to be a mass attack, an assault from all sides.

Nolan yelled to those below to get ready. Then he tried studying the trio of *dhonis* accompanying the fleet. His instincts told him one must be the pirate commander's ship. If so, would sinking it affect the coming battle? Possibly . . . But which of the three was it? Alpha Squad had only so much ammunition, and Nolan didn't want to waste even a single round shooting at the wrong target.

He yelled down to Gunner, asking if he could guess which dhoni was the command vessel. But he was as much at a loss as Nolan.

"No idea," he yelled back up to Nolan. "And one in three ain't good odds at the moment."

The speedboats began revving their engines. Some started circling the freighter; others began closing on it. The pirates were making their move.

Nolan tightened his battle helmet. His clothes still smelled faintly of Emma's perfume.

This was all about her, he thought once again.

He was sure of that now.

• • •

THE ATTACK STARTED at exactly 0300 hours.

There was no diversion this time; none was needed. The reinforced Bom-Kat force hit the *Taiwan Song* from all sides, en masse, even as it puttered along at barely five knots. The pirates had a simple plan, too: brave the gunfire, get on board the ship and overwhelm the vessel's defenders with sheer numbers.

The pirates began throwing up rope ladders all over the ship; their grappling hooks made a distinctive clang when they hit the deck railings. It sounded like dozens of out-of-tune church bells going off at once.

Standing fast in their positions around the deck, the ship's defenders watched all this unfold. Of the seven men of Alpha Squad, six had pistols and a combat weapon with a long carving knife attached. Gunner was the exception. His Streetsweeper was not conducive to holding a bayonet, makeshift or otherwise. So in addition to his Beretta and oversized shotgun, he'd armed himself with the largest piece of cutlery on the ship.

The idea was for them to use the knives to cut the rope ladders off the railings *before* the Bom-Kats could climb up. This way Alpha could still fight off the pirates while saving their precious ammunition until they really needed it.

But Nolan quickly found it would not be as easy as that. Not ten seconds into the attack, a rope ladder clanged onto the railing right in front of his station, which was starboard side, next to the bridge. The hook grabbed on tight and began jerking with the movements of the pirates climbing up.

Like the others, Nolan had used duct tape to attach his carving knife to the end of his M4. Again, by positioning it like a bayonet, he hoped he could both defend himself and slice through the attackers' rope lines. But in his plan, he'd been expecting the Bom-Kats' ladders to be made of something like heavy clothesline, as they'd been in the previous attack. This time, though, the ladders were made of substantial hemp twine, at least four inches around and heavily braided. Just one look at it told Nolan there was no way he could quickly slice it in half. Instead, he would have to cut through it with his makeshift bayonet like a saw cutting through wood. But as soon as he started doing this, the duct tape holding the knife to his gun barrel began coming loose.

Meanwhile, the first pirate climbing the rope ladder was just a few feet away from him. Nolan had no choice but to pull out his Beretta and shoot the man between the eyes. He didn't even stop to watch him fall. Instead, he pulled the carving knife off his M4, threw the rifle aside, and with both hands, began frantically cutting the rope beneath the large grappling hook.

He was still sawing away when a second pirate neared the top of the ladder. Nolan had to shoot him as well. He fell away, only to be replaced by a third pirate who Nolan *also* had to shoot, all while still trying madly to cut the rope.

By the time a fourth pirate neared the railing, the weight on the weakened twine had become too much and snapped on its own, taking him and several more pirates down with it, much to Nolan's relief. But he'd used three bullets from his pistol just to defeat this first tiny group of Bom-Kats—and under these conditions that was way too much ammo to expend. Even worse, when he looked at the carving knife, he realized that trying to cut through the thick hemp had bent and dulled the blade considerably. And a moment later, another hook clanged onto the railing in front of him.

This time he attacked the rope with verve, sawing away as he anxiously eyed six more pirates climbing toward him. But the knife just could not do the job fast enough, so Nolan had to use his Beretta once again and shoot the pirate at the top of the ladder, as well as the attacker behind him. Only then did he manage to cut the second rope to the point where it finally snapped on its own, sending the rest of the pirates back into the sea. But no sooner had this rope ladder fallen away, when *another* hook clanged onto the railing nearby.

This was getting very crazy very quickly. Suddenly everything was moving too fast. The pirates were screaming like madmen. Their comrades circling in the speedboats were blowing air horns. Somewhere, fireworks and flares were being lit off, weirdly illuminating the night sky. And Nolan had already used more than half his pistol's ammo supply *and* he had ruined the all-important knife as a cutting tool—and the battle wasn't even two minutes old.

Even worse, he could see the same thing was happening all along the railing. There were Senegals to the right and left of him and it was apparent their knives just couldn't cut through such thick rope either. He was also hearing lots of gunfire. Valuable ammunition was being used to repel the first couple minutes of the assault. Definitely *not* part of the plan.

As before, he had to shoot the first two pirates coming up this third ladder, then saw away at the grappling hook's rope until the weight became too much and it snapped. It was harder this time though, as the knife was practically useless; it took so long, the third pirate in line came within an inch of grabbing Nolan before he had to shoot him, too.

But even as he tumbled way, Nolan noticed something else was going on here. The blind ferociousness of the attack told him the pirates were most likely on methamphetamines or maybe Indonesian Ecstasy, which was a combination of several highly toxic stimulants. This was no surprise. But he also realized the attackers were armed only with knives. Why no firearms? There was only one reason. The pirate commander didn't want his men to leave any weapons on board the lightly armed ship should they be killed or captured. In other words, Alpha's earlier instincts had been right. The Bom-Kats had done some recruiting and this first wave of pirates, probably all new members, was simply fodder meant to wear down the ship's defenders without giving them any more firepower. The problem was, it was working.

Amid the growing confusion, Nolan spotted one of the dhonis coming up close to the freighter's starboard side. He could see a large man dressed in blue sea camos and lit by a flashlight standing on the bridge, yelling into a walkie talkie. Was this the pirate commander? Was he directing the attack?

Nolan only had a few seconds to yell over to Gunner about this when another rope ladder clanged onto the railing in front of him. There was so much noise and chaos, Nolan was sure Gunner hadn't heard him. Yet a moment later, the telltale streak of a Streetsweeper incendiary projectile flashed high over his head, zooming up at an insanely steep angle before coming down squarely on the bridge of the dhoni.

It was a tremendously lucky shot—and it caused a tremendously loud explosion. Gunner's projectile had hit ammunition stored on the boat's bridge, setting it off like a mini A-bomb. The dhoni came completely out of the water and broke in two before slamming back down again. It quickly sank beneath the waves, leaving only a trail of smoke in its wake.

And suddenly, everything just stopped. The explosion froze attackers and defenders alike. But not for long. Because just like flipping a switch, the attack instantly resumed its ferocity. Nolan banged his fist against his helmet. The meaning was clear: They had sunk the dhoni, but it probably wasn't the one carrying the pirate commander.

Now Nolan began hearing snapping noises all around him. He looked up from yet another frenzied rope cutting to see orange streaks coming at him from all directions. Tracer rounds . . . meaning another element had been added: Those pirates circling the freighter in speedboats were now shooting at them.

Taking cover as best he could, Nolan continued cutting through his fourth rope ladder. But again, it was too slow and the knife too dull, so he had to fire his Beretta twice to shoot the first two pirates before the rope gave way.

And with that last shot, the Beretta's clip popped out.

Nolan couldn't believe it.

The weapon he'd meant to hold in reserve was already empty.

• • •

TWENTY-FIVE FEET DOWN the railing toward the ship's stern, one of the Senegals was also struggling with this new reality.

He'd managed to cut a half dozen of the rope ladders already, but his knife had become irreversibly bent. He'd emptied his pistol of ammunition, too, just like Nolan, and was loath to use his M4 rifle until he really had to.

But again, just like Nolan, he was close to being overwhelmed. Though so far only armed with knives of their own, the pirates looked and acted absolutely crazy.

Now, in just the span of a few seconds, two more rope ladder hooks clanged onto the railing in front of him. The Senegal somehow managed to cut through one ladder with his misshapen knife, but in the time it took to do this, a pirate coming up the second ladder had reached the railing and was climbing over it.

The Senegal quickly charged him with his twisted makeshift bayonet, startling the man even before his feet hit the deck. The bent knife went into the pirate's chest, puncturing his heart. He crumpled backward, getting entangled with the top strands of the ladder and stalling the pirates climbing up behind him.

But when the Senegal went to pull his knife out of the dead

man's chest, it wouldn't budge. The ball of duct tape holding it on the gun muzzle had gotten stuck in the man's wound. The Senegal couldn't even free the M4, that's how jammed up it was. Now the Senegal was without any weapon at all and the two pirates behind the dead man were clutching at him like creatures from a monster movie, trying to pull him over the railing. The Senegal was sure he was doomed.

But then, above the chaos, the shouting, and the gunfire, the Senegal heard a strange rolling noise behind him. He turned his head just in time to see a pair of the Korean crewmen rushing down the deck with their wheelbarrow full of sizzling hydraulic fluid. The African soldier had just enough room to get out of their way as the Koreans, never breaking stride, raised the end of the wheelbarrow and poured the scalding contents onto the pirates still hanging on the rope ladder.

The screams were ungodly; they rose above everything else happening on the ship. Horribly burned, the pirates immediately fell back into the sea, making a terrible sizzling sound when they hit the water.

The Korean crewmen pulled the Senegal back from the railing, depositing him safely on the deck. They somehow retrieved his knife and rifle for him, then returned to their wheelbarrow intent on running back to their fire barrel to get more bubbling hot fluid.

But they quickly realized another pirate had climbed up another ladder behind them and was now blocking their path. They faced the brigand for an eternal second; he was just an arm's length away. The Korean sailors had no weapons and this pirate looked especially crazed. He lunged forward with his knife, intent on stabbing one of the sailors in the stomach—but stopped in mid-thrust. Suddenly his throat began bleeding profusely. He fell to the deck at the Korean sailors' feet, gurgling and dying. Standing behind them was the Senegal the Koreans had just saved, his bent and misshapen knife lodged in the the pirate's neck.

The Koreans regained their composure, high-fived the

Senegal, and then resumed their dash back to their boiling pot of oil.

"We stand and fight," one yelled over his shoulder to the African. "We with you all the way. . . ."

• • •

THE FIGHTING WAS even fiercer on the port side of the ship.

Because the freighter was at a 15 percent list on this side, the pirates had a shorter distance to climb. So they had sent more men against it.

Gunner was doing his best to hold down his midship position. He'd fired his Streetsweeper just the one time, sinking the *dhoni* with a one-in-a-million shot—but it had little effect on the raging battle. He'd used his Beretta a few times as well. But mostly he'd been slicing through the rope ladders as planned, and not having such a hard time of it as everyone else. There were two reasons for this: he was a massive and muscular person, and he was armed not with a carving knife, but with a butcher's cleaver. This and his pure strength had allowed him to cut down more than a dozen rope ladders so far, sending many Bom-Kats into the drink.

But still, the pirates kept coming.

Even now, not five minutes into the battle, as Gunner stopped to catch his breath and try to take in the situation around him, three more rope ladders clanged onto the railing nearby. He rushed over to the first one, and in just three swings of the cleaver, managed to cut it away. He reached the second ladder, punching the first pirate in line in the jaw before severing the rope with another trio of mighty blows.

But by this time, the pirates climbing the third ladder had reached the railing. In a display of crude, blunt force, Gunner managed to backhand the first attacker so hard it caused him to lose his footing. But in falling away, he completely missed interfering with the pirate next in line, and this man came over the railing with a vengeance.

Gunner managed to knock him down with a fist to his

temple, but then a third pirate appeared and he, too, came over the railing. He helped his comrade to his feet and both turned to face Gunner, long razor-sharp knives held out in front of them.

Gunner's cleaver was not much good here. He was swinging it wildly, but because he was forced back on his heels, it was almost impossible for him to get close enough to strike either pirate. Nor could he stop to pull out his Beretta. He had no choice then but to surge forward. He came at the pirates, all 300 pounds of him, still swinging the meat cleaver. And while missing the first pirate's chest, by dumb luck he caught the second attacker on his hand, slicing through his palm and wrist, causing a stream of blood to gush out. When the man fell to the deck Gunner finished him off with a quick kick to the larynx.

The remaining pirate was stunned by his comrade's sudden death; this gave Gunner the chance to back him up against the railing, knock the knife from his hand, and then drive the cleaver into his rib cage. The blow was enough to send the pirate back over the side.

While this was going on, Gunner saw something out of the corner of his eye. It was another of the pirates' dhonis. It was coming up close to the ship, just as the first one had on the starboard side. In a flash of light, Gunner saw a clutch of people on its bridge standing around a man with a walkie-talkie. Some of these people were firing off flares; others were shooting AK-47s in the general direction of the ship. Maybe one of *these* guys was coordinating the attack.

He retrieved his Streetsweeper, leaned over the railing and without hesitation, let his second-to-last explosive shell fly. The projectile streaked through the smoke and sea spray, hitting the dhoni dead center on its engine cowling—and then bouncing off.

There was no huge explosion. The shell was a dud. But just by kinetic energy alone, the casing had severed the dhoni's main fuel line, and sparks from the flares the people on the boat were firing off fell onto the leaking fuel—and *that's* when the huge explosion came. There was a ball of fire, a second deafening bang—and then the dhoni was gone.

Gunner pumped his fist in triumph—but the celebration was short-lived.

Unlike after the first dhoni was sunk, the pirates didn't stop for even an instant this time.

If anything, they began attacking the ship with renewed vigor.

• • •

NOLAN'S KNIFE WAS finally gone.

Bent, twisted and dull, he'd lost it somehow in the frenzy of the battle. His pistol, empty and useless, he had thrown away on purpose. His M4 was serving as little more than a battering club now, his allotted twenty-three rounds gone long ago. He had dispatched so many pirates by hitting them with the assault weapon's stock his hands were bleeding from holding its slender barrel so tight.

How long had the battle been going on? He had no idea. A few minutes, a few hours? He really couldn't tell. All he knew was that his plan to defend the ship was in shambles. Pirates were being killed. Their bodies were splashing into the sea with grisly regularity. The Koreans were running up and down the deck, their wheelbarrows sizzling, their hands horribly burned, pouring the flaming oil on the attackers whenever and wherever they could. And the Senegals that he could see were stabbing, slashing and simply manhandling a lot of the Bom-Kats back over the railing. But just like Nolan, they'd been forced to use their rifles, too—in fact the gunfire sounding out around the ship was nonstop now. Just what Alpha didn't want to do.

And *still*, the pirates kept coming.

• • •

JUST A FEW seconds after Nolan had ducked away from another incoming barrage of tracer fire, he heard someone come up behind him.

He spun around ready to whack them with the butt of his empty M4 when he realized it was Gunner. He had scrambled through the bridge to get away from the fighting on the port side.

"It's *really bad* over there," Gunner managed to say. "They're so many of them coming over the top now, we can't stop them."

Gunner was still holding his Streetsweeper and his cleaver. But blood was running down his right side. Nolan was stunned to see he had a serious wound on his shoulder.

They had to duck as another barrage of tracer fire crackled above their heads. Though the Senegals and the Koreans were still fighting pirates climbing up the sides of the ship, it was clearly a losing battle.

"Might be time to go to phase two," Gunner yelled to Nolan.

Nolan grimly agreed. He let out a loud whistle. A predetermined signal, it cut through the sounds of the battle.

All at once, everyone fighting the pirates on deck pulled back, retreating to the forward cargo hatch. This was a ten-foot raised section of the ship located right behind the bridge. It had a stout safety railing around it and it gave an almost 360-degree view of the deck. It was a perfect fallback position to defend—though to Nolan's mind, it was a little too much like the Alamo.

Only after all of the deck defenders had climbed up onto the forward hatch, did Nolan realize he was the only one among them who wasn't wounded. Gunner had the huge gash in his shoulder and two of the Senegals were bleeding from stab wounds to their legs. Two other Senegals had head wounds, the fifth was bleeding from his chest. Even the four Korean crewmen had sustained wounds to their arms and legs, plus their hands had been burned from handling the hot hydraulic fluid.

The pirates were pouring over the railings now and heading for the small clutch of defenders atop the cargo hatch. Nolan had the Senegals kneel down and form a firing line.

Then he and Gunner stood behind them. Nolan was now armed with Gunner's Beretta pistol; it had just four rounds left. Unarmed and defenseless, the Korean sailors took cover behind him.

The first line of pirates advanced on the cargo hatch.

"On my call!" Nolan yelled above the din. "Acquire target—one shot only. Fire!"

The Senegals' five M4s exploded at once, hitting five pirates closest to them.

"On my call!" Nolan yelled again. "Acquire—aim—fire!"

Again, another barrage spewed out from the M4s.

Five more pirates went down.

"Acquire! Aim! Fire!"

Another barrage came—then another and another. It went on like this for more than a minute. Every shot counted; every shot either killed or wounded a pirate.

But they still kept coming.

• • •

TWO OF THE pirates had avoided the chaos on deck and found their way below.

Both were veterans of the Bom-Kat gang. Though they'd been on ships like the *Taiwan Song* before, they'd never been part of such a huge seaborne assault as this. And unlike the recruits fighting up top, they were carrying AK-47s.

They were here for one prize only. Nothing on this bucket was of any value, except the blond beauty that Commander Kalish had spotted earlier. All the pirates, old-timers and newcomers, had been promised a hefty fee for capturing her and bringing her to Kalish.

Few of the Bom-Kats believed that it was actually Emma Simms on board, even though weird things *did* happen in this part of the world. But the most famous actress on the planet, being on a ship that looked like it was just minutes away from being cracked?

It didn't make sense.

But the promise of a lot of money was hard to resist, especially for bandits like them who were used to being paid as little as $100 a month.

So, they pressed forward through the lower decks, looking everywhere, all the while aware of the sounds of fierce fighting going on just above them.

They came to a series of passageways where the lights were out. The pirates suspected a trap and started to reverse direction. But then they heard something that did not jive with the normal noises found on a ship or of the battle happening one level away.

It was a child crying.

Both men smiled darkly. If the famous blond *was* on this ship, and if this ship *was also* carrying other civilians, then it made sense that these noncombatants would all be hidden away in one place together.

The pirates ventured into the dark passageway, concentrating on the muffled wails. Creeping forward carefully, they eventually found themselves outside the ship's mess hall. The plaintive cries were coming from within.

The pirates checked their weapons, then kicked the door in. It was dark inside, but they found the lights. Though dim, they provided enough illumination for the pirates to see a group of about a hundred people, huddled in one corner of the hall. Women and children mostly, they were all crying and shaking with fear.

And in the middle of them was the most famous actress in the world.

The pirates would have known her anywhere. Both had seen her movies, albeit on crudely copied bootlegged DVDs. And though she was ruffled and devoid of makeup or styling, she looked more beautiful now than ever.

One of the pirates spoke a little English. Still not quite believing this was Emma Simms sitting in the smelly mess hall of the worst ship afloat, he said: "Princess, come with us, or everyone dies. . . ."

Emma didn't hesitate. She knew she was the reason everyone was fighting. And logic said, if she were removed from the equation, then the pirates might stop attacking the ship and maybe leave everyone else alone.

But . . . was this a logical situation? She didn't know.

Nevertheless, she disentangled herself from the hands and arms of the people who didn't want her to go, and walked toward the pirates.

Despite the surreal circumstances, the two brigands were in awe of her. Her beauty, her grace, even in this repugnant place. It was remarkable.

The pirates briefly considered sexually assaulting her. When would they have this chance again? But Commander Kalish was positively obsessed with this goddess and he would have them painfully killed if he found out that they had touched her before he had. So they dismissed the idea quickly.

Instead they told her to put up her hands and continue walking slowly toward them. One pirate removed his belt, ready to tie her hands behind her. They both took a deep sniff and smelled her perfume.

Yes, they had seen her movies. The love stories, the serious Shakespeare role and the action flicks. But as beautiful and graceful as she seemed, Emma Simms had another thing going for her. While she rarely did her own stunts, she'd seen plenty of real stunt people in action. Plus she'd been training, taking jiujitsu, karate, sambu and even some kung fu, so that someday, she wouldn't need any body doubles.

That's why neither pirate knew what hit him. One moment they were about to make her their prisoner, the next they were being hit in the face, the stomach, the groin. She was suddenly not the graceful, helpless American blonde anymore. Instead she was a whirling dervish of fists, knees and feet.

Both men were immediately knocked to the deck, losing their weapons in the process. Emma stood over them, as surprised as they. Then two more kicks, one to each man's temple, and they were out for good.

Emma retrieved their weapons. She gave one to the most

able male in the group and told him to stay put, and protect the others if any more pirates came to the mess hall.

Then, she slipped out the open door, alone.

• • •

ALPHA SQUAD WAS almost out of ammunition.

The Senegals' firing line had delivered twenty-two fusillades, killing and wounding so many pirates, their bodies were stacked like cordwood atop the raised cargo hatch.

Using Gunner's Berretta, Nolan had added to the systematic barrage. But now, with each Senegal only having a few rounds left, they were all firing at will and making sure their last few bullets went where they counted.

As all this was happening, Nolan and Gunner spotted a third *dhoni* coming close to the freighter's port side. No words were needed this time. Gunner immediately aimed his bloodstained weapon over the mass of pirates and fired his last shell. The *dhoni* was so close he couldn't miss. The projectile passed through the boat's exhaust pipe and into its power plant. Once again, there was a spectacular explosion. The engine split in two and the boat's fuel tank caught fire. The *dhoni* was instantly engulfed in flames, sinking quickly under a massive cloud of steam.

It was hard for Nolan and Gunner to tell whether it was because they might have finally iced the Bom-Kats command ship or that the Bom-Cats were simply switching tactics, but as soon as the third *dhoni* went down, the number of pirates coming over the railing stopped.

The Bom-Kats' plan now seemed to be to let their new recruits finish off the ship's defenders and then let their gunmen, the majority of whom were still on the speedboats, take over the ship at their leisure.

The Senegals expended the last of their ammo when a large group of pirates charged the Alpha position. The advance was stopped in its tracks, but that was it—all of Alpha's ammunition was gone. Gunner and the Senegals began battering the pirates with the butts of their assault weapons.

The fight spilled off the cargo hatch and onto the deck just below the bridge on the starboard side. Here, the hand-to-hand combat quickly became vicious.

Nolan put the last bullet from the borrowed Beretta into the chest of a pirate who had climbed the stern cargo mast with ideas of swinging down on the firing line. Nolan then reached into the box of galley knives, pulling one out that looked like an old-fashioned cutlass. He cut a cargo rope and used it to swing down onto the deck, landing on top of the mass of Bom-Kats who were fighting Gunner and the Senegals. He knocked over the pirates like bowling pins.

While the attackers were temporarily sprawled on the deck, Nolan had time to push the Korean crewmen up onto the bridge. With their horribly burned hands and other wounds, they could not help any longer. Two of the Senegals were also badly wounded; they, too, were hoisted up onto the bridge.

That left just Nolan, Gunner and the three lesser-injured Senegals battling for their lives.

About two dozen pirates were still fighting. They were jammed on the starboard deck; Alpha Squad was holding their ground just to the left of the bridge ladder. The pirates' goal was the bridge itself; everyone knew once they seized it, this little war would be over.

The pirates were charging the defenders in fits and starts, trying to slash at the squad members who beat them back with their rifle butts, or stabbed them with the galley knives. Particularly ghastly was the way those pirates unlucky enough to go down near Gunner were dispatched. The big man was still armed with his meat cleaver and he was slashing away at anything that came close to him.

It was brutal and barbaric and endless, and by far, the worst combat Nolan had ever been in. His hands were covered in blood; some of it was his, and some of it belonging to the pirates he'd stabbed. His muscles ached so much from swinging the heavy cutlasslike knife, he was reaching his breaking point. The big knife felt like it weighed a ton.

Making the situation even worse, while the Koreans had abandoned using the burning hydraulic fluid as a weapon, one last pail had been left over the fire barrel. It was sending out billows of acrid smoke, saturating the deck area, making it hard to see and even harder to breath.

Nolan actually thought: *Maybe I shouldn't have lit that fire on board*. It had been nothing but bad luck ever since.

It was inevitable, but the tide of this desperate battle finally turned in the pirates' favor. Nolan could barely lift his arms. Gunner and the three Senegals were struggling just to stay on their feet. Out of the corner of his good eye, Nolan saw two pirates break off from the main group and disappear from sight. They were obviously sneaking around to attack the squad from the rear, but there was nothing Alpha could do to stop them.

Nolan summoned up one last burst of energy and slashed three pirates enough to push them back. Gunner joined in the thrust and the remaining dozen or so pirates were momentarily stopped from advancing.

But then Nolan heard cries from behind them. He looked over his shoulder to see that, sure enough, two pirates were coming at them from the other direction.

Two things went through his mind at that moment. He was sure the toxic fumes were making him delusional, because he found himself thinking back to when he'd brushed the tear from Emma's cheek. It seemed like a million years ago. He could still smell her light perfume as well. And for some reason, these two things made him want to just lie down right there and go to sleep.

Then a voice in his head whispered: "You'll sleep for a long time soon enough."

So now he just waited for the blow. A knife to his back or to his chest. It didn't make much of a difference. This was where it was all going to end—defending a bunch of dying refugees on the worst ship afloat, somewhere in the middle of the Indian Ocean.

But . . . that grim fate was not to be. Because, as it turned out, a guardian angel was watching over him.

Nolan turned to confront the pirates coming up in back of him—a last ditch attempt to simply face his killers—when he saw them stop in their tracks and look down at their chests. Bubbles of blood had appeared all over them.

The next thing Nolan knew, Gunner had slammed him to the deck. He hit hard, and the three Senegals fell on top of him; he felt like they were crushing every vertebra in his back. But in all the confusion, Nolan was still able to see the remaining pirates they'd been battling in front dropping to the deck as well. They, too, were bleeding. They'd all been shot dead. But who was doing the shooting?

Nolan's head was spinning. His lungs were full of toxic smoke. His hands were splattered with blood and he felt half dead already.

But he somehow mustered the strength to turn his head and look behind him again.

That's when he saw Emma Simms standing up on the bridge, a smoking AK-47 in her hands.

17

THERE *WAS* A bad part of town in Monte Carlo.

It was tucked into a corner near the east end of the city; a single block lost in the shadows of the tallest luxury buildings.

The block was comprised of a few elderly apartment buildings, a handful of open-air cafés and what passed for a variety store in this part of the world. An alley snaked through the small neighborhood and down this alley, after a few twists and turns, was a tiny hostel.

It had seven minuscule rooms, stacked one on top of another. Batman and Twitch were now occupying the top floor.

They had no money and they'd exhausted every way they

knew of to get any. Their debit card simply did not work. Nor could they figure out how to successfully make a phone call.

They were able to rent the room in the formerly sold-out boarding house only because they convinced the owner they were expecting funds to be wired to them soon and would pay him twice the going rate once they arrived. Because the proprietor was missing three fingers on his left hand, Batman and Twitch purposely exposed their prostheses while spinning him this tale. He rented them the room for nothing up front.

So they had a roof, albeit leaky, over their heads. And they had a place to sleep, though it was basically two rollouts on a cracked tile floor with folded towels as pillows.

They'd also eaten a little by walking through the Sun Casino, again prostheses in full view, and openly stealing bits of food from the buffets.

But there was no getting away from it.

They were the poorest two people in Monte Carlo.

• • •

THEY'D MOVED INTO the room shortly before midnight, five hours after being thrown out of the Grand Maison.

The next morning was the day before the start of the Grand Prix, and as bad and rundown as their hotel room was—its previous occupant had been arrested for counting cards, creating the vacancy—it actually had a fairly good view of Avenue des Beaux-Arts. Had they wanted it, they would have had an excellent seat for the race. But this had zero interest for Batman. He was still trying to figure a way out of their bizarre situation. Watching multimillion-dollar cars go flashing by their flophouse at 180 mph was the last thing he wanted to do.

The noise of these race cars revving their engines for practice laps roused him after only a few hours of restless sleep. In those first few uncertain moments upon waking, reality hit him like a ton of bricks. They'd arrived in Monte Carlo in first class, were given everything imaginable—the best booze, the best drugs, the best girls, ultraplatinum accommodations—and then suddenly, they'd been turned into nonpersons, virtual untouchables. Just when they should have been on top of their game trying to locate the Z-box, they'd been completely marginalized—and probably robbed.

Whoever was screwing with them was an expert at it.

• • •

FOR BETA SQUAD, the worm began to turn just after Batman woke up.

He was reheating some coffee they'd stolen from a casino the night before when he heard Twitch scream. He turned to see his colleague hanging halfway out of the room's only window, yelling something.

But Batman couldn't really hear him due to the racket of the Grand Prix cars zipping by.

So Twitch began yelling louder: "You gotta see this!"

"No thanks . . ." Batman replied, tasting the foul coffee. "No interest in race cars . . . Had enough of that last night."

But then Twitch walked over, grabbed him by the shoulders and pushed him halfway out the window

"I said 'Look!'" Twitch commanded him. "Down there . . ."

But all Batman could see were the race cars screaming by, taking their practice laps.

"OK—fast fucking cars," he yelled back at Twitch. "So what?"

"Screw the cars," Twitch told him. "Look down on the sidewalk—in that café."

Batman did as told and saw nothing unusual—for the first few seconds.

But then, he saw what Twitch saw.

Sitting at a table almost right below them was a familiar face.

Batman was stunned.

"Wow—is that who I think it is?" he gasped.

Twitch was sure. "It's him . . ." he said.

It was Audette. The CIA agent who'd come aboard *The Immaculate Perception* to brief them in the first place.

But no sooner had Batman seen him than the agent stood up, threw some money on the table, then quickly hailed a cab on a side street and disappeared, almost as if he knew he'd been spotted.

"Freaking spook," Batman said once he had gone. "I wonder what he's doing here?"

• • •

THEY WERE SURPRISED to find a library in Monte Carlo.

It was part of a small culinary and hospitality college run by a consortium of local casinos. While it wasn't exactly open to the public, Batman and Twitch, once again making sure their prostheses were on display, played the sympathy card to get past the head librarian and into the media room.

Twitch was Whiskey's computer whiz, plus he could type faster than Batman. They found an unoccupied PC and he immediately went to work.

Their number one goal was to get a secure communication to Kilos Shipping headquarters in Aden. But though they had the right address and password, after ten minutes and as many attempts, Twitch couldn't get the e-mail to go through.

This was all too familiar. Everything else on the computer worked: browsers, Web sites opened, even Skype popped on the screen. But, for whatever reason, the computer refused to send any kind of message Twitch created.

"I don't get it," he said to Batman. "Do they rig these things so once you're in paradise, they don't want you to talk to people who aren't here?"

"It's e-mail, man," Batman replied, frustration boiling over. "They got e-mail in freaking Siberia. Why not here?"

Even when they switched to another computer, one that they'd seen the previous user sending e-mails from, it simply would not work for them. They even tried to send Kilos a fax on line, but like the e-mail it disappeared into the ethers.

It was just like the ATMs and the public phones the night before. It didn't make sense. It was as if the technology itself was against them.

Then Batman got an idea. "Let's forget the e-mail bullshit for a minute," he said to Twitch. "Do you think you can get past the Grand Maison Casino's computer security system?"

Twitch was already typing. Not twenty seconds later he said: "I'm in. What do we want to know?"

Batman thought a moment, then said: "How about this: Obviously we didn't pay a dime for that penthouse. And we certainly didn't reserve it and now there's a good chance that it was all just an elaborate setup. But it must have cost *someone* something, right? At least for the food and booze?"

"Probably . . ." Twitch replied.

"So then," Batman told him. "Let's see who actually paid for all the Macallan and those Dolce & Gabbanas and Cohiba Behike cigars."

Five more minutes of frenzied typing followed and Twitch was eventually able to get into the casino's encrypted financial files. Then he began a search for who paid for all the accoutrements they'd enjoyed while in their luxurious suite.

It took a few more minutes, but finally Twitch was able to pull up a long list of items that had been "routed" to the Grand Maison's royal penthouse. It was all there: the cigars, the liquor, the cotton robes and the eagle eggs.

Twitch read the total off the screen: "Twenty-two thousand, six hundred and fifty-two dollars, including the meals and booze."

He looked up at Batman.

"This for a room that was still being renovated? A place that wasn't even supposed to be open?" he exclaimed.

"Had to be a bribe," Batman replied. "Someone on the

inside got paid off for making it all look legit. The real question, though, is who *paid* the bill?"

More typing, but Twitch eventually found a name.

"It says some guy named Bobby Murphy paid the bill," he reported. "In cash, no less."

Batman had to read it for himself.

"'Bobby Murphy?'" he said. "Who the hell is Bobby Murphy?"

• • •

IT WAS A slow morning at the Monte-Carlo Bay Casino.

The newest of the handful of gambling halls in the small principality, most of the patrons were out near the casino's front entrance watching the Formula One cars take their practice laps in anticipation of the big race kickoff the next day.

One man was sitting at the Chemin de Fer table, though, counting his meager piles of chips.

It was CIA agent Mark Audette. He was killing time.

His breakfast that morning had been several cups of coffee at a nearby café and nothing else. He'd drank a soda with ice around 10:00 A.M. and another one a half hour later.

Finally, his bladder started calling for relief. It was time to visit the facility.

He left the card table and walked to the nearest men's room. Two men dressed in maintenance worker clothes followed him in. Suddenly one of the men slammed the door shut and locked it from the inside.

The next thing Audette knew, he was looking down the barrel of a Glock 9.

"What the fuck . . ." was all he was able to say before he realized it was Batman on the other end of the gun.

"You?" he gasped. "The pirate guy?"

"And my trusty Boy Wonder, Robin," Batman said, indicating Twitch, who was standing behind Audette.

"How did you know I would be here?" he asked them.

"A government employee—in a place like Monte Carlo?"

Batman replied. "No surprise you'd be staying in the cheapest place in the city."

Audette began squirming.

"Why the hardware?" he said. "We're all on the same side here, remember?"

"Are we?" Batman asked, pressing the pistol a little closer to his nose. "Are you even with the Agency?"

Audette seemed insulted. "Of course I am, you ass . . ."

"Show us your ID," Twitch told him.

Audette laughed. "We don't carry IDs," he said. "You guys should know that. Now, please, lower the artillery."

But Batman ignored him. He reached inside Audette's shirt pocket and pulled out the agent's sat-phone.

"You know the one you gave us was a piece of shit," Batman told him, indicating the sat-phone. "Crap made in China. Defective battery. You name it."

Audette rolled his eyes. "I hope they're not all like that," he said almost under his breath.

Batman checked the nationality of Audette's sat-phone. It looked different from the ones he'd dispensed to the team earlier.

"OK—Motorola," Batman said. "Made in the USA."

Still holding the gun on Audette, Batman dialed their number in Aden. But the call wouldn't go through. He passed the phone to Twitch. He tried—with the same result. The call would not connect.

Batman whipped the phone into the nearest trash basket.

"This thing's a piece of shit, too," he declared.

But Audette complained. "Hey—I need that!"

"Forget about it," Batman told him angrily. "Just tell us what the fuck is going on here?"

Audette shook his head. "What do you mean?"

Batman pressed Audette. "We're supposed to be working for you, right?"

"Yes—you are . . ."

"Then why have you put us out to pasture? Forcing us off

track? Distracting us? And stealing ten million dollars from us?"

Audette seemed authentically confused. "What are you talking about? I didn't know you guys were here until this very minute."

Batman quickly told him everything that had happened to them in the past twenty-four hours. Their five-star welcome. The penthouse. The royal treatment. Maurice's visit. The buy-in fee. The disinformation agent. The chase and the jump jet, and then their transformation into nonpersons.

"When you consider your employer tried to stage a battle against some fake pirates, only to get bested by real pirates," Batman said, "I think what we just went through is just weird enough to have the CIA's stink all over it."

But Audette protested at every turn.

"I guarantee you the Agency had nothing to do with *any* of this," he told them. "We want this Z-box back in the worst way. Why would we stand in your way of getting it?"

The room became silent. Audette was right. It didn't make sense that the CIA would impede Whiskey's progress in getting the Z-box back, not if its contents were as "embarrassing" as the Agency feared.

"What about this 'buy-in' money you were supposed to give us then?" Twitch asked him.

"That's all total bullshit," Audette replied heatedly. "You were there when I got the phone call. I found out about the Monte Carlo connection at the same time you guys did."

"So you say," Twitch challenged him. "That could have been faked, your way of being in on this scam."

Audette pleaded, "But why would I want to extort money from you guys?"

"Because you knew we'd just gotten paid ten million for rescuing the wicked bitch of the west," Batman said. "You saw us as suckers."

"Listen," Audette said. "Let me tell you something. When it comes to my job, I'm like a big city cop. And there are people out there whose job it is to watch my bank accounts and make sure they're not growing bigger than they should and that I'm not squirreling away nest eggs or taking money from the Chink-Coms. Plus, I'm not about to steal ten million from the guys who got close enough to whack Sunny Hi."

"Well, *someone* stole it from us," Twitch said. "And when we catch him, they're going to wish they went as fast as Sunny Hi did."

Audette just shook his head. "Guys—please, we're not in a movie here. All I can tell you is there's no reason me or anyone in the Agency would stand in your way of getting the Z-box back or try to rob you."

Batman finally lowered his pistol. And Twitch did, too.

But they were still certain Audette knew more than he was telling them.

"What are you doing here then?" Batman asked the agent.

Audette was getting perturbed now.

"I'm here because this is where the box is supposed to be," he snapped back. "Where would you want me to be? In Gotta-fuck India?"

"OK then, who *is* this Maurice guy?" Batman asked.

Audette was adamant. "I got no idea. I've never heard that name in any of our operations. Never heard it as a cover name. And I sure don't know anything about any big secret card game."

"OK then," Batman said. "Who is Bobby Murphy?"

That's when Audette's face dropped a mile. His shoulders slumped and he almost turned pale. "Oh, God . . ." he moaned. "Please no . . ."

"Who is he?" Batman pressed him.

"I can't tell you," Audette stumbled in reply. "Just like I couldn't tell him about you . . . if he was involved in this . . . which I don't think he is. But who knows? And that's all I'm going to say about it."

It took Batman and Twitch about ten seconds to let Audette's rambling reply sink in. Then it hit them.

"We're not the only special ops team working this, are we?" Batman spit at him, raising his pistol again.

Audette hesitated a moment, but then relented. He shook his head. "No, you're not," he finally admitted.

"How many?" Batman asked him. "Besides us?"

Audette shook his head. "I don't know," he said. "Some things I'm not privy to. But more than just you guys, I know that."

"One more? Two more?" Batman growled at him.

"Yeah . . . about that. I mean, there aren't many privately run special ops groups around—but we hit them all, I guess."

"So you're saying you hired those assholes from the old Blackwater?" Batman asked him. "And DynCorp? And EOD?"

"I'm not sure," Audette insisted. "I know we got a lot of eyes out there looking for this thing." He paused, then added: "And a few bent noses, too."

Batman and Twitch just looked at each other. "Bent nose" was code for . . .

"The Mob?" Batman asked him. "You got the freaking *mafia* involved in this, too?"

Audette just shrugged. "Hey, it's a tradition with us," he said. "Ever since World War Two. They're watching the ports in the U.S. for us, checking to see if this thing comes in anywhere. Someone's gotta do it."

Batman was growing furious. "So you guys hired a *bunch* of groups like us and then, what? Pitted us against one another? While not letting one group know it was in a competition?"

Audette nodded again. This time it looked painful for him.

"And everyone's going for the hundred-million-dollar prize?" Batman asked.

"Yes—you got it right," Audette said. "I know it was dumb—but you have to remember, we want this thing back *very* badly—and if this doesn't prove it to you, nothing will. We thought if we had more than just one private special ops group going after it, the chances of retrieving it were that much better. I mean, you guys are the pirate specialists, so I was sure you'd have a leg up on the rest of them. But we never dreamed that one group would find out about the other and then throw up roadblocks against them. We went to great lengths to make sure not a word of this ever leaked out."

Twitch spoke up. "You know what this sounds like? This sounds like a fucking reality show. Like you got the big prize hidden somewhere. One team fucks up the other. Winner take all."

Batman looked into Audette's eyes.

"This isn't some kind of weird loyalty thing is it?" he asked him. "Or the Agency's weird idea for a psy-ops experiment."

Audette replied quickly. "No—of course not," he said. Then he thought a moment and added, "At least I don't think so."

Another silence. Then Batman asked him, "So let's get back to this Bobby Murphy character. He's the CO of another special ops outfit, I take it?"

Audette seemed to want to bite off his own tongue.

"I can't tell you *anything* about him," he said. "But yes, he's the alpha dog of another group of operators. *Very independent* operators. In fact, when it comes to busting terrorists, his group is considered the best special ops group in the world, military or civilian."

"If that's true," Twitch said, "how come we've never heard of them?"

Audette just nodded.

"Exactly," he said wryly. "But I didn't sign them up, I swear. In fact, I wouldn't be surprised if he found out about it somehow on his own and just wormed his way in. That's the way his guys are—guys *and* girls, I should say. They're like phantoms. Supposedly they travel around in this old container ship, whacking terrorists, completely unauthorized shit. But they've got a lot of weapons and people who can use them.

So, believe me, I'm sure they're the ones who are glitching you. They probably stole your ten million, too, because while they're in the business of terrorizing the terrorists, they're usually cash-strapped because no one in the U.S. Government wants to fund them—they're just too 'out there.'"

Audette paused for a moment, then asked: "Did you actually meet him? The man himself?"

Batman shrugged. "How would we know?"

"Well, this guy you said came to you in the penthouse," Audette replied. "This guy Maurice? What did he look like?"

"Like the most ordinary person in the world," Batman replied.

Audette shook his head emphatically. "Yep—*that's* him, the bastard," he said. "He looks like your favorite uncle or the guy next door. But he's into some crazy shit. His bunch are like you guys, heroes running around after 9/11. He's the one who punked you, though. I'm sure of it now. Only he could pull off something like that in that casino. It sounds like he arranged that chase to get you out of that penthouse—and the Harrier thing was the cherry on top."

"Son of a bitch," Batman moaned. "So we were sideswiped even before we knew it."

"Fucking dicks," Twitch said. "Trying give us the shiv—*and* steal our money!"

"That's the way they operate," Audette said. "They live, eat and breathe psy-ops. Just ask bin Laden's cub scouts. They're deathly afraid of Murphy and his crew. And if those guys put their mind to it, well . . ."

"Well, what?" Batman asked him.

"Well," Audette answered. "If you guys want that ten million back, never mind your payday, you got your work cut out for you."

Someone started pounding on the men's room door. They were starting to attract attention.

"We gotta get out of here," Batman told Audette. "But believe me this isn't the end of it."

He let Audette off the wall, finally. The agent adjusted his suit and tried to get himself together. Then Twitch unlocked the door and the three of them walked out, to the great curiosity of the man who'd been trying to get in.

Once in the casino's lobby, Audette said, "So, now that we've talked, do you guys mind telling me what you've found out about the box since you arrived here?"

Batman began to say something, but stopped.

But Twitch jumped in. "Yeah, when you open it, a green glow comes out and kills people."

Audette almost bought it. Then Batman said, "Seeing as we might have a security problem here—as well as a competition problem, it's best that we keep anything we've found out . . . proprietary. You can understand that, right?"

Audette shrugged. "Understandable," he said. "But at least tell me, what did Bobby Murphy say about the box's location? Did he think it was really coming through here? Or is it here already? Is it going to change hands here? Or was everything he said wrapped up in this card game?"

Batman hesitated again, more questions flashing through his head. Was Audette telling the truth when he said he didn't know about the Grand Gagnant card game? Did the card game even exist at all? Or was it just more of Bobby Murphy's bullshit?

Before Batman could say anything, Twitch just laughed. "Screw you," he told Audette. "We're not telling you anything. So hit the bricks."

Audette just shrugged again. "OK," he said. "Be like that. Just don't get upset when you see a lot of people running around here in trench coats, sunglasses and big funny hats. Because they'll be going after the same thing you are. And you're already ten million down in the game."

He started to leave, but then Batman stopped him.

"By the way," he said sheepishly. "Do you have any extra cash? You know we lost everything in this scam. We don't have two dimes to rub together."

Audette smiled slyly. He looked at Twitch, then said, "Gee, guys, I'm tapped out. Sorry . . ."

Before Batman and Twitch could argue with him, Audette walked away and quickly disappeared into the crowd.

18

NOLAN FINALLY STOPPED the bleeding.

He'd sustained cuts on his hands, a slash over his good eye and a nasty gash on his shoulder during the recent combat. But once he'd washed the wounds with *cheongju* and covered them over with gauze, he deemed himself in good shape.

It was the rest of Alpha that was badly hurt.

While they might have won the third battle of the *Taiwan Song*—the Bom-Kat fleet had disappeared into the night once all their men on board had been killed—it was not without casualties. Two of the Senegals were seriously wounded, as was Gunner, though he was trying to hide it. The three other Senegals had been slashed on their arms and shoulders during the fight; one had a broken hand. But at least they were still mobile. It was incredible none of the ship's defenders had been killed—not yet anyway.

Besides being banged up and bloody, Alpha had exactly two weapons left on board—the pair of AK-47s belonging to the pirates who'd invaded the mess hall. Neither rifle had much ammunition left in it. The ship's original crew, each with burned hands and other wounds, had just about used up all of the hydraulic fluid in the battle and there was nothing else on board to take its place. Even most of the galley knives were gone.

If and when the Bom-Kats came back, Alpha Squad would be practically defenseless.

• • •

FOREMOST OF NOLAN'S worries, though, was Emma's state of mind.

After mowing down the last of the attacking pirates, she'd dropped the gun, collapsed to the deck and buried her face in her hands. Then she wept uncontrollably for more than twenty minutes.

Finally, one of the Senegals gently lifted her up and guided her to the bow where she sat alone for another half hour. Only after Alpha had thrown all the pirate bodies overboard did Nolan dare approach her.

She was still teary-eyed, looking out to sea and continuously rubbing her hands on her knees. She looked like she was trying to wipe away any evidence that she had fired the AK-47.

She relaxed a little once she realized he was there. Reaching out to grab his hand, she asked, "How are my people below? Did any more pirates make it down to the mess hall?"

Nolan shook his head.

"They're all fine," he reassured her. "Though I'm sure they're worried about you."

She watched the injured crewmen hose off the last of the blood from the deck.

"Do you always feel like this after one of these things?" she asked Nolan.

"Why? How do *you* feel?" he asked her back.

"Sick," she replied. "Sick to my stomach. Sick in my head."

Nolan shrugged. "Well, you have to be alive to feel sick. That's the upside."

Her tears returned. "But I feel like such a criminal," she said. "Do you know how many times I've done something like that in one of my movies? Mown down a bunch of bad guys with some kind of machine gun? But all I was ever concerned about was how my hair looked. Now, I've done it for real . . . I killed how many people? Ten? Twelve? I'll never be the same. I *can't* be . . ."

"You saved our lives," he told her. "And not just us, the

people in the mess hall, too. The pirates would have killed them all—or left them to die."

She wiped her eyes again. "But you've got to know *I'm* the cause of all this. You're all here because of me. I made you take me along. I made you rescue those poor people. I made you steal this boat. Why didn't I just stay on my yacht?"

He sat down beside her. He resisted the urge to put his arm around her, but kept hold of her hand.

"What do you remember about that night in the refugee camp?" he asked her. "Right before we decided to take the Untouchables with us?"

She had to think for a moment. "The whole thing is like a dream to me now. Why?"

Nolan took the diplomatic route.

"Let's just say you've become a different person," he told her. "And I've been in this business a long time, and I've got to tell you, you've shown more guts in the past twenty-four hours than some guys I've spent years with. Now, try to stop dwelling on what just happened—the world is better off without those mooks. The idea here is to save those poor people in the mess hall, and that's what we're going to do. Capeesh?"

She managed a smile. Even in this condition, she looked absolutely radiant.

"Mio *capice*," she replied in a perfect Italian accent.

He raised her to her feet. "Your friends in the mess hall will be very glad to see you. The wounded guys are down below, too."

She wiped her eyes again and then started making her way aft.

But she turned, stepped back to him, and said softly, "Thank you."

Then she kissed him on the cheek and walked away.

• • •

NOLAN WAITED UNTIL she was out of sight before climbing up to the ship's bridge again.

It was now 0400 hours. It was still dark, still brutally hot and the sea was still ominously calm.

With the injured crewmen's help, he got the ship's balky radio working again. He went up and down the dial, hearing a cacophony of chattering voices speaking countless languages at very high speed.

He eventually found one frequency that was clearer than the rest, and just listened. The participants were speaking Hindi, but with a few English words mixed in. After just thirty seconds, he knew it was the Bom-Kats, talking about what had happened less than an hour before. It didn't take long before he heard the name *Emma Simms*.

It just reconfirmed his worst fears. Yes, the Bom-Kats knew the world's most famous actress was aboard the old ship. And like the Somalis who'd snatched her earlier, they undoubtedly knew she would be worth tens of millions of dollars in ransom—and that was after they got through doing whatever they wanted to her.

So, yes, Alpha Squad had foiled the Bom-Kats three times now. But judging from the radio chatter, Nolan was certain the pirates were going to try again. What would happen then? Alpha Squad was out-gunned, out-manned, out of their element, and out of touch—with anybody who could help.

But then one of the crewmen began tapping him urgently on his good shoulder. The man pointed to the eastern horizon where Nolan was heartened to see a bright light approaching. He knew right away that it was not a Bom-Kat boat; it was way too big. The crewman confirmed it; a major vessel heading in their direction.

Nolan started listening to the shortwave radio again. He zeroed in on another frequency. It, too, was filled with a mixture of Hindi and English chatter about the Bom-Kats, and mentions of a disabled freighter coming under attack by the pirates. But the cadence was different and those speaking were using proper maritime radio etiquette—all "rogers," "overs" and "outs." The four crewmen listened to the conversations with growing smiles.

"It's the Indian Navy," one said finally. "They've sent a warship to help us. That's it—coming our way."

• • •

THE SHIP WAS in visual range ten minutes later.

Emma remained in the mess hall; Nolan was hoping she was asleep. Gunner and the two wounded Senegals were in the ship's galley, being cared for by the three less-wounded West Africans. Though he was excited about this development, Nolan did not want to disturb any of them—not until he knew what was really up with this warship.

He asked the *Taiwan Song*'s crewmen to bring the freighter to a stop. Then, with a fading flashlight, he made his way down to the bow to await the vessel's approach.

Once the warship was within 100 feet of the freighter, Nolan used the flashlight to signal his location. Someone on the ship signaled back.

He then played his weak beam onto the stern of the vessel and, for the first time, saw the name of the warship.

INS *Vidynut . . .*

His heart sank to his feet. What were the chances of this?

The second real gig the newly formed Team Whiskey ever took on was to rescue an Indian Navy warship that had been hijacked by Somali pirates. This warship was a new, ultra-high-tech model, wholly designed by the Indian Navy, in hopes of exporting them to many other countries. The Somali pirates had been about to execute the Indian crew when Whiskey came upon the scene.

Nolan and company were able to save the crew, but only after a battle against the pirates that all but destroyed the new warship. The Indian Navy paid the team their hefty fee, but made it very clear they never wanted to have anything to do with Whiskey again.

That warship was the *Vidynut,* the vessel that was now pulling up alongside him.

The ship didn't look much better than the last time Nolan saw it. It had been patched from bow to stern; blotches of new paint were evident all over. The massive deck-mounted rocket launchers that provided the vessel with its firepower were gone. Its futuristic bridge, which had been all but destroyed in the melee, had been cut down by at least ten feet and now looked as ordinary as could be.

Nolan could even hear the ship's radically designed engines sputtering as it approached.

Captain Vasu Vandar was commander of the *Vidynut* during the violent hijacking; it had been Nolan who freed him and the rest of his crew during the rescue mission.

Now, Captain Vandar and a coterie of sailors walked to the deck to inspect the freighter. As soon as he saw Nolan, though, he let out a wail.

"Not you!" he bellowed. "Not again!"

Nolan tried to reason with him. "We're in a bad situation here," he yelled over to Vandar. "We've got refugees on board and we're being attacked by pirates every two hours."

"I don't care," Vandar yelled back, wagging his finger at Nolan. "You a very, very bad man. You almost sink my ship once—I will not allow you to try it again."

"We *saved* your ship," Nolan yelled back. "And your crew. And *you*."

"And my life has been miserable ever since," Vandar yelled back. "I want nothing to do with you."

Nolan couldn't believe what he was hearing.

"At least take the refugees with you," he yelled to the ship captain. "Save them at least."

"Who are these people?" Vandar asked, voice dripping with disinterest.

Nolan explained who the refugees were—a mistake as it turned out, as Vandar almost immediately cut him off.

"These people are Untouchables," he said. "We cannot have them on this vessel. End of story."

Vandar signaled someone up on his bridge; the *Vidynut* started to pull away.

"Wait . . ." Nolan pleaded with him. "We have a very famous celebrity on board. A movie actress."

"I'm sure you do!" Vandar yelled back with a laugh. His sailors laughed, too.

"It's true," Nolan pleaded with him. "And if you take her, then the pirates will leave us alone."

"So they can pick on us then?" Vandar called back to him. "No, thank you. This ship has already had enough bad luck experience with pirates."

With that, the *Vidynut*'s sputtering engines were revved up and it slowly sailed away.

• • •

NOLAN STAGGERED DOWN below decks, greatly disturbed by the strange encounter with the *Vidynut*.

He was furious the Indian Navy would not help them. He hated *everything* about India at that moment: the prejudice, the caste system, rich and poor, haves and have-nots—this in a country that was supposed to be so enlightened?

He found an unoccupied cabin and collapsed atop a pile of rags. He was beyond exhaustion. The last time he'd slept was back on *The Immaculate Perception*, in a lounge chair, taking turns watching over Batman. But that seemed so long ago, it was as if it had happened to someone else entirely.

With these thoughts bouncing around his head, he surrendered to a fitful slumber and was haunted by feverish dreams. Suddenly, he was back in Tora Bora, with two working eyes, chasing bin Laden. The terrorist was riding a magic carpet, though, and Nolan had a ball and chain attached to each of his legs. Then he was in Indonesia, running down a beach, chasing pirates who were dressed like nightmarish clowns. Then he was in the Caribbean, shooting at whales that had sprouted wings and could fly. Then . . . he was fighting the renegade SEALs who'd stolen the nuclear submarine, USS *Wyoming*, but the battle was in the middle of an amusement park.

Suddenly, he was in a movie. He was lying on a deep, feather-bed mattress. Everything was warm and clean and white—and he was looking up at Emma, all gorgeous, huge eyes and flowing blond curls. She was touching his face, trying to tell him something, like: *Please let me sleep with you.*

But just as suddenly, he was awake. And Emma *was* looking down at him, and she *was* touching his face and trying to tell him something. But it wasn't an invitation for intimacy.

She was saying to him: "Please—wake up. The pirates are coming again. . . ."

• • •

NOLAN WAS BACK up on deck in seconds, looking out on the eastern horizon, which was blood red with the newly rising sun.

Emma was right behind him.

The Bom-Kats *were* coming again. They could see at least three dozen vessels heading right for them.

"My God, how many people do they have?" she exclaimed.

"This is India," Nolan told her. "They have access to an unlimited number of bodies, just as long as they're convinced they're in for a big payday."

They had the two AK-47s with a total of twelve rounds between them. That amounted to a couple of very brief bursts from each assault rifle, and after that, the freighter would be practically defenseless.

Nolan's spirits plummeted as the pirate boats approached. Like some wounded animal, the freighter had held off the wolves three times. But there was just no way they could do it a fourth time.

Emma stayed beside him. "I'm the cause of all this," she said softly. "They know I'm here. They want me. And because of me, they're going to kill everyone on this ship— and that's the exact opposite of what this is supposed to be about. . . ."

"There's no way we can change the situation," Nolan said, watching the pirates with his night-vision scope. The pirates were now about five minutes away from the ship and coming on strong.

"Yes, there is," she said firmly. "Let them take me."

He looked over at her. *"What?"*

"Let them take me," she repeated. "They want me. They want to hold me hostage. So let them. Someone will pay the ransom. So, I'll be uncomfortable for a few days, so what?"

But Nolan was already shaking his head emphatically no.

"Not in a million years," he told her.

"But it's the only solution," she insisted. "My life for all of yours? And my people down below? Do the math. . . ."

"No way . . . ," he said again.

"But what about the others?" Emma pressed him, meaning the rest of the people on the ship. The wounded Senegals, Gunner and the ship's crew. "Don't they have a say in this?"

But Nolan didn't answer. He didn't want to think about them. He couldn't . . .

The pirates were so close now, he could see the colors of their brightly painted speedboats roaring up to the stern.

The sun was up, the sea was calm. It was a beautiful morning—and certainly no time to die. But there didn't seem to be another outcome possible.

Nolan was not religious. And he'd been in many tight spots before. But at that moment, exhausted and beaten, he looked to the sky and whispered: "Please . . . get us out of this."

And not a moment later, he heard it . . .

The pirates had surrounded the slow-moving freighter by now and were preparing to send up their grappling hooks. Even worse, these pirates were armed not with knives but with AK-47s. This time they weren't just fodder employed to expend the freighter's defenders of strength and ammunition. These were the Bom-Kats' *real* fighters.

It was strange, because as this battle was beginning to envelop them, Nolan was still staring into the early morning sky, making sure he wasn't just imagining things. That his appeal to the heavens had come true.

Then he saw it.

Right above them.

Like an angel . . .
The *Shin-1* flying boat.

• • •

THANKS TO THEIR special forces training, the pilots
of the big amphibian were able to read the situation below
them right away. The Bom-Kat pirate band was well known
in this part of the world; the Stormo pilots knew them by
their colorfully painted boats.

It was only through their expert navigational skills that
they were able to find the *Taiwan Song* in the first place. But
now they had to save their friends below. They'd picked up
weapons and ammunition when they refueled at an Omani
Navy refueling base. Just speaking Emma Simms's name had
opened many doors for them.

One of the weapons they'd borrowed from the Omanis
was an MK-19 belt-fed 40-mm grenade-launching machine
gun. It resembled a small artillery piece and was similar to a
Streetsweeper but with much more power and range. It could
be fitted to fire huge incendiary shells and even anti-armor
rounds. The pilots thought this was the kind of weapon those
on the freighter might need for protection.

Now the Stormo copilot quickly unpacked the massive
gun and fed an ammo belt into it. Then he opened one of the
observation blisters that dotted the side of the flying boat;
this one was on the left-hand side.

He stuck the weapon's huge barrel through the opening
and propped it up on his knees. He squeezed the trigger, just
for a moment, and was almost knocked backward by the
recoil.

But it was workable.

He yelled ahead to the pilot: *"Scendere al di sotto!"*

"Go lower!"

The huge seaplane went into a steep dive. Only when it
reached a heartstopping 200 feet in altitude did the pilot finally pull up above the slowly moving freighter. Leveling
off briefly, with a scream of its engines, the amphibian then

dipped its left wing. The copilot took aim and began firing the massive gun.

When viewed from the deck of the freighter, it looked like the big plane was crashing. But then Nolan saw the telltale spit of flame come from its lower midsection and understood right away.

He grabbed Emma and pushed her to the deck. The big airplane went overhead seconds later, the huge MK-19 firing intensely.

It was instant madness. The *Shin-1* had turned itself into a crude Spectre gunship. And it was chewing up the Bom-Kat fleet. The danger was the pilots really had no way to control where the MK-19's grenades were going other than moving the plane in order to aim the weapon. Being no-where as precise as a real AC-130 gunship, some of the grenades were hitting the *Taiwan Song* itself.

So Nolan covered Emma completely with his body and just held on.

It went on like this for five terrifying minutes. Emma pressed herself very close to Nolan, especially when the *Shin-1* passed right over the freighter, the MK-19 firing at an ear-splitting volume.

It was only after Nolan heard the huge gun stop firing that he dared to look up. He saw nothing but burning and sinking pirate boats and floating bodies all around the ship. About half the pirate fleet had been sunk. Many other boats were retreating; many of them were smoking.

Finally he helped Emma to her feet. She looked out on the devastation and gasped.

"My God," she finally said. "When will this movie end?"

• • •

THE *SHIN-1* TIED up to the freighter, which had once more come to a dead stop in the calm morning sea.

Nolan and especially Emma greeted the Stormos warmly; it was well deserved. The two ex–special forces pilots had saved the lives of everyone on the leaky freighter.

The *Shin-1* was carrying dozens of boxes of Omani Navy food rations and medical supplies. Also on board were much needed weapons including a dozen M-16s and ammunition, plus the MK-19. The guns and ammo, especially the grenade-throwing machine gun, would help ward off any future pirate attacks. Plus the food was enough to feed everyone on board for at least forty-eight hours.

But as helpful as it was, the delivery of relief supplies didn't solve their biggest problem.

Once the Shin was unloaded, Nolan called a meeting on the ship's bridge. The gathering looked like a scene from a hospital emergency ward. While the four original crewmen all had burned hands, treatments contained in the Omani medical supplies would help ease their distress. Then again, it was obvious that the wounds suffered by Gunner and all of the Senegals needed medical attention as soon as possible.

The quandary was that the ship was still at least a day's sail from the Lakshadweep Islands. And once there, there were no guarantees they'd be allowed to dock or even get anywhere close to the isolated island chain. And even if they were allowed to drop anchor, what then? Arriving unannounced—with a politically volatile human cargo? It might be the story of the SS *St. Louis* all over again.

So, there really was no other choice. While Emma was adamant she would not leave "her people" at this point, Gunner and the Senegals *would* have to be evacuated immediately. That meant they'd have to leave in the Shin.

"But what about you guys?" Gunner protested on hearing the plan. "We can't abandon you here."

True, Nolan and Emma were still in good shape and the ship had been resupplied. But the reality was they could have a hundred weapons on board and a ton of ammunition, and there still wasn't much the pair of them could do if the Bom-Kats attacked again.

But this was the way it had to be, Nolan finally convinced Gunner. His colleague, weakened and his shoulder wound still bleeding and in danger of infection, had no choice but to agree. The Senegals protested as strenuously as Gunner, but in the end, they, too, knew it was the only thing to do.

• • •

IT WAS A bittersweet farewell as the six wounded men were put aboard the *Shin-1*. The Stormos promised to get them to the nearest medical facility—which, ironically, was the Red Crescent hospital in Karachi, Pakistan, the same place that refused Emma's request to take in the ninety-nine Untouchables—and then come back and look for them.

It was with mixed feelings that Nolan watched the *Shin-1* pull away and go airborne. On one hand, he was glad his friends would be getting the medical treatment they needed. On the other hand, the *Taiwan Song* was on its own again. True, it had more firepower, but with far fewer people to actually pull the triggers.

But that's when Alpha Squad got strangely lucky again. Because no sooner had the *Shin-1* disappeared from sight than the ship's dormant radio suddenly burst to life.

One of the ship's crewmen immediately answered the call. He announced it was for Emma. She got on the microphone and discovered it was her old friend, the Sultan of Oman, the man who owned the Shins, and a whole lot of other things.

She broke down when she heard his voice. He told her—tipped off by the Stormos' refueling stop at one of his country's naval bases—the head of his intelligence service had briefed him on her predicament. He'd been trying to contact her ever since.

Emma explained the current situation. She told the Sultan the freighter's approximate location, emphasizing the lives of the innocent people on board and how she felt responsible for them, and how no one in the area would grant them asylum.

The Sultan told her to worry no longer. "Help is on the way," he said.

• • •

THIS GOOD NEWS was enough to relax Emma considerably. She actually lay down on the bridge's cot to rest. She was snoring softly just a minute later.

But her nap didn't last too long. Only a few minutes later, Nolan was gently shaking her awake.

She came to with a start.

"Are we being attacked again?" she asked almost in a panic.

He put his hand on her shoulder and calmed her.

"No, we're okay," he told her. "But come with me. I have a surprise for you."

She followed him down to the deck and he pointed out toward the western horizon. She saw dozens of ships approaching, silhouetted by the slowly rising sun.

"They are not Bom-Kats?" she asked.

Nolan shook his head no. Then he handed her a pair of binoculars. She focused on the vessels and then leaped for joy.

"Is that really the Omani flag I see?" she asked excitedly.

"It is," Nolan confirmed. "That's the Omani National fishing fleet. Your friend has kept his promise. He's sent a hundred little ships to protect us."

• • •

WITHIN THIRTY MINUTES, the fleet of brightly colored wooden fishing boats had surrounded the freighter.

As one, they all started moving southwest again, resuming the freighter's journey to the Lakshadweep Islands. The commander of the fleet sent a message to Emma saying the Sultan had already made arrangements for the Untouchables to live in Oman, to get medical treatment, homes and jobs. It was the ideal outcome for her.

Even as the surrounding fleet and the freighter moved to

the southwest, Nolan could see vessels belonging to the Bom-Kats, some similar in color and wooden manufacture, sailing around the edges, scoping out what had happened and realizing it would be impossible to get at the freighter for another attack.

So, for once, *everyone* on board the *Taiwan Song* felt relaxed. The refugees below received medicine and treatment and then came up to the deck for the first time since the bizarre journey began. They shared a communal meal around the raised cargo deck, the Omani K-rations being supplemented by fresh fish caught by their new guardian angels, all one hundred of them. Around this time, Nolan scanned the horizon and saw that the remaining Bom-Kat ships that had been hanging on the periphery had finally given up and departed.

Morning passed into afternoon; dusk became night. Emma fell asleep again on the bridge and this time for more then a few minutes. Nolan stayed close by, keeping awake all night and watching over her.

He didn't mind a bit.

• • •

IT ONLY GOT better the next morning.

An Omani warship had arrived with the dawn. It came up next to the *Taiwan Song* as the fleet of fishing boats parted the way. A gangway was placed between the freighter and Omani destroyer. The warship's captain greeted Emma like an old friend.

"The Sultan sends seven million blessings," he said. "For the most beautiful flower in the world."

Then he had his crewmen escort the Untouchables onto his ship. All of the unfortunates were in tears as Emma hugged each one and bade them farewell. She promised she would return soon to Oman to see how their new lives were going— and she meant it.

By this time they were within sight of the Lakshadweep Islands. The freighter's crew, also grateful to be alive, had already agreed to sail the ship back to Gottabang and finally put the old tub to rest, its last voyage being its most heroic one.

Now that it was just them, Nolan felt it best that he and Emma get to the main Lakshadweep Island and maybe get a flight out to somewhere. At the same time, he would try to contact Beta Squad.

To this end, one of the fishing boats came alongside the *Taiwan Song*. Its captain yelled up that he'd be honored to taxi Nolan and Emma to the nearby island. This was all right with the Omani navy captain, as it would avoid any complications of his warship entering India's territorial waters without proper authorization.

The warship departed with four loud blasts of its horn. The crew lined up on the deck for the occasion and let out a cheer. Speaking through his bullhorn, the captain said: "To the Earth's most beautiful jewel, 'til we all meet again!"

Then the destroyer turned and was quickly on its way, the dozens of ships of the Omani National fishing fleet turning as well and following in its wake.

Nolan lowered a rope ladder and helped Emma down to the remaining fishing boat's deck. He then said good-bye to the *Taiwan Song*'s crew, at the same time giving them a phone number. It was the private line to Whiskey's office in Aden.

"If you're ever in trouble," he told them. "Anywhere in the world, call us—and we'll come get you."

There was a group hug, a series of bows and then Nolan himself climbed down the rope ladder. He joined Emma on the fishing boat's bow and together they watched the old freighter slowly sail away.

"That will be something to tell their grandkids," Nolan said.

"I'll tell it to mine as well," Emma said, briefly squeezing his hand.

The thought went through Nolan's mind at that moment that maybe they could wait a little while for a flight out of the remote Lakshadweeps. Maybe they could spend some time on the beach, recuperating after their ordeal. Perhaps a few drinks. Some unwinding. Some time to talk.

He was just about to summon up the courage to pass this idea on to Emma, when he turned and saw the captain of the fishing boat was holding a gun on them.

"Bom-Kats very brave pirates," this man said with a toothless grin. "Smart pirates, too. They make enemies do their dirty work for them."

19

Monte Carlo

BATMAN AND TWITCH returned to the shabby hostel and wearily climbed seven floors up to their room.

It had turned into a sweltering day and the sound of race cars revving their engines and taking practice laps nearby provided constant background noise. Even louder mechanical rumblings were coming from the harbor; their vibrations ran so deep, they shook the hostel to its creaky foundations.

The room's version of air conditioning was an ancient electric fan stuck on low. Batman and Twitch, sweaty and exhausted, sat down in front of it and relived the strange events of the morning.

"There's really only one solution to this," Batman said finally. "If we're going to find that fucking box, get our ten million back *and* get paid, we better hope that gagnant game exists, because one of us has to get into it."

Twitch wiped his brow. "Well, it's got to be you," he said. "Last time I was involved in a card game, I wound up shooting four guys in the head."

Batman laughed darkly. "You never know," he replied. "You might have to do it again."

Twitch tried to get the fan to move faster, but the switch would not budge off low.

"But remember," he said. "If that a-hole Maurice, or Bobby Murphy or whoever the fuck he is, is telling the truth and there *is* a game, the buy-in is fifty million dollars. How can we get that, if we can't even make a phone call?"

Batman stared out the room's one window for a long time.

Then he said: "Let me think about that for a while. I might know a way."

• • •

THEY BOTH COLLAPSED on their rollouts and, despite the racket outside, soon fell into fitful sleeps.

Batman's dreams were especially upsetting. In a peculiar vision of the Grand Maison Casino, he was sitting on the balcony, but he was in a wheelchair, a broken down invalid. The casino itself was deserted and in disrepair. The penthouse was in shambles; the concourse below was it overgrown and the Olympic pool empty and cracked. On his lap was a newspaper with front-page stories that kept changing before he could read them.

But one headline he could see clearly. In big, bold type, it read: "Opportunity Lost?"

• • •

BATMAN WOKE AROUND 8:00 P.M.

He left Twitch sleeping in front of the fan and climbed up to the hostel's roof.

He was surprised that this particular part of Monte Carlo had been left to wither. The view from here was spectacular, especially at night.

He looked out over the high-priced penthouses and luxury buildings and the casinos beyond. He wondered how much money was jammed into this half square-mile of seafront property.

A few billion?

A few *trillion*?

More?

All they needed was a small fraction of that—fifty million dollars. Back in his Wall Street days, before Madoff, before the Crash, he could make someone fifty million during a coffee break.

He thought about this for a long time, then recalled the headline from his dream.

"Opportunity Lost?"

What a strange thing to see.

• • •

THE PETITE JUNQUE was the smallest casino in Monte Carlo.

It was two blocks from the hostel, on a back street where the vendors who worked the waterfront area during the day left their idle carts at night.

It was the only casino in town that was frequented more by locals than tourists; it didn't appear on any travelogues. Just one large room, with fifty gaming tables and a bar, there were no frills, no tuxedo-clad doormen and certainly no Rolls-Royce taxicabs. Instead, the place smelled of Noisette, cheap brandy and cigarette smoke. This was Monte Carlo's version of Fulton Street in Las Vegas. Bright, harsh and as far away from the Strip as possible.

Batman arrived just before 9:00 P.M. He was alone; at his request Twitch had stayed behind. What Batman was about to do, he felt he had to do solo. Because if he failed, if he went down in flames, to have a witness present would be unbearable.

He'd sold his pistol to the hostel owner, fifty euros for a $450 weapon, plus ammunition. Batman fought back the sting now as he converted the euros into chips. That gun had been with him since his first day in officer training.

He walked slowly among the tables, hoping instinct would lead him to the right one. But after three times around the floor, he wasn't getting vibes from any table, any dealer, from anywhere. Finally he selected a table at random, close to the back of the place, almost in the shadows.

He sat down and asked for a glass of mineral water. He accepted a free cigarillo from the waitress. Four other people were at the table. The game was blackjack. It was five Euros a hand.

As the cards were being dealt, Batman took out a piece of tinfoil and unwrapped a small herb inside. It looked like a cross between a garlic clove and a small tulip bulb.

It was a parting gift from Chief Bol Bada of the Ekita, the same magic herb they'd cooked him in. Batman believed this plant had led to everything he'd experienced in the past forty-eight hours. For at least part of that time, absolutely everything had gone his way, as if he'd been in direct contact with the cosmos. But then that connection became a little too close, with troubling, mind-bending side effects.

This was the first time he'd looked at it since that long night in Somalia. Should he try it again? Would it have the same effect on him? The same downside?

He was desperate. If there *was* a gagnant game, it was to be played at midnight, now only three hours away. Not to try to find it and get in it would be giving up, an opportunity lost. And he just couldn't stand that.

So, he finally pinched off a little piece of the bulb, put it between his teeth and bit down.

It tasted like vinegar and burned his tongue.

• • •

BATMAN LOST THE next nine hands in a row.

Each time he was but one or two numbers away from beating the dealer, a swarthy Italian with too many earrings and not enough mouthwash; each time he crashed and burned.

Batman questioned everything during the losing streak. Why did he take so little for his beloved pistol—he should have gotten at least a hundred Euros for it. And was this the right casino to start his bizarre quest? Or should he have just gone down to the waterfront and started playing there? And was this place even on the level? How could a dealer win nine close hands in a row?

Had he made a grave mistake, ingesting a bit of the bulb? That was the biggest question of all.

He was down to his last five-Euro chip. He thought a moment, then prayed, hard, for the first time in a long time. Then he threw it in and opened his eyes . . . and saw someone standing behind the dealer.

That person looked at Batman, then smiled and nodded, as if to say: *Take a hit*.

And Batman nodded back, as if to say: *Hello, again old friend*.

• • •

ONE HOUR LATER, Batman was tipping the malodorous dealer 1,000 Euros.

He was also signing a register noting him as one of the biggest single winners in the Petite Junque's history. He was even given a bottle of cheap champagne by the casino's manager to mark the occasion.

None of this was because the casino liked him. They were just happy to see him go. Because when he stepped out onto Avenue des Beaux-Arts, he had $874,000 in his pocket.

He walked three blocks to the Summer Casino, giving the champagne to some tourists along the way. As planned, Twitch was waiting for him outside the casino's front door.

Twitch was surprised to see his colleague at exactly 10:00 PM, the agreed-upon time. Batman was rarely on time for anything. But Twitch was even more surprised to see Batman smiling. Until lately, *that* was a rare sight.

"Are you hungry?" Batman asked him as a greeting.

"Always," Twitch replied.

They walked into the casino; the *Michelin Guide* called it "a moderately expensive place to visit." They were seated at the bar, and with Batman's urging, Twitch ordered a steak and a double scotch. Batman, meanwhile, wanted only a soda water.

Finally, Twitch couldn't take it anymore. He was still completely in the dark.

"What's happened?" he asked Batman.

"My plan is working" was all Batman said.

"You mean that bitch Lady Luck is smiling on you?" Twitch asked.

"Something like that," Batman replied.

He pulled a wad of bills from his pocket. Twitch's eyes almost fell out of his head.

"*Jesus . . .*" he gasped. "Did you play at that casino or rob it?"

"Little bit of both," Batman replied cryptically.

Twitch's steak and drink arrived in record time. "OK, then," he said, diving into his meal. "What's the next part of the plan?"

Batman drained his water. Twitch saw him bite down on something between his teeth.

Then Batman said: "The plan is, you stay here, enjoy that steak and drink it up."

"But where are you going?" Twitch asked him.

"I've got to find the *l'arrière-salle* in this place," Batman told him, meaning: the back room. "I just hope they have one."

• • •

TWITCH WAS FINISHING his third glass of scotch when Batman reappeared.

His smile was even wider now and he looked like he had an aura glowing around him.

"Ready to go?" he asked Twitch.

Twitch was confused. Batman had been away twenty minutes at the most.

"You mean we're done here?" Twitch asked. "Already?"

As a reply, Batman pulled out the wad of bills again. It had doubled in size.

Twitch couldn't believe it.

"Damn . . ." Twitch said. "What *the fuck* are you doing back there?"

Batman paid the bar bill, including a hefty tip. He guided Twitch toward the exit.

"The night awaits" was all Batman said.

• • •

THEY VISITED THREE more casinos in the next hour. The Monte-Carlo Bay, the good old Sun Casino and the so-called Café Casino.

The pattern was the same at all three: Twitch drank at the bar while Batman disappeared for about twenty minutes. When he returned, he'd be happier than ever—and carrying a bankroll that grew so large, they finally had to purchase a travel bag to carry it in.

Twitch had no idea what was going on. Batman was obviously gambling in some way, but he seemed to be doing nothing but winning huge amounts of money in short periods of time. So when they started off toward the fifth casino, the exclusive Casino at Monte Carlo, Twitch drunkenly begged Batman to let him watch. Batman finally agreed.

They walked in and Batman exchanged most of his cash for a tray of gold chips. Each was worth $100,000. They walked through the most prestigious gaming area they could find, where Batman flagged down a floor manager. Slipping him one of the $100,000 chips, they had a brief conversation, and the floor man bid them to follow him.

He led them through an unmarked door that led into a smaller, windowless, previously unseen gaming area. It was ringed by armed plainclothes guards watching over just ten tables. The room was dark and elegant, and hushed. No one was talking over a whisper.

"Every casino in Monte Carlo has one of these places," Batman told Twitch quietly. "No limits on betting. Anything goes. You just got to know how to get in."

Twitch watched as Batman scoped out the various gaming

tables. It took him a few moments, but he finally found a blackjack game to his liking. Three other players were on hand.

Batman took his seat and played five hands for 100 Euros each, losing each one. The low figure of his wager caused snarls from the other players. Why was this man here if he was just betting mere hundreds?

Then, when the sixth hand was dealt, Batman suddenly threw in all of the gold chips. Twitch almost passed out. His colleague was betting more than five million dollars—on one hand.

Twitch tried to get Batman's attention, but his friend's eyes had glazed over. He seemed to be looking at a spot over the dealer's shoulder.

The dealer was stunned by the bet, but tried not to show it. He dealt the next card. Batman was showing seventeen, a high number and risky to take another hit.

Yet he did—his card was a four.

And he won.

Just like that.

The other players gasped as the dealer, now pale and unwell-looking, pushed a mountain of gold chips in Batman's direction. A pit boss appeared and offered to help compute Batman's winnings, but Batman politely declined.

"I know how much I have," he said.

And so did Twitch.

By his count, Batman had just won ten million dollars.

The dealer took out a new deck of cards and, his face slightly ashen, asked the players to put up again.

Batman pushed his new mountain of chips forward and smiled madly.

"All in," he said. "And may the best man win."

20

Indian Ocean

SNAKE NOLAN COULDN'T believe he was still alive.

He'd been beaten about his face and shoulders. His feet had been hit with bamboo sticks. His torso had bruises from the ribcage on down. His head felt like it had been split open.

But it was his knuckles that told the tale. They were scraped, cut and bloody. He'd fought back. That's why he'd been pummeled to within an inch of his life.

It was all still hazy, but bits and pieces were coming back to him. He and Emma had climbed down to the fishing boat to get a ride to the nearby Lackshadweep Islands when the toothless man had pulled a gun on them. In that moment between freedom and captivity, Nolan realized what a fool he'd been. The toothless man was a Bom-Kat. The pirates had taken over one of the Omani fishing boats and when the others departed, it had lingered to offer them a ride to the islands. In a hundred years Nolan wouldn't have thought the Bom-Kats could be that crafty. But then again, he didn't know how obsessed their top man was with Emma Simms.

He remembered throwing punches around when the Bom-Kats started manhandling Emma, but there were too many pirates on the stolen fishing boat for him to defeat.

While being beaten, he recalled one of the pirates holding a knife to Emma's throat and threatening to slit it if Nolan continued to resist. And he remembered Emma saying to the guy: "Don't be afraid. There's no reason to be afraid," and he realized at that moment, it had been the perfect thing to say.

Nolan finally stopped struggling when someone hit him over the head with a bottle. He was just now waking from the deep, painful fog that blow had caused.

He was in a dark compartment, with a single weak light-bulb providing the only illumination. Machinery was chugging all around him and the air was stifling and full of oily steam. As he began to get his wits back, he realized he was locked in the fishing boat's tiny engine room and that they were underway.

Two pirates opened the door and came down the ladder just as Nolan was getting to his feet. They started shouting at him as soon as they realized he was awake.

They were talking in rough pidgin English—but Nolan got the idea. The stolen fishing boat's engine was acting up, and for some reason the Bom-Kats just assumed that he, being an American, knew how to repair it. As they were telling him this, the engine sputtered to a stop, as if on cue.

Nolan knew enough about engines to change the oil in a car, but that was about it. Still, when one pirate stuck an assault rifle in his ribs—oddly it was an old M-16—Nolan knew he had no choice but to try to fix the damn thing.

He took off what he guessed was the access panel and found himself looking at what was basically an old Chevy eight-cylinder engine. Half of the eight spark plug wires were off, causing the problem. It was an easy fix, but Nolan was smart enough not to repair it very quickly. As they had recently stolen the fishing boat, it stood to reason the Bom-Kats knew little about how its engine worked, especially since it was an American design.

So he told the Bom-Kats he needed a gallon of cold water and a screwdriver and that they should be quick about it.

When they hesitated, he yelled at them: "Do you want to sink or not?"

They finally left and only then was Nolan able to fall to the seat of his pants and catch his breath.

He figured he'd been a captive of the Bom-Kats for about ten hours now. He was sure it was dark out and he could hear the wind picking up outside. Once again, he became furious with himself for falling for the Bom-Kats simple ruse. After he had beat them so successfully during their murderous assaults on the *Taiwan Song,* the pirates had skillfully tricked him when his guard was down. It was a real blow to his ego.

Worst of all, though, he had no idea where Emma was.

The pirates returned with the water and screwdriver. They left just as quickly, but not before spitting at him.

Nolan drank the water greedily, and poured some over his wounds. His head began to clear a little more. He went back to the engine, connected two of the four hanging spark plug wires and then started the engine manually. It coughed to life.

He heard the pirates up top let out a cheer. Someone in the control room hit the throttles and the boat started moving forward again.

Nolan's instinct told him they were heading east, back toward India, and the Bom-Kats hideout. This was not good. He knew once they reached the pirates' lair his chance of survival would be nil. As for Emma? Who knew what awaited her—if she was still alive.

He had to find out. He located a sturdy steam pipe and climbed on top of it just under a deck brace. With much effort, he unscrewed the brace and gently let the plank it was holding fall down a bit.

He peeked through the opening and saw . . . nothing, except the bare feet of pirates on the deck above, lit by torches. Nolan returned that brace, unscrewed another and peeked through that opening, again, to no good end.

He unscrewed and replaced a dozen braces until he finally saw what he wanted to see. Another pair of bare feet on the deck, but definitely not belonging to any of the pirates.

It was Emma. She was bound to a crude wooden stool on the starboard side of the boat, next to the railing. She did not look bruised or cut, but she was very frightened and crying.

Even worse, she was not wearing the combat suit Nolan had last seen her in. Rather, she was clad in a very small woman's bathing suit. And he could see many pirates were crowded around her, poking at her, laughing at her, but mostly ogling her. These brigands were getting inebriated as well; it was obvious by the way they were stumbling about.

Nolan replaced the brace and tightened it back up.

What would happen to Emma when the pirates *really* got drunk?

He didn't want to know.

Just about that time he noticed the boat was beginning to rock. It was strange because since they'd left Gottabang in the old *Taiwan Song,* the sea conditions had been nothing but smooth and calm, almost too much so.

But now, with each passing second, he could tell the seas were getting rougher. Then he heard the sound of rain beginning to spatter on the deck above. Then came the sound of thunder, the crackling of lightning, and finally footsteps frantically running in all directions right over his head.

The wind began to screech and soon enough, waves were crashing violently against the side of the fishing boat.

The typhoon hit full force about a minute later.

• • •

IT HAD BLOWN up so quickly, Nolan could barely stay on his own two feet. Still, he climbed back up on the steam pipe, unscrewed the specific plank brace and looked up onto the deck. He saw that Emma was still bound to the seat, getting very wet, her hair blowing crazily in the wind. Meanwhile he could see the drunken pirates staggering around the deck not knowing what to do, even as the storm grew worse.

Now was the time for him to act. He went back to the engine, reached into the access panel and unplugged six of the eight spark plug wires, bringing the engine as close to a stall as possible without it actually going dead.

This brought the same two pirates back. Nolan barked at them as soon as they appeared: "You want to save that girl? You want to ransom her? Then get her down here. And give her a life jacket."

The pirates seemed confused about his orders, but they didn't question him. They were too scared.

One disappeared but returned a minute later, and Emma was with him.

Nolan pretended to be engrossed with the engine—and he yelled at the pirates: "Tell everyone up top to strap in and hold on tight. I'll try my best to get this running again."

The pirates didn't hesitate an instant this time. They went back up the ladder as quickly as they could.

Once they were gone, Emma fell into his arms. Soaking wet and crying, she would not let him go.

The boat began bouncing around the wild sea. Water was splashing up top and draining into the engine room. It hit the hot pipes, caused them to steam, and before long the steam filled the small compartment. But she did not let go.

Nolan managed to free one hand and replace two of the disconnected spark plug wires. The engine surged and the boat started moving a little faster through the gale.

Still, she would not let go.

They were being thrown all over the engine room, and when they stumbled together, she just held on tighter.

Finally, still without a word between them, they both sank to the dirty, oily floor, to ride out the storm together.

• • •

THE SEA GREW even wilder, and the wind began to absolutely howl.

The stolen fishing boat was made primarily of wood and aluminum, meaning it bobbed in the rough water like a toy. Nolan could hear the pirates running around up on deck, ignoring his orders to find a place and strap in. They were all drunk and obviously inexperienced in how to properly take a vessel like this through a storm. They had given Emma a life jacket when they brought her below, though—and at the moment that was the only comfort Nolan could find. If the boat broke apart and she had a life jacket on, then at least she had a chance to survive, small as it might be.

The storm grew even more. She was hugging him so tight, Nolan could barely breathe, but that was OK with him.

Finally, she spoke.

"You're brave and you're strong," she said. "Can you share some of that with me?"

"Like I told you back on the freighter," he replied. "*You're* one of the bravest people I know."

"But what did you think of me before that?" she asked him. "Before what happened happened? Tell me the truth . . ."

Nolan was stuck for a moment. It was a strange conversation to be having as a typhoon roared outside.

"I guess I thought you were the type of girl who'd sit in a guy's lap even while he was standing up," he finally replied.

She would have laughed had she not been so scared.

"I guess that's better than you thinking I was someone who liked to pull the wings off flies," she said. "Or stomp little bunnies."

"It was never that bad," he lied.

"I know it was—and worse," she said as a massive wave hit the fishing boat. It was so powerful it seemed to knock them sideways. "I've done so many stupid things in my life—and I'm not that old. I've screwed people over. Ruined careers. Destroyed marriages. Lives. I was born to be a monster."

"The best thing to do with those kind of memories is to just forget them," he told her.

"But what if you can't?"

"Then just get drunk," he replied. "That's what alcohol is for."

Another massive wave hit them. It sounded like the boat would come apart at any moment.

"I guess I figured that out when I was about twelve years old," she finally replied. "When I was a little kid, I used to hear a voice in my head. I thought it was God. Hell, we talked all the time, though He did most of the talking. I finally got worried about it and told my mother. She was an actress and she was making a movie at the time. I thought sure she'd send me to a shrink, but instead, she and my father decided that it was 'precious' and never did anything. I started boozing right after that."

The boat was hit again by a huge wave. Nolan waited for the vessel to settle down.

"So what did this voice tell you?" he asked her. "Did it say you should become a movie star?"

"No," she replied through some tears. "The voice told me I should save the world and do it some good—but I did the exact opposite. I became an actress."

Nolan thought a few moments and said, "Someone told me once that when a person goes to sea, they should forget about everything that happened on shore. It took me a while to figure it out, but I did eventually. Do you know what I mean?"

She thought about it a moment and then nodded. "I think so," she said, pulling him even closer.

"People can be whatever or whoever they want to be as long as they are fighting for something," he said. "And you gotta take a stand. I mean, if you don't believe in God or the devil, you're never disappointed. But what fun is that?"

He actually got her to laugh at that one.

And about a minute later, the sea around them started to calm down.

They heard the rain stop. The wind died away. The thunder was gone.

The storm had passed quickly—and they had talked through almost all of it. The sun eventually poked through the cracks between the fishing boat's beams. They were highlighted by the steam coming off the still-chugging Chevy V-8, giving the engine room a surreal noir look.

Finally Nolan could see her face again and she could see his.

He said to her, "Throughout those battles on the freighter, I smelled a bit of your perfume on me and I knew I would have given my life just to see you one more time."

She replied, "I don't know anything about war or politics—but I believe in you. And what you do must be right. You know, brave men are never forgotten. And like I said before, you *are* a brave man."

He laughed. "Well, that might be true, but sometimes they don't last long enough to be remembered."

She looked him straight in the eye.

"I'll remember you," she said.

Nolan felt like he was floating in space. He was dirty, wet and wounded—yet nothing around him had any effect on him. He was lighter than air. He figured, it was now or never.

He went to kiss her—and just as their lips touched, there was a huge explosion.

It nearly knocked him out, the concussion was so bad.

All he could think was: Wow!

But then he opened his eyes and realized that this was not from the kiss—someone had fired at the fishing boat, and in fact a shell had come right through the hull, passed through the engine room and gone out the other side.

Before they could say anything, there was a second explosion; this one on the top deck. It shook the vessel from one end to the other.

Four pirates quickly appeared. Nolan had never seen these guys before. But it was clear they were all scared and angry.

They grabbed Emma and began dragging her away. Nolan tried to stop them but they began beating him with their rifle butts. He retaliated by stabbing them with his screwdriver, but this just made them beat him more.

All the while, Emma was screaming and crying as they carried her up the ladder way.

"I will remember you!" was the last thing Nolan heard her say.

One pirate stayed behind. He was the fiercest-looking one of them all. He pointed to the engine and screamed at Nolan: "Make fast, now!"

Then he, too, hustled up the ladder.

Another shot came in. This one blew off a large chunk of the hull just in front of the engine. The resulting hole was so large, Nolan could see out onto the water. About 1000 feet off their port side, a police boat was firing at them. He could clearly see the flashes coming from its deck gun.

"Make fast . . . now!" another pirate screamed down at him.

But Nolan did the opposite. He knew this was their only chance to get out of this thing alive. So he pulled out all the spark plug wires and the engine ground to a halt. A few seconds later, the fishing boat stopped moving.

Nolan tore off his battle suit top, ripped off his white t-shirt from underneath and frantically started waving it through the hole in the hull, hoping to attract the attention of the police boat.

But whether they saw him or not, he would never know, because they fired their deck gun again and this shell exploded on the other side of the engine, effectively cutting the fishing boat in two.

The boat's fuel tank went up a second later, blowing Nolan right out of the engine compartment and high into the air. He stopped in midair just long enough to see the fishing vessel sink in a ball of flames. Then he came down and hit the water hard, plunging at least twenty feet under, before he was able to stop himself.

He madly fought his way through the turbulence to get back to the surface. But when he reached the top again and looked around for Emma, all he saw were the dead and the dying amidst the smoking remains of the fishing boat.

He began swimming through the burning wreckage, searching for her—but then he noticed the water was snapping all around him. The police boat was now just 100 feet away and they were machine-gunning anything that was moving in the water. As there was no way they could tell him from the bad guys, they were shooting at him, too.

He had no choice but to swim for it.

He went under and with all his might began swimming away. When he surfaced again, the police boat was circling the wreckage, still firing into it as if doing it for sport.

He looked around and saw there was an island about 1,000 feet away from the scene. With tears spilling out of his one good eye, Nolan started swimming toward it, Emma's last words still ringing in his ears.

It was not an easy go. The current carried him one way for a while and then the other. Though the small island was always right ahead of him, it never seemed to get any closer.

But then came a shift of tide, or a lucky wave, or something else, because one moment, Nolan was close to going under for good, and in the next, he'd been thrown up on the island's rocky beach.

Still, he couldn't move, he was having trouble breathing and he could barely feel his legs. He had water in his lungs and his stomach. He began throwing up and didn't stop for a long time.

Only after this nausea finally passed, did he try to crawl further up on the beach, but his legs still didn't want to work. No matter how hard he tried, he was stuck in the same position.

He thought: "I meet the girl of my dreams—and *then* my life is over? Thanks for nothing, God—you bastard."

And at that point, he just gave up. Emma was gone. He was out in the middle of nowhere. And the tide that had swept him up onto this beach was now about to overwhelm him and drown him after all.

So, he stopped trying to move.

He stopped trying to breathe.

For Snake Nolan, it was finally time to die.

21

Monte Carlo
On the waterfront

TWITCH CHECKED THE clip in his handgun for the third time in the past ten minutes.

It was still full, as it was the last two times he looked.

He knew he was obsessing, but he couldn't help it. They were sitting at an outdoor café on the Monte Carlo waterfront. The large travel bag was on the table between them—with slightly more than fifty million dollars inside. Anyone with a bigger handgun and younger legs could make off with it in a snap. That fact alone was driving Twitch nuts.

But Batman did not share his concern. He was still glowing from his fantastic streak of luck at the gaming tables. He'd made the $50 million-plus in less than two hours, all by taking hits at blackjack when it seemed suicidal to do so.

Twitch wouldn't have believed it if he hadn't seen it himself. It was almost scary the way Batman had gone about it. Staring into space before a big hand, eyes glazed over, not moving, as if in a trance. Twitch knew there was a secret behind how Batman was doing it, yet his colleague had chosen not to reveal it to him.

But even that didn't make any difference at this point.

What was important now was what to do with the money.

"We know the gagnant is being played at midnight tonight," Twitch said, once some nearby patrons had moved off. "The question is, *where* will it be played? That's just about the only thing Bobby Murphy never told us."

Batman had been thinking about the same thing ever since they'd left the last casino.

"Remember back on the yacht," he said now. "When Audette first heard about the pirates making all those phone calls? He said some were to the Stazi guys in Bad Sweeten and some were to the top casinos here. But he said one call was to the Prince's Palace. The place the Monaco Royal Family lives."

"You think the gagnant is being held there?" Twitch asked. "That's pretty far up the food chain."

"But why else would mooks like the Tangs call there if it wasn't?" Batman replied. "I doubt they dialed a wrong number."

"OK, so let's assume it's at this palace," Twitch said. "And we know it's being played at midnight. And we've got the money—though it might be giving up fifty million in hand to get a hundred million in the bush, which is insane. But I guess that's where our patriotism comes in. Still, how are we going to get into the game?"

Batman replied, "Murphy did say, while most people send in the entry fee and back it up with a surety, if someone walked in and had the cash with them, they wouldn't turn them away. They must figure if he's connected enough to actually know about the secret game and has the money to play, why not let him in?"

"Are you saying we go . . . uninvited?" Twitch gasped. "Walk up to this palace and just knock on the door?"

"That's our only option," Batman replied. "We try to fake our way in and see what happens."

Twitch checked the time. It was almost 11:30 P.M. In his own little world, nothing was *too* crazy. But this was coming close.

"We'll need better clothes," he finally told Batman. "We can't go dressed like this. But I don't think we'll find a tuxedo store open right now."

Batman thought a moment, then he said, "What size suit do you wear?"

Twitch shrugged. "I didn't know when I was asked that in Shanghai. I still don't know today. Why?"

"Let's go talk to some cabbies," Batman replied.

• • •

TWENTY-FIVE MINUTES LATER Batman and Twitch were riding in the back of a Rolls taxi, climbing the road that led from Monte Carlo up to the Prince's Palace.

They were now wearing tuxedos, courtesy of two other cab drivers who, in exchange for $1,000 each, took the rest of the night off and turned over their penguin suits to them.

The palace was not as lit up as usual. There was no state dinner going on or some glamorous party to celebrate the beginning of the Grand Prix the next day. This alone struck Batman as odd, and fed into his theory that the gagnant was being played here tonight.

"It seems that if you lived here, this would be the night to party," Batman said to Twitch.

"Depends on what you call a party," Twitch replied.

The front gate was wide open. Two uniformed guards were on hand, as were a small group of men in plainclothes.

At that point, Batman and Twitch were ready for anything. They'd exchanged the bag of money for a bank cheque, a two-minute procedure at the Sun Casino. This made transporting their funds a lot easier. And they thought they looked the part of high rollers. But how much ID and security would they have to deal with here, at the palace gate?

As it turned out, absolutely none.

The taxi approached the gate—and was waved right through.

So far so good.

The taxi pulled up to the only lighted entrance on the palace grounds, a stairway on the east corner. Batman and Twitch bucked themselves up for a moment and then climbed out of the cab. They *had* to look like they belonged here—that would be the key to their success or failure.

Its driver paid, the Rolls departed and the two pirate hunters stood alone before the palace entrance.

That's when Batman looked over at Twitch and suddenly realized they were wearing the wrong tuxedoes. When they'd made the deal for the monkey suits, they'd selected two cabbies milling around outside the Grand Maison's driveway, two guys who looked to be about the same size as them. But they'd hastily changed in the back of the cab that brought them here and in doing so, each had put on the wrong suit. Batman's was way too small and tight in all the wrong places, while Twitch was swimming in his.

But it was too late to switch now.

They went up the steps to the huge door. It opened before they could ring the bell. A man in an eighteenth-century butler's getup peered out at them.

This was the moment of truth. . . .

Batman looked the guy straight in the eye and said, *"Un Grande Gagnant?"*

Twitch quickly added, *"Si'l vous plaît . . ."*

The doorman didn't hesitate a moment, but bowed and swept them right in.

The inside of the palace was just as they'd imagined. Huge long rooms with massive chandeliers hanging from the ceiling; ornate furniture, expensive rugs, medieval art on the walls, lots of marble, crystal and gold. And that smell: of royalty, of landed wealth, of pure money.

"Now we know who's making half the profit tonight," Twitch grumbled, taking in his surroundings. "I'm guessing a quarter billion pays the light bills here."

They were escorted down a series of hallways, each more grandiose than the last. They passed small groups of well-dressed men with tiny earphones in place, obviously private security agents. Batman guessed these people were hired heat for the high rollers attending the game tonight.

Finally he and Twitch reached an enormous oak door. Their escort knocked three times and the door opened to reveal a small room lit mostly by candlelight.

The first thing Batman saw inside, though, was a round antique card table.

This was the place.

An elderly man in a more modern livery bid them to enter.

Batman repeated: *"Un Grande Gagnant?"*

The elderly man bowed by way of saying yes. But then he asked in a thick French accent: "Do you have credentials, good sirs? Our game table is already full."

Batman reached inside his jacket and took out the bank cheque. He held it up to the man's eyes and saw them widen with surprise. Showing up with "cash" was somewhat ostentatious; most players simply brought surety bonds for the remainder of the $50 million buy-in. But it also meant no one was going to kick them out just because they didn't have a proper invite. It was exactly as Batman had hoped.

The butler led them deeper into the room. It was smaller than Batman had imagined, but extremely well done and elegant in dark mahogany and crystal. There were about three dozen people already here; a dozen of them were armed guards standing in the shadows, their Uzi machine pistols on full display.

Ten people were sitting around the table, but the lighting was so low, it was hard for Batman to see any faces clearly.

Three Arabs, complete with headdresses, stood out though. Persian oil money types, no doubt. A couple Asian men were sitting beside them. All bling and sunglasses and scowls, they looked like criminals from a James Bond movie.

Two elderly women were seated beside them. Both looked like they might be queens of some European country. In fact, if Batman didn't know better, he would have sworn one of them was the Queen of England herself.

Sitting next to the ladies was a middle-aged man who was obviously a Russian gangster. With hands like beef, a red nose and lots of gold teeth, he reminded Batman of the team's odd acquaintance, Bebe, the Red Mafia strongman.

The two remaining people were sitting with their backs to him. As Batman was ushered around to the last place at the table, he saw one of these people was none other than the Asian woman who had first shown him and Twitch the penthouse at the Grand Maison Casino. She was simply gorgeous: perfect face, long black hair, stylishly dressed. She was probably the most beautiful Asian woman Batman had ever seen.

And obviously she was here working for Bobby Murphy. She took one look at Batman and froze. It was clear she had not expected to see him here.

Her presence proved Bobby Murphy had been out to get the Z-box all along, as opposed to going in and busting up the gagnant before it even started. While Batman was fairly certain Murphy and his people would give the Z-box back to the USA should she win it, he was also sure the rogue private security operations group would ask for more money than they knew Whiskey was going to make. Audette was right, Bobby Murphy *was* an extremely crafty individual.

The last person at the table was a large dark-skinned man in an ill-fitting white suit. He looked like he was either from northeast Africa or the southern quadrant of the Middle East.

But something about him caught Batman's attention right away. Every finger on both his hands had a shiny silver ring on it.

Batman's temple began to throb. So did his back.

Where had he seen this guy before?

• • •

EACH PLAYER WAS allowed to have a second person accompany him to the game room, so Twitch took a seat behind Batman.

There were no introductions. The round table was clear of everything but a single deck of cards. A cashier simply said: "Time to play."

The dealer explained the game. It would be one hand of blackjack. The kitty would be each player's fifty-million buy-in. Whoever won the hand would get the "grand gagnant." If the house won, they would reset and start all over again.

The dealer asked if there were any questions. There weren't.

So the hand was dealt: two cards down to each player.

Because he was the late arrival, Batman was at the end of the deal.

He peeked at his pair when they came to him—and his heart immediately dropped. He'd been dealt a king and a nine. Two *very* bad cards for blackjack.

The dealer started around the table once again. One by one, every player took a hit—and the dealer beat each one of them.

Now it was Batman's turn. He spied his cards again, not sure what to do. If he took a hit and lost, there would be a reset, and another hand would be dealt. But this was exactly how he'd won all the money earlier that night—taking hits when he shouldn't have.

That's when he looked up and once again realized his old friend had joined them. He was nodding and smiling, just as before.

Batman leaned back to Twitch and whispered: "Do you see him?"

But Twitch had no idea what Batman was talking about. Why would he ask such a weird question at a stressful time like this?

"Just play the God damn hand," Twitch whispered back to him. "The suspense is killing me."

Batman looked at his hand again, then back up at his old friend.

Then he took a hit.

It was a deuce.

He won.

There was a collective gasp. Those around the table were astonished—and very upset. They'd all been expecting a re-set. Now they were convinced Batman had used trickery to win the big prize.

The tension grew in the room. All the armed guards took a giant step forward. Twitch visibly fingered the massive handgun he had in his belt. He didn't have to remind himself that the last time he'd been involved in a high-stakes card game, he'd shot four people to death. He was perfectly willing to do it again if it meant he and Batman walked out of here alive.

The palace help hastily ushered all the other players out of the room. Bobby Murphy's gorgeous proxy was the first to leave and did so quickly.

Once they were gone, the cashier handed Batman an envelope resting on a silver plate.

Still beaming from his win, Batman asked, "What's this? A receipt?"

The man shook his head. "No, monsieur," he said. "This is your prize."

Batman was confused. He opened the envelope and found a simple gold key inside.

He growled at the cashier: "A fucking key? Where's the box?"

The cashier replied in a hushed tone: "This is the key to open the box, sir. *It* is the gagnant. Who told you it was a box itself?"

Batman looked at Twitch and rolled his eyes. Who told them?

Maurice. Bobby Murphy. Take your pick.

His aura gone, Batman was about to explode. Sensing this, the cashier added, "But you are lucky, you see, as the box is of little worth unless you have this key."

Batman got very close to the cashier, grabbing his collar with his mechanical hand. "So *where's* the box then?" he asked him.

The man shrugged. "I have no idea, sir . . ."

Batman tightened the grip on his mechanical hand.

"Well, how the fuck do I find it?" he spat at the man.

The guy kept his cool.

"I don't know that either," he said. "No one here does. We have been dealing only with this key from the beginning."

"A lousy key for fifty million bucks?" Twitch spoke up angrily. "Sounds like bullshit to me."

"Bullshit?" the cashier replied dryly. "On the contrary,

gentlemen, this is the straightforward unadulterated truth. Had you not been such late arrivals, you would have been told all this beforehand."

• • •

WITH THEIR GRAND prize in hand—be it dubious or not—Batman and Twitch knew they had to leave the palace quickly.

They weren't sure what the key was for—but it had been worth a combined half a billion dollars to the people who'd come to play the gagnant. So, at the moment, it had to be protected at all costs.

They walked out of the game room to see the rest of the players still being escorted down the long hallway by butlers in eighteenth-century garb.

Batman knew this was not a happy crowd—and why should it be? They'd all lost at least ten million in cash, with another forty million to go, in less than a minute.

So he and Twitch walked slowly down the hallway, letting the others drain out and avoiding any confrontation with them.

When they reached the main door, the same butler who'd let them in was waiting, seeing everyone out.

"Do we tip this guy?" Twitch whispered to Batman.

"Yeah, tell him not to play the horses," Batman whispered back.

They went out the door bowing and smiling to find the driveway filled with various limos and SUVs waiting for the losing players. It looked like a hired goon convention on the cobblestone entryway. While there was no sign of Murphy or his lovely proxy, each of the remaining players had a small army of guards waiting for them—all except Batman and Twitch.

They watched the other players climb into their vehicles and roar away, one at a time, tires squealing, almost as if the mass departure had been choreographed ahead of time. It took less than thirty seconds for the driveway to empty out, leaving Batman and Twitch all by themselves, with no protection at all.

Even the light above the palace door went out, throwing them into a cold darkness. They'd failed to plan for this part. Here they were, holding what might be an essential element in getting their $100 million fee, but also what might be one of the most important items in the world at the moment, if indeed the Z-box was a WMD. And yet they had no quick way to get it back to civilization.

They had no choice. They would have to hoof it.

They walked out beyond the palace gate and contemplated the winding road ahead. It was surprisingly dark and deserted. They could look beyond it, down into Monte Carlo and see the place was obviously hopping. But it would take quite a hike to get back to their crummy little hostel room, especially for Twitch and his artificial leg.

They set off, though—and immediately began imagining that people were following them.

Then a bit of luck: Looking over their shoulders about a minute into their journey, they saw headlights approaching. It was a Rolls taxi coming down the road. They flagged it down.

Batman explained to the driver they were heading for the east side of Monte Carlo. The driver indicated they should jump in. They did so and finally felt safe.

They began making plans: They would go to the hostel, pay the owner the money they owed him and then get information about flying out to Aden. Monte Carlo didn't have an airport, so they would have to get to Nice, France, to catch a flight. But that was not a problem as there were both train and bus services that would get them there quickly. Before all this, though, they would use some of the money left over from their casino winnings to call someone at Kilos Shipping who could get a message to Alpha Squad telling them that Beta had made some progress.

They'd ridden only about a few hundred feet when the taxi driver suddenly pulled to the side of the road. Batman thought he was stopping to pick up someone else—something Batman was definitely not in favor of.

But instead the man put the car in park and turned around to face them. He was holding a massive .45 automatic.

"OK, guys," he said in an American accent. "Let's make it easy and just turn over the key."

Batman and Twitch were stunned—but it only took a few seconds for them to figure it out.

"DynCorp?" Batman asked the guy. "Or EOD?"

The guy smiled. "Just for the record, it's DynCorp. But really, what difference does it make?"

"It doesn't make any difference," Twitch responded. "Whether its DynCorp, or EOD or Blackwater—we got the same message for all of you."

"Oh really?" the guy with the gun said. "And what message is that?"

"Two simple words," Twitch replied. " 'Fuck you.' "

The guy was shocked. "You do see this gun I'm holding on you, right?" he said.

"Sure do," Twitch replied. "But what are you going to do with it?"

"Shoot your ass," was the guy's response.

"Do it then," Twitch challenged him. "Go ahead—shoot us. I dare you."

Batman was trying to nudge his colleague to get him to calm down, but it was a waste of time. And Twitch did have a point. This guy wasn't an enemy—not exactly. He was just part of one of the other private special ops groups that Audette and the Agency had hired to recover the Z-box—and now the guy was trying to get $100 million for his group by taking it away from Whiskey.

But would he kill them for it?

Batman didn't think so.

The driver realized this, too—and an awkward moment was upon them.

"Look, just drive," Batman said, breaking the impasse. "We'll figure something out."

The driver thought about this. And though he didn't exactly put the gun away, he did slip the Rolls back in drive and resumed driving down the winding road.

As they approached the next corner, though, Batman was planning to open his door and jump out, dragging Twitch with him.

But as they went around the bend they were surprised to see two Fiats with spinning lights on top and three men in police uniforms wearing reflective vests and using flashlights to flag them to a stop.

The man driving did as told; everyone in the luxurious cab thought it was a simple security check set up in preparation for the big race the next day.

But then one of the men walked over to the window and told the driver and Batman and Twitch that they all had to step out of the car.

Batman did not like the sound of this; he and Twitch didn't move. Neither did the driver.

But when the guy in the cop uniform pulled out his gun, they all complied.

It was clear at that point that these guys weren't cops at all: they were Americans from yet another PSO firm. It was easy to tell.

All three had their guns out, though, and as soon as the driver climbed out of the Rolls he had his gun out, too.

Seeing this, Twitch pretended to stumble coming out of the backseat, and doing it only as Twitch could do, knocked into one of the fake policemen—and somehow came up with his pistol.

Suddenly they were all standing in the middle of the road, three sets of special ops groups, holding guns on one another.

But despite all the gun waving and posturing, no one was going to shoot; they all knew that. The only danger was if one of them fired by mistake.

"Which one of you guys has the key?" one of the fake

cops asked out of desperation. "We're from EOD; we can make a deal with you."

Twitch kicked one fake cop in the ass and yelled "We got the key . . . but we know none of you girls will shoot us for it."

But no sooner were those words out of his mouth than bullets started flying.

Twitch was the first to get hit. He was knocked off the side of the road and into the ditch below. The driver of the Rolls went down next, then the three fake policemen.

In a surreal moment, Batman found himself standing alone, with writhing bleeding bodies all around him. Yet he had no gun—and it wasn't like the fake cops or the fake cab driver had shot anyone.

He turned to see a large dark-skinned man standing behind him. He was the player at the gagnant, the guy with all the rings on his fingers. He was holding a smoking Lugar-style pistol. Now he pointed it at Batman and pulled the trigger.

The bullet hit Batman square in the chest. He was thrown backward and slammed against the side of the Rolls taxi.

Crumpling to the pavement, the last thing he saw was the man's hand, with silver rings on every finger, taking the Z-box key from his bloody shirt pocket.

22

Somewhere in the Indian Ocean

NOLAN KNEW HE was dead because an angel was looking down at him.

She was smiling and laughing and he could see her wings. There was a halo around her head and a bright white light behind her. This light was as bright as the sun and it felt warm and safe and it made Nolan feel like he'd wasted way too many years suffering on Earth, when the afterlife was so much better.

In the next second, though, he was awake for real, feeling cold and wet, with just about every body appendage feeling like it was falling off.

But . . . still, there was an angel hovering over him.

The blond hair flying everywhere. The enormous blue eyes. The wide smile . . .

It was Emma.

Alive, somehow . . .

As soon as he opened his eyes, she hugged him as hard as she could. He thought she would squeeze out what little life he had left in him.

"How?" was all he could mumble through his salt-cracked lips. *"How . . ."*

"I swam here, silly," she replied, squeezing him even tighter.

"I mean, how did you make it off the boat?"

"The fat guy threw me on a life raft just as the other boat shot at us," she explained breathlessly. "But when he tried to jump on, he missed—and that was the end of him. The raft had some bullet holes in it, but it got me far enough away so I could swim for it."

She finally released him from the monster embrace and touched his face.

"At least I was dressed for it," she said, referring to her very brief bathing suit.

At this point, at least one of Nolan's appendages was beginning to get some feeling back.

"How long was I out?" he asked her.

"A few hours at least," she replied. "I looked all over for you."

Nolan wiped the grit from his eye. "At least I got some sleep," he mumbled.

"Think you can stand up?" she asked him. "You've got to see what I've found here."

"Please tell me it's a bottle of scotch . . ."

"We're not that lucky," she replied. "But I'm sure you'll find it interesting."

She got him to his feet and steadied him.

"Where are we?" he asked her, looking around as his faculties slowly came back to him. The island was like something from a travel brochure, all palm trees and lush tropical vegetation.

"I've got no idea," she replied. "We traveled a long way last night. I was trying to keep track. I wish I knew how to navigate by the stars, but I think we were going north. Then that storm blew up—and *then* we got sunk. So, we're lost, I guess. We could be anywhere."

"Sounds like something from a film," he said, only half-kidding.

She nudged him. "Please," she said. "That's now a four-letter word in my book."

They walked up the beach and over a rise. On the other side they could see the northern tip of the island. It was made up of a small lagoon bordered on three sides by tall palm trees and extremely thick jungle foliage. The flora was so dense, it completely hid the small bay.

A typical pirates' lair.

"But I see nothing but more trees and more water," Nolan said.

"Come with me," she told him.

She led him down a winding path that brought them through the jungle. After a minute or so, they reached a smaller beach lining the lagoon.

That's when Nolan saw the bodies.

There were at least a dozen of them lying in the sand. Some had been shot. Others had been stabbed. Most appeared Asian.

About a hundred feet out in the bay, partially hidden by a coral reef and overhanging trees, were the remains of a sea-going tugboat. It was about three quarters sunk and had been partially burned. And just at the water's edge, there were several large deep grooves in the sand, indicating a helicopter had landed here recently.

Nolan knew what he was looking at. It was the aftermath of a battle.

But who had fought who—and why?

Emma walked him over to the nearest body and lifted up an arm.

"This is totally gross," she said. "But look at his tattoo."

Nolan saw the stylized scrolling on the man's bicep. It read: *Kupak Tangs*.

He couldn't believe it. The Tang pirates? Here?

"Aren't *these* the guys you're supposed to be looking for?" she asked him. "The guys who had the box?"

Nolan scratched his head. "Yeah, these are them. And that tug out there is the kind of vessel that guy at Gottabang said the Tangs were using. But what were the chances we'd stumble upon this?"

Emma just laughed at him. "After what we've been through in the past few days?" she said. "I wouldn't question anything."

They walked further onto the beach. It was clear the Tangs had been overwhelmed by an opponent who had more firepower and who had gotten the drop of them. It was more a massacre than a battle.

Emma was proceeding gingerly amidst the carnage. She told him: "I want to go on record as saying that being near all of these dead bodies is icky."

"Duly noted," Nolan replied.

One of the bodies was different from the rest. It was dressed in black camos and the person wearing it was not Asian, but rather looked European. He'd been shot once, and stabbed a few times. But his legs were also broken.

"This guy is a long way from home," Nolan said. "Just as the Tangs were."

"Just like we are," she added.

Nolan tried to take in the whole scene and divine what had happened here.

"I think the guys in black camos came here in a helicopter," he began, pointing to the dead European. "They got the Z-box from the Tangs, maybe as a business transaction at first, but then they started shooting. They killed a lot of the pirates, but this guy might have been wounded and fell off the copter as it was trying to get away."

"But who were these guys on the helicopter?" she asked.

It was a good question. Nolan went through the pockets of the dead guy in the black camos and came out with just one thing: a sales receipt. It was for chocolates—and it was written in German.

Germans? Nolan thought. The ex-Stazi guys from Bad Sweeten?

Who else could it be?

"So the Stazis come here," Nolan said, continuing the reconstruction, "and they rip off the Tangs, take the box and kill them all, with a loss of one of their guys."

"So the box *was* here?" she asked him.

"It could have been," Nolan replied. "Take a look at this place. It's a perfect hiding spot for pirates. It has access to the sea, but you can't see it unless you're right up on it."

He studied the helicopter marks again and determined they were made by a substantial aircraft, probably something along the lines of a Russian-made Hind.

He said, "The question is, where did the box go from here?"

Emma found one more clue. It was a bunch of packing receipts, the kind used for overnight shipments. There were maybe a dozen, held together by a rubber band, not far from the dead German's body.

"These must have fallen out of the helicopter maybe?" she said, handing them to Nolan.

He agreed, but this just made it even more of a mystery.

"So, the Stazis got the box," he said. "And they're going to ship it somewhere. But where?"

Emma studied the receipts. They were all blank, but she thought she could detect some indentations on the top slip, as if someone had started writing on a packing slip a couple on top of this one, made a mistake and started writing another.

She took the top slip from the rest of the bunch.

"I was in a kid's detective movie once," she told him. "We solved the case like this."

She took a dab of seawater and ran it over the address box of the receipt. Sure enough, some scribbling caused by the indentations on the receipt showed up.

The package dimensions were filled in—it was four feet by two feet and weighed about twelve pounds. This was just about the size of the Z-box as Audette had explained it to them. But the entire address had not been filled in, only parts of it had.

What *was* clear was the street address: 45 Park Place. And the zip code: 10007.

"10007?" she said. "That must be in the United States. But where?"

Nolan just shook his head. "You asking the wrong person," he said. "I've been out of the country for more than ten years. But if they're shipping the box to the United States, where does the Monte Carlo connection come in?"

At that moment they heard a dull roar approaching from overhead.

For a second, Nolan thought it might be the helicopter returning to the island. But then the noise changed, got deeper. That's when they both recognized it.

They ran—through the jungle, over the rise and back to the place where Emma had found Nolan, half dead on the shore.

Their eyes skyward, they started waving their arms madly.

High above them, the unmistakable shape of the *Shin-1* appeared and began wagging its wings in reply.

"They said they'd look for us," Emma said excitedly. "Isn't that great?"

Nolan was torn.

Here he was, on a quasi-paradise island, with the most beautiful girl in the world—and in a bikini yet.

Not exactly the best moment to be saved.

"Duty calls," he whispered.

23

Monte Carlo

BATMAN FELT LIKE a cement block was sitting on his chest.

He was lying on his back, barely able to breathe, barely able to open his eyes. He could see the stars, though, and that was strange. They seemed to be spinning and spinning, and getting closer. Or was he falling into them?

He didn't know where he was. When he brought his mechanical hand close to his face, he saw its prongs were misshapen and shooting off at weird angles.

His first thought was: "If I'm dead, why do I still have an artificial hand?"

Suddenly, the weight was lifted off his chest and he could breathe again. His eyesight started to clear and he lost the sensation that he was falling.

Someone was slapping his face, urging him to come to.

At first, he thought it was an angel. But then everything came into focus and he saw this was hardly a seraph hovering over him.

It was Audette, the CIA agent.

"Are you still with us?" he was asking Batman. "Can you hear me?"

Batman finally nodded and, with Audette's help, was able to sit up.

"What the hell happened?" he asked the agent, realizing he was lying in the middle of a road.

"You got ambushed and you got shot," the agent told him soberly. "But you're the lucky one."

Batman saw four people lying on the asphalt close to him. The taxi driver and the three men who'd impersonated cops. They were all dead.

"But why not me?" Batman asked Audette.

Audette held up a thin piece of metal. Batman had to

look at it for a few moments before he knew what it was: the platinum players card that Murphy's beautiful female accomplice had given him when they first went into the penthouse.

"They tried to kill you, but the bullet hit this," Audette said, holding the bent and distorted card up to his eyes. "I don't know what it is, but it saved your life."

Batman started breathing deep again. In just a short while, he'd been shot in the back and survived, and now shot in the chest . . . and still survived.

"Next time they'll have to aim for my head," he said. He gratefully shook hands with Audette, then asked, "How did you find me?"

Audette just shrugged. "I've been tailing you—I was about a half hour behind. You made some noise in those casinos winning all that money, then I found the taxi drivers you got the clothes from and . . ."

But suddenly a panic rose up inside Batman.

Where was Twitch?

He jumped to his feet and almost fell over. Audette steadied him.

"Was your little buddy with you for this?" the agent asked him.

Batman's head was pounding with pain.

"I'm pretty sure he was," he replied groggily.

With Audette helping him walk, he staggered to the side of the road.

"The real cops are going to be here at any minute," the agent told Batman. "We probably want to avoid that."

Batman tripped over something. He looked to see pieces of Twitch's artificial leg next to the Rolls taxi.

Then he looked over the edge of the road and saw a crumpled body below. Batman didn't even think about it. He immediately slid down the side of the embankment, Audette close behind.

He reached Twitch, turned him over and went to feel for a

pulse. But his colleague surprised him by sitting up and shouting at him, "What *the fuck* took you so long?"

Batman almost had a heart attack and came close to dying a second time. He could have punched Twitch right in the mouth.

"I've been trying to crawl up this fucking hill for a half hour," Twitch complained. He seemed not the least bit harmed, except his artificial leg was no longer attached to him. Oddly, the same thing had happened to him on their previous mission.

"You have a hard time holding on to that thing," Batman told him. "Why don't you just grow a new one?"

Again with Audette's help, Batman dragged Twitch up to the roadway. Then they quickly told the agent everything that had happened: winning the gagnant's buy-in fee, getting into the Palace, playing the very brief game and getting not the Z-box but a key that apparently opens or activates it. The story ended with Batman telling Audette of seeing the man with the rings on his fingers stealing the mysterious key.

Audette listened in disbelief.

"This is the first I've heard about any key," he told them. "But it must have *something* to do with the Z-box if only because a bunch of people just lost a lot of money trying to get it."

"Well, we had it, for about three minutes," Twitch said. "But who's got it now? And where the fuck is the box?"

"Lots of rings on the fingers sounds like Jihad Brotherhood," Audette told them. "They're usually gofers for al Qaeda's African operations, but it looks like they've expanded their sphere of influence and are flexing their muscles."

"But how the hell do guys like that get into Monte Carlo?" Batman asked him. "Aren't they all over the watch lists?"

Audette shook his head.

"I'm guessing they slipped through when they let all the

vendors in for the race week," he said. "But that doesn't mean it's going to be that easy for them to get out."

He pulled out a sat-phone and started dialing

"You'll recall I've got a small army of private PSOs running around this city?" he said. "Well, they're all going to be pissed off these Jihad monkeys just killed some of their brothers up here. So I'm going to use them to seal this place tighter than Tupperware. All the roads, the bus station, the train station—I'll get people to the Nice Airport. Key or no key, box or no box, those assholes ain't getting out. And when we're through beating the crap out of them, you guys can take over . . ."

Full of rage now, Audette was ready to start giving orders. But his cell phone wouldn't cooperate. No matter what he did, he couldn't get a dial tone.

"Are we in a dead zone here or something?" he asked Batman and Twitch, looking in all directions. "I mean, we're up on fucking hill. What's blocking the signal up here?"

They both shrugged. "Nothing works when we're around," Twitch murmured.

Audette finally gave up and said, "I got to get back to the city and get on a landline. How are you guys feeling? Need to go to a hospital?"

"Not me," Twitch said.

"Same here," Batman replied.

At that point they heard sirens approaching.

Audette told them, "OK, I say we all get out of here before the local cops start asking questions we don't want to answer."

• • •

IT WAS 3:00 A.M. by this time.

Audette drove like a madman back to Monte Carlo, agreeing to drop them at their hostel.

Squeezing his rented car into the alley nearby, the agent parked next to the hostel's dumpster long enough for Batman to get Twitch out of the backseat.

Then Batman awkwardly thanked Audette for being there in their time of need. The CIA agent waved off his gratitude and handed him an umbrella. He said Batman might be able to fashion parts of it into a temporary leg for Twitch.

Then the agent drove off with a squeal, leaving Batman with the distinct feeling that he wanted to get away from them as quickly as possible.

Twitch felt the same vibe. "He must think we're a jinx or something," he said.

Batman helped Twitch up the seven flights of stairs leading to their tiny room. It was a tough climb. Batman was full of aches and pains, the worst being a huge throbbing in his chest. But it was Twitch who had the biggest problem; without his artificial leg, he needed to hop up each step, one at a time, with Batman holding him under the shoulder for balance.

They finally reached the top floor, sweating, dirty and exhausted. Twitch pushed the door open about halfway when Batman suddenly stopped him. He pointed down at the doorsill. Going across it was the shadow of someone waiting on the other side.

Neither of them was armed, but it wasn't like they could go back down the stairs either. Batman toed the door open a little more. The shadow did not move. He peeked around the corner and saw the silhouette of a man sitting near the room's only window, the moonlight illuminating him from behind.

All he had was Audette's umbrella. He felt its point and found it fairly sharp.

"Unless you're the cleaning lady," Batman called out. "Don't move a muscle."

The intruder complied, so Batman finally switched on the light.

Only then did he realize their uninvited guest was the man Batman and Twitch knew as "Maurice."

When Twitch realized who it was, he grabbed the umbrella and lunged at him, hoping to stab him with the sharp point.

But he wound up falling to the floor just two feet into his attack.

"Help me up so I can kill this guy!" Twitch yelled at Batman.

But the little old man just smiled. He didn't seem nervous or scared. But he did look worried.

"So, we meet again," he said to them shyly.

"This already makes it once too often," Batman replied, helping up Twitch and settling him in a chair on the opposite side of the room. "And if you're here to scam us out of the key, you're too late. We just got our asses kicked and saw four other guys get shot down by someone who wanted the box just as much as we do."

The little old man nodded glumly.

"I know all about the key," he said. "Last time I talked to her, my person at the gagnant gave me full report. My people are out there trying to find those guys who robbed you."

"So, you *are* 'Bobby Murphy' then?" Batman asked him.

The little man bowed slightly. "Guilty as charged," he said.

Batman studied him for a few moments, contemplating him now in a different light. He was dressed the same as when they first met him, except now he had a tie on. And despite all he'd heard about him, the little man still looked very ordinary. Like the retired neighbor you chatted with over your back fence.

"That was quite a sting you pulled off at the Grand Maison," Batman finally told him. "You had us looking like assholes right from the start."

Murphy shrugged. "It's just what we do," he said apologetically. "We've whacked al Qaeda financiers in just the same manner, after we've robbed and beat them first, of course. You go with your strengths."

"Don't flatter yourself," Twitch told him harshly. "For all we know, you've just been making it up as you go along. Or maybe you're double-dealing with these Jihad assholes somehow."

Murphy stared at him for a long moment. "I've been called a lot of things, but never 'treasonous.'"

"How did you find out about the Z-box then?" Twitch challenged him. "Or about the gagnant or even any Monte Carlo connection?"

Murphy almost laughed. "You really want to know?"

"I sure do," Twitch shot back.

Murphy shrugged again. "Me and my people have been listening in on the CIA for years," he said starkly. "At Langley; their field stations. While they were busy trying to figure out what bin Laden had for breakfast, we've had our ears to the wires, taking it all in, blow by blow."

Twitch laughed at him. "Eavesdropping on the CIA? I'm sure . . ."

Murphy straightened his tie. "Do you really think their crappy sat-phones made by the Chi-Coms are so impenetrable?" he asked. "Do you think *no one* can hack into their field stations' database? Into Langley's database? There are hundreds of people around the world who will do just that for a price and we paid a few of them to do it for us."

"Well, I'm guessing that's total bullshit," Twitch declared.

"If you don't believe me," Murphy countered. "Perhaps you'd like me to recite word for word the action report the crew of that spy ship had prepared to release after the Agency had sent the Z-box and the fake pirates to the bottom of the Java Trench? That thing had everything but dancing girls and a sound track."

Twitch fell silent for a moment. Audette *did* tell them such an action report was written and possibly lost somewhere in cyberspace, but very few people knew about it beforehand.

But then Twitch erupted again: "Well, asshole, if you're here looking for more money, we're tapped out. That's what happens when someone steals ten million from you and then you almost get killed figuring a way to get it back."

Murphy was in full agreement. "I'm very sorry about that," he said. "But you have to remember, while I have the same goals as you, I don't have the CIA approaching me to do their dirty work for them. I'm sure you know all about my group by now. We might be the best PSO around, if I say so myself. But because of politics, we're on the outside looking in. No one gives us funds; no one approaches us with multimillion-dollar missions. So, unfortunately, we have to get in between the seams."

"So—*why are* you here then?" Batman asked him. "To gloat?"

"To the contrary," Murphy replied. "In light of the key slipping through your fingers and its obvious connection to the box, I came here to urge you to pool your talents with me and try to get it back immediately."

Twitch laughed. He said, "Translation: He wants a cut of our payment if we wind up recovering the Z-box."

But Murphy was emphatically shaking his head no. "Not exactly," he said. He thought a few moments, then went on. "Remember when I saw you guys the first time? I listed three groups of people who might want access to the Z-box: People who thought it was a terrorist weapon and wanted to use it against the U.S. People who wanted it to sell back to the Agency at a high profit. And people like you guys who'd been hired to recover it for a fee.

"Back then, I admit I thought of myself being in that middle group. If I got it I would have ransomed it back to the U.S.—for twice or more of what you guys were getting paid. That was an important thing for me. But I would have used that money to continue my private war against al Qaeda, because that's what we do best. We do it better than the whole freaking U.S. government. But yes, I would have extorted as much money out of them as I could."

He paused a moment, collected his thoughts, then went on.

"But now—things have changed. Because now *I know* what this thing is. *I know* what's inside the Z-box. And now

I don't care about the money so much. It's secondary, down a bit on the list. Now, priority number one is, I just want to prevent a catastrophe. Something a thousand times worse than 9/11."

Batman and Twitch were stunned. Suddenly the hostel began shaking again. There was a huge sound coming from the harbor.

"But how could you know what's in it?" Batman asked him. "I mean, even the Agency doesn't know that—or at least their field agents don't. So it wasn't like you picked it up sniping their communications."

"I know because we did something those guys should have done a long time ago," Murphy replied strongly. "I sent two of my best operatives into the worst part of Bangkok. And not ten blocks away from the CIA station there, we found the guy who dreamed this whole thing up back in 1968.

"He's an old, old guy now, and he's got a very bad opium addiction *and* a huge drinking problem, afflictions that are the direct result of him coming up with the original Z-box design and what it was built to do. He was so ashamed of himself that he couldn't go back to the U.S. after the war was over. He had to keep the secret inside, especially after the Goddamn box got lost. But, let's just say, when he met my two guys, they persuaded him to educate us."

Murphy pulled out a small DVD player from his coat pocket and activated its screen. Then he revealed two unmarked DVDs.

"I just got these," he said. "And they're both bombshells."

He pushed one into the DVD player and hit play. The screen filled with static, but then slowly, a grainy video materialized. It showed a hotel room smaller and grungier than the one they were in now. Two men in ski masks and black clothes were talking to a third man, who happened to be tied to a chair.

This third man was elderly and looked sick, both mentally and physically. He had long scraggly gray hair and a beard to match. He was wearing a traditional Thai silk shirt and yoga pants, but they were stained and ripped and filthy.

The men in masks were injecting him with something: narcotics, truth serum, a little of both? It was impossible to tell. But after a few editing dissolves, the old man started talking

"The box was designed to be the ultimate booby trap," he began in a raspy voice, with captions appearing at the bottom of the screen. "The idea was to turn the North Vietnamese Army's worst weapon on themselves. So many of our guys had been killed and maimed by their booby traps. We wanted to give them a taste of their own medicine—but just do it in spades.

"The packing case was exactly the same kind used by U.S. troops to transport classified material, documents, even secret weapons in and around Vietnam. These boxes were built of the same material as an airplane's black box, and they all had a small 'artificial atmosphere' inside to preserve the contents over long periods of time.

"Several had been captured by the communists during the Tet Offensive, and a bunch of our secrets were compromised. We learned Hanoi had ordered its troops in the field that should they find one of these boxes, they were not to open it, but rather get it and if possible, the key, back to Hanoi as quickly as possible."

The old man started mumbling, so one of his interrogators gave him another shot in the arm.

"Remember the neutron bomb?" he started up again. "It kills people, but leaves the buildings standing? That's approximately what we dreamed up. Again, that box was the ultimate booby trap. An atomic booby trap. But of course, it was also against the Geneva Convention."

That's where the first DVD ended. Murphy put in the second one. It was a black and white film converted to video.

"He had this with him," Murphy told the others. "It's a Z-box test from many years ago."

The footage showed a flat, snowy, frozen setting, perhaps

in the arctic. There were hundreds of steel cages arranged in a huge circle within camera range. They contained everything from dogs and cats, to birds, rats, and larger mammals like a bear, and many, *many* chimpanzees.

The Z-box was placed on the back of a jeep by men in hazmat suits. The jeep was then driven into the center of the animal cages and parked. The driver got out and quickly walked away.

An undetermined amount of time went by, and then a timer appeared in the upper left-hand corner of the screen. It began ticking down from thirty seconds. On reaching zero, there was a tremendous flash of light, so much so it blinded the camera lens for at least a minute.

When the image could be seen again, it showed some fire, some smoke, but mostly just a thirty-foot-deep crater where the jeep had been. Also many of the hundreds of animal cages around the crater had been destroyed, their occupants incinerated. But just a few hundred feet farther out from the center of the blast, many of the cages were still intact and their occupants alive but in a very high state of agitation.

Someone pushed a button somewhere and all the animals that survived were released from their cages. But on getting out, all of them began flopping about, stumbling or moving in a highly disoriented manner.

"What's the matter with them?" Twitch asked. "Are they irradiated?"

Murphy just shook his head slowly.

"Worse," he said. "They're blind. *Permanently* blind . . . from the flash."

Batman and Twitch were shocked.

Batman said, "We had no idea this is what the box contained. Whatever it is."

"It's a nuclear weapon, is what it is," Murphy told him strongly. "But not a typical one. Even Nixon knew if he started lighting off tactical nukes in Vietnam, the Russians or the Chi-Coms would probably supply small nukes to the

NVA and then we would have had nuclear-armed guerillas running all around southeast Asia. But somehow the Agency talked Nixon into this weapon disguised in a Z-box.

"Technically, it's called an 'extremely low-yield gamma-neutron TNW,' for tactical nuclear weapon. It was built to do three things: First was to explode in such a way that it would be very hard to prove if it was even nuclear. You can see it had a relatively small blast area, maybe a quarter mile or so. We had some conventional blockbuster bombs in Vietnam that could do at least that much damage and probably more.

"Second, this bomb would also send out vast quantities of neutrons that would kill many people while leaving structures relatively unaffected. But third, and the worst of all, it was built to release huge amounts of gamma rays as well. Anyone within twenty miles of the explosion, who looked at the flash even for a second, would be rendered permanently blind.

"The CIA figured the Z-box would be opened somewhere in Hanoi, a tightly packed city of 1.5 million people at the time. There would be an explosion, which again wouldn't be very big, but the flash would be tremendous. The Agency figured, while only a hundred or so would be killed in the actual blast—more than seven hundred thousand attracted by the noise of the blast would be blinded forever by the flash.

"Can you imagine the crisis that would cause? Three quarters of a million people suddenly and permanently without sight? All in one city? The effect would have been so paralyzing that the North Vietnamese government would have collapsed. No matter how much aid Russia and China poured in, this thing would have ruined them.

"And it probably would have won the war for the U.S., too— but we would have been morally bankrupt in the eyes of the world, or even more so than we are today."

He pointed to the DVD, still showing the hundreds of

blind animals in confused agony, stumbling about. Then he said: "Gentlemen, *that's* what's in the Z-box. . . ."

A stunned silence descended on the room. It lasted for a long minute.

"But how did they expect it to get into the hands of the NVA?" Batman finally asked.

"Like I said," Murphy replied. "The CIA knew if it were found by NVA or Viet Cong troops, it would eventually get to Hanoi, where they would try to open it. But the Agency didn't want to be obvious about it, like leaving it behind on a battlefield or in the backseat of a car.

"So they tried to fake an airplane crash with the Z-box on board, along with four already-dead bodies dressed up like the crew, hoping the box and the key would be found and immediately taken to Hanoi as ordered. But the plane was shot down long before it got where the Agency wanted it to go and it wound up being lost in this rice paddy that was covered over with water and mud for years afterward."

"Man, the Agency was goofy even back then," Twitch said. "I mean did they just expect it to work, just like that?"

"Yes, they did," Murphy nodded. "Because they kept it simple. You open the box with the key, and the first few layers contain what look to be classified documents. But once you get down to the bottom layer, like a VC spinning mine, it starts ticking down and it's impossible to stop. Unless, you turn the key again, and shut it off. And you have exactly one minute to do that. After those sixty seconds, the bomb goes off fifteen seconds later."

Another silence came over the room.

Then Murphy said, "Now, can you imagine such a weapon being detonated in a large American city? With *millions* of people in the affected area? It would make 9/11 seem like a tea party."

The hostel shook again with the loud noise coming from the harbor.

Murphy continued to pull on his tie nervously; at times he

seemed like an intensely shy man. "I guess I always hoped this thing was just a box of feathers," he went on. "Or LBJ's stained pajamas or something. Because then, it really *would* have been a game, getting it back, trying to block everyone else out, just to save the Agency some bad press.

"But now that I know what it is, it's frightening that I thought so cavalierly about it."

He fumbled with his tie some more. Then he added: "And I swear to you on my life, I thought the gagnant prize *was* the box—and not just a key."

"Well, you fucked that up, genius," Twitch roared at him again. "And now that key is out there on the loose, and so is the Z-box."

Batman raised his hands as a request for calm. Then he said, "Look, we all fucked up here in some way, shape or form. And pointing fingers won't solve anything. What we've got to do now is figure out how these Jihad Brothers are planning to get the key out of Monte Carlo and bring it to wherever the box is."

"The only people who know that must be the ex-Stazi guys," Murphy said. "They were the brokers; they're the ones who handled all this."

Batman said, "Then I suggest we go back up to that Palace and beat the piss out of everyone we see. One of them has *got* to know where these Stazi guys are."

Murphy nodded, but then replied, "Normally, I would say that's not a bad idea. But I really doubt the Stazi guys were ever even here in MC. They're too smart for that and I doubt we can ever catch them. As for the Palace, they're just doing what every other European royal family is doing these days: They're strapped for funds and have a lot of debt and they just made themselves a quarter of a billion dollars for doing nothing more than hosting a card game. For all we know, they were told the players were vying for an antique or a precious art collection. Far worse things have been done inside those four walls, I'm sure."

"But here's what's bothering me," Twitch said. "If the

game was just for the key, then why would those people even play in it? Why would they put up fifty million if *they* don't even know where the box is?"

"The answer is simple," Murphy replied. "Everyone in that game *does* know where the box is—*but us*. Don't you see? You two guys and my beauty queen were the only ones not in on it. We were late arrivals. My proxy was in just under the wire and then you guys walk in uninvited. We were the only *good guys* there. The rest of them were crooks or terrorists or a little bit of both. They all had to know where the box was already and that the key was super-important. We were just left out in the cold."

"Then let's face it," Batman said glumly. "There's only one guy in MC who definitely knows where the box is—and that's the guy who just stole the key. Like I said, we got to find him before he slips out of town."

"I agree," Murphy said. "But he's too smart to try to get out by plane. Or bus or train or car because he'll know, or the person pulling his strings will know, that the Agency or all their PSO guys will have all those places sealed by now. I'm sure your friend Audette is doing that as we speak.

"Now we all know those Jihad Brothers are smart—or at least smart enough and brutal enough to get the one thing a lot of other people in this town wanted. What we have to do immediately is figure out the *real way* they're going to get out of town."

The building shook yet again. The noise from the harbor was even louder than before.

That's when it came to Batman. He suddenly realized he might know how the Jihad Brotherhood was planning to escape.

He signaled Twitch and they both began climbing out of their mismatched tuxes and into their old Versace clothes.

"We've got to go right now," Batman said. "The three of us . . ."

"Where are we going?" Murphy asked him anxiously.

"To the harbor," Batman replied. "Of course . . ."

24

IT ALL CAME down to traffic.

It was now almost 5:00 A.M. and it was still dark. Yet Monte Carlo's winding streets were crowded, bumper to bumper. The traffic was made up almost exclusively of taxis and limousines carrying race drivers, race officials and the glitterati. Because it was just a few hours away from the beginning of the Formula One Grand Prix, there was a mad rush to get to the race staging point before the sun came up and the crowds descended on to Avenue Albert I.

Batman, Twitch and Murphy stood on the corner near their apartment building for fifteen minutes trying to hail a cab, but none were available. They finally walked out onto Avenue des Beaux-Arts, their goal being the harborside roadway of JFK Drive. But even though they could see the waterfront, despite the glare of all the headlights, it seemed like a hundred miles way.

Through it all, Murphy was trying to call his people on his cell phone, but with no luck. He seemed legitimately concerned as he went through a litany of numbers, dialing then redialing them all, but not connecting with any of them. He was muttering that he never stayed out of touch this long with his PSO group, and he was clearly worried that his people might have been trying to get in touch with him.

They finally gave up trying to find an empty cab. They would have to go down to the harbor on foot, though they'd be slowed by Twitch's lack of mobility. He'd hastily fashioned a temporary prosthetic out of the umbrella stem and shoelaces and it worked surprisingly well. But he could not move fast with it.

In the end it didn't matter. For the entire trip down to the harbor side, they kept hearing the same distinctive and tremendous roar; Batman and Twitch had been hearing it since they'd arrived in Monte Carlo, always on the periphery of everything else that was happening in the glittering city.

Mechanical, powerful, and very loud. It was not a race car; it had nothing to do with Formula One. It was a gas turbine engine, not too unlike those used in jet fighters. Two gas turbines, in fact.

Power plants attached to a pair of the fastest yachts in the world.

Two yachts that were racing each other to New York City.

• • •

THE POWERFUL RACING yachts were gone by the time they reached the waterfront.

Unlike the beginning of the Grand Prix, there was no crowd on hand, no fanfare for the start of the waterborne high-speed race.

The two vessels had to leave on the tide—and the tide had started going out at 5:00 A.M.

Batman, Twitch and Murphy began walking down the pier nevertheless, heading to where the two yachts had been housed. Murphy still had his cell phone out, was still furiously dialing his people; it was crucial they knew where he was and what he was up to. But he just couldn't connect.

He was getting frantic . . . until suddenly he slapped himself upside the head.

He stopped Batman and Twitch in their tracks.

"Are you guys still carrying those platinum cards my girl gave you?" he asked them.

Twitch meekly took out his card. Batman showed his too—with the dent made by the terrorist's bullet.

"A lot of good they did us," Twitch said. Then he looked at Batman's, and added: "Except for saving his ass."

Murphy took both cards and immediately tossed them in the water.

"Those are EIDs," he said as Batman and Twitch watched them sink into the harbor. "Electronic interference devices. You guys haven't been able to make phone calls, use ATMs and so on? Those things were the reason why. It was all part of our plan to isolate you. Sorry . . ."

Twitch just looked at Batman and shrugged. "*Now* he tells us?"

By that point they had reached the support shack for one of the two racing yachts, the vessel dubbed *Numero Two*.

The building was actually a substantial structure about the size of a one-story house, built onto the dock itself. Its support crew was sitting outside, relaxing after a hectic few days. There were six of them—mechanics, electricians, computer techs. They were drinking mimosas under a string of party lights.

Murphy struck up a conversation with them, as Batman and Twitch, ever aware of their prostheses, hung back. The support crew were all Italian; their yacht had been designed in Pisa and built in Milan. This would be its first race across the Atlantic.

At Murphy's folksy prompting, the support crew explained they'd spent the last forty-eight hours getting all the provisions onto the *Numero Two* in time, making sure it was mechanically in tune and getting its drivers ready for the trans-Atlantic contest. Each turbine-powered racing yacht had a two-man crew, a pilot and an engineer, though either man could pilot the boat if necessary. Ninety-nine percent of the work was done by computer anyway, with all of the steering done by GPS.

Their own particular launch had gone off like clockwork, the pit crew said. No problems. No drama. Now that their work was done, they could relax and enjoy Monte Carlo for a change.

"And how did the other entry get off?" Murphy asked them, nonchalantly.

The Italians shrugged as one. "*Chiedere loro*," one said. "Go ask them, if they can still speak . . ."

By Murphy's expression, they knew he didn't understand.

"Even before the race begin, they have drug dealers and hooker on a visit to them," one man explained. "Must have been big party, premature."

Murphy bade the support crew good luck. Then on his cue, the three of them continued strolling down the pier to the support shack for the second racing yacht.

"Drug dealers and a hooker?" Twitch said, once they were out of earshot. "That's an odd way to say 'bon voyage.'"

The second vessel was named *Smoke-Lar.* A twist on the Dutch word for "Smuggler," it was built at the famous shipyard at Oss, Holland. Its support shack was located at the end of the isolated dock, away from just about everything else.

But there was no partying pit crew here. It was all very quiet; the shack and its dock seemed deserted.

"*No one* is around?" Batman said. "That's a bit suspicious."

"If the Jihad Brothers stole this yacht," Murphy said. "Then they would have had to whack the support crew and the guys on the boat."

"Well, we know they're not averse to whacking people," Batman said.

The door to the support shack was locked. Murphy used a small knife to pick the lock and they piled inside.

The interior looked like a typical suburban house garage. Lots of tools, fuel cans, electric cables running everywhere. Technically, it was a wet dock, meaning one section of the base had no floor. This allowed the yacht to float in and get serviced while staying in the water.

"No drug dealers, no hooker," Twitch announced after a quick look around. "No party . . ."

He was right. Nothing was out of the ordinary inside the building. The place looked so normal, it was more likely that the support crew had simply gone into town after their yacht departed.

But then Murphy spotted something. Floating in the water of the wet dock was a handful of small brass-colored items; they looked like thimbles. Murphy reached down and scooped them up.

They were shell casings that had failed to sink.

Batman examined one and said, "They might be from an Uzi. Maybe recently fired."

Then Twitch found something even better. He pointed to the shack's fiberglass ceiling. Each corner had a tiny security camera hanging from it.

They found the small operations room in back and Twitch was soon pulling up the video feeds of the last few hours. At first they saw the yacht's crew hurrying through some last-minute work on the bullet-shaped racing vessel. But then, about 4:30 A.M., two dark-skinned men entered the support shack, guns drawn.

"Are those our 'drug dealers?' " Murphy asked.

The video was blurry at this point as the yacht's power plant was turned on and massive vibrations from its turbine engine were shaking everything inside the structure, including the cameras. But the tape was clear enough to show the intruders murdering the support crew, one at a time, and then putting their bodies on the boat.

The video went a little crazy at that point. It almost looked like a third person was suddenly with the terrorists, forced into the boat but not killed. It looked like a woman, though she had a coat pulled over her head.

"And could that be our 'hooker?' " Batman asked

The video showed the vessel then leaving the wet dock. The vibrations calmed down and the camera went back to simply recording the static scene.

"So they killed the crew here," Murphy said after the video ended. "And obviously the racket from that freaking engine was enough to mask the sound of the gunshots."

"And they'll probably dump the bodies at sea, once they're under way," Twitch added. "I mean, that's what I'd do."

"The question is, what do *we* do now?" Batman asked.

"Call the Monte Carlo police?" Twitch offered. "Or the Monaco military? Does Monaco even have a military?"

Batman shook his head. "If not, we can call the French military, I guess?"

But Murphy vigorously disagreed. "You want to *call* someone and *lose* everything?"

"But *someone's* got to stop that yacht," Twitch said.

"I agree," Murphy said. "But if we call in the French military now—or any military for that matter, this thing will blow sky high. God, especially involving the Frogs, it will be headlines inside the hour. Remember, this isn't just a WMD that might be heading to the US. This is a WMD designed and built for the CIA for God's sake. If it goes off, that whole '9/11 was an inside job thing' will erupt again and that could tear the country apart."

He paused a moment, then added, "Besides, didn't Audette tell you guys that you couldn't ask for any help from anyone in this thing?"

"But that was before we know what the freaking box was," Batman replied harshly. "Those mooks stole that yacht for two reasons: It was a way to get out of Monte Carlo with no one looking and it was a way to get to the U.S. again without anyone being the wiser, at least until they got there.

"So the box *must* be in the U.S.—I mean, if the key is going there, then the box has to be there, too. And the way that yacht can travel, it's already a hundred miles away from here by now and once it gets out in the open ocean, it could really go anywhere, Florida to Maine. The way I see, we got no choice but to call for help."

But Murphy was still shaking his head no.

"What do you propose we do, then?" Batman asked him.

"How about this?" he replied. "What if *we* were able to sink that yacht somehow? And the key went down with it? That would be almost as good as sending the box to the bottom of the Java Trench, right? If that thing works the way we think it works and you need the key, then eliminate the key and you eliminate the immediate threat. Then we can tell the Agency what we know about the Z-box—after they pay us, that is. Then they can track down everyone else who was at that card game, waterboard them and go find it. Make sense?"

Twitch said, "What do you mean 'pay *us*?'"

"I mean will you cut me in for a percentage if this works out?" Murphy replied.

Twitch rolled his eyes. "I knew it," he said. "It's *always* about the money with you. Stealing it. Conning it. A half hour ago, you said you didn't care about the money."

"I said it was farther down on my list." Murphy corrected him calmly. "But my goal had always been to continue the work my group and I started right after 9/11. To do that, we need money, and this will be a way to make a tidy sum, courtesy of the Agency, and get rid of this horrible thing."

Twitch started to protest again, but Batman stopped him short. The little man was making sense.

"How much?" he asked Murphy.

He thought a moment. "Well, you guys won the key, but you lost a substantial amount of money doing it. Plus, you figured out the Jihad Brothers would be taking the yacht for their escape.

"Plus, we suffered mental distress," Twitch added. "You know, in the penthouse, and then suddenly *not* in the penthouse . . ."

"Thirty percent," Murphy said.

"Plus you return our ten million you stole," Batman told him.

Murphy thought a moment, but then nodded.

Batman looked at Twitch. "Instead of a hundred million, we get seventy, plus our ten back," he said. "Plus, Murphy here does all the heavy lifting."

Twitch thought a moment then just shrugged. "OK, deal . . ." he said.

They all shook hands, but it was very quick and perfunctory.

Then Twitch asked, "Now, how are you going to get that

boat sunk? It's already been thirty minutes since it left, and the goddamn thing is moving at eighty miles an hour."

Murphy just smiled.

He pulled out his phone—and finally got a dial tone.

"Leave that to me," he said.

25

Off the coast of France

FAHD FAHIM SHABAZZ had grown up on a yacht.

For more than thirty years, his father was the chief maritime engineer who oversaw the upkeep and repair of a fleet of yachts owned by members of the Saudi Royal Family.

That fleet contained more than two dozen yachts and involved so much work, around the clock, over the years, that the Fahim family lived on the fleet tender, which, in fact, was an old yacht converted to carry tools, spare equipment and replacement parts. Fahim Shabazz was two years old before he'd set foot on dry ground. Until he turned twenty-one, he'd spend the majority of his life on that old yacht tender, with only the water rolling beneath his feet.

Now he was at the controls of the *Smoke-Lar,* one of the most fantastic yachts ever built and going almost eighty mph. It was fifty-six feet long, constructed mostly of lightweight composites, with a gas turbine that was powerful enough that, with a few tweaks, it could produce enough electricity to light a small city.

The yacht was shaped like a bullet that had melded with a knife. Everything in its design was about aerodynamics; every ounce of weight, every contour, even the special glass in its sleek cockpit was made to let the air slip past it in the most efficient way.

When all this was working together, Fahim Shabazz

could get the yacht moving at *more than* eighty miles an hour and nothing on the ocean's surface could catch him— with the exception of the yacht currently following him, of course.

• • •

FAHIM SHABAZZ WAS also on a suicide mission—and he couldn't have been more excited about it.

He was a soldier of al Qaeda, by way of the Jihad Brotherhood, and he'd been hoping for just such a mission ever since being sent to Somalia to stir up trouble there. Because of his nautical background, he'd been imbedded with local Somali pirate groups, such as the Shaka, and had gone on several raids with them, all in hopes that a suitable opportunity, like this one, would arise. So, in a way, he was a bit of a pirate himself.

When word came down from the al Qaeda leadership that a powerful weapon needed for a retaliatory operation against the Americans would soon be in place and all that was required was for an activation key to be smuggled into the United States, possibly by boat, Fahim Shabazz jumped at the chance to serve.

So now here he was, piloting what was probably the fastest yacht in the world and making great time. If everything went right and this unusual way to circumvent U.S. security actually worked, Fahim Shabazz hoped to reach his goal in fifty-five hours and start the operation with no problems whatsoever.

Getting to this point had been challenging, however. He'd slipped into Monte Carlo among the deluge of street vendors allowed in to sell their wares during Race Week. He'd made contact with officials from the Pakistani consulate in Monaco. They gave him clothes, funds, weapons and lastly a place to stay, which was probably the most difficult arrangement of all. The Pakistani Intelligence Service, the notorious ISI, secured a seat for him at the Grande Gagnant by paying the ten million dollar buy-in fee up front and then wiring a surety bond for the remaining forty million in his name to the game's organizers.

Fahim Shabazz had also been led to believe by the ISI that some sort of fix was in for him in the game, but when the late-arriving pair of Americans wound up winning the key, he had to fall back on his al Qaeda training and ruthlessly get by force what he could not win by chance.

He'd been lying in wait for the Americans to come down the Palace Road; that they were subsequently kidnapped and then stopped by their friendly rivals worked in his favor. It set up the massacre on the road—and put the key in his possession.

Had he won the key, he would have just left, as he'd come in, through the airport at Nice and then on to America. But obtaining the key by violence led him to Plan B, which is where his nautical background came into play, which was why he'd been selected for this mission in the first place.

Plan B required he kill the original drivers and support crew of the *Smoke-Lar.* This was done without a problem. Weighted down, they were thrown overboard as soon as the *Smoke-Lar* was out of sight of land. And now, with a little last minute insurance aboard, Fahim Shabazz wasn't expecting any trouble from anybody.

Off in the distance, maybe ten miles behind him, was the second racing yacht, *Numero Two.* As there would be no radio contact between the two competitors—indeed no radio contact with anyone, barring emergencies, until they were in sight of the U.S. coastline—there would be no way the crew of the Italian boat would know anything was amiss on the *Smoke-Lar.*

The other member of his crew was Abdul Adbul. Typical of al Qaeda operations, for security reasons, Fahim Shabazz had met Adbul just the day before when they both stole into Monte Carlo pretending to be street vendors.

Like Fahim Shabazz, Abdul was a Saudi. He'd been Fahim Shabazz's second at the Grande Gagnant, and when they didn't win the key, he'd helped gun down the group of men on the Palace Road and then assisted in the murders of the *Smoke-Lar*'s crew and support team.

Abdul Adbul was here for one important reason. He'd worked as an engineer at the vast Ghawar oil field in the Saudi desert. He knew about gas turbines, which meant he knew that if you just left them alone, if you didn't mess with them, they would run forever on their own.

They hadn't spoken much since stealing the *Smoke-Lar*. Abdul knew very little about driving racing yachts, not that he had to. The entire trip was programmed into the vessel's onboard guidance computer, which used the same integrated navigation technology as a modern jet fighter or airliner. Basically the humans on board confirmed the course set in for the race, at the maximum speed allowable and the guidance computer and the GPS unit did the rest.

What Abdul didn't know was he was just along as a backup in case anything went wrong during this transatlantic dash. But once they reached America and the time was right, just to uncomplicate things, Fahim Shabazz was under orders to send Abdul to paradise early.

This was the perfect situation for Shabazz. He hated Americans, hated the West, and he loved fast boats. He looked for this to be the best way to spend the last forty-eight hours of his life on Earth.

He'd already recorded his martyr video; he hadn't seen his family in years, not that it mattered. He would get to cross the mighty Atlantic and invade the hated USA, the land of the Great Satan—with a key to a weapon more powerful than an entire army.

So everything was going smoothly.

For the first three hours.

Then the jet fighter appeared.

• • •

THE *SMOKE-LAR* WAS on the other side of Majorca when Fahim Shabazz first spotted the jet.

He was three hundred miles out of Monte Carlo by this time and making great headway. He'd just passed a small fleet of sardine boats, making sure he waved to them just as he did any vessel that came within 1,000 feet of him, when heard the unmistakable sound of a jet overhead.

It rocketed very high above the yacht, then banked sharply and started circling. It was at least two miles up, too high to identify its make or country of origin. But on the face of it, it seemed innocent enough. There was always a chance the aircraft was just curious to see such a large boat going so fast. Or maybe it hadn't noticed him at all and was just on a training flight or something.

Still, it was enough for Fahim Shabazz to get worried.

He watched the jet for about five minutes, aware only that by continuing to fly in wide circles it was keeping pace with him. But then, once he was out of sight of the mainland or any island or any other vessel, it began diving on him.

For Fahim Shabazz, this was like something from a bad dream. He'd been having nightmares since being selected for the honor of martyrdom. He was told this was normal, that the Devil was trying to tempt him into not obeying God's will.

But one of the bad dreams was about the sky itself falling on top of him—and almost as soon as that thought went through his head, the jet fighter was down at wave-top level, coming right at him. Any notion that this might be just a curious pilot was dashed.

The jet went by his port side at tremendous speed. Not fifty feet away, and no more than ten feet off the top of the water, just the disruption in air pressure around the *Smoke-Lar* violently rocked the racing yacht back and forth.

Fahim Shabazz knew by now what kind of a plane it was. It was a Harrier jump jet. He'd seen plenty of them as a boy growing up on the Persian Gulf. Flown by both the U.S. Marines and the British Navy, they made a distinctive high-pitched sound when they flew overhead.

But this jump jet had no national markings. Instead, it was painted in sinister black camouflage. And it was turning again.

The second time, the jump jet went by so low and so fast, Fahim Shabazz thought for sure it was going to crash into the sea. Through the clear cockpit glass, he could see the pilot glaring at him as he flashed by. The pilot actually gave him the thumbs-down sign.

Fahim Shabazz knew it would be foolish to disconnect from autopilot and try to evade the jet. One deviation from the planned course could put them off course by hundreds of miles. And besides, where would he go? There was no way he could outrun the jet fighter.

As he was thinking all this, the jump jet turned again and this time he saw its nose light up with flashes of cannon fire.

The plane was shooting at him!

But physics worked in Fahim Shabazz's favor at that moment. As a result of its tight, low-altitude turn, the jump jet was now flying due north, while the yacht was racing due west. The window for firing on the yacht was a brief one. Of the dozen or so shells fired at him, only two pinged off the long yacht's snout, the rest ripping into the water on his starboard side.

But then the jump jet turned once again and was coming back at a much better firing angle.

There was no real mystery now. Fahim Shabazz knew that someone had obviously caught on to him.

Luckily, he had made provisions for just sort a thing.

He screamed for Abdul to come up from the engine room, then he started nervously playing with the silver rings on his fingers as he watched the jump jet approach again.

Abdul appeared and quickly appraised the situation. He disappeared below but reappeared a few moments later— with a third person.

She was an Asian woman—her name was Li. To a non-zealot Muslim, and to just about the rest of the world, she would have been considered astonishingly beautiful.

They had snatched her shortly after they'd swiped the key from the winners of the gagnant. She'd secreted herself near the bend in Palace Road, and at first they took her because she'd been a witness to the killings and they weren't sure what to do with her. But then they decided to keep her for just such a thing as was happening now. She was their extra insurance.

Fahim Shabazz made her stand out in the open in full view of the oncoming fighter jet. He drew out his razor-sharp knife and put it up to her throat.

The jump jet streaked by—but did not fire this time. It turned and went by slower; the pilot was fixated on the beautiful woman, almost as if he knew her.

Then finally, the airplane slowly rose into the sky and eventually disappeared from sight.

26

Monte Carlo

IT WAS 8:00 A.M. when Murphy's phone finally rang.

The three of them were still holed up in the support shack for *Smoke-Lar*. Twitch was presiding over the late support crew's Power-Mac suite; it contained a Kestrel 4500 weather-tracking station and a GPS-slaved Earthworks program that allowed him to uncover the predetermined course of the two racing yachts. Batman, meanwhile, had been watching the door, on the lookout for any unexpected visitors.

Murphy had spent all this time on the phone. Outside, the preliminaries for the Grand Prix had begun, and between the sound of the Formula One cars and the noise made by the thousands of spectators awaiting the race, it didn't seem like Monte Carlo would ever be quiet again.

But this did not deter him. He was constantly checking in

with his network of operatives, especially the ones who were keeping an eye on Audette's PSOs, who in turn were watching all the local transportation points where the terrorists or the other participants in the gagnant could leave the area. He spoke with other operatives who were watching for any suspicious activity around the Pakistani consulate.

Murphy was also in touch with his base of operations, which was a nondescript container ship anchored about fifteen miles to the west, off of Nice. While using cargo vessels as cover for special operations had been around since the Q-ships of World War Two, Murphy's ship, built with funds he'd managed to weasel out of the U.S. government after 9/11, was not just for transport; it was a self-contained floating headquarters complete with advanced communications and eavesdropping equipment for his small army of spies and special ops experts. It was also part aircraft carrier: It was from here, still shrouded by the morning darkness and fog, that his unit's jump jet had taken off.

Murphy had not been entirely successful getting all his people on the phone, though: at least one was not answering his calls. At one point, he blamed the growing commotion in town for screwing up his phone reception. "Monte Carlo is one big EID," he said.

What Murphy was *really* doing, however, was waiting for someone to call him—namely the pilot of his jump jet. *That* was the one phone call that could change everything, the call that would tell them the key and the terrorists were sleeping with the fishes somewhere off the coast of Majorca. Only good things could come from that. The calamity that could be caused by the Z-box would be lessened tremendously. The box could then be tracked down in a much more rational manner. And the CIA could write a big fat check and reward those who'd pulled its collective ass from the fire.

So when Murphy's phone finally rang—someone was calling him, and not the other way around—he hit the TALK button with much anticipation; Batman and Twitch were listening in close by.

But not five seconds into the conversation the little man literally slumped to the greasy floor, his face turning white, his eyes tearing up.

The call did not bring good news.

To Murphy's credit, he pulled himself together just as quickly as he'd collapsed, getting back to his feet and brushing himself off even before Batman and Twitch could reach him to help.

"My fly guy found the yacht," he told them after hanging up. "And he was ready to take it out, but then he realized the mooks had a hostage with them. One of *my* people."

Batman and Twitch couldn't believe it. "One of *your* people?" Batman said. "Who?"

"The woman you met twice," Murphy said, his eyes red. "The woman who showed you the penthouse. The woman who sat in for me at the gagnant. Her name is Li—and no wonder she wasn't answering my calls. They got her and they made it clear they'd kill her if we interfered."

Batman's mind flashed on the face of the gorgeous Asian woman, clearly one of the most attractive females he'd ever met, and that included Her Bitchiness, Emma Simms. She made the perfect special ops operative because just about anyone with an ounce of testosterone in his body would be charmed into submission just by meeting her.

"But how could they have kidnapped her," Batman finally asked him. "Her, of all people?"

Murphy could barely speak now. In a halting voice, he revealed that after she'd reported in to tell him that Batman and Twitch had won the gagnant, he'd told her to tail them. He could only guess that's what she'd been doing on Palace Road when the shootout took place. The terrorists must have captured her in the process, and seeing her value as a hostage, didn't kill her when they whacked the four PSO guys and the racing yacht's support crew.

"So *she's* the 'hooker' on the videotape?" Twitch asked.

"She's hardly a hooker," Murphy shot back. "And I know it sounds corny, but she's like a daughter to me."

But she was now a huge complication, this beautiful Asian woman who, up until then, had been haunting the edges of this very strange adventure.

Batman and Twitch eyed each other—they were thinking the same thing.

"I know it's difficult to accept," Twitch tried to explain to Murphy. "But this isn't a time for sentimentality. We could have an enormous catastrophe in a major U.S. city if that boat isn't dealt with."

Murphy knew what he was proposing—and was immediately incensed.

"No way," he said sternly. "Not in a *million* years."

"But you're talking about one life as compared to millions of permanently injured people in the United States," Twitch said. "These things aren't easy, but look at the big picture. Someone has to take the hit."

Murphy just waved him off. "Well, it's not going to be her. The least of the reasons being the guy flying the jump jet happens to be her significant other. So, you can just forget about that option, because it's not an option at all."

A tense silence came over the three of them. Meanwhile the racket of the race cars outside provided the perfect sound track for what was happening inside the shack.

Finally, Batman broke the silence.

"OK, then," he said to Murphy. "Will you at least admit now that it's over? That this thing is too big for us? *None* of us is going to get what we want, so what's the fucking point? We've got to call in the military . . . *someone's* military. We've got to come clean about this whole thing to someone who can do something about it."

"And say bye-bye to one hundred million," Twitch mumbled. "But I guess that's better than blinding everyone in Washington, Boston or New York."

But Murphy was still shaking his head.

"If we call in the military now, especially the *U.S.* military, what do you think they're going to do?" he asked harshly. "If they're made aware of the magnitude of this threat, they'll hit that yacht with a couple Harpoon missiles and then tell everyone it was lost at sea. End of story. But I'm not going to allow that, not with Li on board."

"What else can we possibly do then?" Twitch pleaded. "We can't swim after that fucking boat. We can't just snap our fingers like ghosts and suddenly be there to stop these assholes."

That's when Batman held up his hand—asking for silence.

"Wait a minute," he said. "Do you hear that?"

Twitch and Murphy had no idea what he was talking about.

"*Hear* it?" he asked them again.

"How can you hear anything over all those race cars?" Murphy replied.

Batman looked out the shack's only window, and then ran out to the dock.

That's when he saw it.

High in the sky, but getting closer.

The answer to their prayers—maybe.

It was the *Shin-1* flying boat.

27

THE ITALIAN-BUILT *NUMERO Two* racing yacht was like the *Smoke-Lar* in almost every way.

It, too, was shaped like a sharp-point bullet; it had special paint, aerodynamic glass, a semi-enclosed cockpit and a gas turbine for propulsion. And it, too, could reach speeds in excess of eighty mph on water.

They were virtually the same vessel, except *Numero Two* was painted red and the *Smoke-Lar* was painted white.

Michele Savoldi was *Numero Two*'s pilot; his cousin Giuseppe was his engineer. They'd left Monte Carlo at the same time as the *Smoke-Lar,* but had fallen behind the Dutch-designed boat almost immediately, losing sight of their opponent not ten minutes into the race.

This was not so unusual; it was just a difference in racing philosophy. Going at a moderate speed early, as Savoldi had, saved fuel for later on. If you start out at full throttle, as the *Smoke-Lar* had, you might get a big lead, but that could diminish as the race went along, especially if you ran into mechanical issues that sucked up more fuel than expected. Per the competition's rules, Savoldi had never met or talked to the *Smoke-Lar*'s pilot, and every driver had his own methods. But in Savoldi's opinion, his opponent did seem to be pouring it on a bit prematurely.

In fact, Savoldi had been out of sight of the *Smoke-Lar* during most of the Mediterranean leg of the race. It was only after both vessels passed through Gibraltar in late afternoon and were out on the open ocean that he increased his speed and finally resighted his rival.

Savoldi did not have any binoculars with him; only absolute essentials could be brought on the race because any extra weight meant loss of speed. This was why when he finally saw the *Smoke-Lar* again it was simply a dot on the horizon leaving a faint spray of water and smoke in its wake.

He'd been keeping a close eye on the Dutch boat ever since, though. His plan was to gradually increase his speed during the night and creep up on his opponent. Even though they were trying to outrun the sun, if Savoldi could get within five miles of the *Smoke-Lar* by dawn the next morning, he would be happy.

• • •

GIUSEPPE HAD JUST changed out a fuel tank when Savoldi realized something was about to fly over them. He'd seen all kinds of aircraft during the Mediterranean leg—everything from airliners, to private planes, to TV helicopters taking pictures as he roared along below. But since moving out into the Atlantic, only the contrails of the airliners remained and even they became few and far between.

But there was an aircraft above him now and it wasn't an airliner or a private plane. It was a huge flying boat—and it was flying extremely low.

It had come up from his aft starboard side, making no noise until it flew right over him not fifty feet above the mast.

And now, as he and Giuseppe watched, the big plane turned violently to the left, and started coming back at them from the opposite direction.

Savoldi had no idea what was happening. Giuseppe was equally baffled. This huge hulking airplane seemed so interested in them—but why?

The flying boat went over a second time, again very low and extremely loud. Its four propellers even drowned out the roar of the *Numero Two*'s turbine engine. Savoldi didn't know what to do. He didn't want to deviate from his precise, predetermined course—that might cost him time and speed at the finish line. But he didn't want to collide with the huge plane either. Yet it was flying so low that seemed like a possibility.

The plane turned a third time, and came at them now from the starboard bow. It went by no more than twenty-five feet off the water, its wing almost touching the boat's nose. Then it turned once more, sped up—and landed with a great splash about a half-mile directly in front of the *Numero Two*. Incredibly, it began taxiing toward a collision course with the racing yacht.

Savoldi had no choice. The plane had succeeded in outmaneuvering him. With great reluctance, he disengaged the autopilot and pulled back on the throttles. The boat slowed down to almost nothing.

That's when he saw a person frantically waving something from the flying boat's open cockpit window.

It was an Italian flag.

This person was also yelling for Savoldi to come to a stop.

• • •

INSIDE TWO MINUTES the flying boat had come up alongside the idling *Numero Two*.

By now Savoldi and Giuseppe were convinced that something had gone wrong and the race had been canceled. But then they saw a raft deploy from the rear of the flying boat with several heavily armed people on board. They began paddling madly toward the racing yacht, reaching it in seconds.

The first man to climb aboard was an Italian; he identified himself as one of the pilots of the flying boat. He told Savoldi and Giuseppe that he was ex–*Stormo Incursori* and that the people with him were an American special operations unit that had to take over the *Numero Two*.

By this time, the rest of the strange group had climbed aboard. Four of them were wearing futuristic battle suits and huge helmets and carrying large combat weapons. But Savoldi was mystified to see this small army was made up primarily of a man missing an eye, a man missing a leg and a man missing a hand. A fourth man was not in a battle suit; he was dressed like an average American citizen, someone's grandfather out for a leisurely stroll. And the fifth person was not only the most beautiful girl Savoldi had ever seen, she looked like his favorite movie actress.

He couldn't believe this was happening.

"*These* people are taking over my vessel?" he asked the *Stormo* pilot in Italian. "In the middle of this race?"

The *Stormo* nodded yes.

"*Come pirati?*" Savoldi asked. "Like pirates?"

The *Stormo* pilot thought for a moment and then nodded. "*Preciso . . .*" he replied. "*Sono proprio come i pirati . . .*"

They are just like pirates.

• • •

THE *SHIN-1*'S MONTE Carlo stopover lasted only thirty minutes.

The flying boat had taxied up to the amphibian dock on the edge of the busy harbor to be met by Batman and Twitch. They knew right away this was the airplane that Alpha Squad had taken to Gottabang because of the detailing around the cockpit and tail section.

Nolan had jumped out of the open hatch even before the flying boat had stopped moving. He greeted Batman and Twitch warmly—as if he hadn't seen them in years, when actually it had only been a few days.

Nolan looked especially strange to Batman. He was battered and bruised all over, like he'd been shipwrecked, beaten-up, through a major battle and more. Yet he seemed . . . happy. Batman had never known his friend to be anything but in a dark mood and angry at the world, especially after the team's misadventure at Tora Bora. But now, he appeared to be a changed man.

Nolan told them he knew Monte Carlo was the only logical place to look for them. They were full of gratitude he'd followed his gut. Then a reunion that should have taken hours or even days, was accomplished in a matter of minutes, right on the dock.

Batman and Twitch talked first. They quickly told Nolan what had happened to them in the past forty-eight hours. Their arrival in Monte Carlo, their brief stay in the world-class luxurious penthouse, their fall to pauper status. They explained their comeback via Batman's vast gambling winnings, the events surrounding the gagnant, and its tragic aftermath—and finally, their unusual alliance with a guy named Bobby Murphy, and his revelation to them just how dangerous the Z-box was, and how the key needed to activate it was now in the hands of terrorists.

In the retelling, each chapter sounded more fantastic than the one before it. The money, the intrigue, chasing jump jets, mysterious women. But as incredible as it all was, nothing could have prepared Batman and Twitch for the surprise Nolan had in store for them.

Only the need to get properly dressed in an extra *Stormo* flight suit had delayed Emma Simms's arrival onto the dock. But as soon as she stepped out of the airplane, Nolan saw the look on Batman's face and said, "You look like you've seen a ghost."

To which Batman replied, "Better watch what you say . . ."

They'd had no idea she'd smuggled herself aboard the *Shin-1* for the trip to Gottabang. No idea that she'd been with Nolan all along.

But then it got *really* weird.

On first seeing them, Emma greeted Batman and Twitch like they were long lost brothers.

"We were *so* worried about you two," she told them breathlessly, embracing them and kissing their cheeks. "We were off doing our own thing, but we were always wondering how you guys were. We had to rescue a bunch of really unfortunate people from Gottabang and then these really bad pirates called the Bum Cats kept attacking us, but we fought them off because of these poor people—we just *had* to save their lives even though they're wracked with disease and malnutrition, and . . ."

She went on and on . . . and on, telling it all, at times hugging Nolan, at times laughing and then almost crying, and then laughing again.

It was so unexpected, that at the end of it, in perfect deadpan, Twitch had asked her, "And who are you again?"

• • •

THEIR CONVERSATION CONTINUED while the *Shin-1* was being gassed up and the Alpha Squad was introduced to Bobby Murphy.

It was clear that a lot of strange things had gone on with both teams, especially when Batman pulled Nolan aside and told him the unusual spiritualized way he'd so quickly won the immense fortune playing cards.

But they really didn't have enough time to ponder any of it. They had to concentrate on the two most important items of information: that Beta now knew what the Z-box was, and that Alpha had a good idea where it was—at an address with the zip code of 10007.

When a quick Internet search told them that 10007 was located in lower Manhattan, frighteningly close to where the Twin Towers once stood, everyone agreed that, considering what had transpired and what was at stake, it was up to Whiskey to stop the Jihad Brothers *before* they got where they were going.

Which is why they were now on the *Numero Two*.

• • •

THEY HAD A plan.

They'd worked it out during the flight from Monte Carlo to this point almost 800 miles off the French coast.

The plan was typical Whiskey: highly improvised and held together by Band-Aids and duct tape. That's what had worked best for them in the past. They had no time to change their technique now.

Most of the team's special combat equipment had remained aboard the *Shin-1* after Gottabang, so now they had access to it again, including their sniper rifle, a Barrett M107 LRSR capable of firing a .50-caliber round almost four miles, an astonishing distance. If the person firing it knew what he was doing, the M107 could be an extremely effective weapon.

It would have to be for Whiskey's plan to work.

They'd immediately discounted any kind of ship-to-ship boarding action as a way of stopping the *Smoke-Lar*. Though it was more their forte, attempting such an attack would almost definitely cost Murphy's protégé Li her life, not to mention it would have to be done while both vessels were traveling in excess of 80 mph.

So their idea was this: If they could get within four miles of the *Smoke-Lar,* then they would use the M107 to shoot the terrorist who was piloting the boat, and hopefully his engineer as well.

It seemed crazy, killing the two people who were in control of the high-speed vessel. But in theory it would work because just like *Numero Two*, the *Smoke-Lar* was basically run by a computer. As long as its autopilot was engaged, whether a human was at the helm or not, the boat would continue going where it was supposed to go.

But Whiskey also figured that, with both terrorists dead, the beautiful female hostage would be able to figure out how to take the computer off-line and stop the boat. Or even if that failed, by not changing out the fuel tanks, the vessel would eventually stop on its own.

Another advantage of the plan was that the Jihad Brothers would probably never know what hit them, at least not until the last moment. The roar of the *Smoke-Lar*'s turbine engine would be Whiskey's ally here. Just as its racket masked the sound of the terrorists killing the Dutch support crew back on the dock in Monte Carlo, so now it would mask the sound of any gunfire being aimed in their direction.

The hope was neither terrorist would realize anyone was even shooting at them until the first sniper bullet hit. And as far as they knew, as the race was still on, the only people following them were the two people trying to beat them to the finish line.

Finally, because they were still about 3,000 miles from the U.S., mainland, Whiskey would have almost forty hours to carry out the scheme.

• • •

BUT, AS WAS usually the case when Whiskey took on these high-risk endeavors, there were potential complications.

Though the M107 rifle could indeed hit a target four miles away, that was based on an expert doing the shooting and that expert being on solid ground. A non-expert firing the weapon from a racing yacht going 80 mph over six-foot ocean waves might prove a bit problematical.

The second dilemma was how to get close enough to the *Smoke-Lar* to get off a good shot. The *Numero Two* had already been ten miles behind the Dutch vessel when Whiskey appeared on the scene. The midocean stop took another ten minutes, putting the *Smoke-Lar* another fifteen miles in front, for a total of more than twenty-five miles.

The *Numero Two* would have to somehow make up a lot of that distance if they hoped to get within decent firing range of the lead boat.

• • •

BUT ON HEARING the plan, Savoldi, *Numero Two*'s pilot, simply laughed at them.

"*Non si può fare,*" he told them. "It cannot be done."

The *Shin-1* had departed and the Italian racing boat was climbing back up to 80 mph, its nose pointing northwest. While Savoldi's main concern was to get moving again, he'd been quickly briefed on who was driving the *Smoke-Lar* and how they had killed the racing yacht's driver, engineer and support crew. As it turned out, the pilot was intensely sympathetic, as he'd had a close relative slain by al Qaeda gunmen while serving in Iraq. And he wished he could help Whiskey in catching these terrorists.

But, he reiterated, their plan was unworkable. Why? Because the *Numero Two* had become seriously overloaded.

"This boat is built for two people," he explained to them in rough English, shouting to be heard over the roar of his recharged turbine engine. "And Giuseppe and I are thin on purpose. We diet just to make this trip. The boat goes fast not just because of the engine but because everything else on board is built lightweight or it does not come with us at all. We don't even have binoculars or sat-phones or more than one radio. We drink energy drinks instead of bringing food and water, and we pop pills so we won't need a place to lie down and sleep."

He used his hands to indicate all the equipment Whiskey had brought with them. Their weapons, their ammunition, their heavy battle suits. And the fact that there were now five extra people on the boat.

Savoldi guessed they were at least six hundred pounds overweight. And while there was one extra person on the *Smoke-Lar,* she was probably less than 100 pounds at the most, which equaled Emma's weight. So the two females were a wash.

But that still left the fact that Nolan, Batman, Twitch and Murphy were all extra poundage, as was all their gear, something that never dawned on them while they were en route, cooking up this plan.

To put it in numbers, Savoldi explained the *Numero Two*'s turbine contained a sensor that, in simple terms, indicated how hard the engine was working. That information could then be translated into how much the boat weighed at any given moment.

When he checked this sensor, it showed they were 575 pounds overweight.

"I am with you one hundred percent in this endeavor," the surprisingly even-keeled Savoldi concluded. "But we have no hope of catching the lead boat, because we'd have to get rid of almost 600 pounds just to get back to even—and that seems impossible."

In other words, with the *Shin-1* long gone, and with no way of calling it back, Whiskey was now stuck aboard the racing yacht whether they liked it or not.

So much for off-the-cuff planning.

• • •

BUT WHISKEY COULD not just give up.

Once Savoldi's cold truths sank in, they began accounting for anything aboard the racing boat that was not necessary and could be thrown overboard.

The first to go was most of Whiskey's weapons. Over the

side went their beloved M4s, all their ammunition and their sidearms. Next went the teams' heavy battle suits, their helmets, utility belts and even their boots.

They knew this was not nearly enough, but still wanted to know how they did. Savoldi checked his sensor

They'd shed only eighty pounds.

Next to go were the two gunny sacks containing MREs, some water, medical supplies, blankets, an assortment of things usually needed by special ops groups.

Another check of the sensor. They'd only lost another thirty pounds. And that was just about all the equipment Whiskey had brought aboard the vessel.

With Savoldi's blessing, they started searching for items belonging to the boat itself that weren't necessary. The racing yacht was made up of three basic components: Its extended nose was empty; its main purpose was to provide the aerodynamics of a long narrow snout. The semi-enclosed cockpit, where they were all congregated, was also where all the navigation and steering controls were located, as well as all the computers. The third component was the engine compartment, the claustrophobically small, brutally hot rear space where the turbine sat surrounded by a slew of twenty-five-gallon fuel containers. Once a container was used up, it was thrown overboard, thus making the vessel that much lighter, and making it go just a little bit faster.

Whiskey crawled all over the vessel, inspecting every bit of it. But as Savoldi had said, the intricately designed boat had been built to be lightweight in the first place, so there really wasn't much on board that could be discarded.

Then Twitch said, "Just before they went to the moon, they discovered the Apollo lander was too heavy. So the first thing they did was get rid of the seats."

The *Numero Two* had a pair of seats located in front of the control panel. Again, on Savoldi's OK, Whiskey went about dislodging these seats from the deck, using their combat knives as screwdrivers. It took more than an hour, but they finally came loose and we're thrown overboard.

Each seat weighed twenty pounds, so an additional forty pounds was gone.

But they were still more than 400 pounds from their goal.

• • •

SCOURING COMPARTMENTS ADJACENT to the engine compartment, Nolan found a steel box that contained many unusual and exotic tools. Giuseppe, the engineer, indicated the tools were on hand in case the vessel's turbine broke down.

This began an extensive discussion. While the chances of the turbine breaking down were remote, it wasn't impossible, especially considering the many hazards of the sea. Finally they asked Giuseppe what were the most important tools he would need if a problem arose.

He pointed out a handful of ratchet extensions and wrenches, then told them in broken English: "If I can't fix it with these, then I can't fix it at all."

That's all they needed to hear. Giuseppe took out the tools, then the box went over the side.

Savoldi checked his sensor. It was a total of sixty pounds gone.

But about 350 pounds of dead weight still remained.

• • •

THEY SPENT THE next two hours going over the racing yacht yet again, picking up scraps, like deck mats, extra seat cushions, even some lightbulbs.

But discarding things like this had minimal effect; less than ten pounds for all their efforts. Plus, it was getting dark and the *Numero Two* had made up little if any distance separating it from the still out-of-sight *Smoke-Lar*.

They'd all worked hard at it—even Emma and Murphy. But slumping back down in the cockpit after yet another hour of searching, the universal feeling was obvious: Their plan wasn't going to work and the terrorists would probably reach the U.S. unchecked to do their dirty work.

"We still have the option of calling in help," Twitch said finally, even though Murphy's sat-phone had run out of juice a long time ago. "If we sent a radio message to someone in a position of responsibility, they could pass the word along and someone can still deal with these guys before they're within sight of the U.S."

"But you *know* what that means," Batman said glumly, having heard the argument before. "The Navy will get involved and more likely than not, they'll cream that boat and apologize later."

Twitch just shrugged. "I still think we should consider it," he said. "Because what we've been doing here just ain't going to work."

Overhearing the conversation, Murphy slowly got to his feet and calmly made his way over to the boat's control panel. Without a word, he pulled the small two-way radio out of the console and nonchalantly tossed it overboard.

Then just as calmly he sat back down again.

"That was at least ten pounds," he said.

• • •

ONCE AGAIN, THEY started searching, this time concentrating on the cockpit and the various tiny compartments that ran off it.

Batman found a box tucked way behind the control panel. It was so heavy, he needed Nolan's help to pull it out.

"This is got to be at least a hundred pounds," Nolan said. "Maybe more."

"Actually it weighs almost one hundred and forty pounds," Savoldi told them.

"Christ—what is it then?" Nolan asked. "Can we toss it?"

That's when Savoldi pointed out a tag on the side of the box that read: EMERGENZA ZATTERA

Loosely translated: LIFE RAFT.

There was a slight gasp from the others.

Batman looked up at Nolan. "Remind me again how much

we want to do this?" he said. "I mean, no radio, no phones *and* no lifeboat?"

Nolan did a quick calculation. "We'd still be more than two hundred pounds overweight," he said.

"We should vote," Twitch said.

But Nolan knew this was hardly the time for democracy. Besides, it really wasn't their decision to make, especially now that the radio was gone.

He turned back to Savoldi, who'd been amazingly gracious as Whiskey had ripped apart his boat.

Nolan said to him, "You have the right to tell us to stop all this right now," he said. "Bottom line, you guys are the victims of circumstance here."

But Savoldi shook his head no. "I want to beat the man in that boat more than anything now. Race or no race. I have trained for something like this my whole life. *He's* a fraud. Plus, he killed people like me. People who do what I do. It is my duty to help you catch him."

Giuseppe was vigorously nodding in agreement.

"But this is not something we can do half-ass," Batman said. "Once it's gone, that life raft, like the radio, ain't coming back."

Strangely, it was Savoldi and Giuseppe themselves who settled the matter. They each took an end of the box and hurled it overboard.

No one said a word. For five long minutes, as they roared along, hammering against the Atlantic waves, everyone was silent.

Savoldi checked his weight sensor. It was down 140 pounds, but still that had only a minimal effect on their speed. They had 200 pounds more to go, and that was just to break even. And according to Savoldi, those 200 pounds were more than enough to prevent them from even seeing the *Smoke-Lar* again, never mind catching up to it.

This had a huge dampening effect on the uninvited passengers. Hearing it, they all collapsed to the deck of the cockpit, tired and beaten, and contemplated this unexpected disaster. They'd been aboard the boat for six hours now. They were wet, they were cold, and there was no food or water for them, only energy drinks for nourishment. And as these were highly caffeinated, they would only serve to put people on edge. It might have been the worst predicament Whiskey had ever found itself in.

His back pressed up against the rear panel, Nolan spied Twitch across the cockpit and could almost feel frustration oozing off of him. Truth be told, he'd been of little help in the weight search because, due to his makeshift umbrella-parts prosthetic leg, he had an especially hard time moving around the boat.

Now Nolan could almost hear him thinking, "If I just throw myself overboard, it might be enough to get close to the terrorist boat."

This vibe was so intense, Nolan leaned over to Batman, told him his fear about Twitch, and then said: "Please keep an eye on him. Don't let him do anything rash."

Batman replied, "OK—but who's going to keep an eye on me?"

• • •

NIGHT HAD FALLEN by this time. As was always the case at sea, one moment it was dusk, the next it was the dead of night and the stars were out in all their brilliance.

Still sitting in the back of the cockpit, Nolan saw an airliner going over their heads. Way up there, all lights and contrails, he thought: *You lucky bastards.*

Emma was right up next to him as always, her head pressed against his shoulder. He couldn't imagine what she was feeling about all this. It was embarrassing that after all they'd gone through he'd fucked up so royally with such an unworkable plan. As everything had more or less gone their way in the past few days, he'd never considered the string of good luck would so suddenly run out. And that had been a big mistake.

But all she said to him was: "Who will tell our story if we all die?"

• • •

NO ONE SLEPT. No one spoke.

The racing yacht roared on, bouncing constantly by riding atop the ocean waves.

Nolan watched Savoldi, as if he was waiting for a miracle to occur. The pilot was continuously checking his computer readouts, checking the weight sensor, checking the GPS screen and tracking the little red dot that represented the *Smoke-Lar.* But he could tell every time Savoldi went through this procedure, it was not good news. They just could not get close enough to the terrorist boat, and if even the slightest thing went wrong with *Numero Two,* they would probably be lost for good.

Who will tell our story if we all die?

Those words were now stuck in Nolan's head.

Through it all, Murphy sat off by himself, staring into space. He looked so out of place, like an old man lost at the supermarket. He'd said nothing for the longest time, so Nolan started to worry about him as well.

At one point Savoldi pulled a notebook from underneath his control board. It was the operating manual for *Numero Two* and probably weighed a quarter of a pound if that. Yet the pilot considered throwing it overboard as all the information within was duplicated on his computer.

But Murphy stopped him.

"May I?" he asked the boat pilot.

Savoldi shrugged and said, "Be my guest."

Murphy took the book and sat back down.

• • •

THEY PLOWED ON into the night.

The roar of the turbine first became physically tiring, and then painful. Again, the team was huddled at the very rear of the semi-enclosed cockpit, definitely not a space designed to carry people. A lot of spray made its way onto their heads and the temperature was plummeting. Their hopeless condition made them more miserable by the minute.

But suddenly, Murphy came alive.

He sprang to his feet, operating manual still in hand, and made his way up to Savoldi at the control board.

"Turbine engines have a tendency to leak fuel, am I right?" Murphy asked him.

Savoldi thought a moment, then nodded. "More so than other types of engines, *si*."

Listening in, Nolan also knew this to be true, especially on some jet aircraft or turbine-powered helicopters. When turbines were first started, they were flooded with fuel, and some of that fuel inevitably leaked out. It was the nature of the beast.

"What do you do with that leaking fuel?" Murphy asked him.

Savoldi had to think a moment. "It's found and used again," he said in the best way he could find to explain it.

Murphy's eyes lit up. "So, your engine has an attachment that captures and then recycles this leaking fuel?"

Savoldi called for Giuseppe. His cousin crawled out of the engine compartment having just changed out a fuel container.

Savoldi explained Murphy's question to him and Giuseppe nodded. "When the turbine stops, we take extra fuel back," he said.

"So, your engine has a fuel recycle and recovery tank?" Murphy pressed Giuseppe directly.

Giuseppe nodded. "*Si* . . ." he said. "A big one."

Nolan was up beside them now. Murphy explained to him that the turbine's recycling attachment and recovery tank must weigh at least four hundred pounds. Yet according to *Numero Two*'s manual, they really didn't need it, as the amount of fuel it would save in a couple days was negligible. If they were able to take it off, along with the recovery tank, it would be a huge weight savings.

Nolan and Savoldi both understood, but then Savoldi

said, "Such a thing can't be done while turbine is running—everything in the engine is too hot to touch. And we can't stop to do it or we'll be way too far behind. Plus, fuel usually caught by the recycler would wind up on the floor of the compartment."

"But the engine *can* run without this attachment?" Nolan asked Giuseppe.

He nodded again, but confirmed the fuel would collect on the bottom of the engine compartment.

He said, "Kerosene. One spark—*boom!* All over . . ."

Nolan turned back to Savoldi. "If we were able to lose all that equipment, would we catch up to the *Smoke-Lar*?"

Savoldi checked the Dutch boat's position and then nodded. "It's a better possibility," is how he replied.

Now Nolan had a million thoughts shoot through his head. If they could somehow get rid of this nonessential engine part, then they might still be able to make this all work.

But how could they detach it? Giuseppe was indicating that he knew how to do it, but how could they work on a piece of equipment that would be red hot?

"I can do it," Batman suddenly said from the corner of the cockpit.

Nolan turned to him. "You? Why you?"

Batman held up his twisted prosthetic hand and said, "Because I got nothing to burn."

• • •

SIX HOURS.

That's how long it took for Batman to disconnect the fuel recycler and its recovery tank from the boat's massive gas turbine engine.

All the work had to be done inside the extremely tight confines of the engine compartment, a hot, smelly greasy place that had no headroom, no legroom, and only a dull fifty-watt-equivalent bulb to light it.

Add in the constant bouncing of the boat, and the thunderous roar of the engine itself, it equaled a little piece of hell traveling at 80 mph.

Batman stuck with it, though. The attachment was located at the front and on the underside of the turbine, the most inconvenient spot imaginable when attacking it from the rear. It was held on by a flange of countersunk bolts, designed to be removed by a universal wrench, which was one of the tools Giuseppe had retained. The problem was, there were three-dozen of them, and each bolt took many minutes to slowly come undone.

Batman worked the wrench with his good hand, using his mechanical hand to hold the loosening flange in place and to collect the bolts each time one needed to be removed. Nolan sat just outside the engine compartment hatch throughout, passing in a t-shirt soaked with seawater for Batman to cool himself off, however minimally. Giuseppe sat just inside the cramped room, providing encouragement and collecting the bolts each time one was removed.

Nolan found himself thinking more than once the engine room was so small, even Crash's ghost would have a hard time fitting inside.

The attachment was finally separated from the turbine five hours into the operation. The sixth hour was spent trying to position the heavy, four-by-five boxlike recycler so they could work it out of the engine room. This proved to be the hardest part of all, and for a few scary minutes it seemed that after detaching it, the recycler was just too big to take out though the engine compartment's hatchway.

But with a lot of pushing, pulling and even some kicking, they managed to squeeze the 400-pound attachment out the engine hatch, where Nolan, Twitch, Savoldi, Murphy and Giuseppe triumphantly pushed it over the side. The recovery tank was also given the heave-ho. Then Savoldi checked his weight sensor again.

The *Numero Two* was lighter by a whopping 422 pounds.

They could feel the boat moving faster already.

• • •

BUT THEN THEY extracted Batman from the engine compartment, and one look at his other hand—the one without the prosthesis—told just how painful the procedure had been. All of his fingers and his palm down to his wrist were horribly burned.

Emma immediately wanted to take care of him, but all their first-aid supplies had gone overboard. The only thing she could treat it with was salt water from the spray coming into the boat. She gathered it up on the t-shirt and gently rubbed the burns.

It must have been hugely painful, yet Batman just sat there and took it.

"How do we get ourselves into these situations?" he asked Nolan darkly through gritted teeth. "I had more fun when the IRS was chasing me."

28

WITHIN TEN MINUTES of Savoldi telling them that *Numero Two* could now catch up to the *Smoke-Lar,* the Whiskey contingent were all asleep.

It was strange. Whether the situation had become a little more hopeful, or a little less stressful, or that exhaustion finally set in, everyone found a place at the rear of the cockpit and just drifted off.

Nolan was the last to succumb; Emma was the first. She was pressed tightly against him and he could hear her breathing softly despite the roar of the turbine and the constant slamming of the boat's hull against the ocean waves. Above it all, she felt warm when everything else felt cold.

No surprise that when he finally dozed off, she was in his dreams. They were back on the deserted island. They had built a house, and were living their lives in paradise, everything unfolding just like a movie. But then things started to go wrong. The weather over paradise grew nasty, dark and gray. A typhoon hit and he lost Emma in the jungle, and then he himself became lost. During all this, Nolan felt his head aching and his good eye burning up. There was a fire in his throat; his lungs seemed filled with hot water.

Then . . . suddenly he was awake. It was morning and the sun was pouring into the *Numero Two*'s cockpit. But the cockpit smelled horribly—of kerosene.

He knew why. The recycler and the recovery tank they'd removed. The fuel they were designed to catch was now dripping onto the hot engine-compartment floor. The fumes were seeping into the cockpit.

Nolan started shaking Emma, but she would not respond. He looked at the others. The way everyone was sprawled about, they seemed to be not sleeping but unconscious—or worse.

Then he looked up at the control board and saw Savoldi slumped over the steering column. At that moment, Nolan was convinced everyone but him was dead of carbon monoxide poisoning.

But then he felt Emma's hand touch his face. She woke up—groggy but looking beautiful as always.

"I just had the strangest dream," she whispered to him.

"Join the club," he said.

He hugged her tight, thrilled that she was alive.

Then everyone started waking up—bleary-eyed, but all still breathing.

The fumes were real, though. Everyone was aware of them; they were thick in the early morning air.

"This ain't good," Twitch said with a cough. "Sniffing fumes can make people crazy."

"You mean, 'crazier' don't you?" Batman replied.

As for Savoldi, he'd just been leaning over his tracking computer, making sure what he was seeing was really true.

Finally he called out to Nolan, "Major—you should look at this . . ."

Nolan made his way up front. He looked down at the tracking screen, thinking this is what Savoldi wanted him to do. But instead the pilot directed his attention through the windshield to the sea beyond.

Nolan was astonished. There was a boat out there.

He saw the spray first and then the exhaust plume. Then they went up on a wave and he was able to see the whole vessel.

It was a racing yacht, moving just as quickly as they were.

Savoldi nodded and smiled. "It is no dream," he said.

It was the *Smoke-Lar*.

Not a mile in front of them.

A cheer went up. Everyone was quickly on their feet and looking out at the hijacked Dutch boat. Murphy was especially happy. He cried out: "Behold the white whale!"

But even as they were watching it, the boat seemed to be streaking away from them.

Savoldi turned serious.

"You never know what's going to happen at sea," he told them. "So if we want to shoot these people, it's best to do it now."

Whiskey didn't have to be told twice.

They brought up the last weapon they had left on board— their M107 sniper rifle.

It was a monster. Nearly five feet long, and weighing a precious twenty-five pounds, it was all muzzle, metal and stock. It had a built-in collapsible bi-pod assembly for support, and a night-vision-equipped targeting scope that looked powerful enough to peer deep into the Milky Way.

Its .50-caliber bullet could seriously damage something like an armored car, a helicopter or even some tanks. As for a human body, one round in the right place could simply blow it apart.

They assembled the gun quickly and jammed in the ten-round magazine.

But then, another problem.

Where would they set up the gun?

Both racing yachts were traveling in a virtual straight line. Trying an angle shot would mean the *Numero Two* would have to deviate from its predetermined course, and reprogramming the computer to make that happen would take some doing. Plus, there were no guarantees if they did go off course that they'd be able to get back on track afterward.

So the sniper rifle had to be aimed straight out over the *Numero Two*'s bow. But the only way to do that was to take out a piece of the forward cockpit glass and stick the M107's barrel through the hole.

But that brought up more issues.

The *Numero Two* was now moving at more than 85 mph—but this was not a smooth, clear pond they were traveling on. It was the middle of the Atlantic Ocean, with swells that ran at least six feet high, mixed with the occasional rogue wave that could go up to ten feet or more.

At the very least, firing the M107 under these conditions called for an expert. The problem was, the team's sniper was no longer with them. Jack "Crash" Stacks had passed away a month before. In fact, the M107 once belonged to him.

A second Whiskey member was semiqualified on the rifle—but that was Gunner, who at that moment was still in a hospital in Pakistan, recovering along with the Senegals.

So after removing the section of windshield and anchoring the weapon as best they could, it fell to Nolan to peer through the sniper scope first.

As soon as he got a good look at the man at the controls of the *Smoke-Lar,* Nolan felt his body freeze up. This was the guy who'd started all the trouble. The guy who'd slaughtered the Dutch crew, and the four PSOs on Palace Road. The guy who'd snatched Murphy's adopted daughter. The guy who was holding the key to one of the most merciless weapons ever made.

Nolan wanted nothing more than to pull the trigger and erase him from the face of the Earth. But because of the high-speed, bumpy conditions, he couldn't keep him in the sighting scope for more than a second at a time. Plus, in situations like this, Nolan really needed his specially adapted helmet-mounted telescopic lens; it had been designed to fit perfectly over his good eye. But it had gone overboard with the rest of the team's equipment.

And he also felt he shouldn't be the one to take out the Jihad Brothers. Considering what they'd gone through, it was really up to Batman or Twitch to have the honor.

He told this to Batman, but his colleague just held up his hands. One was burned and one was artificial.

"As much as I want to," Batman said. "No can do."

All eyes fell on Twitch.

And he tried—but because of his crude prosthetic leg, he couldn't set himself properly. As a result, he could barely keep his eye on the sniper scope, never mind hold the rifle long enough to make a shot.

In desperation, Batman whispered to Nolan, "How's your girlfriend feel about shooting people?"

Nolan shook his head. "That ain't going to happen," he said. "Take my word for it."

That left Bobby Murphy . . .

The little old man made his way up to the rifle, took off his glasses and put his right eye to the scope.

"What should I aim for?" he asked with some uncertainty.

Savoldi thought it best to explain where *not* to aim on the *Smoke-Lar.*

"Don't hit anything from midships to the stern," he said. "That's where the fuel is stored and where the turbine is located. One big bullet in the turbine could cause it to come apart, sharp pieces flying everywhere.

"And a big bullet in the fuel supply? *Poof!* There will be nothing left."

• • •

Aboard the Smoke-Lar

FAHIM SHABAZZ WAS a happy man.

This was an unusual state of affairs for him. When the

sun came up that morning, his autopilot told him the *Smoke-Lar* had passed the two-thirds marker in crossing the Atlantic Ocean.

This is what brought joy to his essentially joyless heart. He was accomplishing his mission. He would soon be a martyr. He would soon bring great destruction to the homeland of the Great Satan.

He felt on top of the world.

But there was another reason for this. He'd been taking regular injections of Adrenalin since the previous afternoon, another item provided him by the Pakistani ISI. The shots made him feel like he had superior strength and superior mind power. They also kept him awake and alert, even though he'd been doing little else but watching over the autopilot all this time.

Abdul had remained below throughout, keeping an eye on the *Smoke-Lar*'s power plant. He was constantly checking their fuel supply and changing out the fuel tanks when needed. The only time he and Shabazz saw each other was when Abdul came topside to throw one of the empty fuel containers overboard. Each time Abdul did this, Fahim Shabazz imagined the vessel going just a little bit faster.

Their hostage, the beautiful Asian woman, was locked in the forward bow compartment, a space barely large enough for one person to fit into. Fahim Shabazz had praised Allah regularly for giving him the wisdom to keep her alive when he did. He had not had any interference since the bizarre incident with the jet fighter. To Fahim Shabazz, feeling almost superhuman in mind and body, that seemed like it had happened years ago.

The yacht was running perfectly. Everything from the mechanicals to the computers to the turbine had been flawless so far. The support crew they'd killed back in Monte Carlo had done their jobs well. And even the weather was cooperating. Though he saw the occasional high wave and had gone through a few rainsqualls, for the most part nature had been good to him, too.

As for his unknowing opponent, the boat named *Numero Two*? Fahim Shabazz had stopped monitoring his tracking screen hours ago. In fact, his challenger had fallen so far behind, his boat wasn't even registering on the computer the last time Shabazz checked. He suspected the Italian vessel might have had engine issues and had probably dropped out, not that it made any difference to him.

To his mind, this had ceased being a race a long time ago.

• • •

SHABAZZ WAS ALSO consuming energy drinks to keep up on his nutrition.

He'd just finished a can and was in the act of throwing the empty container overboard when something strange happened.

The can never hit the water. It disappeared in a puff of smoke as soon as it left his hand.

It happened so fast, Fahim Shabazz wasn't even sure it happened at all. One moment the can was there—the next it wasn't.

He immediately wondered if the Adrenalin was making him see things. Or was it exhaustion? He hadn't slept in nearly four days, and while the Adrenalin was keeping him feeling strong, the energy drinks *did* contain a lot of caffeine. Maybe this wasn't the best combination.

But when he factored in the excitement of his pending martyrdom, Fahim Shabazz decided the incident with the can was probably just a slight figment of his imagination.

And that's how it stayed—for about a minute.

That's when he heard an odd crackling sound and saw one of the LED screens on his control panel disappear in a cloud of smoke. It was strange because, at eighty-five miles an hour, this smoke hung in the air for what seemed like a long time, before finally blowing away with the wind.

Once again, Fahim Shabazz wondered if he was seeing things. But unlike the vanishing Red Bull can, when he looked down at the computer screen there was no doubt that it had been shattered. In fact, there was nothing left of it, the glass or any of the gear behind it.

Now Shabazz was very worried. It appeared to him the panel had exploded from within, and this meant something was going wrong with the heretofore-perfect racing vessel.

The blown-away panel was their weather service screen—something that was important but not crucial. But still, Fahim Shabazz was concerned about the boat's overall condition.

He called for Abdul, screaming to be heard over the never-ending roar of the turbine. The engineer climbed out of the engine compartment, looked at Shabazz, as if to say: What do you want?

But before he could open his mouth to speak, a piece of Abdul's left shoulder suddenly flew off in an explosion of blood and skin.

Abdul stood there in shock. Shabazz was equally stunned.

It was only then that Shabazz realized someone was shooting at them.

• • •

BOBBY MURPHY WAS not a soldier.

His best weapon was his intellect. He killed terrorists by outsmarting them. By fooling them. By scamming them.

But unfortunately not by shooting them.

He had fired four shots at the *Smoke-Lar.* The one that hit the energy drink can and the one that took a chunk out of Abdul's shoulder were pure luck. The round that went into the *Smoke-Lar*'s weather display panel had come within inches of destroying the boat's autopilot, exactly the opposite of what Whiskey was trying to do. A fourth shot came dangerously close to hitting the boat's fuel supply before falling into the sea. It was only that the *Smoke-Lar* was going up one wave while the *Numero Two* was coming down another that the Dutch boat didn't blow up in a million pieces.

A lot of factors had worked against Murphy. The recoil of the massive M107 was enough to crack the shoulder of the most muscular rifleman; it was brutal on the bones of a sixty-five-year-old man. Then there was the noise. The M107 was basically a .50-caliber machine gun that fired one round at a time—and the noise that one round made going out the barrel was deafening, even drowning out the clamor made by the boat's turbine engine. The standard operating procedure for deploying the M107 called for mandatory earplugs on the shooter. There were no such luxuries aboard the *Numero Two*.

After the four shots Murphy was essentially deaf and, for a few moments, thought he had a dislocated shoulder.

After that, he knew it was best to leave the shooting to someone else.

So the job fell back to Nolan.

• • •

WHEN HE TOOK over, Nolan was just praying the cosmos would finally take pity on them and steer any round he fired into the head or the heart or the backside of the terrorist driving the *Smoke-Lar*.

But it didn't happen. There was just too much physics involved. The functions of wave motion, the combined speed of both racing boats and the constantly changing distance between them, the vicious recoil of the sniper rifle and the auditory disruption caused by the shooting of the gun. Bottom line, the physical act of firing the M107 had turned into a huge pain in the ass.

Worst of all, by this time, it was obvious the terrorists on the *Smoke-Lar* knew someone was shooting at them—so the idea of a quick kill was long gone. The terrorists were desperately trying to get the boat out of firing range, pushing their throttles to the max, but Savoldi was able to stay within a mile of them. Never closer, but never falling too far behind either.

Yet as the seas grew rougher, and both boats poured it on, the opportunities for any kind of accurate shot diminished proportionally. While at first Nolan was firing the M107 every thirty seconds or so, the conditions soon stretched that time frame to just one shot a minute. Then that became one attempt every five minutes as the terrorists were doing their best to stay down and under cover, not easy to do when one was bouncing around so much. Still, from there it went to one attempt every ten minutes, then fifteen, then twenty—with all of these rounds falling harmlessly into the sea.

Soon enough, as their ammunition, which had also been spared from being thrown overboard, started to run low and the ocean waves ran even higher, Nolan found himself attempting only one shot every half hour or so.

Then this thing they'd been waiting for, this thing they thought would take just minutes to accomplish once they were in range, stretched into an hour. Then two.

Then three.

Then four . . .

• • •

NOLAN STAYED WITH it, though. By midafternoon, six hours into the hunt, his good eye was red and running with tears from trying to sight his prey for more than a fraction of a second. He wasn't able to squeeze off more than a handful of shots in that time—all misses.

Night arrived and the others in the Whiskey contingent, with little else to do, retired back to their corner of the cockpit and began to doze. Emma had stayed by Nolan's side for a while, but when he told her she should get some rest, she listened to him and retreated to the back of the cockpit, too.

Eventually it was just Nolan and Savoldi: he at the gun, the pilot watching the controls. Even Giuseppe took the time to nap.

The stars came out, the moon came up, and the crazy, frustrating high-speed chase continued, with no real end in sight.

At one point Savoldi told him: "In a lot of Italian literature, the ship is used as a metaphor for the soul. That is why you just can't give up. This is in your soul."

"Maybe," Nolan replied, his eye still glued to the scope,

as it had been for almost the entire day. "But it should be easier than this."

Savoldi laughed. "And why is that?" he asked. "Now that I know what you have gone through in the past few days, and what your friends have gone through, and what this terror weapon you are pursuing is, *nothing* about any of it has been easy. So, what makes you think this particular part would be that way?"

Nolan took his eye from the sniper scope for a moment and looked over at him. "Are you saying we've been wasting our time out here?"

Savoldi shook his head no. "You are on their trail, yes? You are chasing them. You are not letting them get away. But my heart tells me this will not end until the last chapter is written, not until you chase them down to where this bomb is located. I might be wrong, but I just think anything less would just be *troppo facile.* Too easy."

As if to prove Savoldi's point, at that moment, it started to rain.

The bad weather came as a bit of a surprise; most of their trip had been free of annoying atmospherics. But the clouds had gathered, the wind began blowing up, and according to their weather readout screen, the occasional rainsqualls had all coalesced into one large front. Soon they were in the middle of a steady, blustery downpour.

The wind was blowing up from the south, so it didn't affect the speed of the *Numero Two*—or that of the *Smoke-Lar,* either.

But the rain all but killed Nolan's chances of getting a good shot at the terrorists.

• • •

ONE HOUR INTO the storm, Nolan made the mistake of asking Savoldi for one of his energy drinks.

It tasted like bad soda pop but it did give him a rush—for about thirty minutes. Then he began to lose this artificial vitality as its effects quickly wore off.

Savoldi recognized the problem and handed Nolan two tiny white pills. Nolan knew what they were—amphetamines. He'd downed a lot of them in his special ops days as well as during his more recent pirate-hunting gigs.

Nolan swallowed both with another can of energy drink. The combination kept him sharp, alert and wide-awake for the next three hours. But this did nothing to help him achieve that elusive kill shot. And as the rain got worse, he found himself taking his eye off the scope more and more and just wanting to breathe.

Finally, he had to take a break. He visited the tiny commode located in the aft part of the forward compartment, then he made his way back to the rear of the cockpit to check on Emma. She was sleeping peacefully, or as peacefully as could be expected. The others were as well.

Nolan sat down close by and stuck his head out the cockpit vent window, hoping to breathe in some fresh, if damp air. That's when he saw a cargo ship passing them in the near distance.

This seemed odd. They had not seen any other vessels during the trip. Now this one was no more than a quarter mile away.

But Nolan quickly realized this was not some ordinary ship. It was a container vessel, painted mostly black with some green and white on the upper decks.

He was stunned. He didn't even have to read the two words on the side of the ship to know its name.

He knew it was the *Dutch Cloud*.

Batman had his ethereal visions—and Nolan had his. Both men were haunted by things they couldn't explain. For Nolan, it all started a few months before, during Whiskey's gig for the Russian mafia. Protecting a cruise liner full of mobsters as they took a "business trip" through the Aegean Sea, their client, a gangster named Bebe, had told Nolan about the *Dutch Cloud*.

It was a near-mythical vessel, a phantom ship said to have disappeared shortly after 9/11. Endlessly sailing the seas ever

since, its contents were unknown but subject of much specu-
lation. Bebe said that if Whiskey were ever able to capture the
Dutch Cloud, they would be in for a *huge* reward, payable by
none other than the CIA.

It had sounded like drunken Russian bullshit at the time.
But then Nolan actually *saw* the ghost ship. It happened while
Whiskey was heading toward an island near Zanzibar to help
recover a buried treasure containing a billion-dollar micro-
chip. He was out on the rail one particular stormy night and
saw the spectral ship passing just off their port side, only to be
quickly lost again in the gale and fog.

Then just a month later, Nolan saw the ship once more,
this time while the team was crossing the mid-Atlantic to
the Bahamas for another gig.

Now, he was in the northeast Atlantic—and here it was
again.

In the middle of a storm, just like before.

• • •

THE NEXT THING Nolan knew, he was awake again,
slumped against the vent window where he'd just paused for a
breath of fresh air.

Yes, the pep pills and the energy drinks had delivered him
a great rush, but then they hit him with a sudden crash. He'd
gone to sleep in a very awkward position for about two hours.

When he awoke, the first thing he saw was a seabird flying
overhead. Then he looked out on the brightening sky and saw
other ships, all shapes and sizes, plying the ocean.

He took in a deep breath and for the first time in a long
time, detected something more in the air than just the smell
of the sea.

This time, he smelled land.

• • •

FAHIM SHABAZZ HAD done nothing for most of the past
twenty-four hours but duck bullets, both real and imaginary.

Shortly after the first three shots were fired at them, he'd peeked out the back of the boat and was astonished to see that the rival Italian racing yacht had not only gained on him, but was practically right behind them. This didn't seem possible, as he thought he could see more than two people crammed into its cockpit, vastly overloading it. But after a few more large caliber rounds had gone zipping by his head, Fahim Shabazz had stopped wondering how it happened, and started worrying about how he could get away from his pursuers without getting killed first.

As a result, he'd spent a lot of time crouched down below the *Smoke-Lar*'s control panel, checking his settings only occasionally, but always making sure that the autopilot was still engaged. This gave him a lot of time to think as to why he was being chased—and eventually he started to put it together. The Italian boat was from Monte Carlo and there were people in Monte Carlo who knew he had the key to the Z-box. These people must have discovered that he and Abdul had stolen the *Smoke-Lar* for their escape and so in turn had somehow commandeered the *Numero Two* and had been chasing them across the Atlantic.

So for Shabazz, a weird set of circumstances was at work here. He was trapped on a boat going more than 85 mph, a boat he didn't dare divert from its preplanned course, with another similar boat right behind him, apparently carrying expert marksmen ready to take him down the moment he presented them with a hittable target. These fears were reinforced anytime Shabazz saw the sparkling trail of a bullet going by.

It was so distracting, so unsettling, he never even bothered to crawl over and check on Abdul, who'd managed to stagger back into the engine compartment after being shot, and had stayed there ever since.

• • •

AS TIME AND the miles dragged on, the euphoria Fahim Shabazz had felt earlier had drained away.

He didn't want to die, at least not like this. Not at the hands of these people who were so relentlessly pursuing him.

All throughout the stormy night, he was certain he saw bullets whizzing overhead and on either side of the *Smoke-Lar,* leaving their long trails of smoke and sparks. He felt if he moved even one inch this way or that, a bullet would find his gut or his cranium, so good were these people trying to shoot him.

His biggest fear, though, was if he was killed here, out at sea, then all his efforts will have been for naught. He would have failed in his mission and the Great Satan would escape punishment once again.

But when morning finally arrived and the sky started brightening, Fahim Shabazz began rethinking his predicament. He began to wonder why his pursuers had not killed him yet. One bullet fired on the boat's turbine would have torn it apart, sinking the boat immediately. One bullet hitting a fuel line would have blown the racing yacht to bits. They could have done either one of those things at any time.

Even in these crazy conditions, his would-be assassins were trying to be too precise, like the SEALs who'd shot the pirate hijackers of the *Maersk Alabama.*

Why?

And then it suddenly became obvious. This wasn't about *him.* Just like it wasn't about those *Maersk Alabama* pirates on that Easter Morning. It was about the hostage he had stashed below. His pursuers wanted to kill him and Abdul *without* harming her because with them out of the way and the autopilot still engaged, she could probably get the boat under control somehow. Or at the very least it would run out of fuel eventually and just come to a stop. Simple . . .

Yes, now that daylight was coming, Fahim Shabazz was sure he had the situation right—and he knew there was only one way to counteract it.

He, too, could smell the land, meaning his goal wasn't that far away. In fact, he was close enough that he could steer the boat manually from here.

So he boldly lowered his cockpit top, making sure he'd be in full view of his pursuers and with the butt of his knife smashed the autopilot's computer screen. The message was clear. If they shot him or Abdul now, the girl would probably die when the high-speed boat went out of control.

From that moment on, no more bullets came his way.

But now with this done, Fahim Shabazz had to get as far away from his pursuers as possible. But how?

Both boats were reaching speeds of 85 mph plus, even though the Italian boat had as many as a half dozen people on board. Logic told Shabazz its passengers had somehow discarded a lot of weight in order to increase their speed.

He had to do the same thing.

He ordered Abdul out onto the deck. The engineer timidly crawled out of the turbine compartment, still bleeding, terrified he'd be shot again.

Fahim Shabazz yelled over to him to find anything on board that they didn't need and to throw it overboard. Two could play this game, Fahim Shabazz thought.

It took Abdul about a half hour to crawl around the boat, finding nonessentials and with his good arm, throwing them over the side. Then Fahim Shabazz told Abdul to hook up the last fuel container and, when this was done, to bring the girl up.

The end game was about to begin.

· · ·

THE GIRL NAMED Li had been tied up below for almost the entire trip, yet she still looked as glamorous as always.

Making sure the rope binding her hands was tied tight, Fahim Shabazz forced her to stand at the rear of the boat in full view of his pursuers with Abdul at her side, holding her upright. Then Shabazz checked his turbine weight gauge and found Abdul had done a good job; he'd lost about two hundred pounds of nonessential items. Shabazz could actually feel the boat going faster—but he needed even more speed. He'd lost a lot of extra poundage, but at this point, every little bit more would count.

So Fahim Shabazz made his way back to the rear of the open cockpit—and promptly pushed Abdul over the side.

Then he pulled Li down to the deck, threw his throttle to full maximum power and off he went, quickly pulling away from the *Numero Two*.

• • •

ABDUL ADBUL COULDN'T swim. He began panicking the moment he hit the water, splashing about and trying madly to breathe. He just couldn't believe Shabazz had done this to him. They were supposed to be partners in this. But now his desire for a great martyrdom was gone.

He was still bleeding from his gunshot wound and the salt water brought excruciating pain. Though he was far out at sea, he could make out the rim of the land to the west. The buildings, the early morning lights—this had been their goal, New York City, not twenty miles away.

But Abdul was beginning to sink; his wounded arm prevented him from even treading water. His only hope of being saved was the Italian boat coming up on him fast.

He raised his hands and started waving them madly, pleading with them to stop.

But the *Numero Two* was now off autopilot, too, and at maximum power, roared right past Abdul, leaving him in its wake.

29

THE FINISH LINE for the Great Racing Yacht Competition was at Coney Island, New York.

The location was selected as part of the iconic amusement park's modernization and revitalization. A temporary dock had been put in place near the park; it stretched out into New

York Harbor, about a mile south and west of the area called The Narrows.

A review stand had been erected on this dock, along with a set of bleachers and seats for media, sponsors and guests on hand to witness the end of the race. About a hundred people were in attendance.

Chief among them were representatives of the racing yachts' design teams. The designers of whichever boat actually won the race would have bragging rights to the title of World's Fastest Yacht for at least a year, a desirable position when it came to future sales.

Also on hand were members of the yachting press and a couple New York City TV news crews.

Exactly when the yachts would reach the finish line was not known; estimates ranged between 6:00 and 6:30 A.M. The actual finish line was about a half mile south of the review stand and was represented by a laser beam bouncing between two pilings installed for the occasion. Whichever yacht broke the beam first would be the winner.

From there, the plan called for both yachts to pull up to the reviewing stand for photos and interviews.

• • •

IT WAS A warm muggy summer morning.

Even at 6:00 A.M., the temperature was climbing into the 80s and early thunderstorms were forecast.

At 6:10 A.M., a traffic helicopter owned by one of the TV stations spotted the pair of yachts about a mile off Sandy Hook, New Jersey. The pilot reported that one yacht had about a half-mile lead, but the other vessel was coming on strong. This put the people on the reviewing stand in high scramble mode. The yachts would be passing the finish line within five minutes, and would be slowing down to tie up at the dock just two minutes after that.

The guests went to their assigned seats; the TV crews turned on their camera lights. Per agreement, there was no radio contact with the yachts as the race organizers didn't want to distract either crew. A TV camera set up on the laser beam piling would record the finish; only then would radio contact be made.

The helicopter radioed the reviewing stand at 6:12, saying the yachts were about a minute away and that both were going at tremendous speed, one right behind the other.

At 6:13, those people on the dock who had binoculars were able to see the two yachts coming out of the early morning haze.

The video feed from the TV camera on the finish line piling was put up on a monitor on the reviewing stand. The yachts were now only about thirty seconds away from crossing the finish line. The TV reporters got on their marks, ready to broadcast the finish live.

At 6:14:40 the first boat zoomed across the finish line. It was the Dutch boat, *Smoke-Lar*. Right behind it was the Italian boat, *Numero Two*. The Dutch boat had bested the Italians by less than ten seconds.

Those on the review stand burst into applause. Crossing the Atlantic in a yacht in fifty-five hours was a huge achievement for the yachting world. They could clearly see the pair of boats now roaring up the channel, as if they were still in a race.

"Competitors to the end" was how one on-air TV reporter described it.

But then, something strange: Once the two yachts reached the point where they should have slowed down in order to come into the dock as planned; they kept on going instead.

They blasted right past the reviewing stand, causing an earsplitting racket, and continued up the channel toward New York Harbor.

It happened so fast the people on the reviewing stand weren't sure what was going on. Race officials immediately tried to contact the boats to tell them to turn around, but neither boat answered the call.

In less than thirty seconds both vessels had disappeared into The Narrows. Beyond that, lay Manhattan.

Totally confused now, one spectator told another: "That is not a race—that's a chase."

• • •

LONGSHOREMEN WORKING THE docks on Red Hook Pier 19 saw the racing yachts pass at about 6:25.

It was the noise of the gas turbines that first attracted their attention. This being New York City, nothing was really surprising, even two yachts shaped like bullets screaming up toward Governors Island.

However, among the dock crews were a couple soldiers in a local crime family, and they'd be told to report anything unusual they saw along the waterfront or in the harbor. Anything at all.

A few phone calls were made, some texts were sent, and within minutes, word of the two racing yachts was spreading up and down the inner harbor.

This is why two other low-level mobsters working the fish pier near Maiden Lane were on alert when they saw first one, then a second racing yacht heading in their direction at high speed. The pier was a place where anything from stolen furs to trash bags full of marijuana were known to pass through, always under heavy protection. Even the police gave the place wide berth. Anyone intending to dock here better have a very good reason.

Yet, no sooner had the first yacht come into view, when it suddenly cut its engines and began pulling up to that part of the pier normally reserved for fishing boats.

It didn't bother to tie up. Those dockworkers nearby saw a swarthy-looking man jump off the racing yacht, holding a beautiful Asian woman by the arm.

Even in this rough-and-tumble part of lower Manhattan, this just didn't look right. Two crewmen of a nearby fishing boat tried to stop the man as he made his way up the gangway to the street, practically dragging the woman behind him. The man never broke stride, though. He pulled out a gun, shot both workers and kept on going.

At that moment the second yacht screamed to a halt in front of the pier. That's when it got *real* confusing.

Of the dozen stevedores working on the dock, more than half were armed or had personal weapons nearby. As soon as the two pier workers were gunned down, these weapons came out and Fahim Shabazz, potential suicide bomber, found himself in the middle of an unexpected gunfight.

To step on American soil for the first time was a moment he'd been waiting for. But the reception was not what he expected. He knew it was dangerous in America, but did *everyone* own a gun?

He had no choice but to fire back, even though bullets were flying at him from many directions. Shabazz's first thought was to return to the dock, get back on the high speed yacht and escape. But upon turning in that direction, he saw the *Numero Two* had now arrived and at least one person on it was firing in his direction with a huge weapon.

That's when Shabazz put Li in front of him to use as a human shield. All the shooting stopped immediately and Shabazz resumed making his way off the pier, heading for the street.

A stretch van was parked almost at the water's edge, not ten feet from the pier. It was a shuttle for tourists wanting to take the scenic harbor tour offered at the Fulton Street pier, three blocks away. The van's driver was having his morning coffee when he saw the bizarre gunfight unfold. Before he could put the van in gear and drive away, Shabazz ran up to him, ordered him out, then shot him on the spot.

Li was just baggage now. Shabazz put his gun up to her head and began to pull the trigger. Suddenly he saw a glint of light come from his right. The next thing he knew the sharpened tip of an umbrella was sticking out of his right forearm.

It was such an odd thing, that he stared at it for a few seconds, enough for Li to break free and run. He wanted to shoot her—as well as the strange little man who'd hurled the razorlike umbrella tip at him—but the wound in his forearm had temporarily frozen his fingers, making it impossible to fire his gun.

So, Shabazz just pulled the piece of metal out of his arm, jumped into the van and roared away in a cloud of exhaust.

• • •

AT THAT MOMENT, it started to rain. Suddenly there was very heavy thunder and lightning and high winds. It was so violent, and came so fast, it even surprised the people who'd just been involved in the strange gun battle.

Fighting the sudden gale, Nolan and Batman put down the M107, jumped off the *Numero Two* and ran up the gangway to the street.

Batman was in the lead. He quickly sought out the dock workers' foreman and explained as best he could who he and Nolan were and what was going on, including their connection to the CIA. He made it clear that he and Nolan had to pursue the man who'd just stolen the van, but that everyone else on the pier should stay in place, get under cover and shield their eyes should they hear any kind of explosion.

The boss understood eventually. He brought Nolan and Batman over to his tool truck and gave them two highly illegal AR-15 rifles. He also gave them some extra construction boots, as everyone on board the *Numero Two* was still barefoot.

Now armed and shod, Nolan and Batman ran out onto Dalton Street, trying to determine which way Shabazz had gone. People were starting to drift down toward the waterfront now, alerted by the commotion. To them, Nolan and Batman, with their camos and heavy weapons, appeared to be a couple of actors about to shoot a scene for a movie. It was the only explanation that made sense.

They were tempted to tell these people to seek cover and to shield their eyes if they heard a loud explosion, but they were sure no one would take them seriously.

Instead, they peered up and down the long street, but had no luck spotting the van in any direction.

Cabs were flying by, and they tried to wave one down. But none of them were about to stop two guys dressed for a costume party at 6:30 on a hot summer morning. Especially in the rain.

Then Batman spotted something strange. It was a newspaper box for the *New York Post*. The headline read: "Where's Emma? Hollywood Star missing for 4 days."

It was at that moment that everything just stopped. They didn't know why, maybe it was just the absurdity of it all, but whatever energy they had left just drained out of both of them. Standing in the downpour on the dirty New York street, with borrowed guns and borrowed shoes, looking at the newspaper headline, the whole adventure suddenly seemed over.

"We'll never catch this guy now," Batman said. "Even if that address you found is right around the corner, he's got a big head start on us."

Nolan was devastated, but he had to agree. Even if a cab stopped for them, they had no money to pay the driver, and every second that passed just meant the terrorist was driving deeper and deeper into New York City.

"After all this," he said. "And we lose him *here*? Of all places . . ."

Batman just nodded glumly. "I think it's time, Snake," he said.

Nolan knew what he meant. There was no sense fighting it. It was finally time to call the authorities and report what they knew.

"Who?" Nolan asked him wearily.

"Call 911," Batman suggested. "Hopefully the cops will catch him—then maybe they'll give *them* the hundred million."

Nolan borrowed a cell phone from one of the dockworkers and dialed 911.

An operator answered quickly and asked what the emergency was.

Nolan wanted to keep it simple, so he just said: "There's a bomb about to go off at 45 Park Place. I have to talk to the bomb squad."

The weird thing was, it almost seemed as if the operator laughed at him. "Bomb in 45 Park Place?" she said. "Right. OK—hold on."

Nolan explained to Batman the operator's weird attitude.

Batman just shook his head. "New York's always been a weird place," he said.

The line clicked twice and a NYPD officer came on, announcing he was from the bomb squad.

Nolan repeated his message—and this guy laughed for real.

Nolan couldn't take it. "Why the hell are you laughing at me?" he demanded to know.

"Because," the guy replied, "we get four or five bomb threats on that building every day. And it's against the law to call in prank phone calls."

Nolan was pissed. "But why do you assume this is a prank call?"

The cop yelled back: "Because that's the address of the Ground Zero Mosque . . . that's why."

Nolan immediately hung up. Again, he told Batman what had happened, then said, "Well, damn—it all makes sense now."

Their enthusiasm revived, they started hailing cabs again—but once more, to no good luck.

But suddenly Emma was beside them. Wearing a pair of borrowed construction boots herself, she was disobeying Nolan's order to stay on the boat.

She raised her hand for no more than a half second and three cabs screeched to a halt.

"That's how it's done," she said to Nolan.

He and Batman piled in—she started to come with them but Nolan blocked her at the door.

"No way," he said. "Not this time. Get back to the boat and make sure everyone covers their eyes if they hear anything go off . . ."

But she knew him too well now. She waved his protest aside by saying, "They already know that."

Then she climbed in the backseat with him.

The cabbie looked back at them. He first saw Emma and nearly flipped out. Then he saw the guns and said, "Shooting a movie Miss Simms?"

"Something like that," she replied. "Take us to forty-five Park Place and please step on it. . . ."

• • •

FOR NOLAN, THE ride from Maiden Lane to 45 Park Place seemed to take forever.

It wasn't even 7:00 A.M. but the traffic turned awful once they'd left the waterfront. The rainstorm wasn't helping. It was coming down so hard, Nolan had no idea how the cabbie could even see. But even without the weather, it would have been tough going. Lots of trucks, lots of cabs, lots of pedestrians.

Not that long ago, Nolan had been on an island paradise. Now—he was here. In the busiest city . . . in the United States. A place he wasn't even supposed to be.

He saw at least one cop on every corner, patrol cars parked everywhere. Should we tell them? he thought. Would they believe us? Or would they be arrested for riding in a New York City cab carrying illegal assault rifles?

If he knew the team would still get the CIA reward money if they brought in outside help, what would he do then? Or was the CIA even going to pay them at all?

Nolan just sank deeper into the cab's backseat as the driver ran a red light.

It's not always easy to do the right thing. . . .

The driver turned right off Maiden Lane onto Church and what Nolan saw here was a lot of chain-link fence, a lot of construction equipment, and what basically looked like a big empty space in a canyon of skyscrapers.

This was Ground Zero.

He turned to Emma—he wanted to make sure that, no matter what happened, she knew where they were. But he saw her looking out the window, her eyes getting watery. After what she'd been through, after what *they'd* both been through, no words were necessary.

The driver took three more turns and suddenly they were on Park Place.

The van stolen by Shabazz was out in front of number 45, parked askew, two of its wheels up on the curb, its driver's door still open.

The Jihad Brother had gotten out in a hurry.

It said something about New York City that people were walking past the oddly parked truck without giving it a second look.

The taxi pulled up and, though they had no money, Emma paid the driver by autographing his Yankees cap. Then the three of them jumped out.

They hesitated—just for a moment—when they realized this place really didn't look like a mosque.

"That's because it isn't," Emma said, reading their thoughts. "We were going to shoot a movie here. It's a center for Muslim religious study. There's a difference."

"Tomato, to-*mah*-to," Batman said dryly.

And Nolan agreed. They checked their assault weapons and then they ran inside.

They came upon an unexpected scene in the lobby. Three people, two men and a woman, were lying on the floor. All three were wearing traditional Muslim garb; all three were shot dead. Nolan knew this could only be the work of the terrorist. He imagined the gunman had stormed into the building, shooting anyone who got in his way.

So much for Brotherhood.

There were at least a dozen people cowering in the lobby; they were behind chairs, hiding in corners and crouched beneath the reception desk.

There was a collective gasp from these people when Nolan

and Batman burst in, Emma trailing close behind. But it was an expression of relief. Many of those in hiding thought Nolan and Batman were a NYPD SWAT team.

Several ventured out of their hiding places and greeted them with hand kissing and frantic gestures. Others simply ran for the door.

"Where is he?" Nolan was asking the people as they were fighting to kiss his hand. "Where did he go?"

All the people remaining in the lobby pointed upward.

"The roof," one man said as he was making a quick exit. "He went up to the roof."

Though there was a bank of elevators off to the right, Nolan, Batman and Emma made for the stairs. They climbed quickly but carefully. Emma was staying close to them; there was no way Nolan could tell her to stay behind now.

They reached the second floor and found two more dead bodies—security guards, gunned down before they could take their weapons out. Nolan took their pistols and gave one to Batman and kept one for himself.

They climbed up to the third floor. They could see people peeking out of doorways. In each case, Nolan told them to stay where they were.

On the fourth floor, they found a seriously wounded man collapsed outside the building's mail room.

Batman covered the hall as Nolan and Emma hurried over to the wounded man. He'd been shot in the neck and shoulder, but could still talk.

"He has the box," he said weakly. "It arrived here on overnight delivery two days ago. It was being held for him. But I didn't think he'd shoot me for it."

Nolan and Emma pulled the man into the mail room and closed the door.

Then they carefully returned to the stairway and resumed their climb. Seconds later, they'd reached the top floor of the building.

There was a long hallway in front of them, but off to the

left was a fire exit door slightly ajar. The light and rain coming in told Nolan this door led to the roof.

Just as they were about to move, the door opened wider and Fahim Shabazz walked in from the roof.

Nolan felt his body tense up. He recognized this guy as the one he'd seen so many times through the M107's sniper scope, if just for fractions of a second.

The terrorist took two steps and then realized there were three people in camo clothing standing ten feet away from him, two of them carrying assault rifles.

Shabazz wasn't armed. He put his hands up, as if to say I'm innocent.

But Nolan and Batman weren't fooled.

They cut him down in a hail of bullets before he could say a word.

Then they ran forward; Shabazz was literally full of holes. There was no need to check if he was dead or not.

They burst out onto the roof in the pouring rain. And there it was, in the northeast corner of the flat roof. The Z-box.

Nolan stopped in his tracks. They all did. This thing that had consumed their lives for what seemed like years was now right here in front of them.

All this time, Nolan had pictured it as a briefcase. A black briefcase. But of course that didn't make sense.

It looked more like a small footlocker. Not black and shiny like it would be if this were a movie, but painted in typical dull Army olive drab.

And sure enough there was a 'Z' carved into its top.

But more important, the key was in the lock and it had been turned.

"It's activated!" Batman yelled to Nolan.

Nolan ran to it, suddenly soaked by the rain again. A clap of thunder went off over his head, then a flash of lightning.

He slid to a stop in front of the box. It was ticking—strange that it would work after all these years.

Murphy had told Whiskey the only way to stop the Z-box

from exploding was to turn it off with the key. But this would have to be done before a minute had elapsed after the box had been turned on. After that, the box would blow up fifteen seconds later, no matter what happened.

But how long ago had Shabazz activated it? There was no way to tell. Nolan knew he had to turn the key anyway.

But the key wouldn't budge. He tried it again, very aware of the ticking. But it would not move—it was stuck.

There was another clap of thunder above him, along with the crackle of lightning. He was suddenly aware that there were also helicopters overhead. Police copters, TV news copters. He could see searchlights and TV lights cutting through the rain.

All the while, he was trying to turn the key with all his might, but it just wouldn't move.

He turned back to see Batman and Emma standing right behind him, watching and feeling helpless.

"Run!" he told them. "Get out of here!"

"No way!" they both yelled back at once.

"Go!" Nolan yelled at them again. "I'm half blind *anyway!*"

But they did not move.

Nolan tried the key again—but again no luck.

Then Emma yelled, "Try taking it out and putting it back in again."

It didn't make sense, but Nolan did as she suggested. He pulled the key out and then put it back in.

Then he twisted it—and this time it moved.

There was a click and then suddenly, the top of the box sprang open.

And then there was a tremendous flash. . . .

• • •

TWITCH, MURPHY AND Li had stayed back on the docks.

Murphy was so happy that Li was still alive, he wanted to keep her out of harm's way, no matter what the situation, no matter how much money was involved. She meant that much to him and his PSO.

For his part, Twitch stayed behind because he wasn't too mobile after using the sharp tip of his makeshift prosthesis to save Li's life, something she had not stopped thanking him for.

They waited on the pier, under a boat shelter, a coterie of mobbed-up dockworkers keeping an eye on them, keeping them safe. Savoldi and Giuseppe were there as well.

They weren't exactly obeying Nolan's last order. Instead they were all just talking and waiting for the other shoe to drop, awaiting the final outcome of the strange chase.

So everyone on the docks saw the tremendous flash of light. It came so quick, and was so bright, there really was no time to cover their eyes.

There was also the sound of a huge explosion in those same few seconds. Yet amidst the confusion and the storm, it was impossible to tell if it had come from an incredibly loud clap of thunder, or something else entirely.

Twitch, Murphy, Li and the two Italian crewmen had immediately put their hands to their eyes anyway, at the same time knowing if they had to think about it, then it was probably too late—if the Z-box had gone off, that is.

But after a few moments of what seemed to be total silence throughout Manhattan, Twitch uncovered his eyes. He looked over at the beautiful Li and saw she was smiling back at him.

"I can see?" he asked.

They all lowered their hands and opened their eyes and it was still raining and thundering, and lightning was still crackling everywhere.

But yes, they could all see.

• • •

BACK ON THE roof of the "mosque," Nolan regained consciousness to find a hectic, confusing scene around him.

He had no idea what had happened. He recalled opening

the Z-box, just as it appeared a lightning bolt had hit the roof nearby. Either that or one of the searchlights on one of the helicopters overhead had exploded. In any case, it was a tremendous flash of light.

He remembered seeing Emma, bathed in this light, being thrown backward and hitting her head. He remembered seeing Batman blown right through the roof exit door and back into the hallway.

But the strangest thing was that Nolan remembered seeing all this as if *both* his eyes still worked, as if his eye patch had been blown away. And in that briefest of moments, while the tremendous light was still all around him, he also thought he saw his old friend Crash, standing in front of him, smiling and giving him two thumbs-up.

Shortly after that, Nolan lost consciousness.

Now he was awake again. It had stopped raining and the roof was crowded with NYPD SWAT team members, firefighters, EMTs and *lots* of spooks in bad suits.

Nolan's vision was still blurry, though his eye patch was back in place. But among the crowd, he recognized one person right away. It was Audette, the CIA agent who'd started the whole Z-box thing. He was with a couple of other people who Nolan was sure were government bomb disposal experts. They were carrying away the now-deactivated Z-box.

As they were walking past him, Nolan overheard a conversation between Audette and two NYPD cops.

One of the cops was saying to Audette, "If there was a bomb here, we need to know that for our report."

To which Audette replied, "There was no bomb here. Capeesh? No one ever saw a bomb here."

Then Audette looked down at Nolan, paused a moment, and said, "Good to see you again."

Then he disappeared into the crowd.

Two EMTs were trying to keep Nolan in a horizontal position at this point, but he fought them off and got to his feet.

He had to find the others.

He located Batman first. He was on a stretcher, out in the

hallway, an IV already plugged into his arm. Eyes closed, he was still unconscious.

Nolan grabbed the EMT treating him. "What's the matter with him?" he demanded to know.

The guy just shrugged. "Most immediate problem is a severe concussion," he replied. "Long term—a quick saliva test says he's got some kind of highly unusual toxin poisoning his blood stream. Has he been eating any weird foods lately, wild herbs or something? Was he having hallucinations, things like that? Before he passed out, we found him in the corner talking to someone who wasn't there."

Before Nolan could say anything, two more EMTs arrived and wheeled Batman away.

"What about the girl?" Nolan asked a cop nearby. The cop was already drinking a cup of coffee and eating a doughnut.

"The cute blonde?" the cop replied with a wry expression. "I heard she's got a grade-three concussion."

"Where is she?" Nolan asked him desperately.

The cop pointed to a room down the hallway. "Right down there," he said. "But be sure you protect your private parts before going in."

Nolan ran down the hallway, fighting his way through more cops and firefighters.

He arrived at the doorway expecting to see a gaggle of medical personnel surrounding Emma.

But what he saw instead was Emma, looking like she was in fine shape, sitting on a chair surrounded by a small army of what looked like Hollywood handlers and flunkies preening her. She was drinking a large glass of water—and Nolan noticed it had exactly five ice cubes floating around in it.

Before he could say anything, Emma spotted him and started yelling, "That's him! *That's* the guy! I want him arrested. Kidnapping. Holding a person against their will. Destruction of personal property. Arrest him! Now!"

And strangely enough, Nolan *was* arrested. But not by the NYPD and not for kidnapping. Rather two Federal agents had come up behind him and put him in handcuffs.

One said to him: "Philip Nolan, you're under arrest on charges of violating a military court order barring you from entering the United States. You have to come with us. If you need a lawyer, one will be provided to you . . ."

Nolan was in shock. He was numb. He just couldn't fathom what was going on around him.

But as he was being led away he managed one long look back at Emma. The flash of light? Did she hit her head again when she fell? What *the hell* happened?

He didn't know—he was just heartbroken at the result.

She saw him staring at her and yelled at him: "Just keep walking, you one-eyed freak . . ."

• • •

AFTER THE FLASH, Twitch had fashioned a new prosthesis from materials given to him by the dockworkers. Then he, Murphy and Li found a taxi and headed off for 45 Park Place.

By the time they arrived, a huge crowd had gathered outside. Strangely, it was not because word had gotten around about a possible terrorist incident on the roof, but because people had heard that the missing superstar Emma Simms had miraculously appeared inside.

The three of them were just getting out of the cab when Emma herself emerged from the building, led by a flying squad of handlers. There would be no ambulance for her. A stretch limo had made its way down the street and was waiting to take her away.

Hundreds of cell phone cameras went off as she made her way through the crowd, shielding her face from them, her entourage setting up a phalanx in front of her.

But just as she was about to climb into the limo, she spotted Twitch, Murphy and Li standing in the crowd nearby.

She quickly sized up the beautiful Li, then said to her: "What are you looking at, bitch?"

Then she got in the limo and roared away.

30

NOLAN WAS HELD in the federal lockup in Manhattan for the next three weeks.

In that time he recovered from his many physical wounds and was able to sleep and eat three meals a day.

He'd learned that he'd been arrested so quickly that day because, as one federal officer told him, his picture was on the wall of every FBI office in the country.

He was questioned a dozen times by the Bureau, then the Defense Department investigators, and then by people who never identified themselves, but who he knew were from the CIA.

He said nothing to the FBI or the DoD guys. To the spooks he said only the same two things over and over again: "Where's our money?" and "And what happened to my team?"

Neither question ever got answered.

He was never given the attorney he'd been promised. He was kept in a cell, alone, twenty-four hours a day.

The only information anyone would tell him was that he would soon face another secret military court, similar to the one that had convicted him years before, and that he was facing a life sentence, and *then* deportation.

In that time, he wasn't allowed any newspapers, was not allowed to watch any TV. He was given no information on what happened to the other people in Whiskey. He was not allowed visitors. He wasn't even sure if anyone knew he was there.

• • •

ON HIS TWENTY-SECOND day in custody, he was told to pack up his meager belongings, and that he was being transferred to another, more secure facility upstate.

He was given some plain civilian clothes and then two faceless agents led him out to a black van by way of the lockup's rear entrance.

He was put into the back of the van and driven to a small airport just outside New York City, in Rye, New York.

A small white business jet was waiting there.

The agents undid his handcuffs and turned him over to a pair of other faceless agents standing at the door of the plane.

Nolan climbed aboard, was led to a seat in the otherwise empty passenger cabin and left there alone.

The plane took off, but instead of turning north, toward upstate, it veered east, out over the Atlantic Ocean.

Only then did the cockpit door open and he found himself staring at three familiar faces.

Batman was flying the airplane. Twitch was sitting in the copilot's seat.

Sitting behind them, smiling widely, was Bobby Murphy, the genius who'd just broken him out of federal custody.

"Sit back and enjoy the ride, Mister Nolan," Murphy told him. "We'll have to stop a couple times for fuel, but with any luck, we'll be in Aden by tomorrow morning."

Nolan was stunned. He couldn't believe it. He had a million questions to ask. But the one that came out first was: "Did those bastards ever pay us our money?"

With that, a fourth person came out of the cockpit. Long blond hair, perfect shape, huge blue eyes and absolutely gorgeous face. It was Emma, wearing a very short, very tight 1960s-style-stewardess uniform.

She smiled at him, and then said: "How do you think we got the plane?"

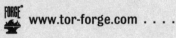